# DIXON,
## DESCENDING

# DIXON, DESCENDING

## A NOVEL

## KAREN OUTEN

**DUTTON**

**DUTTON**

An imprint of Penguin Random House LLC
penguinrandomhouse.com

Copyright © 2024 by Karen Outen

Penguin Random House supports copyright. Copyright fuels creativity, encourages diverse voices, promotes free speech, and creates a vibrant culture. Thank you for buying an authorized edition of this book and for complying with copyright laws by not reproducing, scanning, or distributing any part of it in any form without permission. You are supporting writers and allowing Penguin Random House to continue to publish books for every reader.

DUTTON and the D colophon are registered trademarks of Penguin Random House LLC.

Map: © 2024 by David Lindroth

LIBRARY OF CONGRESS CATALOGING-IN-PUBLICATION DATA
has been applied for.

ISBN 9780593473450 (hardcover)
ISBN 9780593473467 (ebook)

Printed in the United States of America
1st Printing

BOOK DESIGN BY DANIEL BROUNT

*For my parents, George and Peggie, whose love story endures,*
*and my sister, Gwen, who sustains me*

# DIXON,
## DESCENDING

The mountain doesn't care whether we're here or not.
Everything it means to us is only what we bring to it.
It's only what the mountain reveals about us
that has any lasting value.

—DAVID BREASHEARS, ALPINIST

# MOUNT EVEREST, SOUTH COL

**1** Camp 1 (19,500'/5943m)  **2** Camp 2 (21,000'/6400m)  **3** Camp 3 (23,500'/7162m)  **4** Camp 4 (26,300'/8000m)

Mt. Everest Summit (29,035'/8850m)

South Summit (28,500'/8690m)

Lhotse (27,940'/8516m)

SOUTH COL

LHOTSE FACE

NORTH COL

NORTH FACE

SOUTH WEST FACE

WESTERN CWM

TIBET NEPAL

RONGBUK GLACIER

KHUMBU ICEFALL

KHUMBU GLACIER

Base Camp (17,500'/5334m)

# I.

## CHAPTER

1

*March 2011, Mount Everest*

This first time, as they hoisted themselves onto the hip of the mountain, they had to simply learn to survive. Survive the landscape, the thin air, the unbelievable cold, the exquisite suffering. Each step of Dixon's crampons on ice was accompanied by a headache so intense he thought a tiny demon jabbed a pitchfork endlessly inside his ear. His stomach cramped, his tongue swelled against the roof of his dehydrated mouth, he inhaled heavily—at 18,000 feet and rising, his every breath was hard won. A perfect, exhilarating orb of suffering.

His brother Nate climbed just in front of him along a narrow path that stretched between ice boulders. Nate looked back at him, panting lightly but smiling, his black goggles gleaming on his face, rock star–like. "Man! We're in rare air. Black men on Everest." Dixon repeated it with awe: Black men on Everest, which was to say freed men. Because their burdens here were of their own making.

Blue-white ice glowed above their heads. They were climbing just above Base Camp, deep in the Khumbu Icefall, a once-cascading river frozen mid-flow. A surreal landscape of ice boulders at improbable angles perched along cliffs. The ground rumbled beneath their feet. A game of dodgeball, judging which boulder might tumble toward them. And this only their first acclimatizing trip up the mountain; there would be three climbs, up ever higher, then back down, before they attempted the summit. Three more chances to lose this survival game. An improbable game growing ever more ridiculous: not just skimming boulders but spanning crevasses so impossibly deep they might emerge on the other side of the earth.

They had chosen this, Dixon reminded himself, and squinted into the glare ahead of him. A stunning flash, a warning flare: the sun bounced off the aluminum shell of a ladder—four ladders, actually, lashed together and spanning a crevasse slit deep and jagged in the ice. And he was expected to cross it. Unfathomable, all of it, crevasses, ice blocks, mountains. A thrill seized his groin. He turned toward his loosely tethered band of twenty team members, sherpas, and guides, their red and blue and yellow down suits iridescent against the snow. Lunatics did this kind of thing, lunatics and heroes, Dixon thought, laughing, and which did he think he was? "Both!" he said aloud.

Nate waited for Dixon near the ladders, hands on his hips. "Well, this might be it, know what I mean?" Nate leaned close so Dixon could hear him above the wind. "That oh-hell-no moment." He made a sweeping gesture across the Icefall. Ahead of them, the ladders were strung with safety ropes and bolted into the ice on either side of a crevasse. They still didn't look like a good idea.

Dixon lifted his goggles and squinted at his brother, who stood

4

one hand on his hip, a sly smile on his face: a challenge Dixon knew well. "You expect me to believe you're throwing in the towel?"

"Hell no." Nate laughed. He flexed his fingers against each other, tightened his gloves.

"How 'bout I go first," Dixon said. He did not wait for an answer.

Don't look down, Dixon warned himself, but how could he help it? The pale-blue walls of ice below him darkened into a bottomless midnight. He stepped onto the ladders, his crampon spikes clunking on the metal rungs. The ladder swayed and complained under him, his body both weighed down and weightless in the thinning air. The wind howled around his ears. His heartbeat resonated in every vein, every muscle, every clench of his hands around the safety ropes. Thin ropes in his hands, slender rungs under his feet, he teetered above Earth. A gust of wind bellowed in his ears and seemed to lift him like a kite. A belly drop, Dixon gripped the ropes as he felt himself caught up by the wind. The frightening roar in his ears. Dixon suspended midair. It seemed an endless ride on the bounce of wind. He was sure he would be swept away. He could not breathe. He might have expected his life to flash before his eyes, but he saw only sky, endless blue clouds swirling shapeless above him. It wasn't death he feared, but the feeling of nothingness, of expendability at the whim of the mountain.

That jolt of air swept under him only momentarily, but Dixon was badly shaken. Mountain peaks loomed around him, the crevasse beneath him like a dare. He scrambled across the ladder to the other side, his breath heavy, his body trembling, a bead of fear trickling down his spine. The mountain had given him a stiff warning.

LIKE GOD, EVEREST HAD A SENSE OF HUMOR, WHICH DIXON DIS-
covered days later climbing through the Western Cwm halfway
between Base Camp and the summit. He wore a thick down suit as
he trudged through dense snow, and unbelievably, it was hot as
hell. Just that morning his socks had been frozen stiff. Now, sweat
poured down his cheeks and welled along his collarbone. He tried
to imagine convincing anyone back home that Everest could be
this way. Wily. Winsome. In the snow-covered bowl of the Western Cwm, the wind died down and the sun sparkled along the
snow until Dixon saw stars twinkling and dancing off the ice; he
tripped lightheaded through the galaxy.

"Practically beach weather," Nate croaked out, his voice thin.
Nate's dimpled cheeks wet with sweat, his medium-brown skin
tanned a reddish-chestnut in the sun. Dixon flashed to their childhood summers at the Maryland shore, slathering on their mother's
concoction of iodine and baby oil as suntan lotion, then sliding
slick and dark as eels into the water. He might be there now, they
might be boys playing if he squinted his eyes just right, the glare
of sun off the brittle snow like the glare off water.

In the nearly eighty-five-degree heat, Dixon slipped his rucksack from his shoulders, removed the jacket of his bright blue
snowsuit. He tossed his head back, drinking up sun, and Nate piled
a handful of snow under Dixon's hat. Nate laughed. A tease, a comfort, Dixon let the snow melt and trickle down his neck.

Nate unzipped his one-piece snowsuit, slipped out of the top
half, and let it bounce around his waist. Hadn't Dixon warned him
to get a two-piece suit for just this reason? Dixon frowned.

"It's like a reprieve before the execution," Nate joked and

swept his hand wide. In the gentle slope of the Cwm, which spanned the mountain's belly, they had stripped to T-shirts and bandannas, their sunglasses tightly secured. They might be miners or the Seven Dwarfs coming home from work in lockstep across the snowy field. Their smallness stood out; their impressions on the landscape were only minuscule. The surface vast and snowy, they were surrounded on three sides by mountains, one a looming glacier that stood between them and the top of the world. Just now, Dixon thought, they were safe and warm, weren't they? The altitude must be already making his thoughts fuzzy. Because all of this, the sun, the feeling of brightness, all of it was deceptive—ah, Everest was always up to something. And as if she had heard him, the mountain rumbled and shifted, the snow dust of a far-off avalanche blowing toward them, a sprinkler on a hot summer's day, so they threw back their heads to drink it in.

Soon, Everest returned to form as they ascended the Lhotse Face, a steep, vertical sheet of glacial ice. Nate let out a bemused laugh. "You gotta be half billy goat for this."

"Don't see any of those living up here."

"Nope, just us paying fools." Nate latched onto the safety rope.

They headed up the Lhotse Face, their sherpas beside them, their teammates before and behind, but they may as well have been alone. Dixon focused only on Nate in front of him. Clipping their jumars onto the rope, sliding the jumar up, kicking their crampons into the blue ice of the Face, they lifted themselves, then rested; slide, kick, pull, rest; slide kick pull rest over and over, a steady rhythm echoing their breath. When he was a runner, Dixon had loved following the cadence of his breath, the sound of his spikes hitting the track. He had loved the gift of his body: the span of his arms, the strength of his calves, the fluid grace that propelled him over high hurdles. He simply did what was in him to do. In high school, coaches had said he could be the next Renaldo Nehemiah, and for a time he had willed it, posting signs around his bedroom: "High Hurdles Under 13 Seconds like Nehemiah!" He had so deeply imagined that triumph, smelled it, tasted its sweetness, cradled it in his arms at night. He had missed qualifying for the Olympics at national trials by two-tenths of a second. Two fucking tenths! For weeks afterward, his failure so raw that his skin felt bruised, he had not been able to bear being touched. Never again, he had decided, would he give over to such excruciating wanting. And he had not. Until now.

He yielded to the kick, rise, pull, the sheer desire for this mountain.

Sheer desire. It wasn't a gentle thing. He couldn't decide when the wanting was worse, when the mountain's bare rock shone like obsidian, or when clouds veiled the sharp bones of the summit. Sometimes desire overtook him with an angry impatience. Like now, as Nate climbed in front of him up the Lhotse Face, moving with more ease while Dixon fought through each miserable, withholding breath. Nate was taking to altitude the way Dixon had always taken to running. Nate's ease—a thing Dixon had imagined rejoicing over—rode hot under Dixon's collar, rising into full-blown fire across his cheeks. Because Nate moved closer to the summit with each step.

Dixon slid, kicked, pulled up the icy face of Lhotse, lulled away from the mountain's dangers by sheer tedium. But discipline was Dixon's forte. He trusted himself, and with a chill, he glanced at his brother. Did Nate double-check his clip, did he hold the safety ropes, had Dixon taught him well enough? Dixon mouthed up toward Nate, "You got it?"

Nate gave a slow smile that soon faded, the hard work of climbing etched on his face, but then he smiled again. Charming Nate. Even as a toddler, he could peek out from his stroller, bat his long lashes, flash his dimple, and make women swoon. Dixon, only sixteen months younger than Nate, had learned to lean to the right in the twin stroller to let himself be passed over. With a disarmingly handsome older brother, Dixon had to become someone in his own right: he became a good boy.

Wasn't it natural, then, that Nate would be the one to woo Everest? At Base Camp the day they arrived, when they had finally stood at her feet, Nate had squared himself, rising to her glance, and the sun had broken over the mountain's face. Of course. For his part, Dixon had been stunned by how the mountain dominated the sky. He had sucked in a hard breath and stumbled backward, tripping over the uneven ground and landing on his butt. The mountain was so beyond his imagining, with terraces of slate and ice that spiraled up toward the summit, their broad, imposing presence like the arms of God.

"She's beautiful," Nate said with a calm admiration while a bewildered Dixon found himself only able to steal looks toward the summit.

As they ascended, Dixon noted his brother's slow, steady pull up the rope, the intensity and sweat on his face—he did the hard work! Dixon quietly congratulated himself: he had trained Nate over the past six months, and wasn't that training paying off? A steady calm fell over Dixon; the cool, clear wire that had always been his recompense for goodness resounded in him, a measure of the world and of Dixon's place in it.

A hundred feet higher, the mountain revealed the depths of the crevasse below. At first, Dixon thought he saw below him the colorful prayer flags that waved above Base Camp. A lightning jolt of recognition as the forms morphed: a blue arm, a yellow torso, a red elbow, the black stretch of snow pants, the green toe of pricey climbing boots. A wash of terror flushed through Dixon. Bodies lay below him like broken marionettes, legs akimbo, arms overhead, lifeless in snowsuits still stalwart against the cold. Dixon stalled. A long, trembling beat. And then the high siren call of wind, the tickle of snow against his cheek. The call, the awful call. He slid, kicked, climbed.

Later, he would remember the many ways the mountain had revealed herself, and he would wonder: why did they excuse her fits of temper, cajole and caress and long for her, as if they would be spared?

CHAPTER

2

Everest was Nate's idea. In March a year before their climb, Dixon and Nate Bryant sat at their parents' kitchen table. It was a few months after their mother's death, a few weeks before selling their parents' tidy suburban split level. A last drink in the family home with everything just as their mom had left it: the crisp yellow café curtains above the kitchen sink, the pale-blue teacups swinging on hooks above the marble counter. The brothers would not pack a thing, only pick through the house for what they wanted: photographs and high school trophies, their dad's records, a rusted shotgun of their grandfather's. To the church bazaar and the women's shelter, they would leave the floral sofas and solid-wood tables, the dresses with lace collars.

At the kitchen table, they drank gin and tonic from tall yellow tumblers. Their father's favorite drink, Dixon recalled. Their mom had scoffed at it until after her older brother's sudden death when she had taken it up, too, quietly, the way you might pick up the loose edge of a blanket and slip beneath. Dixon and Nate talked, half whispering as they often had at that table.

"How come I didn't marry Terry?" Nate asked suddenly. "You see those beautiful girls she has? And how good she still looks?"

Dixon thought: You're so full of shit. "How come you didn't marry any of 'em?"

"Shoulda married *her*." Nate swirled his tumbler, sloshing his drink near the edge of the cup.

"You didn't want a wife. Not even somebody else's, as I recall." Dixon reared back in his chair, amused, a parade of Nate's women passing before his eyes.

"You're lucky. Kira."

Dixon pictured his daughter's face. His brother had always been a doting uncle, but over the past year he had ramped it up, sending Kira gifts out of the blue, writing her long letters, calling. Dixon stretched his hand out on the table toward Nate.

"I think . . ." Nate's mouth pursed, he studied Dixon, weighing his words. "I think I missed out, man. I was just . . ." He shrugged. "I didn't, I didn't think the average life was . . ." He spun his hand around in the air. "But you built something. No, no, don't shake it off, divorced or not, you built something, Dixon." Dixon twitched in his seat. Nate cleared his throat. "Heard this guy on the news last week, just climbed Mount Everest. He said, 'I'm an average guy, I work, I date, I pay taxes. But this mountain just filled something in me I can't explain.' You believe that?" Nate sat back hard, bouncing lightly in the chair. "Never told you," Nate began, then took a deep swallow. "I went to climb Mount Rainier. Trained for six months."

Dixon raised his eyebrows.

"Find that unbelievable, do you?" Nate took a swig of his drink. "Because you're expected to do that kind of thing, I'm not."

"Why didn't you ever tell me?" Dixon leaned forward. "When I went to Kilimanjaro, man, you could've come."

"You acted like it was some kinda quest, turning forty and goin' to the mountain," Nate joked. "You thought you were the Dalai Lama."

"You dogged my ass out about that trip," Dixon recalled with a flash of anger. His ex-wife Pamela had fought against that trip, too, insisting that Dixon use money from his retirement account, not from their joint savings. Dixon's arms tight across his chest, hands gripping his triceps. Nate continued to laugh, the jagged sound prickling Dixon's skin. "I can't believe you didn't tell me. Asshole."

Nate shrugged. "Now, why I gotta be all that? Anyway, I told Mom. She was secretly pleased, I think. You know what?" He paused, a wistful smile. "She said, 'Good for you, son. Stretch yourself.' Ah, she used to tell me that," a confession, his voice soft.

Dixon had thought it was his own secret with their mother: *You're the one, Dixon. You're going to rise. Stretch yourself.* Of course, of course: she would never leave out her Nate. Dixon shook his head fast, a quick self-chastisement. The cold wash of shame seemed like something he should've outgrown.

That night, Dixon was dozing on the sofa when Nate's voice filtered in. A high call, then a long whistle. Dixon stumbled toward the sound as he'd been so well trained to do. He careened down the wide hallway, navigating the grandfather clock and the duo of striped silk chairs grouped "in conversation," toward the attic stairs, up and across to the dormer window. Nate half in, half out of the window, straddling the dark attic and the bright moonlight outside, between worlds. He kicked his inside foot against the wall insulation, and small pink clusters of the stuff rose under his feet like ash. Nate thrust his tumbler toward the moon and gin sloshed along his arm. "Look! Look!" Nate called. "See how close the moon is?"

Dixon stood on the balls of his feet, ready to spring forward. Nate thrust his body up and forward through the window. Did he think he could fly? Shit. Nate never could hold his liquor. Dixon lunged forward, grabbing at his brother's shoulder, catching a handful of his shirt.

"Look at that," Nate said. "Can you *imagine* what it looks like from the top of the world? Huh?" Laughing, raising his drink toward the sky, and leaning almost sideways out the window. Dixon gripped with both hands and glanced below. A row of boxwoods near the house—they could break a fall. Nate's shirt balled in Dixon's fists, Nate's shoulder blades against Dixon's arms.

Nate stared close at Dixon. "You can, can't you, I mean, you can imagine it, right? Can you just let yourself loose?" A hint of disappointment from Nate, and Dixon registered a low-riding guilt. They might be children again: Dixon, three, and Nate, four and a half, Nate challenging him to eat the purple and red nasturtiums in their mother's window box, the flowers she uses to decorate the fancy cakes she's known for. Nate drags a chair across the linoleum floor and boosts Dixon up so he can tear the leaves from their stems. Nate holds the chair again so Dixon can reach the granulated sugar on the pantry's high shelf. The hard box, yellow like crayons, Nate instructs. At the table, they dump globs of sugar on the leaves, their pudgy fingers leaving sticky evidence all over the table and chairs. The front of Dixon's overalls turns syrupy sweet with sugar and drool. Nate giggles, but Dixon, that wire of alarm tight in him, repeats, "Is she gonna be mad? Is she gonna be mad?" and Nate chastises him, "Can't you just eat?"

Straddling the attic window, Nate grabbed his brother's lapel, his breath all liquor. "Man, I been looking at this Everest thing." Dixon pulled back and Nate slid with him inside and down onto the floor. Thick dust rose from beneath them in plumes, making them cough, turning their jeans nearly white. Nate laughed. "Like this! It's like this, Everest snow, see, it's a sign!"

A sigh of relief, this has been Dixon's whole life: latching onto his brother—that errant kite—always arresting him from danger. Exhausted, Dixon rested his hand on Nate's shoulder. "Yeah, all right," he sighed.

Nate reached for a dog-eared magazine. "Look. Just look." Nate held a photo too close to Dixon's face. "Everest," Nate began, breathless. "I'm thinking, the way the clouds wrap around, see, it's an eye on the whole world. Dixon, don't you think, don't you think, you can't go to a place like that and look at anything the same? I mean, man, tying your shoes," Nate slung his hands wide for emphasis, falling sideways and spilling the last of his drink on Dixon's pants, "would have to be a different thing after that."

"Yo, watch out!" Dixon wiped his pantlegs.

"We gotta, Dixon. We could do this!"

"Yeah, a'right, just let me get some sleep first."

Nate slumped, arms drawn in at his sides, both hands wrapped around the thin yellow tumbler. He seemed so small. At forty-eight, Nate's temples were newly gray, his brow settling into age, and this became clear: his face would darken over the years, like their father's, and small moles like constellations would rise around his eyes even though Nate's face was softer than their father's, his chin delicate. Nate was, in fact, an aging boy, something Dixon's ex-wife Pamela liked to note with derisive glee, "Boy Wonder's getting a little jowl." And when Dixon would reprimand her, she would say, "I'm on *your* side!" as if she fought some implicit war against Nate.

Nate sat quietly, his hands folded in his lap, then he said, "We all need something to show for our time."

———

WHO HAD TIME FOR THIS EVEREST NONSENSE? NATE HANGING sideways out of the window, shouting, *To the moon, Alice!* It made Dixon laugh out loud at work in the middle of an Intervention Team meeting. A disapproving eyebrow raise from a colleague, an audible pause in the room, and Dixon morphed his laugh into a clearly faked cough. Wiley Fitch at the blackboard, chalk midair, his nose wrinkling in displeasure, asked, "I'm amusing you?" Dixon's cheeks hot, he waved it off. "Sorry, sorry, remembering something a kid said earlier. Just got his meaning." A slow rumble of chuckles. But the idea of Everest rode the back of Dixon's neck, pawing and pawing so that his friend Benny Lewis, the only other person on the counseling team who had been at the school as long as him, chuckled. "You itching, buddy? One of these little knuckleheads give you scabies?"

And that's how the idea of Everest arrived at Medgar Evers Charter Middle School Academy for Boys in the D.C. suburbs of Maryland, where Dixon was school psychologist. It arrived as an itch, a goddamned infestation of thought. A deep, private thrill along his spine.

That school building was a 1990s marvel of steel and glass, a high, round metal roof the kids called the spaceship. The circular hallways were flooded by skylights, the concrete floors shimmered with embedded sea glass, and the sounds of conversation and movement echoed in disorienting bursts. Dixon took up his regular station in the hall between classes, Dixon the guardian, the shepherd. "Jamal, why weren't you in class last period?" "Blaine, are you not feeling well? Let's go to the nurse." Boys ran to him, hugged him, banged against him. He loved it. Nothing was more tactile than a pubescent boy, clanging his way through the world. Nothing more awkward. Dixon felt compassion for the ones with glasses sliding off their noses, the ones who half walked/half ran in a clumsy gallop, the ones with pants pulled just a couple inches too high.

Ah, look at this kid, towering over his classmates and skimming the walls trying to be invisible. Wouldn't Dixon's father hate the sight of that? With a swift palm press in the middle of Dixon's back, he'd say, "Straighten up, son, take your God-given space!" as he folded a handkerchief square into the pocket of Dixon's Sunday suit. "You're going to be a suit-wearing man." And didn't Dixon still love a suit? New counselors showed up at school in shirtsleeves and slacks, casual shoes, but Dixon sported a suit—tailored, out of necessity; he was six-five so few things off the rack fit him—and even though he'd abandoned the tie, he'd wear an impeccable crewneck sweater or maybe an open-collar shirt, put a crease in his trousers, a good leather belt, a shine to his lace-up shoes.

As the slouching boy passed, Dixon placed a hand on his spine, pushing him to straighten up. "Own it," he said.

A couple older boys darted out of study hall to tell Dixon their high school plans. Shona Mason waved from her classroom, then pantomimed a scream as kids poured through her door. Dixon rode the wave along the crowded hallway, the boys' voices a cacophony of octaves, their grubby hands pawing at him, a tap on the back here, a knock on the arm there, Dixon's name ringing out through the hallways: "Hey, Mr. Bryant!" A cool wash of an idea, fresh as cloudburst: he saw the bright, bare shoulder of a mountain, saw himself there facing downwind with sun and blowing snow stinging against his skin. He stopped mid-stride, turned toward the library's wide window. Outside, the sun was bright and wavering with the flag and he squinted into it, imagining the fresh snap of mountain air. Something building in him, low and tight below his ribs. What if he left?

Late that afternoon, Marcus Hollinger came to see him. One of his favorite kids, part of a small group who hung onto Dixon—"The Acolytes," Benny Lewis teased Dixon—Marcus had a pudgy, round face, his hair close-cropped. Marcus, whose mother visited her son's teachers so meekly, as if she were about to fail seventh grade and full of shame about it. Marcus sat down amid a semicircle of upholstered chairs. "Oh, Mr. B., I got health, right?" he jumped in, theirs an ongoing conversation. "It's, like, the body and everything."

Dixon laughed quietly. "So I hear."

"You know I wanna be a doctor? For kids."

Dixon recalled Marcus's disabled twin brother and sister, his father who commuted to a job over two hours away, his mother who lived at the end of her rope. "You can do it," Dixon said matter-of-factly. "Just keep working, son. How's everything else?"

Marcus filled Dixon in on his week. His hands moved animatedly as he talked. Dixon relaxed into Marcus's tales, the way he leaned forward to make a point. "Oh, Mr. B., you shoulda been there!"

The first time Dixon saw Marcus, the boy had been running through a hallway, his binder spewing papers behind him, Marcus clueless and so ungraceful that Dixon hadn't been able to suppress a laugh. "Hold your horses, son." Dixon had gathered the trampled papers. How boundlessly grateful Marcus had been, the boy's face had glowed as if he had never been helped before. As if Dixon had saved his life.

"So, how's our problem?" Dixon asked.

Marcus pressed his arms tight to his sides. "He's, like, tryina hurt somebody or something."

"Still?"

Marcus shrugged. "He doesn't like me."

"I'll have another talk with him."

"That won't, like, make it worse?"

"He needs to know you have people looking out for you."

There it was again, Marcus's beguiling gratitude. And here he was, thinking of abandoning him for Mount Everest. It landed like a shoe in his gut. He sucked in a fast, hard breath.

Marcus's problem, Shiloh Evans, had quickly become everyone's problem. Not a week went by without that kid ending up in detention. He'd been suspended twice so far, and there were still three months left in the school year. From the first day of school, he had shown himself to be trouble, arriving late, bounding up to the front door, a suppressed explosion in each step. An oversized black windbreaker, a hood pulled low over his head, as if to announce, "I'm your nightmare." Dixon had been front-door greeter on Shiloh's first day: "Son, second bell has rung. Get a move on." The boy had paused and let the hood drop, revealing his face: pockmarked and scarred with trails of burned skin down the slope of his cheeks, the skin a dark, worn leather. Hard as hell to look at. The boy had leaned into Dixon's space, but Dixon didn't budge. The boy's look a long leer. Clearly this was his power.

The day after he began thinking of Everest, Dixon monitored the cafeteria during lunch: rows of long white dining tables and red plastic chairs, boys' voices echoing up the walls. Dixon joked with a few kids, commented on their lunch selections, keeping a light banter. At a far back table, he spotted Marcus eating a pitiful lunch of a few crackers and a few slices of apple—a lunch he likely made for himself, his mother too overwhelmed with the twins this morning. Dixon beckoned and Marcus bolted toward the lunch line. With one hand on Marcus's shoulder as he joked with a group of kids, Dixon slipped a five-dollar bill into Marcus's hand and guided him into line. Dixon spun around. Behind him, perched wide-legged on top of one of the dining tables, sat Shiloh, darting his look to Marcus and back to Dixon.

"Young man," Dixon said, "off the table, please." He offered the boy a chair. They stared each other down, and finally Shiloh slid from the table. "Are you finished with lunch, or have you not been through the line yet?"

"Why? You gonna buy me lunch, too?"

Dixon was taken aback. "Do you need me to?"

"Yeah, slip me a fi'ty." He let out a snort.

"You need lunch? C'mon. I'll get you a voucher." The boy didn't move. "C'mon. You gotta eat, right?" Dixon was determined to disarm this boy. He lowered his voice, softened it. "We can get you hooked up with a free lunch program, if you need. Confidentially. No one will be the wiser."

"No, no." Shiloh shook his head, an earnest look on his face. "I want *you* to do it, I want it out your pocket, you know, like I'm your *bitch*," he spit out the last word.

Dixon cocked his head to the side. Oppositional defiant disorder, he recalled from his assessment of this kid. "You think I'm looking out for Marcus? Well, I am. Just like I look out for all my boys."

"Oh, you just Big Money, giving out duckets like it ain't all that."

"You don't know where that money came from—from his mother, from his locker, from the lottery—not that it's your business." He crossed his arms over his chest, squared his stance. "Let's not talk about other people, let's talk about you. Do you need us to help you with lunches? We can do that."

"Not us, *you*."

"Say it's from me, then. I'll do the paperwork. How 'bout that?"

"Not good enough."

Dixon gave a short laugh. "Man, you just want us to have a problem here, huh? You just wanna get all in your own way?"

"I take care myself." He sprang up. "We done?"

Dixon stood unmoving a long time—making that boy wait on *his* timetable—a long, measured time before he stepped aside and let the boy leave.

That kid needed something to shift his focus away from his miserable self. Dixon might've considered it longer, but the day soared along loud and frantic: a boy sparked a fight in class, another had a panic attack and was taken out by ambulance, and a parent wept for fifteen minutes straight in Dixon's office.

He left at the end of the day as the activity buses were loading, the sky a watercolor of purple and yellow, the air crisp and green with spring. He felt happy enough, satisfied with the work of the day. Glancing at his car after he tossed his briefcase inside—a flat tire. Not just flat, ripped. Dammit. He examined the slit, a knife slice. Shiloh. Who else? He opened his trunk—this was why you kept a clean trunk, so you could get to the damn tire; you had to be prepared—and set to work. "No Shilohs on Everest, at least," he mumbled, then pushed away the thought of Everest, embarrassed, agitated.

"What happened?"

Dixon glanced behind him at Marcus. "Flat tire."

"You not supposed to call triple A for that?"

Dixon frowned, his eyes steady on Marcus. "You don't know how to change a tire?"

The kid shook his head. So Dixon instructed him: "You want a full size, not one of those donut things. Messes up your alignment. You'll end up needing a new tire anyway, nine times outta ten."

Marcus absorbed the lesson, watching Dixon's face, following every movement. "Like this?" he asked when it was time to replace the lug nuts. He ought to know this, Dixon thought, and recalled Marcus's father, the look of gentle disappointment on him, the hard furrows in his forehead, his jowliness even though he was clearly younger than Dixon. When would he have time for this? They had only met once, the rare time both parents could attend a school event. The man had shaken Dixon's hand hard and said, delighted, "I was in junior high, but I remember you, breaking all those state records. Wow! You were something."

"See now, when your mom gets a flat, you can be the hero." Dixon helped the boy stand when they were done. "How's that?"

Marcus rocked toward Dixon like he wanted to say something. Finally, he blurted out, "I wanna get strong."

Dixon considered. "We can do that."

⎯⎯⎯

HE THOUGHT ABOUT MARCUS AS HE WENT FOR HIS EVENING run. What could it mean for a kid like that to get strong? To count on his body? As if to prove himself, Dixon ran longer that night, uphill, watching day slip to dusk, running into the soft, black lure of night. His calves began to burn. The voice of the body overtaking him. A delicious giving over, a kind of sex, the heat of muscle and speed. The stab of longing. If he turned his head just so, he could see it: that guy just at his left flank, 1981 Olympic trials. Dixon's stride so good, his rhythm all his own—that feeling of being unbeatable spreading like a bright light through his limbs—and yet that runner to his left gaining on him, the sweep of heat from the other runner's body. For the first time, Dixon digs down and finds an empty well. Churning, churning but going no faster. That guy passing him. Then another, a hot spike of air. Only the top three go forward to the Olympics. He must hold his ground, *he has to!* Dixon digs into himself but finds no upper gear. A third guy at his arm so close Dixon's hairs stand up. A chill snaking through him, the splash of air and sweat on his arm, the rhythmic sound of another's breath. Dixon careens forward, arms flailing—*Don't go wild, don't break form*—a wild lunge as if he is drowning. At the tape, another runner leans in first, Dixon just at his heels, just out of contention, Dixon who is never left behind.

The memory seized him, bent him over, he stumbled to a stop in the darkness. Hands on his hips, panting, memory's hot grip in the center of his chest. He dug his fist into his rib cage, pushing back against it, erasing. A long time before he could stand upright, before he could turn his head just so. The girl he dated in high school, Desiree, when he found her on Facebook after his divorce, had said, "I remember pining for you a long time." His eyes closed. Pining. He would have to crack himself wide open again to do Everest. Because you had to want a mountain above all else or it was simply cold and miserable and thankless. Who could stand the wanting? Less than two-tenths of a fucking second between him and making the team. Flags draped over the winners, Olympics-bound. At night for weeks after, he had awakened leaning in, chest pushed out, weeping. *I remember pining for you a long time.* Such old-fashioned language, and it snapped like a whip against him. He didn't wish that feeling back again. He didn't want to latch onto Everest.

⎯⎯⎯⎯

"LOOK AT THAT. LITTLE SHIT," BENNY LEWIS SAID. THEY ALL shook their heads, Benny, Dixon, and Kurt, the school resource officer. They stared at Shiloh on the security footage from the previous day. He sauntered into the teacher's parking lot, strolling through rows of cars. Just before he reached Dixon's car, he ducked out of sight, remained invisible awhile, then reappeared two rows away and jogged out of frame. "He did it, no question."

"No footage of him actually doing it," Kurt said. "Could've been anybody. Look at all the other people out there."

"The teachers, you mean?" Dixon asked.

"Look, you know and I know that he probably slit your tire, but if we present this, we just look foolish. Not enough proof. I'm sorry."

*Not enough,* a sour taste in Dixon's mouth but one he'd just have to swallow. And he did. Later, when he passed Shiloh in the halls, Dixon said, "Don't be late for class, son," as if nothing was wrong.

But he had an extra beer that night at his cousin Charlaina's. Kira watched him with raised eyebrows. He was known for being a one-drink man.

"What's wrong, Dad?" Kira asked. She curled her feet up under her, sitting lotus-style on Charlaina's immaculate carpet. Tonight, Kira was preppy: polo shirt, khaki jeans, tortoiseshell schoolboy glasses. A relief, really, because you never knew what you'd get from her: retro '60s with frosted lipstick and side-flipped hair, unisex in oversized black clothing. He focused on his daughter. "Kid at school, nothing to worry about, Monkey."

Nate walked toward him, bent down to his ear. "Or maybe you're dreaming of Everest?" He straightened up, raised his brows twice, and plopped down in a chair opposite Dixon, who rolled his eyes. Nate threw back his head and laughed.

"What are you two up to?" Charlaina stood before Dixon with a tray of drinks. Dixon shrugged it off. When Charlaina reached Kira, she said, "The club soda and lime's for you." Kira glared at her. "You're not legal yet, I'm sorry, I changed your diapers."

Kira made a disgusted sound. "You know, I, like, literally drink at school, right?"

"And that's why we sent you away, so we don't have to witness it," Charlaina added.

Kira cut her eyes toward Dixon, who couldn't help laughing. "Why's this funny?" she demanded, then slapped her knee. "I'm grown!" Totally undermining her claim. From the slump of her shoulders, she knew it, too.

"Poor baby girl," Nate chimed in.

Charlaina foisted the tray toward Kira, nodding to her drink.

"Y'all make me sick! For real!" Kira took her designated drink, her face a pubescent scowl.

"Well, you know what makes me sick? Look at this." Charlaina pointed toward the wide-screen TV. "You guys are watching hockey? I mean, this sport builds in a break to let them fight in the middle of a game. And they end up with busted jaws and concussions! Putting themselves in deliberate harm. I have no respect for that."

Nate's eyes darted to Dixon, a quick check between the two. Later, in the kitchen, Dixon whispered, "Do you want to be the one to tell her? Because I'm not doing it!"

## CHAPTER

3

Early in April, Dixon drove Marcus to his house after school for the first time. When he'd asked Marcus's mother for permission, she had been ecstatic: "Praise the Lord! He needs more of your influence, Mr. Dixon." Dixon and Marcus walked to the soccer field across the street from Dixon's house. They would work up to circuit training and jogging but started with basic sit-ups. Marcus had a hard time, sitting up sideways, his feet kicking out for stability. Woefully out of shape but Dixon was patient with him. How could he not be? Despite how hard it looked for him, Marcus was so eager.

Had this plum of a boy ever been a miracle to his parents? Nate had been the miracle in Dixon's family, Dixon the moral barometer. In her later years, their mother used to say before any decision, "See what Dixon says." But Nate had been the gift. For more than five years, their parents had tried to conceive, feeling more than a bit cheated. They were good middle-class Black folks with college degrees and coveted jobs as teachers, career paths that would lead them each to become school principals. They were ready to raise a family in comfort: a hand-painted cradle, a bedroom decorated with kittens-and-puppies wallpaper, a layette set from Hecht Company, and a matching changing table and small dresser bought on time from Van's Furniture. All empty. Waiting. Just as they had nearly given up hope, along came Nate.

Nate had asked Dixon: *Come with me to Everest.*

Dixon called his brother, 3 a.m., his heart racing. "You gotta explain this to me. It makes no sense."

"Sure it does." Nate groggy, yawning. Dixon could picture the childlike way Nate still rubbed his closed eyes with the edges of his fists. "It's just audacious. You're not used to that."

"But where did this come from, Nate?"

Nate shifted the phone, cleared his throat. "There was this client I was wooing, cocky white boy. Makes me meet him at a fitness course. Short, bulky little dude. Turned out this class was some, some climbing fitness course to train you to climb Mount Rainier, then prep you for any summit, right? Kept saying all the North American peaks are 'tame,' not the 'real ones, but it's a good start, do this, you can do any of the others.' Same technique, just a different scale. I can't say I was thinking about it, really, just trying to win over this guy. But he duped me, man, never had any intention of hiring me, just fucking with me. By the time I figured that out, I was into it. I mean, I was good at it, you know? Then the idea got good to me, the challenge. Can't wave a red flag in front of a bull and not expect him to charge."

"And you told Mom?" He didn't mean to sound brokenhearted.

"You know Mom. She always wanted us to surprise her in a

good way. Maybe I had something to prove. I don't know. I wish now we'd done Mount Rainier together. I really do."

"We can't do this, it's not who we are." Dixon pictured the garage of their childhood home, strewn with sports equipment. The Althea Gibson and Arthur Ashe wooden tennis rackets with color sketches of each namesake on the handle—Dixon had grown embarrassed to use them during tennis club when everyone else had newer and anonymous aluminum rackets, embarrassed enough to stop playing, which confounded his father, who held such pride in the racket, in the players. The basketball signed by Wilt Chamberlain. Dr. J's line of Converse sneakers and his basketball hoop. A soccer ball signed by Pelé. For every sport, a hero, a tacit approval. Who in the world ever heard of climbing Mount Everest?

"We get to decide who we are," Nate said in a matter-of-fact tone.

This was less a strike against their father than it sounded. A concession, instead, toward their mother. The one who had whispered into both their ears: *Stretch. Grow.*

"I know we can do this. Bryant Boys. Look, I've watched you train before, you know what to do. And I'll do whatever you say. What*ever*."

"We aren't rich, how 'bout that?"

Except that they had newly inherited money, Nate repeatedly pointed out.

Dixon argued the climb would take nearly half of what each had netted from the sale of their parents' house. "All that money to climb a goddamned mountain? We could do some real good," Dixon said, his hands balled up in his lap.

"This *is* good for *us*."

KIRA WAS A RUNNER. WHEN SHE WAS A CHILD, HER MOTHER had signed her up for soccer, that middle-class cure-all. But Kira always looked so distracted on the soccer field. Dixon realized she was watching the teens on the adjacent track, so he had taken her over there one day. "Come race me," he had joked. He was easy on her at first—she was only nine, after all—but just after they began, she had glanced at him, a split-second look that made it clear she meant business. She instinctively understood not to overpump, to keep her strides long and even, to let her torso propel her. *Look at her go.* It had felt as close to giving birth as Dixon could ever come.

"I wanna see you back at the Penn Relays next year," he said. Her spring break at an end, she was about to return to college. They sat across from each other at a restaurant with white table-cloths, candles in crystal holders, waiters who laid your napkin in your lap. A treat for his nearly grown-up daughter—appeasement for not letting her drink alcohol.

"I'll make it," she said, and her easy confidence made him proud. Kira held her fork between two fingers, bouncing it slightly. She had her mother's small hands, petite fingers, and small, oval nail beds. Not descended from peasants, his ex-wife used to joke, but born to the manor. Kira gazed up at him in that way she had since babyhood, no artifice, just a searing hook into his heart. "Do you think," she began, frowning her mouth in thought. "Do you think I might get to be as good as you?"

A flood of emotion, he had to open his mouth to let it escape before he spoke. "Better."

"Nah, couldn't be." She blushed and beamed at him, then burst into chatter about her coach, her friends, her classes, an excited flow of "have you read this, have you seen that?" peppered with pronouncements: "It's excellent!" with a quick nod of her chin or "It's not that serious" with a sideways glance. Dixon listened, relaxed, studying her persona for the evening: she wore an Afro carefully shaped into a flawless dome. She wore large gold hoops, which sparkled against her caramel skin, a black turtleneck, and black jeans. An homage to the '70s, and he appreciated that glimpse of his own youth.

At last, she paused to eat a bite of her chicken. Dixon cleared his throat. "So, Monkey, I'm thinking—"

"Dad, oh my god, you literally can't call me *Monkey* in public. Ever heard of negative stereotypes?"

He was taken aback. "Your favorite toy?"

"Yeah, yeah, but not in public." She leaned forward, a grimace.

"Sorry, sweetheart." He drummed his fingers on the table, chastised, regrouping. "Listen, I'm thinking. I may—" He looked her in the eye. "What would you think about me climbing again? Me and Uncle Nate."

She sat back, blinked fast. "He climbs?"

"He's done, yeah, little bit." He shrugged. "We're thinking about Mount Everest. Just thinking, mind you. Haven't told anyone yet."

"Okay." Her eyes flashed. "Okay."

She was so like her mother, measuring, weighing.

"We'd only go when we're ready. We'd have to train hard. I'll insist on that."

Her look just this side of terror.

"I'm saying, Monk—sweetheart, we're just batting the idea around." He paused. "Looks like it's not my most popular idea, huh?"

"Well," she said in a fast exhale, "I mean . . ." her mouth stuttering with movement. "Good luck? Don't do it? *Damn*?"

"Watch your language," he scolded lightly, then folded his arms in front of him on the edge of the table. "It's just a thought." Flustered, he shook his head, rebuffing himself. "See, it's a dream, you know, you need a dream now and then." No! That was Nate. "I mean," he said sternly, "that is, something you work hard for, something above all else, something you *earn*."

"Is this, like, your red sportscar? Mom said that's what middle-aged men do. Divorce, red sportscar, that kind of thing."

He dabbed his mouth with his napkin. "Your mom left *me*."

"You mean she released you." Kira laughed and at that moment looked far too knowing. It chilled Dixon. He didn't want to think about what she might've learned watching his marriage. "Don't look so shocked. I know she's hard on a man. For real. So, you gonna tell her about Mount Everest? I mean, are you ready for that?"

Prepared for Pamela? As if he had ever been. Kira would come around, he was sure of it. He could imagine her cheering him on, helping him train—an image of them on the track running side by side.

Wait. Wait. He was getting ahead of himself. This was all his brother's doing. Such old roles they each played: After Nate has convinced three-year-old Dixon to eat their mother's flowers, Dixon lies on the living room rug, his heart thumping in terror. "Act normal," Nate says, and they try to concentrate on watching cartoons. Their grandmother dozes on the living room couch, as she does most afternoons. Dixon, on the verge of tears, has to stop that gnawing, buzzing feeling of wrong. Hands behind his back, trembling, a tiny boy in sugar-crusted overalls, his little arms and legs frail as twigs, he confesses soon after his mother gets home, "I ate the flowers." His mother hesitates. "Just you? What about your brother?" Dixon shakes his head. "I did it." Their parents make a big show of punishing Dixon to incite Nate's guilt, Nate who sits silently as his brother takes a spanking, then he cries softly, too, his face in his hands. That night, Nate crawls into Dixon's bed and wraps himself cat-like around his brother. "I'm sorry, I'm sorry," he repeats. And that becomes their pattern, as if Dixon has been born to the task.

Enough, Dixon thought, but he could not separate himself from his brother's persistence. Sending Dixon articles on climbers. Not pro climbers, not real alpinists, but guys like Dixon, the used-to-be and wannabe athlete in his forties who trained in that focused way Nate knew Dixon could. A former triathlete—Nate had circled that part in the article and written in the margins: "You came in twelve spots ahead of this guy in that same race." He sent glossy photos of the mountain at dawn, the sunlight burning gold and red across its face. Photos of men at high camp in gleaming yellow tents, holding tin cups of steaming coffee. Nate courted and tormented Dixon, who began to feel helpless to desire. He day-dreamed about the sound of crampons crunching into snow, about the view so far above the world, about the high-pitched tune like strummed wire that the thin air calls into your ears. This was how Nate operated. All those girls who had stopped Dixon on the street back in the day, their longing spilling at his feet: *Can't you get him to call me? Please?* Because there was something about being caught in Nate's relentless crosshairs.

"CAN YOU PROMISE ME YOU'LL COME BACK? I MEAN, I DON'T want to be almost an orphan. That is not the journey I'm trying to have. I know I said 'Do what you need to,' but this is crazy!" Kira paced Dixon's living room after their dinner. "Okay, I read about that, that famous thing way back where all those people died on Everest? And then one guy, his wife was about to have a baby and then from the mountain, he's like dying, and he calls and they name the baby and then he's dead. And that's so tragic and stupid, I mean, why would you do that, go, like, oh my god, where you could *die* and you're about to be someone's father, I mean, like you are literally about to have a child come into the world? That's not fair!"

He was silent. He slipped his hands beneath his thighs, sitting hard on them.

"Can you promise me?" She plopped down beside him on the sofa, her breathing fast.

He gathered himself. "There's nothing decided. Nothing."

"I know you, Dad, and I believe you can do it. I really do." Her look so full of confidence in him that he blushed. "But Uncle Nate," she said quietly. "Can he do it? Can you say no to him?"

He felt called out. He stammered, "I haven't, I haven't decided, I told you." Too defensive. "I won't go if you don't want me to," he blurted out and immediately regretted it.

"And you wouldn't hold that against me? Really?"

He could not look at her. But he dreamed that night of Everest, of the clean smell of snow, of standing on a high ridge with Nate, the world indistinct below them, a swirl of cloud and snow and land. They seemed outsized on the side of the mountain, their footsteps carving craters that became valleys. They sculpted the world.

He awakened breathing deep, his hand across his chest. Was it so outrageous an idea? Wasn't it in fact time for him to do something audacious like Nate was always saying? And there was this tremulous thought: What if he succeeded? What if he made it?

JUST BEFORE MEMORIAL DAY, TWO MONTHS AFTER NATE'S FIRST proposal, Dixon agreed to meet his brother and a guy who had summited. The café where he awaited them seemed a place happily left behind. Original Bobby Darin album covers sat dusty and curling with age along the back shelves. The glass saltshakers were filled with rice to prevent clumping, the way Dixon's grandparents had done on their farm. Women in flower-print housedresses, men in plain white shirts tucked into dark slacks. It could've been the 1960s. Dixon frowned into his coffee cup. Instant coffee, like brown acid-water. Yuck.

The roar of a souped-up motorcycle announced their arrival. Of course, Dixon thought, the kind of guys who climb Everest would ride hogs, fly airplanes, and probably jump out of them. Nate entered the café with a tall, godlike man, fit and broad-shouldered with golden-tanned skin, a square jaw, and muted green eyes. Dressed in a polo shirt and khaki shorts, he blazed a perfect white smile, tucked a few loose strands of dark blond hair behind his ear. Here was a long-haired Troy Donahue, straight off a '60s-era movie set. Nate darted in front of the man and beckoned toward Dixon, urging him to stand.

"This is Peter Sands," Nate said to Dixon. He turned to Peter. "My brother, Dixon Bryant." Pleased, Nate stepped back and let the men shake hands.

They were nearly the same height, with Dixon an inch taller but Peter wider, bigger boned. Sturdy, Dixon thought, and examined the man's wingspan, the tightness of his grip as they shook hands. Upper body strength, certainly. But average-looking legs. Short hamstrings, the kind that seized up over long distances. The kind of guy Dixon could cruise past in long, easy strides. Dixon relaxed and said, "Nice to meet you."

Nate gestured for them all to sit around the table, and Peter perched between the two brothers. Once they had ordered coffee, Nate leaned in. "He's been to the mountain," he said in a pseudo-conspiratorial whisper. "Tell him," Nate urged.

"Nate says you've done Kili? You can do this. Only real technical part is near the summit, the Hillary Step. Just learn how to use crampons, to belay, which you probably know. Get some technique with your ice axe, you know, self-arrest. Mostly, you need stamina. It's just one foot in front of the other, all day long."

"Sounds easy," Dixon goaded him.

"Well, no." Peter folded his muscular arms across his chest. He leaned back in his chair, straightened out his legs in front of him, and crossed his ankles. "This is rigorous, no doubt. No doubt. You'll be tested. So don't go into it cold. Get high before you go."

They frowned at him, and Peter paused, replaying his own words, then burst into a deep, full laugh that became contagious.

"High," he gasped, "altitude. Get some high-altitude climbs in."

"Right, right," Nate said.

Peter dabbed his eyes. "It's the altitude that fucks with ya." Peter offered advice about how to choose a climbing team. Dixon nodded patiently; Peter didn't tell him anything he did not know from his research.

"And I say, spend the money. Go with the right team," Peter pronounced. He unfolded himself and placed his elbows on the table. He looked at them plainly, a break in his hubris: his smile faded and the shadow surrounding his wrinkles bared his age. He was Dixon's age, easy. Maybe Nate's. "Lookit," he said quietly. "It's the worst and best thing you'll ever do. This is definitely not fun, but you know that. You'll suffer. Headaches. Worse. And we're not the real climbers, not these guys you'll meet up there who must've teethed on mountain ice. I'm a science professor. Blowing up things in the backyard as a kid, setting the garage on fire, you know? Ahhh!!" He made an exaggerated screaming face. "My mother threatened to send me to boarding school, but my father talked her down. That was my adventure. Just a guy who fell in love with a mountain. Only climbed two before Everest, nothing above five thousand meters. Yeah, yeah, compared to those other guys, I played it safe. A team with a doctor, a cook, a manager, a sherpa, and guide just for me. I paid my money. Good money to get to the top. *Still* only a handful of us can say that." He sat back, the smile reappearing and settling across him.

Dixon asked quietly, "You never climbed Everest before? And you summited? That's rare, isn't it?"

"Yep. Did a couple triathlons. Was really a swimmer, high school, college, Olympic trials."

Nate shot a look at Dixon, who realized he was being slowly, carefully reeled in.

"Swimming was my game. Came this close to the Olympics. The prelims in '82, I swam a 22.96, just missed the finals by two-tenths of a fucking second."

Dixon's stomach congealed around what felt like a fist. He sipped his weak coffee. Swallowed. "Been there, all right."

"Hard to shake off, isn't it? So, you know how to train? You look in shape. You can do this, you can do this." Peter's certainty fell like confetti onto Dixon, who owned it for the first time: I could.

"Listen, I'll tell you," Peter continued, "those mountain men deserve their rep. But it doesn't just belong to them. You sit down there, Base Camp, look up at that peak, you know, the way the clouds and snow blow around it, and it's just another flag, 'on your mark, set, go.' It's that white tape at the finish line. It's touching the wall of the pool."

The three sat for a good while. They lingered over Peter's photos from the climb—the blue tongue of glacial ice exposed beside him, the boulders of ice pouring through the Khumbu Icefall. Dixon felt the rising hum of desire in his body and thought of his ex-wife Pamela before Kira was born: At a dinner party with friends who were out for the first time since the birth of their son, Dixon had come upon Pamela in a corner with the new mother, bent over photos of her baby, Pamela's fingers tracing across the baby's cheek. She had gazed up at Dixon, glassy-eyed.

He was the one seized now with longing. He studied Peter's photo, the backlit mountain behind him, the spool of cloud that unrolled across the sky. The clear, rarified air. A mere few thousand had ever stood in that spot. Peter had said it: Sure, the alpinists deserved their props. But it wasn't all theirs. With a sudden, swift certainty, Dixon fell hopelessly toward Everest. Just as Nate knew he would. Nate, reading Dixon easily, sat back in his chair.

Peter retrieved his photos. "Anything else I can do for you guys, let me know. You won't regret it, believe me."

They stood and shook hands. Peter took a long glance at Dixon. "You might want to beef up. Gotta have some margin for what you're gonna lose on the mountain. Fat, muscle."

Nate clapped Dixon on the back. "Eat up, mountain boy."

## CHAPTER

4

*March 2011, Nepal*

On the way to Kathmandu, Nate was restless, stretching his legs, rising often. They flew from Washington Dulles to London, then to Hong Kong, and finally to Kathmandu. More than twenty-four hours. As they approached, Kathmandu spread out below them low and wide with buildings the color of clay; here and there, a white temple gleamed, its dome tipped with gold. Once on the ground and out in the streets, Dixon marveled at the newness. They had been warned not to risk sickness by spending too much time wandering the city, but how could they resist? The crowded streets smelled of spices and sewage. A layer of dust covered everything, and the air was thick with smog. Their taxi driver navigated around people, cars, bicycles, all competing for the same narrow road. A jittery, frenetic world. A mix of time periods as if the old and new worlds existed simultaneously. Centuries-old brick and timber buildings with ornately carved wooden window frames nestled alongside squat brick twentieth-century buildings. Stupas that dated back to the fifth century, their pagodas like delicate stacked triangles. Gleaming new signs for Coca-Cola.

In their taxi, the brothers traveled in the mix of worlds. Ancient temples filled Durbar Square. The Western world beckoned from street-corner stalls selling Ray-Ban sunglasses, Seiko watches, computers, cell phones. A sudden alcove between buildings revealed antique brass prayer wheels framing an archway. Inside the alcove, an old man in a simple tunic and linen pants knelt in prayer so devoutly that Dixon found himself bowing his own head. In another grotto before an altar, a young man lay on the floor face down, arms and legs spread wide. He moved clockwise in a circle around the foot of the altar. There was something of the past at each turn, Dixon noted. Also something wild and unexpected. Take, for instance, the resident monkeys who wandered Sway-ambhunath, the city's gilded Monkey Temple. Those monkeys reclaimed their ancestral space. Here, in Kathmandu, Dixon found, all things collided.

In the shopping district, Dixon and Nate traveled on foot. The journey felt real now as they passed the many stores clearly banking on their presence, on Dixon and Nate right here, right now, a row full of signs in Hindi yielding to a blaze of English: "The Everest Equipment Here." Dixon elbowed Nate and pointed out the sign with sudden glee. But Nate had spun completely around, staring into the smoggy sky.

"Everest's hiding somewhere. Which direction?" Nate's voice full of childish wonder.

"Can't see her from here, remember?"

"I feel her. She's so close."

The idea of the mountain's closeness left the brothers slightly drunken but wide awake—had Dixon ever been so awake before? The city reminded him of a wilder Brazil. In Bahia, everyone might have been his direct cousin, the same slave ships having taken Africans to Brazil as to America. Here in Kathmandu, the people were more distantly related: brown faces but not like his. They did not have Black African features or tightly coiled hair like Dixon's and Nate's. So when the brothers walked past four weathered old men with dark brown faces and dreadlocs piled in a tall bun, they were startled. The brothers greeted those old men the way they might do at home. But they were not home, they were not among their own.

"We look American, you think," Dixon asked, "or just 'other'?"

"I'm guessing American. But who knows what they see?"

In the market, which brimmed with colorful bins of fruits and vegetables, local women gazed at them with curiosity—so many women in bright silken shawls shimmering with gold threads, a kind of extravagance neither brother had expected. The brothers spun the golden prayer wheels at the monasteries. The whole time, they attempted to translate the looks they received. Were they welcome, were they not? Were they invisible at this shop because of their color—Nate had to resort to tapping hard on a glass counter with his hotel room key—or was it simply a more leisurely culture? Were they being followed in a shop because of fear they would steal or because they were rich Americans and good marks? This is what Dixon and Nate's family and friends had warned them about.

Two men with inscrutable faces and hands plunged deeply into their pockets wound through the market stalls behind the brothers for a good ten minutes. Nate and Dixon exchanged glances: *You see this? What do we need to do?* The feeling of being so far from home and yet experiencing a horribly familiar wariness.

The men on their heels, down one aisle, cutting over to the next, keeping pace with the brothers. Dixon and Nate shared a quick look then stopped and spun around. The men stopped short. A breath held. They bowed, then handed Nate and Dixon flyers for a nightclub. A cool spray of relief washed through Dixon. Nate stuttered a laugh. So hard to read the world here. The work of doing so was the same enervating activity they had performed all their lives, but its familiar cues seemed lost. They retreated to their hotel room, tired, edgy, seeking a comfort zone.

OTHER THAN TELLING KIRA, DIXON HAD KEPT NATE FROM AN-nouncing this Everest business to their family for as long as he could. Since they wouldn't leave for Kathmandu until late March, there seemed no reason to incite disapproval too far in advance. But the secret lay like a bomb between them, unexploded and un-predictable.

Their cousin Charlaina's holiday gathering proved too big a temptation for Nate. Charlaina's house was a wonderland of lighted garland outlining the imposing palladium windows and not one, but two bejeweled Christmas trees flanking the first floor, with trains chugging along their tracks beneath each tree. The mellow voice of Nat King Cole on the stereo, the smell of cinnamon and Fraser fir and its pull back to childhood.

Skeet and his wife Tania arrived. Skeet, Nate's oldest friend, and by extension Dixon's. Tall like them, not as lean. An easy friend, actually, Skeet had never tried to peel Nate off from Dixon but simply joined in, which was probably why he had lasted so long. Skeet neither blocked their light nor stood fully in shadow but found a niche somewhere between.

On the way into Charlaina's living room, Skeet missed the single step down from the foyer, stumbling forward before catching himself.

"Down goes Frazier!" Nate gave Skeet a bear hug.

"Well, that's a record," Tania said as she greeted Charlaina. "Only ten seconds before they invoked Ali-Frazier Two." Tania shook her head. "Can't they just say hello?"

"And what fun would that be," Dixon said. He kissed her cheek. Her perfume was musky and sweet. She was tall and curvy with rich brown eyes and a tiny sickle-shaped scar on her left cheek that mimicked a dimple. It made her look like she was perpetually smiling. When they'd all met her in college, she'd had a crush on Dixon, he later learned. In Charlaina's living room, she studied him, lingered a minute, then let out a small sigh before moving away.

At the dinner table, amid the sweet buzz of wine, conversation, and food, Nate declared, "I've got news." Dixon's body went on alert. "We," Nate motioned between himself and Dixon, "are going to Mount Everest."

Dixon braced himself: here we go.

"What?" Charlaina looked confused.

"Mount Everest. Dix and I are climbing in the spring. We're already in training. Dixon's done Kilimanjaro, Denali. I did Mount Rainier, mostly. So it's not out of the blue."

"Dixon?" Charlaina leaned forward as if he would set this right. "Yep."

"Wow." Skeet froze, his knife and fork midair. He stared at Tania across the table, a quick gesture that Dixon read as *I told you about them.* Skeet had known the brothers since the height of their legend: the Romeo, the runner.

"That's nuts," Charlaina snapped. "Who the hell climbs Mount Everest? Guys, people die up there."

"People die going to the grocery store." Nate shrugged it off. "We're not going to die, we're going to climb."

Skeet cracked up. "But what Black man wants to climb a cold-ass mountain? What, your lives aren't hard enough on earth? Look, just come down to the job with me, climb that corporate mountain, you want some misery. It's nice and white at the top, too, just like Mount Everest."

"It's that most people *don't* do it. That's what makes it worth it," Dixon said.

Nate looked pleased.

"Most people don't shoot heroin either," Charlaina snapped. "'Cause that shit'll kill you!"

Skeet examined Nate, his brow furrowing then gliding into a look of awe. "A man's gotta have a dream. You can't color inside the lines your whole life."

"How far outside the lines are you allowed to get?" Charlaina argued. She leaned across the table, knocking over the salt-shaker.

Dixon picked up the shaker, tossed salt over his left shoulder.

"Are you two the only ones? I mean, are there others of our folk going?" Charlaina reached for Dixon's hand, her face contorted with worry.

"Not in our group," Dixon answered.

"Well, I hate to say it, but it's good you're both going," Tania said. "You won't be totally alone."

"Of all the dangers in the world, who the hell wants this one?" Charlaina clasped her hands together, rubbing them against each other.

Nate said defiantly, "Why wouldn't I want mountains? Why shouldn't I?"

"You *want* a good education, a good job, a family, you want respect and equality. You don't *want* mountains!" Charlaina banged her fist on the table.

Nate wiped his mouth. He threw down his napkin. "This ain't Mars, y'all. People climb mountains. It's not that big a deal."

Skeet said, "Bryant Boys. Off the chain! I'm down with this." He saw Charlaina's shocked look. "I mean it. Man, I want to brag on this!" He leaned back to laugh, eyes narrowed, the slow, steady light of awe sweeping across his face. It gripped Dixon, spread like fingers along his spine. An addictive thing.

In her kitchen after dinner, Charlaina pulled Dixon aside. "It's a joke, right? You're not doing this?"

"We are," he said, his hand wide around her elbow, rubbing slowly. Fear in her eyes.

"It's his idea, isn't it?"

"I've been training us, Char, and I'm taking off the spring semester to go at it full time. I won't let up on him. We're gonna be ready."

"I'm not ready, Dixon."

"It'll be okay." He had imagined how defensive he would feel whenever he had this conversation with his cousin. But the deep well of fear and love that spilled at his feet swept him toward her. Charlaina had long been by turns exasperating—monitoring whatever Nate and Dixon were doing that would invariably get them into trouble—or protective—patching up a torn sleeve before their mother saw, having talks with brokenhearted girlfriends. Dixon had relied on her to navigate through passages he saw blindly, and this was how he had always envisioned her: intrepid at the bow of their small boat, holding a lantern, and peering ahead in the darkness.

He touched her cheek. "I'll watch over us. I promise." He did not see Nate behind them until Charlaina reached for him. She searched anxiously from one face to the next.

"It's all right, baby girl," Nate cooed to her. "C'mon. C'mon." He wrapped her in his arms, her face just below his collarbone, his hand cradling her head.

"Okay," she said to Nate, and to Dixon, a stern, "Okay." And he knew she was commending their safety to him. She pulled herself from Nate's arms, her hand flat over her stomach, and returned to her guests.

"Yeah, I know," Nate snapped. "'If Dixon watches over Nate, he can't fuck up.' Maybe it's you," he said, poking a finger into Dixon's chest, "who needs me!"

***

HIS FELLOW COUNSELORS DIDN'T BELIEVE HE WAS ACTUALLY leaving for Mount Everest until his temporary replacement was named. Once reality set in, Angela Preston, biology, and Lance Benton, geology, became ecstatic. They accosted Dixon in the hallway. There was so much they wanted to know: Did he plan to keep a log? Could he monitor temperature, precipitation, that kind of thing? They requested soil samples, rocks, artifacts. He would take a camera, of course—of course! Photos from the top of the world!

Lance promised to give him a book on clouds to help him identify them. Angela chimed in, "Look for Levanter clouds, they cascade like a waterfall but are horizontal. Very rare."

"Angela, no, they don't have Levanters on Everest," Lance huffed. "They're just banner clouds. Sometimes they look like waves but . . ."

The two leaned across Dixon, intent on their debate. He backed up slowly and disappeared.

Later, Angela Preston approached him alone. Angela and her heart-shaped mouth; had he noticed that before? She had a friend, a news reporter, who might be persuaded to do a piece on him. What did he think? No, no, he said, that might be tempting fate. He thought of how angry Nate might be to hear Dixon decline that offer. No, not angry. Worse—disappointed. "When we're back and have something to show for ourselves," Dixon said to Angela, "then, let's do it." So instead, Angela made a banner duplicating a grainy, blown-up photo of Everest's South Col featuring Base Camp to Camp 4 and then the summit. At the bottom left corner, she placed a cutout of a man wearing what looked more like an astronaut suit than climbing gear but with a photo of Dixon pasted over his face. "We'll climb with you, see?" she explained, her face bright. "It's magnetic." She marched the Dixon-faced cutout from camp to camp up the mountain. Angela beamed at him, a quick flutter of her eyelashes. Why had he never asked her out?

"I think it's your fault." He answered his own question as he replayed it all to Nate. "You and your 'don't shit where you eat.'"

Nate lifted his shoulders in a quick shrug. "It's true. That's a lazy move, dating at work. And when it crashes and burns, there is nowhere to run. Nowhere." A little shudder of his shoulders.

Dixon snorted a laugh. "Is that right, now?"

Nate glanced up, a lift of his brow. "You don't even want to know."

"Who else you gonna confide in?"

Nate tilted his head back and gazed at his brother. "No one else." A quick grasp of Dixon's shoulder. "Which is why I'll tell you this. Our lives are going to change." He folded his hands in his lap. "I mean, they already have, don't you feel it?" His look anxious. "You gonna be ready?"

Dixon shook his head. "We'll be, you know, yes, it'll be a big thing while we're there, believe me, but then we come home, life goes on."

"No, no, man." Nate sat forward, his breath a little faster. "We can't even fathom this, I'm telling you. What if it blows up our whole lives?"

"You mean, we get famous?" Dixon laughed. "Can you recite the names of the last five people who summited Everest? It only matters to a handful of people."

"Well, we're about to become those people." Nate's face soft and sad. "You're not like me. You like your life just as it is. I want you to be ready. If we can't live the same lives anymore."

His brother's concern like a warm hand spread wide along his sternum. "Ah, Nate, you know me. I'm always ready."

Which wasn't entirely true. His leaving was causing a buzz among the staff and faculty, but he wasn't ready to tell his students yet. Half of them were headed out to high school anyway, and the rest would barely notice. Except for his Acolytes, those boys who swarmed him daily. Except for Marcus. It took a good deal of bolstering up for that chat. "I won't be here in the spring," he practiced saying in his car on the way to and from school, at the breakfast table, and yet he paused and stumbled when he actually said it aloud.

Marcus's face alarmed. "For real? How come? Something happen? Are you in trouble? You need my mom to call up and make 'em keep you?" His questions rapid fire, Dixon had to put up a hand to halt the onslaught. He explained about Everest. Marcus looked confused, then his face lit up. "Oh, you like, going on *The Amazing Race?* You gonna be on television?" He hopped forward in his chair, excited.

"No, son, nothing like that. Just my brother and me, just an, an adventure."

"Adventure?" The boy rubbed his jaw and frowned.

Two days after Dixon's departure became widely known, Shiloh sidled up to him, leering. "I hear you leaving. Do Fat Ass know he be on his own now?" A hot poker across his shoulders. Dixon blurted out, "Man, you just want to be an asshole all your life? Can't you come up with something better to be?" The boy, taken aback—a flash of hope in Dixon: could he grab hold of this kid, could he remold him?—and just that quick, the kid slipped back to his normal smirk.

Later that week, Marcus walked into Dixon's office after lunch period and burst into tears, his head hung low. Dixon lifted Marcus's chin and noticed bruises on each of the boy's cheeks. "Him?" he eked out, and Marcus nodded. Dixon hugged the boy, hard. Anger revved in Dixon, then ignited resolve: finally, he could nail that son of a bitch. Photos of Marcus's face, a statement given in Principal Phil Pious's office, a plan: Dixon had discretion to recommend a course of action. He sat across from Phil Pious, who chewed a toothpick, his glasses teetering on the bridge of his nose. "Well, let's hear it," Phil said, "your plea for mercy for this kid. He's been in the office three times in the last three weeks, I have two teachers saying if they quit, he'll be the number one reason, but go ahead."

"No," Dixon said. "He needs to be dealt with. Give him extended suspension."

Phil pursed his lips, nodded his head slowly. "I was sure he was gonna be a 'Dixon save.'"

And Dixon thought: not on your life. There was something he did not share with his colleagues. How could he tell men who joked about kids being Bad Seeds and WTFs—that is, Waiting To be Fitted for their orange prison jumpsuits—how could he tell them his truth? That you help a kid until he shows you he doesn't want your help. You do not waste your time trying to save the wrong boys. It had been a small, thorny hill to stand on, gazing across all the kids who needed him and taking his own inventory, feeling for that inner resonance that guided him to do the right thing. Could he dig in interminably with even the most difficult kids or just grab and lift as many as he could? The thing was, you wanted a few triumphs.

At night, he closed his eyes and saw Base Camp, the din of voices, the gut check of anticipation luring him. Some days, amid the low-ceilinged hallways of the school, the slam and echo of locker doors, the scuff of sneakers on linoleum, in the same useless what-are-we-going-to-do meetings about this kid or that one, he felt himself expanding, inflating, so he became too big for this place, for this life. In a planning meeting, Wiley Fitch leaned back from the row in front of Dixon and laughed. "Hey, your head's always turned to the window these days. Guess I don't have to ask if you're ready to go."

"Go, go," shooing the kids toward their buses at the end of the day, moving the days and weeks along toward Everest. What might he find there? What might he bring back for his boys? A clear dream space, something vast as a mountain. He might just be free.

So Dixon began making phone calls. He notified Shiloh's

state-appointed caseworker of his suspension, then called in a favor from the principal of a math and science magnet school. And then he escorted Shiloh from the building. Dixon and Kurt, the school resource officer, walking fast with Shiloh wedged between them, a bird of a boy, his arms bent at the elbow like wings. Wriggling but hugged tight between the two men so he could not get free. At the door, Shiloh turned to Dixon, a kid's twisted, angry face, "You thinking we done?"

Dixon had imagined feeling the tug of empathy, of doubt about tossing him out. He glanced at Shiloh's aunt awaiting him, the weary look about her. That look engendered his sympathy. But Shiloh's scarred face? A strange feeling. Not just disliking him, but actively not helping him. Hadn't he usually taken a suspended kid home, talked to the parents, explained what needed to be done, checked up on them? He couldn't imagine doing that for this kid, *this* kid who was sure to be back in juvy in the blink of an eye. Hard head, soft behind, as Dixon's grandmother used to say. "Oh yeah, we're done," Dixon said. He waved the boy off and went back inside.

Dixon called Marcus's parents. A different school, he explained to them, a separate bus ride, an earlier schedule both leaving for school and coming home. Out of Shiloh's clutches. Marcus's parents hesitated. "But you won't be there, Mr. Dixon." No, no, but the principal was a good friend who would make sure Marcus was looked after. Finally, the parents decided that if Marcus's Mr. Dixon said this was the plan, then so be it. Dixon felt calm: a last, good act on Marcus's behalf.

On his final day of school, as Dixon packed his personal artifacts and prepared for his going-away party, Marcus appeared in Dixon's doorway, his bottom lip quivering. The boy stood small and forlorn as Dixon said reassuring things like, "When I get back, man, we'll step up your program, maybe add a little rock climbing? You've gotta keep up the training while I'm gone. All right?" When Dixon could no longer avoid the doorway—his only exit—he squared himself and faced Marcus. The boy flung his pudgy body into Dixon, nearly toppling him over. He latched on and wept. The boy's grief and fear penetrated Dixon and never, never had he wished more to be impenetrable. Instead, he might be drowning, his mouth open, head back, swallowing air, the boy digging so deep into him that he had to push Marcus away, nearly a shove, or he might never have gotten free.

CHAPTER

5

*March 2011, Nepal*

Their hotel in Kathmandu was full of Westerners headed to the summit. In the bar, which Dixon found vaguely Moroccan with geometric tiles in deep cobalt and cinnamon, the climbers chattered loudly in dozens of groups, their anticipation palpable. Dim light floated into the room from behind stained-glass panels. Dixon and Nate stood mesmerized in the doorway. They scanned the room, Dixon wanting to make quick approximations of who they all might be. He recognized two distinct camps. There were the ones who drank and laughed and relaxed, and those who sat at the bar showing off their new hiking boots. Again, he drifted between worlds. He could never mistake himself for a true alpinist. He knew just enough to understand how little he knew of that world. But to think someone might mistake him for one of these yo-yos in new boots? Good grief. Nate motioned toward a small, empty table to the right of the bar, and they made their way across the room.

Behind their table sat a group of seven Europeans, five men and two women, drinking beers and swapping stories. "Stuck on that ledge all bloody night, getting the shit kicked out of us. Thought that sodding tent would blow off. More like a bloody kite than a tent. Dane, he's praying the Hail Mary. I'm near shitting meself. And Dexter turns to me, 'Goddamn shame you're so ugly. I could do with a shag.'" They all laughed. The women pelted the story-teller with peanut shells. They recounted routes and the skin of mountains. "It's sheer fucking slate, black as pitch, with specks of gold and amber." They recalled near disasters like slipping from a ledge or dangling from a rope or sliding for what seemed forever before they could self-arrest. Not bragging. Instead, a casual awe flooded their voices.

One of the women, her hair long and honey brown, noticed Dixon and Nate listening and leaned toward their table. "Your first time here?" She looked under thirty, her face smooth with high cheekbones and olive skin.

Nate smiled. Dixon did, too.

"Ah! Welcome to this club," she said. Not a familiar accent like Spanish or Italian, so Dixon could not place it. "These guys are old-timers," she said, pointing to a couple of men in their group. "I am just a baby." She made a pouty face. "Will be my first time with them."

"But that doesn't mean she's a bloody virgin!" one guy offered, and the table erupted with laughter.

"These guys, they are bad," she said to Dixon and Nate. She tossed her head toward the table. "Jett, you asshole! You better play nice to me. Belay is like karma."

"Whoa!" Jett said. "No threats. I'm not a bloody client." They laughed again, swigging from their beers. Nate and Dixon felt like innocents outside the jokes. They gave each other quickly raised eyebrows: *What have we stumbled onto here?* The table's occupants were lean and muscular. They wore jeans, T-shirts, city boots. They were long and sprawled in their chairs. The woman who spoke to them sat lotus-style, bouncing her knees gently. None of them seemed anxious. Certainly, they were less visibly churned up than the obvious newcomers in the room, the ones in their new hiking boots. Dixon watched one guy at the bar sloshing beer onto his boots and joking that they had been "christened." Just wait till he took those babies on their first hike. New boots spelled new blisters.

"Sorry, mates. You clients?" Jett asked.

"Umm." Nate and Dixon shared a puzzled look. "Climbers. With DX8 Expeditions. Clive's group."

"Right," Jett answered, "clients." He gave a self-satisfied snort.

Dixon decided to ignore the obvious insult. "You all climb together before?"

The table grew lively, all of them talking over one another. From what Dixon could piece together, if they had not climbed with one another before, they had climbed with a common friend. A game of six degrees of separation began, every mountain peak seeming to lead back to one of them at the table and link that person to everyone else there. The woman with the accent leaned over to Dixon and joked, "It's kind of the incest. All the climbers, we are all with each other."

"Nice life," Dixon said, oddly envious.

"Headed to Everest?" Nate asked.

"Ha! Not for a million pounds, mate," Jett said.

Dixon and Nate sat back, surprised.

"Ignore him. He's an elitist," said the youngest-looking guy in the group, who would later be introduced as RedCurl for his wild mop of red curls and deeply freckled face. He waved his hands as if erasing the air.

"Purist!" Jett lifted a finger in correction. "I'm an alpinist."

"Ah," RedCurl sniffed. "Sod off." He threw a cashew at Jett, who balled up his fists and snarled at him.

"But it's not polite," the woman scolded her table. "Look, I am Lena," she said to Dixon and Nate, "and I apologize for the rude of them. It's just . . ." She shrugged her shoulders. "We don't go to Everest now. Maybe, maybe, late in May. But not now." Her eyes darted around the crowded bar.

"I thought any other time was off limits?" Dixon asked.

"Only for clients." Jett smirked. His silver-gray hair sparkled along his temples in the bar light. "We wait till you leave, end of May, we take our window."

"We come now for Pumori," Lena explained. "No Os. Oxygen, I mean, we don't do. We rest, later we start for K2."

"But not Everest?" Dixon sat forward, intent. He had the uncomfortable feeling he was doing something wrong.

"Too dangerous or something?" Nate asked.

"Yeah," Jett shot back.

"You want a story for Christmas dinner, go to Everest. You want to climb, really climb, it's K2," an older guy quipped. "Everest is an outlier. Not like the way we climb other mountains."

"Not the mountain, mate, it's you guys," Jett said.

"No offense," RedCurl added.

"Offense taken." Nate squared his shoulders.

"You American?" The older guy was perhaps in his late fifties with deep-set eyes and a mass of thick hair that spilled across a feathery scar on his forehead. He reached out his hands, a conciliatory move. He was missing the tip of his third finger. "I grew up on the Jersey Shore. Know the best time to go to the beach? September. When the tourists leave. Y'see? Maybe you two know what you're doing, okay? Maybe you've climbed."

"We have," Nate answered tightly.

"Great. But half of 'em haven't. And they'll hold up the line, make stupid mistakes, go cowboy. The experienced climbers have to stop *their* climbs to go rescue 'em. Because we're all connected in this thing. You know? You have to be ready to sacrifice your climb for a mate in danger, no matter if it's just bad weather or bad choices on their part or just bad luck. You don't leave somebody behind, if you can help it. That's the way it ought to be."

Jett lifted his mug of beer in a wide arc toward the bar patrons. "*Ought* to be. Every choice one of 'em makes, it's your choice, too. Could determine what happens to ya, mate. So look around. Bet you can pick out three people you wouldn't trust your life to. Well, you're gonna. This one," he motioned to Lena, "I have her on, but she's a damn fine alpinist. I trust her."

"What about that guy climbing this year." Nate was agitated. "Been climbing for fifteen years, his fifth time on Everest. What's his name? Climbing without oxygen this time. You gonna tell me he's not a mountaineer or alpinist, or whatever you call your-selves?"

"Sure he is," RedCurl chimed in. "Rupert's a damned good one, one of the top."

"So I don't get it." Nate looked confused.

"It's not the same, mate. He fixes his own rope, carries his own gear, knows how to bivouac. He *knows* this mountain," Jett insisted.

"Lighten up." RedCurl slapped Jett on the back. "They just

want to see the big girl up close and personal. Don't you remember your first time?"

Jett blushed. "1991, twenty-second of May, fourteen hundred hours on the nose. Thought we missed the bloody window but we waited. Up there twenty minutes, top of the world."

"'87, fifth of May, 13:48. With Collington Muse, God rest his soul," the older guy recounted. They went like that around the table, a quiet, dreamy recollection as if the question had been *Who was your first love?*

"Ah, shit. Look, don't let me and Beau get to you," Jett said and pointed between himself and the older guy. "You'll make it. It's a finely tuned machine, all them ropes, all them sherpas. You chaps look damned fit. With good weather, you'll summit. So, crack on." He drank his beer, an exasperated expression on his face.

"Right, right," Lena said as she slapped Nate's knee, and he sat with his arms tightly folded across his chest. "Just keep the good enough batteries in the shoes." She pointed rapidly to her feet. "To keep the toes warm. You stand around long time waiting. That's dangerous part. You get so cold, yah!" She faked a shiver.

Toe warmers. Batteries. Got 'em, Dixon thought. "It's what we all want, right? To get to the top?"

Jett and Beau shared a slow smile. Beau leaned in. "Yes, yes, of course, but . . . We're alpinists, see? This is how we live. We know thirty to thirty-five percent, I mean, easy thirty-five percent of the time—"

Jett agreed. "Easy."

"—we're not getting to the top. That's part of the deal. And it sits right with us. You guys, d'you just want bragging rights? I mean, d'you care about the mountain? Do you get that you're just there to sneak in and out, quiet? Like Ed Hillary said, you don't conquer her, you just hope she relents. See? It's about having a good experience of the mountain. It's, it's, not a, a transactional experience. You ought not be able to simply *buy* your way to the top." He extended his cupped hand as if he offered gold coins.

"But that's the world these days, isn't it? There's a good few bob in this lark, hauling your arses to the top. So you pay the mates, and you're clients," Jett pronounced.

Nate scoffed, but Dixon connected with Beau. "You get it?" Beau asked him. "There are rules. You watch out for the other guy. Your partner gets sick, you go back down with him, no questions asked, I don't care how close you are to the summit. You don't get stupid and take dumb risks. You're here for the mountain. You gotta respect her."

"I did Kili," Dixon piped up. "I get it."

"Yeah, well good. I hope you've seen the real culture, not—" he waved his hand around the room—"buying season on Everest. I hope you understand it's better than this."

Jett scanned Dixon up and down, then finished his beer in one long gulp. He burped. "Kili, huh." He pulled a wad of bills from his pocket, counted off a few, and plopped them down on the table. "That's a big hike up a cold hill. Think that'll do ya here? That's what makes you dangerous."

———

DANGER, DIXON RUMINATED, THAT APHRODISIAC. 1971, NATE, nine, Dixon, seven. Walking along the street, the boys share the kind of sugary jawbreakers they are not allowed at home. "We have to eat it before we get home," Dixon scolds, "we have to throw out the wrappers." Nate sucks his teeth and stashes handfuls of candy in his pants pockets so that they bulge. He breaks into a run, stuffing candy into his mouth, down his T-shirt, running backward and mocking Dixon. "You have to follow the rules!" Dixon shouts and chases his brother around the corner until he runs smack into Nate stopped in the street and peering along with a group of boys at a model airplane stuck high in a tree. Five boys argue about whose fault it is, sending it up so high, a tree with no branches low enough to grab onto. Can they send a cat up? No, stupid! Get a ladder? No! Call the firemen? No! They'll get in trouble for bringing it outside at all. One kid yells, "I dare anybody to go up there. Anybody!" Nate gives a delighted snort, and in a blur, Dixon reaches for him, finds him gone, and then someone hollers, "Look at that kid!" Dixon's stomach lurches.

Nate has shimmied up the drainpipe of the house next to the tree and walks now across its pitched roof, his arms balancing him, back straight, head up. He repeats, "Shit! Shit! Oh shit!" but walks slowly, steadily across the roof and toward the tree then jumps straight up, latching his slim arms around a branch. He dangles for a moment, long and skinny. His shirt slips free of his pants and his pockets pucker and empty themselves so that jaw breakers spill from him, colorful as confetti. Dixon cannot breathe. His head feels light. Nate pushes off against the tree trunk with his feet and lifts himself so that he can pull up on the branch. He manages to look both terrified and excited. He grins at Dixon, then takes a deep gulp.

Adults are gathering now. The men cursing silently, the mothers exclaiming, "Whose kid is that? Dear god!" Up Nate climbs, licking his lips, determined.

"That's high enough, boy," someone yells, but someone else says, "The one on your left, try that branch." Left one, right one, the thick one, not that one it won't hold you, the crowd calls. "How much you think he weighs?" someone asks, and then a frightened mother yells, "Shame on you! You all gonna watch that boy get himself killed!" So four men position themselves under the tree to catch him, and two older boys drag a blow-up mattress over and take turns filling it with a bike tire pump. All the while, Nate swings from branch to branch so that one mother says, "Thank god he's not my child." She puts her hand over her heart and begins to pray softly.

Near the tree's top, a branch begins to crack under Nate's weight. Dixon wraps his arms around the trunk as if to hold it together. Nate hugs the trunk and swings his butt and legs around so that he clears the cracking limb. He pushes himself upward, grabs a higher limb, and when he is sure he is on tight, he swipes at the errant airplane, smacking at its wing until it pulls loose and glides down. The crowd erupts in applause.

Nate scampers down to Dixon. He is shaking, giggling. Other boys pat him on the back. Dixon shakes, too, but he does not laugh. He may throw up. They begin to walk home, Dixon's legs like rubber. Both boys still trembling, Dixon says, "I don't know how you did that."

Nate shrugs, then they both stare at his pants, dark and wet with pee.

---

DIXON LAY SLEEPLESS IN THE NOISY HOTEL ROOM IN KATH-mandu. The sounds of cars and motorcycles and bicycles' jangling bells mingled with the dust that swirled overhead in long, moonlit columns. Nate lay awake in the other bed. "What made you climb that tree that day, you remember?"

Nate was silent a minute. Then he laughed. "Because it was

there." He leaned toward Dixon, trying to get him to laugh, but Dixon just frowned.

"Those alpinists think we're wannabes," Dixon said.

Nate grunted. "Man, everybody alive wants to be something. Don't let it get to you."

But it did get to him, the dismissal from Jett lighting a slow fire in him. Jett had said their climb, their *kind* of climb relying on sherpas and fixed ropes, was something apart from real mountaineering. Dixon fought the fleeting idea that he may have prepared like a guy so overfocused on the race, on *winning* the race, that is, that he forgets to just run. The idea collided and kicked in his stomach. *They belonged here! They had worked to get here!* And he was certain that as he climbed, it would be Jett's face in front of him, spurring him up that goddamn mountain.

## CHAPTER

6

Because they *had* prepared for Mount Everest. Dixon had made certain. Researching tour groups whose leaders had actually summited Everest. Avoiding ninety-thousand-dollar trips focused on nonsense like espresso machines and tables set with china and Le Cordon Bleu–trained chefs. "Here," Dixon said to Nate, "this is the one," and tapped his forefinger heavily on the bright blue sky of the brochure. "It's sixty-five thousand dollars," he said. "A guide for every four climbers plus we each get a sherpa, all your oxygen and supplies, a medical team. And they pay the sherpas better. This is the one," Dixon repeated. Nate agreed. Because if Dixon said it was good, it was.

Thank you for choosing us for your mountain expedition. This undertaking is difficult and dangerous. We would be remiss if we did not ensure that you fully understand the potential for all eventualities. Please read this packet thoroughly before signing all consent and acknowledgment forms.

"Skeet wants to come along shopping," Nate said.

In the sporting goods store, Skeet sidled up to the store clerks and said, "Guess where they're going?" A wide grin, a little waggle of his head. Dixon focused on his list. Three kinds of boots. Three kinds of jackets. Down climbing suits. Layers of wool tops and pants.

"This trip, this is going to be the making of you both. It's gonna blow up, man, I can see it," Skeet said. He was a barrel-chested man, his shoulders set back, which came across like a kind of certainty about the world. "You know, I was thinking about you swimming," he said to Nate. "Man, you were a natural. Never understood why you wouldn't compete. You coulda been as great as Dix was at running. Never understood." Skeet ran his fingers in contemplation across the shoulders of a row of down jackets.

Dixon tried to catch Nate's glance, but Nate steadily avoided him. Nate used to insist "it's just for fun," but he would show up at the pool, challenge the reigning swim champ, and handily win. Coach had begged him to join the team, even asked their dad to talk to him. "Why not?" Dixon had prodded over and over before Nate answered, "I'd just be asking to be knocked off the pedestal." Because eventually somebody would beat his time. This way, he was perpetual possibility. A tease. Dixon held up a pack of hats with ear flaps, pretending to examine them but peering at Nate. How far then, from that moment to this, to risking himself for the mountain? It welled in Dixon, a bright, heroic pride in his brother.

Hats with ear flaps. Climbing helmets. Balaclavas. Neck gaiters. Sun hats. Ski goggles.

"What's this?" Skeet examined a long, cylindrical plastic bottle Dixon had put in their shopping cart.

"Pee bottle."

Skeet raised his eyebrows. "Y'all are going full native, huh?"

Ice axe. Crampons. Harness. Ascender. Cord. Belay device. Trekking poles. Headlamps.

"Listen," Skeet said, lowering his voice, "how are we going to play this when you get back? You know, I've got a whole PR team at work. Let's do something with this."

Dixon harrumphed. Skeet had that side to him, that "How do we play this?" side, which was probably why he and Nate were friends in the first place. Probably why Dixon rarely spent time with him alone. "You're just thinking about the glory, huh?"

"I'm admiring the hard work, Dixon," Skeet said plainly, and Dixon felt embarrassed for thinking the worst of him.

"So get your company to sponsor us," Nate said. "You see how much we're spending."

"I didn't want to say anything. What's it, like ten grand?"

"Seven. Each," Dixon answered.

"Whew!"

"Don't worry, it'll all pay off. Trust me," Nate said, which gave Dixon a little stutter in his heart.

**You must first sign and return both the "Release From All Risk" and the "Agreement Not to Sue," along with your $30,000 deposit ($3,000 nonrefundable).**

In Dixon's home, their equipment streamed as rivers across the floors. Dixon liked to walk up and down the rows, studying the odd lifelike form of their down suits, shapely bodies awaiting the animation of spirit. The gleaming yellow blade of his ice axe. The clunky pile of boots. So many supplies, so carefully selected.

Have your physician complete the Physician Approval Form. Please inform him/her that the average temperature on the mountain during the 68-day expedition will be 15 to -45°F and that you will carry a 40 lb. pack and wear heavy mountaineering boots, clothing, and equipment. Although the team will have a doctor available, emergency medical services should be considered nonexistent. Remember, we will not make decisions about your health or fitness for this climbing trip expedition. That decision is for you and your family and your physician.

His doctor reviewed the list of recommended medications. "Hmph," he said, neither condemnation nor admiration. To his surprise, Dixon realized that his feelings were hurt. He had thought his doctor, fit, mid-sixties with a swagger, a head full of gleaming white hair that complemented his copper brown skin, might have a competitive sense of the audacity of this trip. "Hmph," the doctor said again as he sat down behind his desk, still reviewing the list. Amoxicillin for upper respiratory issues, Cipro for GI distress, Diamox for altitude sickness, Tylenol with codeine for headaches. He shook his head. Tagamet for stomach issues and malaria drugs as needed. He tsk-tsked. Nifedipine for pulmonary edema, dexamethasone for cerebral edema. He scribbled quickly on his prescription pad, then handed the pack of prescriptions to Dixon. "Good luck," he said with a blank expression.

Dixon grew cross. The point of getting these meds was not that you believed the worst would happen—no! The drugs warded off disaster. Like talismans, things they might hold up in the night against the nagging cough that threatened to shatter a rib: *See? I can beat you. I have prepared for you.* It was foresight!

He shored himself up like this to share his itinerary with Pamela. "This is so irresponsible!" Pamela shot back at him. He felt a residual stab of guilt, then remembered with relief that he no longer answered to her. He closed and opened his eyes slowly. Before they married, she had appeared generous.

"How can you just desert us? I mean, isn't this expensive? To say nothing about dangerous? And you're doing this with him?"

She had been so the wrong woman for him. Her veneer of generosity had disappeared in small ways at first: hogging the covers in bed, making too little dinner—she was tending to the athlete in him, she said, helping him control his weight. Initially, it had seemed a clumsy kindness, but it had soon revealed itself as a calculated move to keep him unsatisfied, to say, *See how it feels?* He had begun stashing nuts and energy bars around the house, which she invariably discovered. Eventually, he had installed a small refrigerator in the garage, fitting it with a lock. She hacked at it, leaving telltale indents of pliers and a saw, the shallow teeth marks nearly human. He could imagine her crouched like an animal gnawing at that lock.

"You have Kira to think about. It'll change her whole life to lose you." Pamela's father had died suddenly of a heart attack when Pamela was twenty, and Dixon knew she blamed that death for her decision to marry him, an athlete who, unlike her dad, tended to his intake of red meat, had regular physicals, and never smoked. "Nate talked you into this, didn't he? He's a careless man, Dixon," she said.

"He's my brother."

In dreams that night, there was Pamela on all fours in the snow, gnawing at his crampons.

A client may be removed from the expedition by the lead guide at any time for any reason related to the health or safety of the client, the well-being of others because of the client, or the client's failure to follow the rules.

He was relentless with Nate. Six days a week they worked, building up to seven or eight straight hours. That fall before the climb, they took a four-day climbing course in the Colorado Rockies. They trained like their lives depended on it.

One Saturday in October, Dixon and Nate went running on a trail beside the C&O Canal. Dixon ran close to Nate, egging him on: "Keep up." Veering into him so that Nate either had to move over or speed up to get away from Dixon. The canal wound lazily below them. It was early in their training so they carried only ten-pound packs. Nate began to slow down after five miles, and Dixon banged his shoulder into him. "Move it!" he huffed. "Keep. Heart rate. Up."

Trudging around a curve, they ran alongside the river. A six-foot wall of red rock and granite rose at their backs. Nate tripped, stumbled forward about fifty yards before reaching out his hands and falling toward the ground. On all fours, panting, Nate finally sank down, chest on his knees, head propped on his folded arms.

Dixon stood over him, hands on his hips, calming his breathing. He watched the water flow by, heard the echoing silence, noted where they were: only flat ground. His brother folded beside him. Did he think clearly at that moment: don't do it, we shouldn't do this? He would like later to imagine that he had, that he had said to Nate, *Let's stop*. That they had quietly turned around and gone home and never spoken again about Everest.

Instead, Dixon nudged Nate with his foot. He chided him into standing, walking, running again, running until Nate gave out. "No más," he said, Roberto Durán's infamous words—hadn't that phrase marked their youth? The way they had mocked Durán for refusing to get back in the boxing ring with Sugar Ray Leonard. "No más," one of the brothers might say and laugh, and the other would reply, "Punk." But Nate sank down, stretched flat out on the cold ground, and said haltingly, "No. Más."

Dixon, tired as well but taking that exhaustion as a challenge, leaned over him. "That's it? You gonna lay down on that mountain? You gonna. Fucking. Quit on me? I can't carry you!" Dixon yelled, a plea, and he might as well have been five years old.

Nate lay down. "Fuck you."

"Fuck *you* if you do this to me up there. I can't"—Dixon's face so near Nate's—"do this for you."

"Back the fuck off!" Nate spat back at him. "I have to catch up to you. I'm not there yet!" He lunged forward, wretched, and threw up in the dirt.

Dixon sat back on his haunches. When he had composed himself, Nate said quietly, "Just give me a fucking chance." His look a desperate plea.

They emptied the water from their weight packs and walked back to their cars in silence.

After that, Nate worked hard, harder than he did, Dixon thought, spending more time in the gym, taking long runs each day rain or shine. He reported all this to Dixon, adding, "I'm redeeming myself," with a searing earnestness.

Some training days were all Dixon's. The brothers ran side by side on the community college's track. Invariably, Nate would nudge Dixon and announce, "Light speed." Dixon would obey, reaching for that upper gear in himself, taking three deep breaths, and off he would go, churning up speed to take flight, a burst of light spreading through him, Nate beaming behind him. Other days were all Nate's, days when they took to the natatorium at the college. Nate's speed and ease in the water, his grace, were stunning. As the brothers rested at the edge of the pool, a kid who had been watching asked Nate, "Hey, mister, you a professional swimmer or something?" The look on Nate's face part-wistful, part-amused, he said, "I'm a mountain climber. Like my brother." He arched his back and launched himself into the pool, rising into a back stroke that knifed clean and swift through the water, leaving shimmering streams in his wake.

At the first heavy snow in January, Nate appeared at Dixon's door: "Let's go." The two suited up and headed out, their backpacks full of water weights. They trudged for hours. At Dixon's suggestion, they set up camp in the wooded park behind Dixon's condo, pitching their tent on frozen ground. This was the hardening Dixon knew they needed, the thing he knew Nate needed. On Kilimanjaro years earlier, Dixon had discovered an otherworldliness surrounded by wind pawing at the tent walls, the feeling of having slipped from the world but being so keenly present, stripped to an essential nakedness. A terrifying freedom. Unbounded from his life, from the undeniable misery of his failing marriage, he had wept into his sleeping bag that first night. There seemed nothing to moor him in the thinning air. But that air carried, like billowing ribbon, the sorrow from him. He felt alive, the cold spiking each pulse, each struggle for breath a rebirth, each step a moment of grace.

He and Nate had camped out for three days, getting used to the howling assault of wind and sleet against their tent. "Listen to that," Nate said.

"It'll be worse up there. Misery."

"Misery times fifty," Nate added, and they tried to fix their minds on it, lying in their sleeping bags alongside the imagined struggle that awaited them. Nate squinted. "I want this." He propped his chin in one hand and stared at Dixon.

Dixon sat up. "I see that. I'm impressed."

"Just doing what needs to be done." Nate drew imaginary circles along the floor of the tent.

"That's why I'm impressed."

"I've created and sold two successful businesses, you know." Nate's voice defensive. "Must know how to do something right."

"Who says you don't?"

"Listen, when we come back, I'm thinking I might buy a house out here. Do the suburban thing. Whatd'ya think?"

"Could suit you," Dixon replied, but he really couldn't imagine that.

"I think you're right," Nate said, and lay back, dreamily staring at the ceiling. "It'll be a new world by then."

Dixon had believed he knew Nate completely, but maybe his brother was a bit like a prism, and perhaps Dixon had been looking only through a particular slant of light. Take, for instance, this burst of determination in Nate's training schedule. In fact, Nate's quiet willingness to step up had most reassured Dixon. Pushing their way up the modest mountains of the East Coast, their backpacks bulging with weight, the brothers settled into a rhythm, the swish and swipe of their jackets like music. In their climbing gear, bundled in the same dark yellow suits and boots, carrying the same rounded shoulders, the same stance, they were always recognized as brothers; sometimes they were asked if they were twins. On those long, cold hikes, Dixon watched his brother rise to the moment—Nate might pause to adjust his pack, his face furrowing in discomfort, he would shift the pack, settle in, and steel himself to carry on. Becoming the man Dixon had believed all along Nate could be. A blushing need rose in Dixon so full it was embarrassing. Nate might veer toward Dixon, an arm brushing against his, and the absoluteness of his presence would spike through Dixon. He would want so badly to throw his arms around his brother and hold on.

At night, drifting toward sleep, Dixon would imagine Nate's face at the summit, Nate the conqueror, Nate ascending to the best in himself. He had seen it before, a focused Nate working on algebra late at night, his brow furrowed then rising in delight as he got the answers. Dixon had recognized that moment again the first time he saw Nate in action at one of his small-business seminars. Dixon had sneaked into a large conference room at a Hilton, sat low in a padded chair near the back of the room. Nate stood at the front before a white board, a long pointer in hand, his shirtsleeves rolled up. He had become a clean slate, it seemed to Dixon, as if he had slipped off the cunning charm, the sideways glances. Nate was plainly himself, funny, smart, he glided in and out of business speak, he kept the room entranced, and perhaps this was his greatest feat, that he held attention using none of the sweet talk, none of the wily looks that Dixon was used to. A bead of sweat on his brow, an arc of wetness beneath his armpits, Nate talked strategy and business design, cupping his hands as if his words were precious. A truthfulness—Dixon thought it again—a cleanness to Nate, as if he had made himself over, bright and pure.

After the session, once Nate saw Dixon at the back of the room, Nate had darted toward him, wrapping his brother in a hard hug. But when Nate released Dixon, Nate's whole self—what might have been his real self, Dixon would recall over and over—fell, slowly at first, toward the Nate that Dixon knew, Nate's smile easing wide, his shoulders thrown back. "My kid brother," Nate joked to the men around him and flicked Dixon's arm with his fingers. "Sneaking into my seminars for free. Thinks he can steal my secrets," he joked. "Listen, I remember the time he once caught me out back smoking . . ." and like that, Nate became an atavistic self, and Dixon couldn't help feeling it was a show put on for him. A flash of anger yielded to a moment of shame. Perhaps Nate had spun in a separate solar system, and Dixon had merely clung along an outer band. Perhaps Nate had always lived in a place deeper, richer, more sober than Dixon had imagined.

In his bed at night as he prepared to climb Mount Everest, Dixon thought again of the Nate he encountered on their hikes, that man without pretense, embracing the hard work. How long had Dixon awaited that Nate's return? Now, how long could he hold on to him?

### BODY DISPOSAL PREFERENCE FORM

- If you die on the mountain at or above 25,800 feet, your body will need to be left at that location.

- If you die on the mountain above 17,500 feet, your body most likely will be put in a crevasse and marked with a rock cairn.

- If you die lower on the mountain, it might be possible to bring your body to a lower altitude for cremation by the local people. This option costs between $5,000 and $10,000, which your estate must pay. Please check here if this is your preference: _____

- If you die lower on the mountain or on the trek to Base Camp, it might be possible to bring your body down from the mountain to be shipped to your home country. For this complicated and expensive process, your estate will be charged more than $15,000 and travel could take several weeks. Please check here if this is your preference: _____

- If you elect cremation or repatriation, please indicate below who will pay for the costs:

  _____

- Name/Address/Phone/Relationship:

  _____

- Life Insurance Company/Policy Number:

  _____

DX8 Expeditions, Application Form C

CHAPTER

7

*March 2011, Mount Everest*

When Dixon and Nate met their fellow clients for the first time in Kathmandu, Dixon was edgy and expectant. There were eight other clients on their team, including a banker, a doctor, a filmmaker, a priest, a hedge fund manager, and a law firm partner. That's how they introduced themselves, by announcing their status along with their names. They milled about, telling stories that Dixon recognized as establishing their height in the world. Everything would be this way from now on, he was certain, the height of the world measured against Everest the way these men measured themselves against one another, throwing casual mentions of travels to Istanbul or Venice, their private planes and their Mercedes, their climbs on Denali or Aconcagua, matching one another's brags until one by one they were outdone and one stood tallest: the biggest car, the most extensive travel, the most mountains. It was the banker,

Cavit, a freckled, stocky guy with a habit of locking one thumb under his armpit like a rooster about to crow.

Dixon and Nate listened to the jostling—why join the pissing contest? Like always, they'd rather keep them all guessing. The aloof but not unfriendly Black guys at the back of the room, mysterious but not overtly threatening. That mystery was a kind of superpower.

Two other members of their group, Luke and Reg, stood by just as silently, and the brothers were drawn to them. Average guys, as it turned out. Luke, the director of marketing for a college, and Reg, a retired pharmacist. Mortgage, Honda, two-weeks-at-the-beach-in-summer kind of guys. Luke, a first-timer like they were, joked about himself, "Not exactly the athlete," and revealed he had been fifty pounds overweight just ten years ago. "I'm happy just to be up to the effort, really. Being here is enough," he said too many times for Dixon to think it true. Reg, on the other hand, had a quiet self-confidence. In his late fifties, his shoulders just beginning to curve with age, Reg had been an avid climber in his twenties and thirties. "I was about half a foot taller then," he said as he lifted his shoulders a few times quickly. He had climbed Mount Hood, Denali, Rainier, Ama Dablam. Had even lost friends on Denali. "Stopped when my wife got pregnant. Figured it wasn't fair. But I'm old, kids are grown. 'Do not go gentle into that good night!'" he pronounced, raised on tiptoes.

During that first meeting in Kathmandu, their leader, Clive, offered a cautionary welcome speech. "We'll do our best to help you reach your summit goal, but we will not risk your life, our lives, or any life on this team for that goal. Clear enough? All right. Enjoy each step of the journey, but stay focused and careful," he said in a way that made them all feel reprimanded. Dixon noticed Clive's hands. They were full of bruises and scars that gave them the texture of rock. "There's a saying in this sport. You can grow old or you can go bold, but you can't go old and bold. That means careless climbers don't last. Remember that," Clive added.

———

TWO SHERPAS WERE ENGAGED IN DEEP ARGUMENT IN THEIR NA-tive tongue while Clive and his fellow guide stood by, avoiding eye contact with Dixon and Nate. The two brothers shared a glance. A simple, sharp disappointment passed between the two. Nate said softly to Dixon, "So what do you suppose the problem is here?" and Dixon remembered their friends' warnings about being the only Black men on the team.

"I win!" one sherpa shouted gleefully in English. Wiry and very handsome, he looked like a brown-skinned Cary Grant with his chiseled features, salt-and-pepper hair, and cleft chin. Despite his regal look, he giggled like an adolescent but Dixon guessed the man must be close to forty. "Matthew Hensons, I am Pemba Jangbu Sherpa. You know Matthew Henson, yes?" Pemba asked.

"Right man, wrong trip," Dixon answered, wondering how in the world Pemba knew about Henson, the first Black man to reach the North Pole.

"Yes, yes, but it is just my joke, and everything." Pemba intro-duced the man beside him as his younger brother, Angkaji, who flashed a set of deep half-moon dimples. "You are brothers, we are brothers. We carry our families up to Chomolungma," he said, beaming.

———

THEIR PLANE GLIDED FROM KATHMANDU TOWARD LUKLA, THE mountain village from which they would begin the ten-day trek to

Base Camp. As they ascended from the city, they passed over agricultural terraces carved along the foothills in alternating stripes of brown earth and green plants. They drifted above tiny villages whose green and blue roofs sprouted low and tight as mushrooms. Everest rose and fell behind them, teasing. "Where is it?" one in their group asked, and Clive responded, "She's there." They landed in Lukla on an alarmingly short airstrip that pitched straight up and ended smack dab into a hill. They touched down and careened forward, the brakes slamming on, their bodies lurching forward. Dixon gripped the edge of his seat, his eyes dead on the approaching hill. A cheap irony, he thought wryly, that a little hill, not a mountain, could be the death of them. Cursing rumbled through the plane. Clive said loudly, "They always pull it out, don't worry." And just like that, they came to a stop.

In Lukla, they strapped on their backpacks and joined a steady throng of climbers, trekkers, and tourists on the narrow path that led through the mountains. Their fellow adventurers—American, Asian, European—grew ruddy and brown in the sun, their skin burning with the shared anticipation. They moved through lush forest, pungent and sweet with spring, then rose above vegetation and into rocky terrain. In the villages they passed through, they encountered signs in English and village stores stocked with candy bars and soft drinks, then before they knew it civilization had been left behind. One day, they walked over a clattering wooden bridge above a rocky ravine a few hundred feet below, and then the next over a modern bridge, its bottom made of woven steel rods set in concrete boulders on either shore, the world still shifting between old and new. Dixon might be on a sacred pilgrimage or in a post-apocalyptic movie.

He had assumed their miseries would not truly begin before they actually reached the mountain. He was so wrong. The rumble of an unhappy stomach, the attempt to draw a breath that was slow to come. Dixon and Nate checked in frequently with each other. "You a'ight?" one might say and the other would reply, "Yep, it's all good." Blisters swelled on Dixon's feet; Nate had them, too. But in one Namaste Lodge or another—as all these villages had one with that name, decreasing in cleanliness the farther they traveled (Dixon and Nate politely refused the urine-soaked mattresses and used their own sleeping pads, which Dixon had insisted on packing)—each night they tended to their blisters without complaint, and the next morning they wrapped their feet in lambswool and soldiered on.

Along the packed-earth route, villagers lined the road as if watching a parade. Sometimes one pointed at Dixon and Nate and giggled or waved, and the brothers enjoyed an odd celebrity. Late one afternoon, a group of boys, about eight or nine years old, ran up to the brothers and grabbed their hands. Instead of simply holding them, the boys splayed the brothers' fingers wide and swiped their palms along them. "You must be his first," Nate said to Dixon, and sure enough, the boys seemed engrossed in comparing Dixon's and Nate's skin tones with their own, which were darker brown with the deep red undertones of their Indian ancestry. "You speak English?" Nate asked.

One boy nodded enthusiastically. "Give me one pen," he said, smiling.

"A pen? D'you mean a penny?" Nate asked.

The boy repeated, "Give me one pen."

"You got a pen?" Nate asked Dixon, who shook his head. The boy repeated his phrase.

"Must be his only English." Dixon laughed. The boys, eager, clambered all over Dixon and Nate, pulling at their hands.

One of the older boys whispered with his friends, who nudged him and gave their support. The boy puffed up with bravery and pulled at Dixon's shoulder to make him bend down. He plucked off Dixon's baseball cap and rubbed a hand over his hair. The boy giggled, baring a smile budding with new adult front teeth, large and ungainly on his small face. He called to his friends, who came bounding over. Soon the boys surrounded Dixon and Nate, stopping them in their tracks. They pulled at Nate, too, rubbing their hands in his hair. The two brothers laughed, a little embarrassed, and the kids returned that language, amused by the soft, nappy curls of Dixon and Nate. If he were at home, this would have made him recoil, becoming someone's exotica, but Dixon was captured by the boys' innocence, their delight in discovery. A sharp pang of missing his own boys. A glimpse of Marcus's face.

"All right, that's enough." Dixon pulled away from the Nepalese boys and straightened up. "Okay, okay."

Pemba approached, chattering in his native language and flinging his hands, scattering the boys like fleas. "You are exotic, Matthew Henson," Pemba told Dixon.

"I guess they don't see Black folks here."

"Sure." Pemba shrugged. "We see. Couple Africans. They come before you. Bring whole camera people, and everything."

"Really?"

"Yes, have their own team, and everything. They are not famous for you?"

"Don't know." And Dixon considered the bubble in which he and Nate had lived and trained, the way that for Dixon, Everest had been only theirs.

On the third day of the hike, Dixon caught his first real glimpse of her, Chomolungma, Mother Goddess of the World.

They left Namche Bazaar, the last point of luxury with real

meals and alcohol and hot baths and oddly the best German stru-del Dixon had ever tasted, and they began the approach to Thy-angboche Monastery, whose golden bell-shaped dome rose from a solitary hill as if the mountains had backed away in deference.

The first glimpse of Everest was a hard-earned reward. High above Thyangboche, Dixon saw the mountain across a pasture of budding spring flowers and trees. The wide breast of Everest, its dark ridges peeking out beneath snow, a banner of ice cloud bil-lowing across its peak. Dixon stopped in his tracks. They all did, each climber pausing to gaze. She awaited them. They would come to her. They would strive and suffer to earn her. In that pause, Dixon felt something new and bright: *Wait till Nate climbs, wait till he sees what he can do!*

BASE CAMP ENCOMPASSED A DINGY, ROCKY PERCH THAT SPREAD more than half a mile at the foot of Everest and resembled the pit-ted gray surface of the moon. Amid the dusty earth and car-sized boulders, a frontier town grew, its clusters of electric blue and yel-low tents spread low across the ridge, the colors dazzling in the sun so that Dixon had to squint. Electricity rose from the camp as Dixon entered. His every nerve ending at attention: he was here! Nate grabbed hold of him and shook him, laugh-panting, utterly joyous. Dixon could not find words.

He studied the landscape. Arranged in small groups by each expedition team, the tent clusters served as individual neighbor-hoods. Many buildings connected like a long yellow caterpillar with legs splayed out; a central dining tent connected to cooking, com-munications, sleeping, and gear tents. Prayer flags crisscrossed the roofs in the cluster. "They blowing prayers up to mountain, carrying blessings down," Pemba explained. Satellite dishes sprang up throughout, and the camp resonated with song and laughter and loud conversation in various languages. A thrilling circus of a place.

On their first night in this wonderland, amid the glow of the yellow tent that was now home, Dixon and Nate sat very close, their arms around their knees with elbows resting against each other. They were too new to this altitude to exert much physical effort. Too dazzled, as well. Most newcomers reclined in lounge chairs, drinking beer or wine from tin cups. Dixon remembered the Old West of Saturday afternoon movies, the men around them on Everest like loungers outside the saloon. Those who hung at the periphery of the town were as watchful as sheriffs. The unmistakable waft of marijuana. A gritty layer of dirt covered every surface. Except for the blare of TVs, videos, rock, rap, and blues spilling from tents, it could indeed be the set of a TV Western.

Several Nepalese men wandered through camp passing out flyers for a bed and breakfast just below Base Camp. The flyers promised "good bed, clean towel." All the things they had left behind. A native man approached. He was somewhere between fifty and ninety, depending on the way the lamplight illumined or shadowed his wrinkled skin. He raised his cloaked arm in the direction of several young women who posed on the edge of the makeshift city. "Very clean, she is very clean," the man said.

"Heard about this craziness but I can't believe it," Dixon said to Nate once the man had moved on.

"Brother, we are in the 'hood."

---

"WHAT'S YOUR ANGLE?" DIXON WAS ASKED MORE THAN ONCE before it was discovered that he and Nate were brothers: first Black

American brothers on Everest. It was a world that craved firsts. Dixon wondered: would they ask the alpinists the same question, or was this strictly for clients? The idea made him uncomfortable. At dinner, they often talked more than they ate, the altitude making it hard to both maintain an appetite and keep anything down. So, they talked, which was how Dixon learned about the guy two neighborhoods over who planned to hang glide down from the summit, and the one two tents east who would climb without oxygen, and the blind guy, and the first asthmatic epileptic double amputee, and the first guy to broadcast the entire climb via web camera.

"You have sponsorship?" Cavit the banker asked, leaning in wolfishly across the dining table. Nate shook his head. "No?" Cavit said. He jammed one thumb under his armpit. "Aww! You could've gotten some company to pay your way, give you publicity. You missed an opportunity, guys."

Later Nate confessed to Dixon, "I should tell you something." He sat up very straight. "I used the rest of my inheritance, plus some money after I sold the business, to start a scholarship in Mom and Dad's names. Like you wanted. It's from us both, it'll be noted. I wanted you to know, I heard you. I did. This will do some good, Dixon."

Ah, this, this was his Nate.

"Something else, too. You know, I looked into, into the sponsorship thing. I mean, I tried to solicit sponsors." He waved off Dixon's frown. "Yeah yeah, I didn't think you'd like the idea. But if it had worked, man, we could've come here scot-free. But no takers. Half of them thought it was a scam, Black men on Everest. But I think I can gather some interest from the reporters already here. I've got one I'm talking to."

"When did you do all this?"

"When you weren't looking, I guess."

"You saying I don't pay attention?"

"No. Never that." Nate's smile was wan.

———

DURING THAT FIRST WEEK, DIXON NOTICED THAT PEMBA WAS not in the dining tent in the evenings. Neither was Angkaji. In fact, Dixon realized that only the lead sherpa, the sirdar, joined the team of clients and guides in the dining tent. Dixon asked Nate, "You think they're forbidden?"

"What, from the dining tent?" Nate's voice grew louder.

"Yeah. Like in the Bahamas. Guy who lived there told me island folks can't enter the resort casinos."

Each brother rummaged through legacy. Wearying. Dixon had counted on accessing that reserve of energy he used in his normal life to hoist this particular knowledge, thinking it would not be necessary on the mountain—why, indeed, had he thought that? he wondered—and he had envisioned that freed-up energy as a sort of super-reserve, something he and his brother could use for the climb itself. He began to pace, stalking back and forth, sorting the faces around him.

"Matthew Henson Two, you are restless," Pemba announced with his customary giggle. He had begun calling Dixon "Matthew Henson Two" ever since Nate had corrected him: *You know, I am the older brother. I'm One, he's Two.* "Yes, I see you are impatient, and everything."

Dixon approached Pemba, weaving his way between the supply boxes that spilled from the kitchen. Steam and heat poured out of the tent and shrouded Pemba. "You weren't at dinner," Dixon began, his voice a confidential whisper.

"Oh, ate well, thank you."

"Where?"

Pemba's smile froze. He motioned his head toward the steamy kitchen tent.

"Why?" Dixon's voice all breath.

"Do not be insulted, Matthew Henson Two. For us, it is comfort. We hear news of home. We prepare. We relax. It is just our way. Up there," he pointed to the mountain, "we are all together. But here, sometimes is just family."

Dixon had been holding his breath. He exhaled loudly. "You don't have to eat here?" He glanced inside the tent at a large iron cauldron over a bed of burning coals.

"Have to?" Pemba frowned.

"I mean, you aren't made to . . . required to . . . you want to eat here?"

"Sometimes, yes, confessing, we want to eat separate. Meals is very important time and everything." Pemba held his head slightly down.

"And you wanna spend it with your own folk." Dixon's hands on his hips. "You wanna relax and stretch out. Right, right." He swallowed.

Pemba leaned close, his arm on Dixon's forearm. "You come sometime. You bring your brother. Family time."

Two nights later, Nate and Dixon entered the cooking tent. It was not exactly forbidden, but they felt they were crossing a line lightly drawn in the sand, self-imposed, like when all the Black kids sit together in the cafeteria. They were invaders, and a perceptible veil rose, a slight formality and distance in the sherpas' talk and manner. They had never before felt so Western, so American. Nate quipped, "So is this what it's like to be the only white guy in the room?" They stood at the mouth of the tent for a silent beat before Pemba motioned to them. "Matthew Hensons, come." They fell into the room and its wash of brown skin, some much darker than their own, and there was a certain welcome: distant cousins come to visit. In the small, close circle of the room, they listened as Pemba and Angkaji recounted the bloodlines between the Sherpas. *He is from my mudda's village, the son of my grandmudda's sister. He is from my cousin Ang's house. He is the son of my cousin's son.*

Dixon realized those family ties undergirded everything among the Sherpas. Like this: Angkaji, Nate's sherpa, was the younger brother of Pemba, his face boyish and angelically round with a thin mustache that stuck out stiff as straw. He was inclined to sink slightly into his shoulders, his whole body a kind of defer-ence to Pemba. He began nearly every sentence with "My brudda." "My brudda, I tell him this story, when I was on my wedding day, I was filled with so much happiness that I cried." Dixon felt a ten-derness toward Angkaji, who could not be much older than Dixon's boys at school.

Pemba offered Dixon and Nate a refill of their tea, pouring care-fully into their cups, which the brothers held with both hands. "You must tell me something then," Pemba began as if mid-conversation with himself. "You are rich, yes? You are famous in your country?"

Dixon and Nate glanced at each other, their laughter rising. "No, not at all," they said.

"But you are here, that makes you have money. Yes?"

"Well, not really." Dixon fumbled for words. He examined the tent, the sherpas' rucksacks less new than those of the climbers, no designer names on shoes or shirts.

"But you have the money to spend here? Then rich, yes!" Pemba insisted. "How long since you were Black in your country?"

"Excuse me?" Had Dixon heard correctly?

Nate answered, "We are Black. Black and American."

"How can that be?" Pemba held his head slightly forward, his whole body a question mark. "You are not like that TV. *Good Times. Sanford's Son.* But you are still Black, then?"

"Yes, yes, that's just made-up TV. That's not everyone. That's not all of us," Nate explained.

"Ah ha, is not the rich, then. Like you."

It sank like a heavy meal. Dixon didn't have the energy for all this explaining.

"We're middle class," Nate began, an exasperation in his voice. "We're just—the social worker–preacher–teacher class," he said. "There are lots of people like us." He shrugged. "We're just not the stories that sell."

Pemba's face earnest, weathered, his hands like tanned hide, dark and smooth with the hard work of placing rope high up on the mountain, of packing the yaks, of hauling pounds and pounds of supplies. Dixon pictured his great-grandfather's hands, so swollen and arthritic from farm work that he could barely hold his steaming mugs of coffee, the look of hands sacrificed for food and shelter and hope, for this generation and the next. "Yes," Dixon said firmly, "we are rich." Nate gave him a puzzled look, examined his brother's face, and then conceded.

"You are lucky then," Pemba beamed. "We get rich, too, up here." He gestured wide then gave his usual giggle. "Get rich from you! Send children to school in Kathmandu, and everything. It very big deal." His eyes fluttered closed a minute, satisfied. "Very big."

# CHAPTER

8

*Early April 2011, Mount Everest*

ase Camp was filled with generators and satellites, faxes,
cell phones, Internet, and computer software that analyzed
the weather and told them the perfect climbing window. It
bewildered Dixon, who had imagined it would be more like his
childhood Davy Crockett fantasies. He had watched that TV
show as a kid and yearned to be a mountain man, living in the
woods, wearing a squirrel-skin hat, skinning his own animals—
his father had harrumphed from behind his newspaper: "Only
thing they'd skin is you." For Christmas, Dixon had begged for an
official Davy Crockett squirrel-skin hat, only to have some bigger
boys down the street chase him home when he wore it. He had
quietly hidden it in a desk drawer, but he still dreamed of conquering a wilderness.

So here he stood in his mountain wilderness. Just him and
eight hundred others. All awaiting their chance to summit.

Acclimatizing to the mountain, hoping for clear weather. They milled about Base Camp, their flashes of anxiety piercing the group like lightning. They sang and lounged and stared into space, distracting themselves however they could.

Luke, their teammate, splayed out cards, pulled out two and rearranged them. "Can't remember the last time I played so many hands of cards. College, maybe?" Luke, wide-eyed, innocent-looking despite his age—close to thirty-five, Dixon and Nate had guessed—his face round and pale as the moon.

Nate folded up his cards in one hand, tapped them on the table. "I used to play poker till morning in college." A blast of cold air blew open their tent flap. Snow drifted in, and Nate brushed it from his cards.

Dixon raised one eyebrow. "I remember your grades."

"Lotta downtime here waiting on the big girl to give us a pass to climb," Reg said, then stretched his neck side to side.

Luke laughed. He leaned forward on his elbows so Dixon could nearly see his cards. Dixon frowned, annoyed by Luke's careless-ness. "All this time on the mountain. I'll be seeing it in my dreams the rest of my life."

"Well," Reg said, "let's just say, you won't forget her. See, boys, this is my third try." He exhaled hard and fanned out his cards. Dixon stared at him as if he were some foreboding bird.

They were quiet. Dixon knew they all must be thinking: Jesus Christ, what if we have to do this again?

Reg continued, "You know, it really does change you."

"What changed in you before?" Dixon asked quietly.

"Oh, everything." Reg began a long, slow nod and then closed himself.

"Well," Nate chimed in, "no matter what we do back in the world, it can't match this."

Luke, who had been looking with naked fear at Reg, turned quickly to Dixon. "What do you do, Dixon?"

"He saves souls," Nate joked and took a card from the pile.

"School psychologist."

"He's good at it," Nate said, beaming. "A boy whisperer."

Dixon turned in the direction of the mountain. Even from inside the tent, Dixon could picture the slant of snowdrift rising high above the summit, an accent mark. Shiloh. Some days he combed his eyebrows straight up. His tell. He was sure to start trouble on those days.

"What do you mean, like a sixth sense?" Luke asked. "So if I start losing it up here, you'll notice and be my salvation, Dixon?" Luke joked.

Nate laughed. "Why d'you think I brought him?"

———

SKEET COULD HARDLY SIT IN HIS SEAT, POPPING UP AND DOWN on the screen, in and out of the frame as Dixon and Nate talked to him over Skype. "You're making me seasick." Nate laughed. "Sit down, man!"

"Everything, I want everything. How does the water taste, what's the snow feel like, man, how's the *air*!" He flung his arms wide, his laughter contagious. Dixon and Nate sat inside the communication tent, staring into a computer screen at a world they'd left back home. Skeet and four guys Dixon recognized from the old neighborhood plus a few he didn't know were on the call, their faces floating in and out of the screen.

At a desk behind Dixon and Nate, Clive worked on a set of navigation charts spread out before him. He stole glances toward Dixon and teased, "Do you tell 'em about the diarrhea, the nausea, or do you make it a romance?" Clive laughed. "Give 'em the hero version!" he pronounced.

"Outstanding!" Nate said. Magical. Phenomenal. Breathtaking. The sheen of the ice in the sun. The black ridge of the summit. He gave them the best of the mountain, and the men listened, intent. They flushed with the daring of Dixon and Nate almost as if it were theirs, too. Look who they all were! Dixon felt a sweep of excitement overtake him. Skeet raised a cup, leading a cheer, and the brothers laughed until they coughed, winded. You could not tell Dixon at that moment they wouldn't make it to the summit, the two of them, unstoppable. The surety of it lay between him and Nate. They locked onto each other. They had been born to this bond, this promise that gave them one purpose, one body. Dixon had never been more whole.

Outside the tent, the sun piercing and so close, Dixon felt a drunken joy. Lightheaded, giddy, he and Nate staggered into each other, recalling the looks on their friends' faces, laughing at Skeet's restless energy. They plopped down in the center of camp loose-jointed, delirious.

Near a small outcropping of stacked stones that formed a shallow wall, an expedition of women was newly arrived and setting up camp. A gathering of men swarmed the tent like bees as the porters carted boxes and bags and chairs. The buzz woke Dixon from his exhausted nap. He searched for his brother and found that Nate, of course, had ingratiated himself with the women. He sat on the stone wall to the left of a brunette in her early thirties. The woman brushed aside her hair, engaging Nate in conversation about using the ascender on the Lhotse Face. Her smile widened. Nate leaned forward, folding his hands between his knees, returning her gaze.

Groggy, Dixon retreated to his tent. Let Nate do his thing. Dixon slept, dreaming of the meandering brook where they washed their clothes, beating them on rocks like pioneers. The water crystal-clear and frigid, he dreamed he stood at its center, stood solid and bare as rock, his arms extended, the water gushing from his body like a waterfall.

Nate woke him a few hours later, a brisk steady shake. "Wake up, wake up." Dixon lifted his head slowly, sitting up and attempting to focus.

"Ah, poor newbie, altitude is getting to you, no?" Lena from the hotel in Kathmandu knelt down and cupped her hand around Dixon's cheek before leaning her body against his and enveloping him in a hug. Flustered, a surge of heat through his limbs, Dixon was too stunned to hug her back. His face against her head, the smell of her hair lilting past his nostrils freshly washed, lavender. God, how did he smell?

"Surprised, huh?" Nate beamed.

Lena stood up, her hands on her hips, her legs turned out like a dancer's. "I come to see couple of my friends. They are in the women's group down there." She lifted her chin vaguely toward the direction of the women's camp. "I see this one hanging around. You are bad, I see this about you in Kathmandu. Am I right, Dixon?"

Dixon exhaled. "Indeed."

"Well, I guess you've got my number." Nate looked sheepish.

"Oh! Your number! Is plastered like this." She plopped her palm against Nate's forehead and laughed. "Dixon, you come, have a drink."

Outside the tent, around a campfire, they sipped tea. Lena settled in between the brothers as they sat on a blanket before the fire. She seemed cozy, comfortable. They might all have been old friends. More than that, she was sturdy in her comfort on this mountain. She shone so bright, her hand slipping onto his knee as she talked, its texture rough and earned. Dixon noticed the way her hair lay along the nape of her neck, tangled in a thin gold chain. The sun had burnished her a rich golden brown, the firelight gliding and sparkling off her skin. He opened his mouth toward her as if he might drink her in.

"I'm confused," Nate began. "You said you weren't coming to Everest."

"No, no, we are on Pumori. Just ten kilometers away. Is easy from here."

"That's better than Everest?" Dixon asked.

"It was. More alpinists. We practice. But is getting crowded now. Ack! Clients." She made a face. "You don't tell I come visit you, huh? It could ruin my reputation." She scooted away from them. "Seen with *clients*." Her laugh a trill, she leaned slightly against Dixon, then against Nate. She gulped down her tea and stood up. "Well, I am getting tired for the night." She dusted off her bottom and legs and turned to leave. Then she held her hand out for Nate. "Coming?" She smiled.

Nate hesitated, his arms draped around his bended knees. Her hand suspended. Dixon did not breathe. His whole body stopped in that pause: Don't do it. Don't take her. It twitched through him, his breath too long held, tiny stars skittering before his eyes. Nate stood and took her hand, his eyes steady on her face. Dixon exhaled with a cough, a sharp piercing in his lungs, and he sucked in a breath.

"Good night, Dixon," Lena called, and Nate mimicked her, the two never taking their eyes off each other.

That night, just as when they were teenagers, Dixon lay awake in bed, hands propped behind his head, waiting for his brother to sneak in. He kept picturing Lena. The slope of her collarbone. What was it about a woman's skin along that bone, its unbelievable softness, that small well that held heat, sweat, sweetness? Lena suddenly too close, rising high and blocking all light, her lavender scent. He lay awake, alone, waiting. Finally, at about 1 a.m., Nate crawled in and over Dixon, who had lain deliberately by the door to trip him up. Nate smelled of sweat and perfume and sex. "Gotta try it at seventeen thousand feet, man. Something about the lack of oxygen. Makes your head spin. It's wild."

"Sherpas say it's bad luck," Dixon snapped.

"They must not be gettin' any."

---

DURING THE DAY AS THEY WAITED FOR THE REAL CLIMBING TO begin, Dixon paced the camp, gazing up at his mountain, taking her measure. He grew more anxious to climb. Palms-rubbing-against-his-thighs anxious. He had not been a man given to wanting, and this churning desire hung weighty as loose skin, then surged and tightened around him like a harness. Just before dusk one evening as the temperature dropped, he bundled up and wandered across camp to face the mountain. He gazed across her belly toward the black slopes of her limbs. He examined the way Everest sat beside her sisters, Lhotse and Nuptse. Ribbons of ice and cloud wavered across the summit in the rising moonlight. His body aglow. A little fire swept up from his feet and swayed his back. Ah, Lena's face, the sharp, clean angles of her cheekbones. Lena, who understood this mountain. How easily she wore that knowledge in the tautness of her calves, in the sinewy strength of her hands; she carried it, her true beauty, and her prowess left him yearning. His hand bracing his stomach, he closed his eyes. He could not bear to want all things.

The next morning, after taking a walk to the far edge of Base Camp, Dixon returned to his tent and found Lena sitting beside Nate. A quick flush covered Dixon; he may have conjured her from his dreams the night before. Her face bright and warm. "Newbie!" She beckoned to him, and he sat beside her. She embraced him in a quick, tight hug. Really, how the hell did she manage to smell so intoxicatingly clean?

"I was telling her how I taught you to tie your shoes." Nate grunted a laugh. Dixon scratched his brow. Nate had taught him to tie his laces, all right, but somehow in the confusion, Nate had tied their two sets of shoes together. When they stood up and attempted to walk, they had tumbled down the stairs. Dixon had knocked out his front baby teeth a full year and half early.

"Anyway," Nate continued, "our uncle comes to visit a few months later, Dixon wakes up and there's Uncle Davis at the kitchen table with no front teeth. Hadn't put in his dentures yet. Dixon takes one look, bursts into tears and says, 'I wanna have teeth!'" Nate cracked himself up.

Dixon stood silent. Why was Nate telling this story?

Lena, reading Dixon's face, said, "Ah, but you are sensitive always, then? I tell you what, I cry too to have no teeth." She ran her tongue slowly over her front teeth. A shiver slid along Dixon's spine.

"Just messing with you, little brother." Nate slapped Dixon's knee. Dixon didn't respond. "Hey, there's Clive." Nate stared outside the tent and then got up. "Need to ask him something about the next climb." He disappeared.

"You let him get under your skin, Dixon. Don't give him so much of the power," Lena advised. He nodded, sheepish. She sidled closer to him, her shoulder pressing into his chest. "I mean you are more the grown-up."

"I'm not only serious, I mean, I can be fun, too." Why did he sound like a goddamned schoolboy?

She laughed hard. He stared at the tent opening, calculating how many steps to get away. "Oh, yes, yes, I am sure. I just think, the two of you together, I mean." She crossed her fingers. "Little bit of him in you, little bit of you in him, that would be perfect man. But then no woman would be safe, yes?" She kissed his cheek and stood up, brushing her hands against her thighs. "Hey, Newbie. He has envy for you, too."

HE EMAILED PHOTOS OF BASE CAMP FOR BENNY LEWIS TO SHARE with his boys. Just enough to whet their appetites. He wrote emails to Kira and Charlaina, once to Pamela for good measure, and to Marcus. He only hinted at the struggles. It was worth it, he wanted them to hear in his words: this was worth it all. At the airport among the well-wishers seeing Nate and Dixon off to Nepal: Skeet and his wife Tania, Charlaina, Pamela, a woman Dixon had never met who threw her arms around Nate as if he were a long-lost love, and Kira, who had stayed at Dixon's side until the last minute, going through the zigzag lanes at the security gate. "You won't get it, right, that summit fever? I read about it. That's what kills people, Daddy, makes them not turn around and go down the mountain when they should." Her face so earnest, he answered, "When have you known me to get carried away?" Because temperance had always been his best armor. She had taken his hands, turned them palm to palm against her own and kissed their backs, startling and tender.

Startling. Dixon had had to tell Marcus more than once about Everest for it to sink in. One day after workouts at Dixon's house, Marcus had made him repeat it all. The boy had stood silent, a light going out in his face. "Just, just for spring term I'm gone. That's all." Dixon had explained the logistics of the trip, the timelines. The boy had retreated, closing himself down so that Dixon had reached out, latched onto the boy's shoulders, and shaken him. "I'm not going for good. Y'hear me? I'll be back!" The boy had grabbed his gear and left quickly. And this: Shiloh, as he was marched out of school on Dixon's last day, "Oh, we ain't through." He, too, had taken Dixon's leaving personally.

All the people he carried up this mountain. Some days, he could swear he felt them piled on his back, weighing him down like the packs the porters carried. Why couldn't he be the kind of guy who said *Fuck 'em all*? Perhaps, on this mountain, he could try.

———

THE NEXT NIGHT, THEY WERE AWAKENED BY AN AVALANCHE. The brothers bolted upright. Dixon unzipped their tent, grabbed a flashlight, and peered into the night. "Far gorge east," someone yelled, indicating that the avalanche had happened away from them. Relieved, Dixon retreated into the tent and lay down.

Nate asked, "What do you think this is gonna be like?"

Dixon considered a moment. "I can't tell you."

"Not like anything I've ever done before."

"Well, it's a mountain. You did one."

"Right," Nate answered, tentatively. "Well, no. I mean, I started but—"

"You had to turn back, you said."

"Actually, I never made it out of Base Camp."

"What?" Dixon held his breath.

"They brought down this dude, looked like the mountain chewed him up and spit him out. He fell, broke almost every bone in his body. Just bent and crooked on the stretcher. Another guy nearly froze to death. Lost my nerve."

"You said you climbed but got turned around by weather." Dixon's voice was low and tight.

"I was embarrassed." Nate sighed.

"So you telling me this now? Why?"

"I wanna come clean. I want you to know the truth."

"You couldn'ta done that about sixty-five thousand dollars ago? What the fuck? Goddammit, Nate!"

"I'll do it this time. I've got you beside me. You trained me, man. We'll get it done."

Nate's words like spikes through his body, Dixon lay churned, tamping down anger because how could that help things? He would just have to work harder, dammit. Besides, he reminded himself, he had trained Nate hard. He had not let up on him, not once, not once. *Fuck!* But look, look. They were ready. He had to remember that.

Nate's voice haunting in the night. "Look, I could end up one of these guys, go home, make my living lecturing about climbing Everest with my kid brother. How you dogged my ass out in training. How you were reluctant but how now I see that gleam in your eye. She's gotcha. You've got mad love for her, don't you? You stand out there, hands all deep in your pockets, swaying, man, swaggering for her. I know you see yourself on that mountain. Don't doubt."

That was the thing. There was no doubt what Dixon wanted.

On a clear sunny morning, Dixon, Nate, and their fellow climbers gathered for the puja, the Buddhist ceremony to ask Chomolungma's permission and protection during the climb. With handheld drums and cymbals and flutes, the sherpas sang songs as they danced in a semicircle, arms linked as if on a chorus line. Dixon joined in, eager for a blessing. The songs were sung in unison without harmony, singing that sounded chant-like, hypnotizing. Dixon, like most of the Westerners, participated so as not to offend the sherpas but more so as not to offend the mountain. Because it was clear that Chomolungma lived and breathed. As they followed tradition and passed their climbing gear through the cleansing smoke of juniper and incense, Dixon grew solemn. Quietly, he entreated Everest, Mother Goddess of the World, "Have pity on us."

Finally, the sherpas instructed Dixon and the others to grab handfuls of sampa meal to toss into the air and rain down upon one another. "Signify long life, living to hair turn white, and everything," Pemba explained. Dixon tossed high toward his brother. He watched the sherpas rub the meal into one another's hair, so Dixon pounced toward Nate to do the same. Nate complained, ducking and trying to get away from a determined Dixon, who chased his brother and trailed a handful of sampa like ash. Nate protested, "Man, don't nap it up." They tussled, Nate slapping at Dixon's arms and fussing. "How'm I gonna get this junk out?"

The whiteness of Nate's hair.

A good sign.

# II.

*Fall 2011, Maryland*

f Dixon stood perfectly still and leaned his weight back into his
heels, the new partial foot felt nearly like his own. He might not
even recall what the mountain had cost him: big toe, second toe,
pinky, his balance. When he walked, he moved pretty much like
himself, if slower and with more concentration, but he had a constant fear that the contraption might slip off and send him hurtling.
"Not likely," his doctor had said, shaking his head with a flutter of
half-closed eyes, his arms folded decisively across his chest.

No matter, he simply could not get used to that thing, the way
he had to ease the prosthetic onto his two remaining toes, their
skin blackened from the frostbite that had nearly claimed them,
the way he had to position the prosthetic just right. The toes and
the collar of silicone skin that draped the top of his foot were both
molded in a "nude" color. A white man's nude. Were Black men not
expected to lose toes, he wondered, or just not to replace them?

He stood outside Medgar Evers Charter Middle School Academy for Boys on a bright, hot morning, awaiting the first day of a new school year. He had only been gone for one semester. It seemed a lifetime. A mountain had crept in between. He leaned his weight on his intact foot.

A mass of teachers and counselors lined the walkway, all awaiting the first school buses of a new year. At six-five, Dixon towered above them all, enduring the sideways glances at his foot, the sudden pat on the back accompanied by a quick shake of the head, the determined don't-say-anything stare. No one had the nerve to mention Everest. He had noticed, for instance, in Angela Preston's science classroom that the drawings depicting him on the mountain had quietly disappeared from the wall, along with the banner announcing: "Our own Mr. Bryant climbs Mt. Everest." Quite deliberately, there had been no welcome back party, just a short mention of his return over the loudspeaker that morning during all-staff announcements. Now, standing in front of the school building, his coworkers circled. Dixon felt every eye on him.

Beside him, three counselors wrangled over a bet: number of crying mothers on the first day. Wiley Fitch talked loudly, laughing and throwing his head back so that the deep folds of his neck stretched into tight, white bands. "Phone criers count, too! After all, they can pull up little Johnny's schedule on their laptops and cry about it from work." Dixon kept his gaze somewhere in a fuzzy, soft middle distance. His colleagues invited him with their loud voices, their furtive looks, but avoided him, too: a man with a shattered dream. What could be more dangerous? Nate always said, "Beware a brother with a plan." A knot like a fist settled in the middle of Dixon's back.

Wiley leaned toward Dixon. "First day will always be first day." He sighed. "We missed you last semester, Dix," he said quietly. "Glad you're back." And he glanced toward Dixon's feet, a frown washing across his face.

Dixon exaggerated his stance, locking into his heels and steadying his weight. "Good to be here," he forced himself to say.

He focused on the whip and turn of the flag, the clink of its metal rings hitting the flagpole. It would be all right if he could just settle himself. The metal of the school's spaceship-like roof cast sparks of light across the grass. The sun fanned around him, a pale early morning light, and he recalled the spectrum of color that is mountain snow, pure white when new, aging to ochre and ecru and ivory and cream, champagne and bone. Jesus Christ. When would the school buses arrive?

All he wanted was his boys. The feeling of being among them, a radiating light that gathered in the core of him and fanned out.

His boys. He awaited them like a bare tree awaits the lush shelter of leaves.

In an explosion, they finally arrived, a half dozen school buses pulling up to the front walk.

Children poured from school buses and bounded toward the entrance.

In the drop-off lanes, mothers leaned toward flung-open car doors and shouted last-minute orders to their fleeing sons.

The school staff flanked either side of the entrance. They cheered and clapped a welcome as boys walked between them. Dixon stood, a Maypole planted at the mouth of the walkway, the boys' shouted greetings floating like streamers around him.

Boys swarmed past Dixon. The ones he knew best did a double take.

A squawky voice rose beside Dixon, a voice on the verge of change: "Hey, Mr. B.!"

Dixon focused, blinked. Marcus Hollinger's pudgy round face in front of him. Dixon shook his head fast. "What are you doing here?"

"Mr. B.! Mr. B.! They said you were coming back. You did!" Marcus hesitating, a wash of alarm as he scanned Dixon's withered body, then he lunged forward, burrowing his face in Dixon's chest, inhaling him with a sudden, overwhelming relief. Dixon rocked back, clenching his toes—the false foot was anchored to his remaining toes and if he pulled his foot too suddenly, the anchors gnawed at his skin. The boy beamed. "Can I come by and see you this morning?"

"I don't understand why you're here. What about McKelvin? Didn't you like it there?" Pinpricks of alarm rose along his arms. Where the hell was Shiloh? He hadn't thought to look for him on the school roster. Surely, he had to be in juvy again by now.

"But you're back." Trust blooming from Marcus, searing into Dixon. He wanted to wrap his palms around that boy's tender face. "Yes, come see me." And in that moment, Dixon believed it was still within him to be of use.

Standing so long was hard. His foot began to throb, his whole leg ached. He had to ask someone to bring him his cane. He hated doing that, but he didn't want to go inside. He wanted to feel normal.

The morning rush trickled to the tardies, their parents speeding up to the building and casting them out. The main wave of boys had come and gone five minutes before the school bell rang. The final stragglers would arrive soon, the ones chronically late from disorganization and the ones who couldn't give a shit, those problem kids who would invariably end up in his caseload. The Shilohs. Would he be back? Shit. Marcus was here. Goddammit, who did that kid think

Dixon was that he could magically protect him? A glance down at himself, skinny, half-footed. He hid his cane inside a tall hedge, ran his sweaty palms across his pants legs. He let the bush support him, its long, wiry limbs sharp against his back.

Dixon acknowledged two latecomers with steady eye contact, made his voice a notch deeper. "Gentlemen, the pants." One of them lowered his head, hiked up his drooping pants. The other sucked his teeth and attempted to pass Dixon, who, without thinking, stepped quickly into his path, and the boy straightened and hiked his pants up.

Look what he had done! That he had made that instinctive, easy move with his good foot made Dixon want to shout. He stepped forward then back, a mini-dance. A sharp stab of an elbow in Dixon's side, an extra push against him. He toppled sideways, his arms wide to balance himself, pain echoing in his side. He knew immediately: Shiloh. The rank scent of smoke and sweat. Dixon spun around, scrunching toes that weren't there, tipping forward. Shiloh came into full view, a little taller, slightly more formidable than Dixon recalled. The boy a ghost turned flesh, that same oversized black windbreaker, the hood pulled low. The boy let the hood drop, and his scarred cheeks shone in the morning light. His face like bare rock. Dixon had forgotten the jolt of that hardened face.

Shiloh barked, "You best to watch yourself, old man." The boy scanned Dixon, lingering on his foot, on the off-balance way that he stood, and the boy's smile spread slowly. "They say you climbed some mountain? *Your* weak ass?" He began a long, slow laugh, sucked his teeth dismissively, and sauntered inside.

*Your weak ass.*

Snatching the cane he'd hidden in the bushes, Dixon thudded his way toward the staff kitchen. He filled a mug with hot water, stared into it, then poured it down the sink, watching the steam rise. Deep breaths, deep breaths.

You don't wanna be that guy, the one everybody's whispering about. Living in the shadow of your former self. He and Nate used to lay into each other any time one of them could no longer do something. Maybe they had grown too tall to shimmy through that opening at the back of the fence or maybe they had just missed a layup they usually made. They would hear the other brother mimic Howard Cosell when an aging Muhammad Ali re-entered the ring: *The man he once was is no more.* You don't wanna be that guy. The one who left to climb a goddamned mountain and came home in pieces. He was not going to be that guy.

———

THE PHYSICAL THERAPIST HAD TOLD HIM, "TAKE IT SLOW THIS semester. Continue rehab, maybe go to therapy." His ex-wife Pamela had said, "Don't be so damned brave. You deserve to take time if you need it." He sat in his office, their voices replaying in his head. First warning bell rang. Students should finish up at their lockers and head to class. Ah, the order, the rules! A dress code, an honor code, an ordered life. That's why he had come back.

Except there was a perpetual knot in his stomach. All day, in the few quiet moments, he might rest his head back in his chair, close his eyes, and feel himself a traveler, time slipping along a rail that carried him back to the limbo of the summer just past, where he lay in a hospital bed ensconced in sheets white as snow. In that limbo, he might not be fully recovered or fully ailing but simply floating. All that first day of school, he found himself in an afterlife he could not quite make out. And then the phone would ring (a parent wanting to know why her son wasn't in honors classes), the door would open (a colleague, sheepish: "Anything I can do for you, Dixon?"), and he would be ushered into this life. He wanted this life back. He wasn't sure he deserved it.

Even Marcus's visit felt like an out-of-sync recording, the rush of Marcus's speech failing to reach Dixon in real time, a delayed quality while Marcus's mouth moved and Dixon could not keep up. He blinked and tried to listen. Marcus looked concerned. "You okay, Mr. B.? You not . . . you don't seem . . ." and he bounced his leg nervously. Finally, Marcus gathered up his books. "Want me to come later? Tomorrow?" Dixon nodded. Marcus left, head down, a wash of disappointment spilling from him. Dixon hoped the boy didn't think he had done something wrong. And Shiloh repeated *Your weak ass?* on an endless loop in Dixon's head.

At the end of the day, after the school buses had carted away the boys, Dixon set out into the quiet of the building. He crossed the main entryway, following a band of faux marble fashioned into a wave along the wall tiles, flowing, floating, Dixon giving in finally to this place, to something like descent. In the far-left corridor, he heard a scuffle. Someone pleading. He didn't dare try to run, but he walked as deliberately as he could. At the last bank of lockers, he recognized Marcus pressed up against the lockers, an arm wedged between his chin and collarbone.

"Hey!" Dixon yelled. Shiloh glanced as if Dixon were merely a curiosity. "Turn him loose," Dixon commanded. Dixon hobbled forward, not fast enough. "I said, leave him!" He reached out his arm toward the boy. A bead of sweat on Dixon's upper lip.

Shiloh hesitated, as if not entirely sure he would obey. Dixon's anger rose from his feet like a geyser. His body shook. This ugly little motherfucker. "I said let him go!" Dixon bellowed.

Shiloh pulled back his arm and let Marcus slip to the floor, coughing and holding his neck. "I was just saying welcome back," Shiloh said.

Dixon intended to grab Shiloh by his shoulder, to turn him for a good talking-to. He attempted to step into that boy's space, that easy move he had made just that morning. But now, at the end of a long day, the move eluded him. He stumbled and had to thrust out his hand to arrest his fall forward, his hand jamming against the locker beside the boy, Dixon toppling, his foot stubbing against the metal toe kick of the lockers. He winced in pain. That fucking mountain as much to blame as this fucking kid. The boy's slight snicker a lightning rod, Dixon leaned his full weight into him, shoving him against the lockers.

Marcus remained on the floor, huddled in fear. But that scar-faced boy looked Dixon square in the eye. "I thought you was a good cop," he said. "What happened to you?" And Dixon saw that the thing this boy had wanted most, he had gotten: an entry, as if through a fissure, into Dixon's psyche.

His arm pressing the boy flat against the lockers, lifting Shiloh up off the floor, Dixon barked to Marcus, "Go. Now." The boy scrambled to his feet and ran.

Dixon held tight to Shiloh, who hung weightless. Slamming that boy up against the locker. All the things you find you are capable of.

"You gonna jam me up like this forever?" the boy asked. "You know Shiloh ain't gone let you get away with this, right?"

Trembling, Dixon let go, and the boy dropped, caught himself with bended knees, straightened slowly. Fear spiked through Dixon's body. His breath ragged, he puffed out, "Boy, don't. Test. Me."

And the boy smiled. Because he already had.

CHAPTER

10

Perhaps they had not climbed yet; that was Dixon's first thought each morning. The early morning light in Maryland was nothing like the pure white awakening on Everest, his bedroom nothing like the sunny tent where he and Nate had spent the better part of their spring, but nevertheless he awakened to Everest each morning. "Did you sleep?" he would ask Nate groggily and await the reply, long in coming as it had always been, Nate never emitting more than grunts before ten in the morning. Waiting for Nate's reply.

Dixon pulled up from sleep, from the wide, swift blow of Nate's absence. There it was, the ever-present wash of cold that returned each morning, solid in his gut. His whole self might be forming around that coldness, his arms tingling, his head slightly spinning as he rose. The mountain still claiming him. He showered, standing a long time under the near-scalding spray.

Would Shiloh turn him in? He'd been too stunned to even consider it the day before, but now it loomed. He had intended to hurt that boy. The realization settled hard. It had never happened before.

Back in his office, Dixon dug through Shiloh's case file. No mistaking it, as thick as a mattress, full of incidents and reports.

- *He continues to serve as a disruption in class, continues to act out.*
- *Third home visit. Student would not speak to me. Aunt was helpful but had limited influence on student.*

Nothing there made the boy exceptional. An average trouble-maker but a persistent one. What was he capable of?

As Dixon awaited his boys outside the entrance to school, Benny Lewis approached, hands in his pockets, in that sideways stroll of his. Dixon gazed down at him. Dixon, who towered over nearly everyone, recognized most people by the tops of their heads. Benny's growing bald spot, a small, round spotlight in the middle of his thick black curls. The roundness of his belly puffed over his belt. His marriage had ended about the same time as Dixon's, both of them divorced after a long, hard married time. Neither had seen it coming.

Had Shiloh said anything yet about what Dixon had done? Dixon picked up his usual small talk with Benny, pausing, leaving room for whatever needed to be said. No signs from Benny. Yes, it made sense. That boy with all the power: he would hold it awhile, dangling it over Dixon's head. Dixon heard himself say, "I wonder if I didn't come back too soon." His voice quiet, he might have been talking to himself. Benny leaned closer. "You belong here," he said, an affirmation that Dixon leaned toward as if into arms.

WE GOT OFF TO A BAD START THIS YEAR, DIXON WOULD SAY TO Shiloh, let's start over. He would call the boy to his office, a conciliatory move. He would get a handle on all of this—even though that boy's sneer popped into his vision: *They say you climbed some mountain? Your weak ass?* and his anger and embarrassment bloomed again. Why bother with that kid? Why not just turn him in—right! What the hell had he been thinking? Like a light turning on, he remembered his job, its rules and codes and protocols. They rose up before him like a shield, and he felt protected, just as he had intervened to protect Marcus. Why had he been so eager to take on all the fault?

Dixon entered the main office with conviction. He knew what to do. The rush and rattle of a door opening greeted him, and he turned toward the doorway of the principal's office to see Shiloh emerge, his face as unreadable as if he had not seen Dixon at all. The boy walked toward him but never looked at Dixon, and then he raised his hand close to his stomach, pointed a finger at Dixon, and pulled an imaginary trigger. Dixon froze. A cool wash of anxiety.

Dolores Parsons, the school secretary, touched his arm. "You okay?" Her flowery perfume filled Dixon's nostrils.

He could not answer immediately. "That kid, what was he doing here?"

"Oh!" she said, her voice low and confidential. "Cursed out his homeroom teacher this morning, calm and cool as you please, sitting at his desk with his hands folded. And only the second day!" She shook her head. The flowers pinned in her hair shook vigorously. Dixon thanked her and made his way down the hall to his office. Closing his door, standing with his back pressed against it, he tried to remember how to breathe. He thought of how many inevitable things you simply don't see coming: the edema cough, the avalanche, the snow blindness from just a few moments without goggles, the simple slide forward of trouble like a rope slipping from your grasp.

There were boys who needed him that day, ones who sat in his office frightened and leaning forward in their seats, boys in familiar adolescent trouble: a best friend pulling away, some peer pressure to do what they knew to be wrong, a class they felt unprepared for. Ordinary trouble. The two boys in Dixon's office now, sent to him for disrupting class by shouting epithets back and forth, sat alternately scowling and trembling like terrified children. They just needed a firm hand on a shoulder, a claiming. But hadn't he meant just to grab hold of Shiloh, not slam him against the locker? Clearly, he could not trust himself.

"You'll hear something," he told Benny Lewis. "About me and a kid. Yesterday."

Benny shook his head. "I'm sure whatever it was, you did nothing wrong."

Dixon winced. Back at his office desk, he stared at an incident report form. Do it, fill it out, he told himself, but the paper sat there, glaring at him, and he felt immobile. He wasn't prone to losing his way in the world—his had been such a steady existence— and it felt as if a new planet had formed beneath him, and he walked unsteady in its atmosphere.

He remained withdrawn even once Marcus arrived, jittery, his eyes darting around the room as he chattered. He took furtive glances at Dixon. He said the boy next to him in homeroom smelled bad, the boy behind him in algebra snored through most of the class and Marcus couldn't hear. Dixon sat back, listening. Finally, Marcus said, "So like, Mr. B., you saved me. He was, like, tryina kill somebody."

"Marcus?" Dixon hesitated, unsure he wanted to know the answer. "Didn't you like your new school? I mean, why'd you come back?"

"It was just temporary while you were gone, right?"

Dixon blanched. "But didn't you know Shiloh was here?"

"I heard he got kicked out right when I left."

Dixon fanned his hand in front of his face. "Just suspended. He hasn't risen yet to expulsion level. That requires a more sustained . . ." He waved it off. The new regs made it nearly impossible for charter schools to dismiss troubled kids. "Listen, yesterday, I was wrong. He got the better of me. But I just want him to know I mean business."

Marcus let a smile slip. "He pro'ly got that when you body-slammed him. I mean, I'da got the message, Mr. B."

Shit. Marcus shouldn't be proud of him. Dixon's throat constricted. He began to cough.

"Mr. B., you a'ight? You need water?" Marcus disappeared.

Dixon leaned forward and sucked in a breath. Marcus returned with two Styrofoam cups of water. "Here." He held them out to Dixon, who drank each one slowly. Marcus in front of him, watchful. Dixon small and penitent. At last, he said, "Thank you."

Marcus's face remained worried. "You been sick, Mr. B.?"

Dixon raised up, one elbow on his knee.

The boy hesitated. "I see you got, you know, a limp sometimes. And that coughing. You got circles like my moms get when the twins are real bad off and she don't get sleep." He paused. "And . . ."

He pointed to his own cheek, his eyes on Dixon's ravaged face. Dixon hated to think what he looked like, his skin darkened and mauled by frostbite.

Dixon held the empty cups in both hands between his knees. He had not wanted to tell the students what had happened to him. "The mountain was. Hard. I'm recovering."

"Okay," Marcus said, clearly unconvinced. He looked down at his hands and spoke softly. "You didn't call or nothing, when you got back."

Dixon shifted sideways in his chair. "I was pretty bad off."

"'Cause I went to your house. Coupla times." His look plaintive. Dixon squeezed his eyes shut against it.

"My cousin Charlaina took care of me, I was at her house. Till last week, matter of fact." Had he even thought of Marcus during that time? Had he thought of anything? Nate's face, blue-white with frost, flashed before him, and he shifted back from it.

"You better, now, Mr. B.? 'Cause you don't look—" The boy scrunched his mouth, shook his head.

"I'm all right, son." Dixon used his most soothing voice. "Thanks."

"HOW'RE YOU FEELING? CAN I GET YOU ANYTHING?" IN DIXON'S Kathmandu hospital room, a man entered slowly and stood before him. A reporter Nate had introduced. Cal Fierston. The two regarded each other a long time.

Cal's voice quiet. "I'm sorry your journey took such a turn, Dixon."

A turn. As if he'd taken a wrong exit on the highway.

Cal paused a few feet from the bed. He pulled out a Polaroid and stepped closer. "This is you, correct? I have to confess, at first I couldn't quite follow your sherpa—Pemba, isn't it?—his Matthew Henson One and Two, like that Abbott and Costello routine, 'Who's on first, What's on second.'" His laugh was a faint twitter. "Got it eventually. I just need you to confirm."

Dixon studied the photo. An everyman bundled in down suit and goggles, a sliver of brown skin visible on his cheeks, a gloveless hand holding up one finger. Faceless, alone, rising above a soup of cloud. Dixon exhaled. "Nate," he sighed, and sank back onto his pillow and closed his eyes.

"Really?" Cal pushed the photo closer to Dixon.

"Nate," he repeated, turned his back to Cal, and began to weep.

---

THIS WAS HOW THE END BEGAN, ROLLING FORWARD, A SLOW-growing avalanche: In the hallway as boys rushed by in a blur, Dixon stood at the fork of classrooms that led east or west and heard the loudspeaker call, "Mr. Bryant, would you come to the front office, please?" When he entered the office suite, Dolores Parsons moved her lips as if to speak but instead pointed toward the principal's office. Well, Dixon thought, here it is.

Principal Phil Pious sat on the edge of his desk facing Marcus and Shiloh. Even from the backs of their heads, Dixon knew them. The slump of Marcus's shoulders, his anxious rocking.

Phil beckoned him. "Mr. Bryant, please join us."

Dixon sat across from the two boys, catty-corner from the principal.

"We have conflicting stories of an incident that involves you, Mr. Bryant."

Dixon said nothing. Wasn't this all his fault, his presence a lightning rod for Shiloh's anger, which bounced off him and toward Marcus?

"Shiloh has told me he was assaulted by you after school yesterday. He says that he and Marcus were horsing around and you took offense. Only Marcus has been unusually quiet about this story. So, Mr. Bryant, we thought you could help clear this up."

Sound traveled to Dixon as if through a tunnel. Shiloh stared him down, a long, unblinking challenge. Marcus, looking nauseated and pale, shifted in his seat as if it were on fire. "There was an incident," Dixon said finally. "Shiloh had Marcus in a chokehold. He didn't release him when I ordered him to and Marcus nearly passed out. So I had to . . . forcibly . . . free Marcus. I had to act fast." Dixon sat perfectly straight. Marcus would not meet his eyes.

"Marcus," the principal asked, "is this what happened?"

Marcus gnawed on his lip. His eyes filled with tears.

"Marcus?"

"I don't know, I don't know," the boy blurted out.

"You don't know if you were being beaten up?" Phil grew visibly impatient, each exasperated exhalation making the long hairs of his mustache quiver.

Marcus shook his head quickly.

"Are you sure, son? Was he hurting you?"

"I have to go to the bathroom," Marcus blurted out and ran from the room.

"All right." Phil settled into his chair behind the desk and flipped through an overstuffed notebook. "We'll get some outside assistance. Get to the bottom of this. There's too much history here."

"You not jacking me around." Shiloh rose and pointed at Dixon, his face tight, inflamed. "'Cause you did me wrong," Shiloh said.

"Ask my boy. He'll tell ya." Shiloh's look assured. He strutted from the room.

After Shiloh had left, Phil said, "He's trouble, that one. Did you write up the fight?"

Dixon examined his hands.

"You mean, the report is on your desk and you haven't had a chance to file it yet." Dixon said no, and Phil repeated, "You mean, the report is on your desk and you'll file it later today."

"He got under my skin. It's the meanness, you know, I just cannot stand that."

"He's a sneaky little son of a bitch." Phil put on his glasses. "He's obviously strong-arming Marcus." Phil typed on his computer keyboard, then searched the screen. "I hate a boldfaced liar. Really fucks up my day. He's old, did you know that? Nearly two years too old to be in eighth grade."

Dixon said, "I wanted to hurt that boy." His stomach churned, a strange sensation of heat amid the coldness that welled in him.

"I didn't hear that." Phil continued to search. "Don't worry about this kid. Nobody's as good a liar as they think. We'll catch him at it. Here it is." Phil began to read. "Been to juvy four times. And he's fifteen. Almost time to be charged as an adult if he doesn't straighten up." Phil peered over his glasses at Dixon. "Which he won't."

Dixon kneaded his hand, pressing his thumb across his lifeline. "Why isn't he in a gateway program after juvy?"

"Look, just write up the report straight and factual. You know how." Phil Pious rocked back in his chair. "How're you doing, overall? I see you're having some trouble with that foot. I noticed, Dixon. Perhaps. Perhaps you might need more time after all."

Dixon blinked hard. It was like a slow sinking, being taken under by current.

"No shame in that. It's just, you're off your game, buddy. I can see it. This thing with Shiloh could get out of hand. I'll do more internal investigation, see if I can get Marcus to tell the truth before I write a full report. At least I have that discretion. Thank your union. Listen. I think you need to take the time to heal. In fact, I insist. Go back on leave, Dixon."

His body gunning, bouncing forward. "So who protects Marcus when I'm gone?"

"I do."

"I can't leave him here like that, he's, he's got a target on his back." He was talking too fast.

"You can trust me. I'm looking out for you, too, buddy."

---

EVERYONE LOOKED OUT FOR HIM, AS IF HE WERE AN IDIOT OR A small animal. Or worse: On the plane home from Kathmandu, he had navigated the glances and polite smiles of curious travelers. His bandages, his ravaged face, his brittle thinness. He wanted to yell, "I'm not contagious!" When he arrived at the airport, Charlaina, Pamela, and Kira greeted him, the whole of his life right there in that small gathering. They wept in a collective heap, wept long past the point that those around them could look away politely. At last, Pamela and Kira grew quiet, a shell-shocked quality to them, and Charlaina rose into her fierceness, pushing Dixon's wheelchair with her shoulders square, a determined nothing-to-see-here glance that made Dixon wonder at the sight of them, him in bandages and a cast, them standing shoulder to shoulder behind the wheelchair with its rhythmic squealing wheels: Dixon and His All-Girl Revue.

At Charlaina's, where he would spend the next six weeks recuperating, the women had hovered: Tea, Dixon? Time for more pain meds? A pillow for your head? Hovered and examined him silently, dredging up courage to ask. It was Charlaina, of course, who spoke finally. "They said it came on fast. Nothing could be done." She looked at him, her face wide open with desperation. "Is that right, Dixon? Was it fast?" Charlaina on the sofa beside him, Pamela standing in front, squeezing her hands. Kira stiff and wide-eyed on an ottoman facing him.

Dixon wished he could be anywhere but here. No, anywhere but there: he remained on that mountain, Nate wrapped in his arms. He took a long time to speak. "Sudden. Yes." He lied.

"But one of you made it to the top, that reporter said." Pamela spoke slowly, measured. "Him?"

His chest tight—*hold him, don't let go*—he simply blinked, a slight nod.

"Oh, Dixon." Pamela sat beside him. "You must've used all your strength getting him there."

His hand at his throat.

"No, no, I'm sorry, breathe, breathe. Slow it down." Pamela placed a hand on his chest, Charlaina's hand on his shoulder, the two women breathing deeply, becoming his lungs: breathe in, hold it, long exhale, his head light and fluttering, his breath calming. "Kira, honey, get Daddy some more tea, won't you?" Pamela's nod like a hand ushering Kira out of the room. Kira was reluctant, familiar with this trick.

Pamela placed a hand atop his. "This is so awful for you, I

know, Dixon. Just please don't beat yourself up. Promise me that. I'm sure whatever happened wasn't your fault. I know you're disappointed, not reaching the summit. You think you've failed."

He opened his mouth, then closed it.

"Dixon, you're too competitive not to think that. But you didn't fail, you tried. You hear me? Let it go. Please."

He knew what she meant: Don't be Reg, three attempts, three rejections from that mountain and the burning desire never sated. He exhaled. "Don't worry."

———

IT HAD TO BE SOME KIND OF RECORD: KICKED OUT THE SECOND day of the school year. Dixon stood in his office, thinking of what to take with him: a photo of Kira, a plaque recognizing him as administrator of the year. How anticlimactic. So gut-churningly stupid. He looked at his watch. Time for hall duty—he could do that, couldn't he? It felt urgent. It felt like an honor.

In the west-end hallway, Shiloh leaned against a radiator, that dull, amused expression on his face. Dixon walked straight for him. "Get to class."

"What you gone do, chase me?" He laughed, throwing back his head.

Dixon's whole body pulsed. He lunged for Shiloh. The boy's face registering surprise, he jumped backward out of Dixon's reach. Dixon lunged again but slipped, landing hard on one knee. He grimaced in pain. The boy laughed at him, and Dixon lunged up again. He got hold of the boy by both arms and shook him hard. Nate in his grasp now, the two brothers tussling, gripping each other's parkas, staggering across the icy slope of Everest, Nate rasping out, *You have to come with me!* and Dixon yelling back, *Let go! Let me go!*

"Dixon! Dixon!" Benny Lewis behind him, his hands on Dixon's shoulders. A descent from the pitch of anger. Shiloh's look steady and hard. Dixon jerked back, releasing Shiloh. What fell from Dixon was a skin, leaving him raw and formless. Look what the mountain had made of him!

He did not belong here anymore.

He pointed at Benny Lewis and then to Shiloh, Take him, he motioned, and Benny grasped Shiloh by the arm.

Dixon limped back to his office. He gathered his jacket, wallet, keys. He headed for the door. His head ached. Dolores Parsons called after him and when he did not stop, she ran into Phil Pious's office. Dixon walked fast, too fast. He tripped, stumbled, and slammed his foot against the concrete of the front stoop. He heard the sharp snap of his false foot. He dragged himself along, the foot throbbing, the heat and cold in him numbing into an awful dullness.

In the parking lot, only a few steps from the car, the pain in his foot bloomed. He snatched off his shoe, his black-and-white foot exposed, and then removed the false foot, the skin beneath it rubbed raw. He hopped those last awful inches to his car.

He might have returned a hero.

For a full week, Dixon got up, dressed, stuffed his damaged foot into a shoe, and set off for school. No one expected him. He'd been put back on leave through at least the end of the fall term, his doctor hinting he might want him to stay out for the whole academic year.

In fact, he shouldn't be anywhere near the school building, not with Shiloh's complaint looming over him. Once reported, the incident had to be investigated, his union rep had said, even if Dixon was on leave. Even if Shiloh was unreliable and clearly coercing Marcus, he had to be given a full investigation. "Every little jerk deserves his due process," his rep had joked, and Dixon had recoiled. Was he now the kind of guy who talked like that about a kid?

Dixon drove to school each morning—what else was there to do? His whole focus had been getting back to his boys. He had thought of it as a salve as surely as the compacts and masks Charlaina had poured onto his face, swearing she could see improvement in the darkened, rough patches of skin.

He parked at a curb across from the school. A four-lane avenue sat between him and the building, but he had a full view of the front entrance. He watched boys arrive and scatter, some clamoring through the front door in a dense cluster, others scattering around back to the science labs, the gym, the hidden corridors at the back of the building.

*Look how it goes on without you,* he thought.

He flexed his damaged foot. He had, in fact, broken a toe rushing away on his last day. It ached unendingly, making it impossible to wear the prosthesis. Instead, he had to use toe fillers inside his shoes to hold his foot in place. The indignities of his life compounded.

Across the road, Benny Lewis moved into view from behind a school bus. Benny ushered the boys inside, then beckoned the ones who had fled toward the side doors where they might sneak a smoke behind the curve of the building.

Dixon searched for Marcus. At least Shiloh had been suspended, thank god. Exiled. Wasn't Dixon in exile, too? His school life gone. Even the mountain had largely left him. It had become difficult to recall it fully. A blessing, perhaps.

He sat up in his seat, accidentally smacking against the horn, and the loud toot seemed to stop the world. Benny peered across the road toward Dixon's car, and when he was sure he had caught Dixon's glance, Benny lifted his hand in a slow wave.

Flushed, shamed, Dixon sped away. He drove aimlessly, waiting for the flood of feeling to recede. Instead, it welled up at the back of his throat. The plaintive look on Benny's face, the pity he might imagine from Marcus. Marcus! How disappointed he must be in him. Dixon changed radio stations, hoping to change his thoughts.

Eventually, he found himself in front of an old diner at the edge of a neighboring county. The same diner where he and Nate had met that climber Peter and their fate had been sealed. An unexpected refuge—what if Nate was sitting there, nursing a weak instant coffee, waiting for Dixon? A dagger of hope evaporated as sharply as it had come.

From outside, the restaurant appeared friendlier than he recalled, enough so that he almost second-guessed himself about whether he was in the right place. But it was unmistakably the same. Tucked off a nearly forgotten road in the southernmost part of the county, as far from Baltimore as from D.C., the restaurant had been part of a strip mall once the heart of a small exurban neighborhood. One by one the other stores had been razed, leaving only The Beaten Egg, square and white-skinned on three sides, the hieroglyphics of demolished floors and walls etched deep into its walls.

Dixon sat in the parking lot a long time. He examined the etchings on those outer walls. Something alluring in the traces of a now-silent past. He got out of the car and climbed the restaurant's front steps. A green Help Needed sign was propped near the door. Wait. He could call Marcus, he should tell him to go back to the other school before Shiloh's suspension ended. He should do that now. Right now. What the fuck was taking him so long to think up solutions? His brain sluggish, foggy, maybe still oxygen-deprived, maybe still in the Death Zone on Everest. Turning toward the diner, then back toward the car, spinning, unsure, Dixon tripped on the crumbling top step and hurtled first toward the spot where the sign was taped and then right through the front door. He lay sprawled out, clutching the sign and nearly seeing stars from the pain that ripped through his foot. Rocking back and forth, his stomach lurching, his foot throbbing, Dixon panted against the pain. He gazed up at a guy, six-four, three hundred and fifty pounds, and mumbling, "Another motherfucker who thinks he can sue me for that front step."

Dixon sat up. The man in front of him held out his hand but Dixon brushed it away, trying to settle his stomach from the hard fall, his humiliation sliding into anger with himself. He snatched off his shoe and sock, and the toe fillers, like large ear plugs, spilled out. The man reached down to collect them. He held them out to Dixon, who put them back in their place, then slipped his foot inside his shoe. He wanted to leave so badly, so badly, but where exactly was he going? What was he supposed to do now? He jerked his shoelaces. *Fuck, fuck, fuck.* The big man waited patiently. Then he lifted his own pantleg just enough to show the muscle of an artificial leg, an Army insignia etched there. Dixon jerked back, then glanced up. In what felt like a truly cowardly act, Dixon stepped into the clear assumption that his own wound was something other than self-inflicted.

The man pointed to the green Help Needed sign on the floor beside Dixon. "You want the job?"

"Excuse me?" Dixon said.

"Name's Hoss, well, it's not, but that's what they call me. Obvious reason." He motioned a hand over his belly, and Dixon flashed back to Hoss Cartwright on *Bonanza*. Indeed, all this guy needed was a ten-gallon hat and he was the spitting image, that slight hangdog look included. Dixon laughed slightly at the idea. "So then, you ready to work?" Hoss asked again.

Dixon sat back, legs straight out in front of him, his hands propping him up on the gritty linoleum floor. He scanned the triangular dining room, its corners full of stuffed animals and faded banners from a long-closed high school. A high shelf that ran the width of the room was crammed with souvenir salt and pepper shakers: dice from Las Vegas, hula girls from Hawaii, a wedge of cheese from Wisconsin, and nearly a dozen pairs of the Twin Towers. It smelled of real maple syrup and bacon and eggs and coffee, the reassuring scents of morning. He remembered the simple satisfaction of a summer job thirty-five years earlier working the grill at Donny's Dairy Bar. Besides, in this distant hamlet, he wouldn't run into his old life. "When can I start?"

HOSS PROVIDED A HIGH STOOL FOR DIXON TO REST ON DURING his shift. In the first week, his foot swelled and his doctor prescribed a pressure bandage. Dixon wrapped the stump of his foot, disguised it with the prosthesis, and slipped the foot into his shoe. With that motion, he bound his whole self tightly before he left the house each day for a gig where he became someone else. He was Dix here, the guy at the grill, the one who did not smile easily but who made perfect brown hotcakes and crisp bacon. He poured himself into his tasks, methodical and efficient and grateful. He was far enough from his old life not to feel it pawing at him. At home each night, something climbed his spine, a longing for the feel and sound and weight of boys' voices rising through wide hallways, the shrieks of glee and terror intermingled. But at The Beaten Egg, all that fell away.

Strangers rarely stumbled onto The Beaten Egg. First off, the diner was not near anything. The new interstate had turned the state road out front into an afterthought. The restaurant served mostly regulars from the nearby Slavic neighborhood of modest bungalows, the regulars retired and happily so. There was a rhythm, a sameness to The Beaten Egg.

So, two weeks after Dixon began working there, when Charlaina appeared in a silk shirtwaist dress and pearls, she stood out. She had been leaving messages on his answering machine every day for the past week, and he had only texted a short, daily reply, "I'm all right." Clearly, she had had enough of that.

Dixon watched her from the kitchen. She touched the arm of a passing waitress and asked for him by name. Herbert, the lead cook, nudged him. "Girlfriend here for you?" Herbert grinned, absent his molars on either side, the hardness of his life laid bare in that grin and the ashen gray whiskers against his brown skin. "Go on see 'bout that pretty woman," Herbert urged.

"It's just my cousin."

"Cousin, huh? The kissing kind?"

"No, man, she's like my sister." Dixon caught short: *She's all I have left.*

Charlaina waited patiently. He approached her like a kid about to be scolded. "Hey," he said.

"My cousin, the fugitive. I have to hunt you down these days?" she said softly. "What's going on, Dixon?"

In the kitchen, Herbert stepped away from the grill, watching for trouble, catching Dixon's eye.

"Wasn't ready to go back to school, it seems." The feel of Shiloh's bony chest beneath his hands as he hoisted him up against the locker.

"But you can work here?"

"My union rep says it's all right," he lied, but he imagined it could be true. "I'm just—" He could barely face the wounded look on her face. "I didn't mean to hurt you."

"I'm not here because my feelings are hurt." She frowned. "That's not what hurts, Dixon." Her lips parted, closed, parted again. "Who else is gonna miss him like us? We're in this together."

He grabbed the edge of the counter to steady himself.

"You're not sleeping. I can tell." She pointed to the bags under his eyes. "Talk to me. Please."

Did she imagine he had sequestered himself this far from home just to dredge up Everest here? Dixon squeezed a wadded dish towel to control his anger. "Can't you just let it be, Char?"

"You need to talk to someone. If it's not me, okay, but then someone. Will you let me get some names of good therapists?" Her freckles, soft along the bridge of her nose, were his brightest recollection from their childhood.

"Just, just. Give me a minute."

It took an interminable while, but she said finally, "Okay," a capitulation and then a sharp reprimand: "But don't ignore me." She kissed his neck before she left.

He retreated to the kitchen. He didn't hear Herbert come behind him, but he felt the accumulated heat of the grill spilling from him, the pungent smell of bacon cooked and burned. "Yo, Dix man. Your 'cousin'"—he curled his hands around quotation marks in the air—"look cute. She got long legs for such a little thing. I see you a bad man, get a woman like that in this joint looking for you."

Herbert's satisfaction with himself was so great that Dixon had to laugh, too. "You've got the wrong impression of me, man. She really is my little cousin. Little sister, nearly."

"Isthatright?" he said fast, then added, "Family hunting you down." He shook his head slow, his mouth turned down at the edges.

Dixon stiffened. "You don't know the half of it."

"Whoa, I ain't no priest, I 'on't need no confessionals." Herbert picked up his knife and resumed slicing tomatoes.

———

HE MISSED RUNNING. MISSED IT ACHINGLY SO. IT MIGHT'VE worked off the tension, might've kept him from the nights spent climbing in his sleep, his legs and arms in motion, digging into the mountain. He nearly ripped the side seams of his mattress with his grip. He often awakened from the pain of slamming his hand into the wall while dreaming about drawing his ice axe from his harness to self-arrest. All night, he fell, careening across ice and snow.

His days were no better. He limped restless through his small two-story townhouse, "the cocoon," Charlaina called it, a place that just nearly fit him. "Why didn't you let me come see before you bought it?" Charlaina had fussed. "It's too small for you, Dixon. Can't you see that?" Living room, eating area, kitchen on the first floor; bedroom, study, and bath on the second. The stairway was so truncated he had to duck to avoid banging head-first into the overhang, the upstairs hallway so tight that he could not stretch out his arms. In the shower stall, he had to stoop below the fixture and keep his arms drawn in, this entire space built for someone half his height and wingspan. Perhaps he had once thought of it as a lesson in discipline, reining in his body, learning to duck, to endure. Along the now-blank walls of the upstairs hallway, the ghosts of removed photos of himself climbing Kilimanjaro and Denali left dark square outlines. He lived in his cave-like house among shadows and hieroglyphs.

Weekly calls to Kira helped fill his space. He would put on the speakerphone and let her voice and the background sounds of her dorm room fill his home, echoing in his empty corners. One week in September, she called him, and her voice sounded so distant that he might yet be on the mountain. How unreal his life back home had felt then, distant and therefore perfect, a thing cast up like a pearl, miraculous and whole and utterly separate from him. That was Kira now. "Are you in for the evening?" he asked.

"Maybe. I'm not sure. Daddy, you're not worried about me partying?" She'd reverted to calling him Daddy, he had noticed.

"No, no, I know you've got good sense. But it's Saturday night, a college Saturday night." He gave a stilted laugh.

She was quiet, drifting. "I don't know," she sighed. "What's out there, anyway?"

Quiet another beat, he asked, "What's going on, sweetheart?"

"Tell me something," she said. "I mean, just, like, literally, anything good about it all."

He didn't know what to say at first. "Are you asking, asking . . ." he stammered, "asking if it was worth it?"

"No, I don't mean that. Not that. I mean, just give me something to hold on to."

His mind so blank, he pictured a whiteout of dense, billowing snow. "You'll have to give me a bit," he said softly. "I'll have to dig for it."

Dig for something comforting. Charlaina's voice on the answering machine left comfort, if also a raft of guilt: he could not reassure her he was fine. Perhaps that's the same reason why he had answered only one of Skeet's calls. Luckily, Skeet's wife Tania had answered the phone. "Is he doing okay?" Dixon asked. She hesitated a long time. "He's taking it hard, you know?" she answered. "But he'll want to talk to you, I'm sure." That was what Dixon feared: talking, talking, Skeet was a "Let's hash this out" kinda guy, processing everything aloud from what to order for lunch to which investment might pay the bigger yield.

Alone, tumbling through flashbacks, he often envisioned Lena at his hospital bedside in Kathmandu, the way she had floated near him when he'd awakened shouting for Nate. "Okay, it is okay, Dixon." Lena in civilian clothes: a white button-down shirt, jeans, a small gold coin around her neck. She had stroked his cheek, then cupped it in her hand. "Darling Dixon." For three days, Lena had appeared and disappeared as Dixon drifted in and out of consciousness, he heard her warding off visitors, scolding the nurses for being late with his meds.

Dixon the protector, in need of protection.

---

"I WENT FOR HIM," HE CONFESSED TO BENNY LEWIS, A SUDDEN blurting out of truth Dixon had not planned. Benny had simply called to offer a cheerful "How ya doing?"

"Shiloh, you mean. Dixon, you were protecting a student in danger, that's well within your responsibility, you know that."

"I mean that last day. When you stopped me. I wanted to hurt that kid."

"Dixon." Benny shifted the phone audibly, lowered his voice. "I didn't see how it started but I'm sure you were provoked. Defending yourself. I'm sure he started it."

Dixon shook his head. "I put my hands on him."

"I haven't heard that story going around. In fact, word is, he hurt Marcus, then you. That's the buzz from the kids. He's the big man in the story. He's not gonna want to upset that narrative."

"Unless he decides he'd rather screw me."

"Then I'm a witness. Look, let's not dig up more trouble. You've got enough on your plate. Have you been talking with your union rep?"

"Little bit. Not so great about checking my messages these days."

"Do it, Dixon. You need to be ready."

---

MARCUS STOOD AT DIXON'S DOOR THE WEEK AFTER HE'D LEFT school. Marcus in sweatpants and a workout T-shirt. Dixon noticed for the first time that the boy seemed a little beefier than last year. More muscular. "You ready, Mr. B.?" Surprised to see him, Dixon offered only a weak "Yeah." Marcus frowned. "You ready?" Dixon halted: Nate on the narrow pass through the Rockies as they trained for Everest, Nate in that blue two-piece down suit carrying water weights, matching Dixon stride for stride, that look of determination on his face, the flash of dimple, a quick twinkling glance. Dixon gripped his mug of coffee, stared into it to clear his vision. Marcus said firmly, "Okay," and marched past Dixon into the small backyard.

The weakness in Dixon made everyone around him fierce. At the airport as he finally prepared to fly home, Lena had appeared again. She stood patiently at his gate, a backpack riding low on her back, her arms folded in front of her. Dark-wash jeans, a tight pale-green T-shirt pulled sideways by the backpack. She wore gold hoops and a necklace of small red stones interspersed with gold beads. She was nothing like the woman on the mountain—bejeweled, the sheen of lip gloss on her pale brown lips. She was absolutely that woman—the curve of her forearm muscles, her straight, sturdy spine. She leaned down to him in his wheelchair, her face beside his. He braced, unsure how unbearable it might be if she kissed his cheek. She whispered, "I will call you." She straightened up. She did not kiss him. What was it about her face, so different from before? In this light, in non-mountain air, her face held tiny lines around the eyes, fissures, wells of sorrow.

Marcus said, "Stretching first, right? Then the weights?" They stood in Dixon's small fenced-in yard.

"Right. Warm up first."

Stretches, leg lifts, squats. Dixon stepped down wrong sometimes and pain splintered through his foot. The tremor of his biceps straining with the hand weights, the stiffness of his lower back. When Marcus dropped to the ground—"I can do one hundred now. I kept it up while you were gone"—and elongated his body for push-ups, Dixon froze. Marcus's feet flexed, he held his body aloft, arms outstretched. He looked at Dixon with pure glee. "You go ahead," Dixon said quietly.

"You 'on't wanna race me? See can I beat you?"

"I can't, son." He sat on the ground beside Marcus. He glanced at his foot. The boy didn't know. Dixon drew his arms tight against his body. "Go ahead."

Marcus studied Dixon then turned to his task, rising and falling easily for a long time, calling out his own reps. Dixon took over counting at sixty, Marcus grunting and grinding out the last ten reps. Look at his determination. At one hundred, the boy teetered a moment on straight arms then tumbled onto his belly, panting, spent, then laughing, so pleased with himself. It was an illusion, the idea of your own strength. It was a trap.

"You have to go back to McKelvin to school. You can't stay. You have to get away before Shiloh comes back. Listen to me."

The boy turned his face toward Dixon but did not lift his head.

"I can't . . ." Dixon had to take a breath, calm himself. "Protect you."

"That's why we doing this, right? Getting me strong?"

"It's not just, just getting strong, son, sometimes it's just not putting yourself in the way."

———

IT FELT GROUNDING AND DISORIENTING TO WORK WITH MARCUS again. Three days a week after school he came over. Dixon startled himself by how eagerly he awaited the boy, sitting coiled on the edge of the seat. At the sound of the doorbell, Dixon would spring up and toward Marcus, exploding in a hug so hard and fast that Marcus let loose a laugh. As if the boy knew that he saved Dixon.

They worked up to tandem lunges, which were consistently punctuated by Marcus's farts, and they might both topple over with laughter, the two of them fully themselves. Dixon gave in to his limitations haltingly. Modified push-ups, then, the old-lady kind his PT had shown him—Dixon might've been more receptive if he had not glanced across the therapy room and seen a couple of grandpas doing it just that way.

"I called the principal at McKelvin," Dixon began after they'd finished one Friday afternoon. "He hasn't heard from you or your parents."

Marcus sat on the grass, his legs crossed, fiddling with his sneaker. "It was kinda far, you know, I had to get a ride, then two buses. It was hard for my moms and them. Besides, he mess with me away from school, too. He, like, wait for my bus and mess with me."

"You keep your friends close by?" The boy said yes. "Do your parents know?"

"I gotta, like, testify. About that day, you know. He wants me to say he didn't really do nothing, like, I wasn't hurt and you just—" The boy would not look at Dixon.

"Right."

"I don't want to lie on you. He, like, threatening me all the time."

"Did you tell the principal? Tell your parents to make a police report against him. Don't just take it! Look, I can call your parents. I'll tell, I'll tell the school." Something sour at the back of Dixon's throat. "Listen to me. You have to get out of his way. Y'hear me?" His hands gripped the boy, insistent.

Phil Pious said their hands were tied with Shiloh suspended and off the property. Benny Lewis said he'd call Shiloh's case-worker. Marcus's parents thanked Dixon for his concern, then his mother fretted about whether she could possibly send him to live at his aunt's house for a while. Marcus's father said, "The boy has to learn to deal with trouble, like us all," and hiked up his pants against his own vulnerability.

Dixon might be the boy crying wolf. Even the Board of Education chief psychologist shined him on—"Aren't you on leave now, Dr. Bryant? And isn't there an incident under investigation concerning you and this boy?"

"Doesn't that make this more credible!" Dixon blurted out, hopping up slightly in his seat as he recalled the conversation. He glanced around the Metro train as it whizzed between stations. The other passengers took little notice. He was heading across town for a doctor's visit. A new problem, sciatica, had just flared up and he could swear, just the thought of that fucking Shiloh had started it. He twisted and stretched his back, which seemed to clench harder. He let out a groan.

"Hey, man, look like you could use a little help." A skinny, solemn dude leaned toward Dixon from the seat opposite him. He raised his chin, then opened his hand, offering the small, round white pill in his palm. "Cuts that edge, boy."

A young guy, maybe eighteen, his shoulders knobby and high, holding himself in as if he knew the parameters of the world and how to remain just inside. Not as innocent as Marcus, not quite as wily as Shiloh, but somewhere in the wide in-between. He was so young. He could be one of Dixon's former boys. The kind Dixon might have been intent on reaching. Or one who had slipped by unnoticed. Or one his colleagues might have called a BSer, a Bad Seed, a code name for a kid with a case file, a probation officer, a kid they'd closed the books on, a kid they usually worked to weed out of their charter school.

The young guy thrust his hand out again toward Dixon, the pill perched in his palm.

"Did you go to Evers Charter School?" Dixon asked and thought, Should I have helped you?

The boy pulled back his head. "Naw, man." He seemed to grow irritated. "You want it or not?"

Dixon stared at the innocuous-looking pill being offered to him. "What is this? What're you doing with it?"

"Free-market enterprise, I think it's called. Give you a good deal." It was the smirk, the cocksureness of the snap of his neck.

"Get away from me," Dixon snapped and slapped at the boy's hand, the pill popping up in the air and landing somewhere between the seats.

"Motherfucker!" the boy shouted. "You owe me five dollars."

The train rolled into a station. "Fuck that," Dixon said and rose to leave.

"Hey!" The boy hard on his heels. "You limping motherfucker, you better give me my money!"

The boy followed Dixon off the train and onto the platform. He shoved Dixon hard once, twice. "You gimp somabitch. You gonna pay me my money!" He punched Dixon in the middle of the back, tipping him halfway over. Once Dixon caught his breath, he came up swinging, landing a lucky punch first on the side of the kid's head and then on his chin, snapping the boy's head back. Dixon charged into him, the two toppling down to the platform, Dixon on top, pummeling the boy, his heartbeat thumping. The boy landing punch after punch on Dixon's head, back, sides. Dixon taking his punishment, he leaned down, the boy's collar in his fists, the windbreaker a familiar nylon, Nate's face floating in front of Dixon, Nate flailing under him in the snow, fighting him, and Dixon screaming to him, *You're going to get us killed!*

For the second time in his life, he had to be pulled off a kid, pulled from behind, up and away. He struggled to get his footing, his back, his foot, his body a mass of pain. He staggered toward a concrete bench on the platform and sat panting. The boy was lifted, too, by transit cops who jerked his arms behind his back and restrained him. Two older Black women pointed at the boy, telling the tale: "He followed that man off the train and assaulted him." Dixon leaned his elbows on his knees, covered his face. Nate lying limp in the snow, a fistful of his blood in Dixon's palm. "I'm sorry, I'm sorry, I'm so sorry," he repeated.

CHAPTER

12

The incident inquiry would be held the first Friday in October, Shiloh and Marcus interviewed in front of a panel of administrators before they heard from Dixon the following week. "You sure you don't want your own lawyer, buddy," Benny Lewis asked, "not just the union guy?" Dixon brushed it off, a willful denial. The things he had to answer for were piling up. At least the cops seemed satisfied about that thing with the kid on the train. They focused on the drugs in his possession more than the assault, which Dixon could hardly think about—what the hell had that been about?

The Wednesday before the inquiry, Dixon awaited Marcus. October remained warm enough for their outdoor workouts. Dixon had bought a jump rope to add to their routine, something he might have done earlier if he hadn't dreaded his own inability to use it. Not yet, not yet. He cringed just thinking about how that might feel, jumping up and landing on absent toes, their ghosts spiking pain through his foot. He sat, then paced to the window to watch for Marcus. He nursed a banana smoothie—he was careful to leave enough for Marcus. It had become his post-workout reward. Dixon parted the slats of the blinds and scanned the street. Stay calm, he told himself: there could be tons of reasons why he was late.

By dusk, it was clear Marcus was not coming. Don't worry, Dixon told himself, it could be anything, but it seemed like those final moments before the world changes for certain. Dixon put the last of the smoothie in the refrigerator, just in case. He rubbed his sweaty palms along his pants legs, then dialed Marcus's home number. The phone rang a long time and just as Dixon was preparing himself to leave a message, Marcus's father picked up. The muffled sound of the phone after Dixon asked after Marcus, as if it had dropped away from the father's mouth and scuffed against his chin, then up again. "You hadn't heard, then?" Marcus's father said, his voice tremulous. "Yesterday. Coming home from school . . . he's in the intensive care. Beat real bad. It's not good, not good."

Dixon jerked forward, then arrested as if he were falling. "Uh-huh," he managed. Marcus's nervous hands, balled into fists and pounding on his knees, flashed in front of Dixon.

Benny Lewis picked up his phone immediately, and Dixon blurted out what he knew. "Yeah, buddy, found out this morning. I was waiting to call you tonight. I know this isn't what you wanted to hear."

"They know who did it, right? Did you give the police all my notes?"

"The police have his file. We've told them everything. They're looking for him. We have to let them do their job." Benny's voice became that cloyingly reasonable counselor-voice Dixon knew so well. Fuck that.

Fuck this.

He moved quickly to his car. Driving too fast, grinding his teeth. He should have done something about Shiloh long ago. He drove down a long, divided highway to the neighborhood near the school, a trek through five zip codes, from newer to older neighborhoods, from greater to lesser privilege. Dixon drove fast, passing cars, tailgating, courting disaster. He accelerated the car with the force of his body alone.

A familiar route toward school and the narrow streets beyond. Usually to this kid's house or that one's, or to a workplace of a parent who only got a half-hour lunch break. Courting some kid's salvation. He wasn't looking to be anybody's missionary today. His hands itched, and he tensed them around the steering wheel. He sat high in his seat.

He reached Capitol Crest, the neighborhood that fed the school. From the main road, he turned onto the first residential street, its corners flanked by a coin laundromat, a dollar store, a car wash. He drove through the web of streets toward the places he knew kids gathered and landed finally on a corner two blocks from Shiloh's address—he had memorized it; he could see it typed on the crisp, white page of a student record. Even more, he could sense that boy around him: the way he held his head slightly to the left, his raw smell.

The stoplight stayed red for so long. Dixon scanned up and down the intersecting streets. A Chinese food carryout and liquor store with black bars on the window faced him on one corner, another liquor store and God's Armor Christian Church of Faith on the other corner.

His adrenaline drained, his body descending from that awful pitch of anger. The low quiver of his organs settling back down. He must've lost his mind. Had he really come gunning for Shiloh? Who had he become?

At the top of the hill in a vacant patch of grass, boys were pooled. A mix of older boys whom he knew, mostly—boys who had graduated from middle school and disappeared from his life— and younger, current students. Dusk settled across the yard. The boys far back on the lot glowed in borrowed snatches of light, the flame of cigarettes, the catch of metal around their wrists and necks. Even in the dimness, Dixon knew their faces, knew their older brothers' faces, their cousins' and baby brothers'. So much of what he held was intimate knowledge: a hand on a shoulder, a wipe of tears, a steady pinch on the bridge of a bloody nose.

He slowed down. Several boys stepped to his car and draped themselves around his door. "Hey, Mr. B., you workin'?" A bewildered curiosity on their faces. Because they must have heard. They must know.

"Hey, guys. Just passing through," he answered. "How ya doin'? You're at Northeast High, right?"

They nodded, his former boys: Marquise, Dontay, Michael, Jerome, and then Denzel, who cleared his throat self-consciously; Dixon had heard he dropped out.

"You guys see Shiloh Evans around?" Dixon asked.

Marquise and Dontay straightened and gazed up the hill. "Naw, Mr. B. He run his own way," Michael said in the slow, exaggerated drawl Dixon recalled.

"You see him, tell him I'm looking for him."

They murmured a collective grumble. "I 'on't know 'bout that, Mr. B.," Marquise said. "You oughta let that one go. He crazy. Cops looking for him, you know."

"I know. Tell him, he needs to turn himself in. Before he gets caught." *Before I catch him.*

"True that." Dontay gave a stern frown. "Before he get caught and shot, the way they do."

"You gone help him, Mr. B.?"

The idea caught in Dixon's throat. Help him? Hell no. But what could he say? He waved and sped away.

He crouched in his seat, feeling battered by the cold evening. The streets were narrow and winding. The bungalows clustered tightly. Trees hung overgrown across the road. The place deceptively quiet. Capitol Crest had always struck him as an amplified place, everything closer, louder, tighter, and it reminded him that he had had space growing up, an endless yard backed by a small creek overflowing with tadpoles and guppies and turtles and all manner of discovery and triumph for a kid. He might've been able to see clear around the county from that sloping back lot. And his was just a small slice of the world. When he was twelve and his family drove across country for the first time, he was stunned by the vastness. West of the Mississippi River, the land unfolded into rivers and mountains, broad golden plains, endless blue sky. They would drive west for days across the upper states and see only a handful of cars. They owned the roads that wound through valleys swollen with grain, skirted by mountains. The landscape bathed them in grace and possibility. Did his folks back home in all those crowded-up cities know about this land? Hadn't a trick been played to keep them all sequestered? It had angered him, and he had envisioned leading caravans of Black folks to all this space, this richness and privilege. Because he had stumbled onto what seemed a well-kept secret, he let that space invade him, inform him, let himself dream inside of it. Now, in the small, dark streets of Capitol

Crest, he wondered: Was that where the dream of Everest had been made possible? Where the nascent idea of himself, vast, uncontained, had begun?

He turned onto a darkened street, the air dense with spices and sweet cooking grease. The shadows wide and deep along the curb. Had he trained Marcus too well, had he made him overconfident? He emitted a small, feral cry.

The now-darkened streets he had driven into the neighborhood became unfamiliar. His eyes cloudy and wet, he second-guessed which way to turn. He drove in tense circles, up the wrong street and back out again, the chill of autumn rising. The world around you could shift so quickly and so could your place in it.

---

HE HAD NEVER PARTICULARLY FEARED HOSPITALS, BUT DIXON dreaded the one where Marcus had lain unconscious for the past three days. It felt like an awful homecoming, and he imagined himself being whisked back into a room, forced into a hospital bed, being told he had been released in error. As he walked toward Marcus's room from the elevator down the long corridor, his back clenched. He had to sign in at the reception station before being buzzed into the unit. The nurse's station sat at the center of the space, each room opening from the core like spokes on a wheel. The nurses barely noticed him as he passed, although he was sure one nurse made a mental note of his gait: prosthesis patient. Down the corridor to the left, Dixon found Marcus's last name on the door plaque.

There was one bed, a pastel striped curtain drawn partway around so that only the bulge of Marcus's legs was immediately visible. Dixon drew back the curtain. He would not have recognized Marcus, his face swollen into a soft, bruised mound, his nose camouflaged beneath a swath of tubes. Dried blood clung to one side where tubes escaped, bending like long tendrils and draining into a bloody bag. Beaten up, knocked down, his head hitting the sidewalk, the boy had been left to this.

Dixon circled the bed, his hand trailing along the bed rails. He sat in a chair beside him and took the boy's hand, which was cool and baby-soft, yet Marcus's presence fell hard against him. Dixon bent on one knee, his head so heavy that he rested his forehead on the bed. He breathed slow and tight and jagged. He lifted Marcus's hand and placed its palm atop his own bowed head, awaiting pardon.

Later, he sat back in the chair and held Marcus's hand. Dixon laced his long fingers through Marcus's and leaned toward the boy's bandaged ears. "I'm here, Marcus. I'm here." He conjured that part of himself that had fallen away, the counselor, the protector. "It's going to be all right, son. You're safe, you're safe."

There had been no time for tending like this with his father, who had passed in his sleep. Only his mother's death had been a long, lonely march. He could see her being erased, her skin tightening toward her skeleton, her memory and sense of humor leaving her. Even her hair fell out, remaining on the pillow against the imprint of her head. Finally, she had said, "Get my shoes!" He had gone to find them in the clutter of her closet, and when he came back, she was gone, a wide, ecstatic grin on her face.

Sitting beside Marcus, Dixon traced the tubes attached to him, decided on a function for each one. This one fed his brain, this cleaned his blood, this pumped his lungs, this soothed his pain. In this way, he passed the afternoon sitting before a wide window, the passage of time marked by the sun's movement along his arm.

The nurse who came to check all those machines reminded Dixon of his night nurse in Kathmandu. Her hands large, her thumbs thick and pale, unusually long. Good for gripping rock. She had a casual way of unwinding the bandages on his foot, never seeming to dread what she would see: the toes crispy black and blistered. The day nurses steeled themselves, taking a deep breath before the room filled with the fetid smell of his dying toes.

Marcus's mother arrived late in the afternoon. Her walk was burdened, her shoulders pushing back and forward, her mouth angled down. She stopped in the doorway when she saw Dixon, trying to place him. "Oh!" she said and rushed toward him. The unexpectedness of her smile, the sudden light of it illuminating her face, startled Dixon. She was so suddenly pretty. "Mr. Dixon!" She wrapped both hands around his, her square, matronly purse dangling from her arm and banging against his knees, her presence all clumsy gratitude so like her son that Dixon could feel Marcus's lurching hugs. "Oh, you're here! Praise the Lord!" She released his hand. "It's a grace, you being here. I believe my boy knows you. Look. See that little smile?"

He wanted to see it, but there seemed no change. "Minimally conscious," the nurse had said.

"I know how you always took up for my boy. Marcus told me," she insisted, grasping his hand hard.

He winced. "I wonder if I didn't make it worse."

"Oh no, not you." She released his hand and sized Dixon up. She scanned his whole body before looking back at his face in alarm. "You took sick?"

"No, no, I—" He could not find words.

"I understand. You don't need to tell me your business. My boy says you went to live in the mountains last year." She let out a short laugh. "I know that can't be right. I told him, we don't like the cold, now."

He cleared his throat. "I was in the mountains, Himalaya. Climbing." It sounded nearly shameful right this minute, telling his tale to this particular woman in this particular room.

She widened her eyes, a look that reevaluated him as if within clear sight he had turned alien. "Well now," she said quietly, "I forget, other people got a whole world." She prattled on: She wished she could stay here twenty-four hours, but she could only manage a short visit in the mornings, then she had to get back home to take care of the twins—still not walking, still not potty-trained at four years old. After her husband came home from work, they switched off and she came back to the hospital. "Seems like life is just one set of trouble feeding another." She strung together aphorisms: "What doesn't kill us makes us stronger," "The Lord doesn't give us more than we can bear." These sayings a drug that soothed her, her face calming, her shoulders less tense. She stood beside her son's bed and something dropped from her so that she grew bright and clear in the late-day sun.

He envied her ability to turn darkness to light. But it angered him, too. "Weren't you able to get Marcus away? Couldn't you have—" He shouldn't say this. He shouldn't yell at her: *Didn't you see this coming, goddammit?! I did! I did!*

"That's an evil boy that hurt my Marcus. Never shoulda let him out of juvenile jail, that's what they're saying now. Been in and out nearly five times. Sometimes the devil gets his way but that don't mean he won't get his due. They're gonna catch him. You mark my words."

---

WHEN HIS PHONE RANG THAT EVENING, HE THOUGHT QUICKLY, *Nate*, that thought a gut check. Longing swelled in him.

"It's Cal Fierston, Dixon," the voice said.

"Umm," Dixon uttered, a cloud clearing across his memory. The reporter.

"How're you doing?"

One hand on his hip, Dixon stared down at his feet. "Great," he deadpanned.

"I can only imagine." He paused a respectful beat. "The reason I'm calling is, I'm wrapping up some stories on the climbing season, and I'm including a profile of you and Nate." He let the idea sit between them.

Dixon clutched the phone. He could not seem to catch his breath. His eyes closed, he rolled slightly back and forth on his heels—he knew just how far forward he could roll before the false foot began to tug. He leaned forward hard into the tug.

"Listen, I'm in the D.C. area next week. Can we set up a time to talk?"

"I'm pretty busy these days."

"No problem. I'll work around your schedule. Let me email you a list of dates and times, you pick one. Okay?"

He could hear Nate: *Ain't this some shit? Now they wanna do a story.* "Say, what is it you want, really?"

"Look, most people climbing now are just trying to check off some 'first' this or that, you know? You two seemed like something more, maybe."

"Ah, so we're wild birds. Exotica," he said and turned his mouth down.

"Or you're the start of a revolution. I mean, I've never encountered Black American men on Everest, Dixon. This isn't nothing."

"A revolution," he repeated, and at the corner of his eye, he saw Nate, ninth grade, in front of the bedroom mirror blowing kisses and singing: *You brought me fame and fortune and everything that goes with it / and I thank you all . . . We are the champions.* He dropped his head and laughed.

"Don't laugh. I really mean it. Listen, all right, I'm hoping to tell a good story, yes, I'll give you that. But its, its . . . aftermath," he said cautiously. "No one tells the story of after. The cost." Cal was nearly whispering. "It's important. It matters. Not just to you."

Dixon sighed, nodded. Of course, that's what this was about. Ghosts.

CHAPTER

13

As if Cal Fierston's call had summoned her, Everest returned to him. It began as a subterranean shift, a repositioning of his liver or spleen, and rose into pain: a stab in the palm of his hand like he gripped sharp rock, or a knee that locked and threw him forward, or a throbbing behind the eyes like a high-altitude headache. The mountain springing to life in him.

At a stoplight, he might peer through the windshield of his car and find the clouds had arranged themselves into peaks, shadowed and backlit as the Himalaya. A TV ad might blare at him: "Savings as big as Mount Everest!" On his way to visit Marcus, he passed a sign for "Everest Moving and Hauling" with a sketchy drawing of the mountain's peak in the background above the tagline "We take service to new heights." He dragged those casual assaults with him to Marcus's bedside. Dixon whispered to the unconscious boy, "Every day, I'm back there, I'm, I'm climbing. Every day, I'm making an awful choice and Nate's dying. Every. Day."

The relentless mountain. There was no leaving behind its silt, even within the cocoon of family that Charlaina constructed. They carried on regular Sunday dinners like the ones his parents and Charlaina's had shared. Kira came, too, one weekend when she was home from college. His daughter entered the house looking shrunken, dressed unremarkably. He scooped her into his arms, then examined her. The ashen cast of grief on her bare skin was startling. His fingers grazed her bottom lip. He expected lip gloss, at least. Since she hit her teens, her kisses had left his cheek sticky with it. Her bare mouth brown and flat. He pulled her tight to him, emotion diffuse in his body. It was so hard to release her. She had to pat his arms, whisper, "Daddy, okay."

In the kitchen, Kira shadowed Charlaina, absorbing family lore, learning family recipes, Kira carrying forward tradition because his generation was diminished now. There was the feeling of fleeting time—he turned his gaze to an empty chair. At dinner, Charlaina, Kira, and Dixon sat around the polished walnut table, and there was normalcy, a cloak extended warmly to Dixon. Something he could not name welled in him as he ate the rich beef stew and drank the burgundy wine, as he tore off chunks of fresh-baked bread. Kira and Charlaina on either side of him cast a proprietary rope between them and latched on, holding Dixon buoyant and tight. But they could not ward off the swarm of memory. A snow squall, a blast of cold, foggy air, that indescribable smell of high-altitude snow, cold and crisp and pungent.

HERBERT WORKED AT HIS GRILL, WATCHFUL OF DIXON. "YOU look like a man got a lot on your dance card."

"Yep, that's me. Dancing my ass off." Dixon began a new order. Not thinking about anything but the task before him. That's the way to do it, he told himself, focus, focus. He held the pan's handle, jiggled it too hard, and it slipped from his hand, slamming down onto the grill and spilling eggs. A clumsy move. A Marcus kind of move.

"Careful, man," Herbert said. A concerned frown on his face, he eased slightly back and at an angle from Dixon.

"Sorry, sorry." Dixon wiped up the egg and started over. "You believe in evil?"

"Depends. Any man can find the bad in hisself. Just don't e'er'body's life bring it out. Depends on your people, on luck maybe, on what people expect from you. I 'on't know, man. I'mma cook, not some philosophizer."

"You know the world, man, you know things."

Herbert looked satisfied. "Indeed." He paused. "'Luke, I am your father,'" he said in his best Darth Vader voice. "'Give in to the dark side.' That what you talking 'bout? 'Cause, see, that's e'er'body's fight."

"This kid beat up one of my boys, Marcus. Beat him bad. He's lying there, half-dead, half-alive. I don't know, maybe there is such a thing as evil, a bad seed."

Herbert made a guttural noise. "Sound like that boy a predator. It don't make him evil, necessar'ly. Depends on what he got to fight against."

"We all got something."

"Yeah? Even a good boy like you?" Herbert smirked, and the insult landed sharp against Dixon. "Man, I can read you. You was raised to say 'yes ma'am, no ma'am,' help ol' ladies cross the street, you sang in the church choir. Hustlers like me be waiting for you 'round the corner after church, take your candy money. Right?" He shook his head, a faint laugh. Dixon was caught out. "Ah, look, Dix man, don't nobody end up standing at a grill, forty-some years old and grateful to be here wit'out somethin' kicking his ass, right?"

Dixon agreed. The men tended to their grills. "I may have done something stupid. Found out what he did to Marcus, I went looking for that kid, put out the word." He glanced at Herbert, whose eyes grew wide with alarm.

Herbert grimaced. "Whatchu gone do when that boy come looking?"

"I have no idea." He gripped the handle of a pan more tightly. He looked down at his body. He was in the worst shape of his life: spindle-thin and his arms and legs without their customary strength. A sitting duck.

"Shit." Herbert sliced a steak slowly, then patted it with surprising gentleness. "You worry me, Dix man."

Herbert stood with his back just so to Dixon while he cooked, blocking himself from Dixon's probing. Later, Dixon would recall that turning away, the way Herbert protected himself like the flip of a collar. As if he had taken up the habit Dixon was just becoming conscious of in himself, a small gesture that recurred in the middle of talking or while driving. He would place his hand alongside his face to block the ever-present ghost of the mountain.

The morning after Dixon's regular day off, the restaurant nearly overflowed with a busload of senior citizens who arrived at 7 a.m., slamming the waitstaff and the kitchen. Dixon and Herbert hummed along, keeping a steady rhythm of work and banter. There was a small joy in the anticipation of each other, Herbert's steak ready just as Dixon's eggs were finished. But Herbert stood back every now and then, sizing Dixon up in a way that baffled him. By 1 p.m., the rush had subsided.

"Man, where's Long Legs?" Herbert's voice musical. "Ain't seen her in a minute."

Dixon shrugged. "She's fine."

Herbert gave a long, slow smile. "Yes, she is." He laughed quietly to himself and Dixon felt a bit protective of his cousin. "Say, reminds me I been meaning to say, you had a visitor yesterday while you was off. Wa'n't no Long Legs, let me just say that. Tall, thick beard, underbite. Guy said, he said, you and your brother was the first Black men in America to climb some, some Mount Everest. What's he talking 'bout? You know this guy?"

A cool wave swept through Dixon. "Yeah, I know him."

"Yeah?" Herbert raised his eyebrows and tilted his head, his look both awed and perplexed, full of *are you crazy*? "He telling the truth?"

The sounds of the diner filled the space between them, the clang of dishes in the sink, the call of orders from waitresses, the dull din of voices in the dining area. For a while, the sound drowned out Dixon's voice, he guessed, because Herbert left his place at the far grill and came next to Dixon as he told all, an unexpected unburdening. He related the story of their beshitted climb, of his brother's death. Almost the whole truth.

As Dixon talked, Herbert grimaced. When Dixon finished, Herbert said, "Dude aksed me how do I feel about it. Was I proud. I ain't know what to say, man. Not dissing you, just . . ." He lifted his hands in apology. "That don't even figure for me. It sound like such a wild story, man, I can't fantom it."

"A wild story, indeed. Well, there's no happily ever after to it, I can tell you that."

Herbert kept his eyes on Dixon awhile. "You a surprising dude, Dix man."

HE HAD NOT BEEN RAISED TO BE A SURPRISE. HIS PARENTS' OR-
derly card parties flashed into his head: the women wear broad-
collared blouses and beaded necklaces, and the men sport knit
pullovers and pleated slacks. The women drink sherry; the men,
gin and tonics. The kick his mom Lonette and her sister, Charlaina's mom, get from the sherry. He can see his mother, head thrown
back in laughter, the glint of pearl earrings in the light, the giggle
she and Aunt Flo share. Once, Nate, Dixon, and Charlaina had
sneaked some sherry, then nearly gagged on its sweetness. "I don't
get it," they'd all declared, and only now could Dixon understand.
Daughters of the teetotaling Rev. Dr. Harris Dixon, Lonette and
Flo were giddy with their daring at breaking out of their box, however genteelly. It seemed tender and sad now.

Aunt Flo and Uncle Lloyd gather around Dixon's father, who
plays the piano badly, laughing at his own mistakes but making
music good enough to sing along to. Here is the first time Dixon
declares himself: Aunt Flo taps Dixon's knee. "What're you going
to be when you grow up?"

He is ten. He reaches for the most towering figure he knows.
Mr. Bevins at school, strutting the hallways, commanding, "Ladies
and gentlemen, heads up, shoulders back." Dixon says, "I'd like to
be a guidance counselor."

"Oh, you can do more than that. How about a child psychologist?" Dixon's mother nudges.

Aunt Flo nods. "It's the stronger professional move. You'll lift
us all a little higher."

After that, every time he soothed a crying kid or chastised a
bully, he rose into himself. It had fit Dixon, his box. No, it had been

his truest self. Until he had been seduced away by that mountain. God Almighty, when would he stop paying for that lapse?

———————

BETWEEN 3:30 AND 4:30 P.M., THE NURSES AT THE HOSPITAL where Marcus lay met to change shifts and switch off patients. Dixon could slip into Marcus's room nearly unnoticed, before the evening nurse came to check Marcus's monitors, before the boy's mother brought her burdens. He could find peace. "Swelling's gone down," Dixon said. "You look more like you, Marcus. You'll be back to us soon." He picked up the boy's hand. His chronically bitten-down fingernails were beginning to grow. Dixon rubbed the boy's fingertips under his own like small, loose stones.

After he left the hospital, Dixon drove around, sure that anywhere he landed, Shiloh might be waiting. Herbert had admonished him each afternoon all week as they left work, "Don't go looking for him again. Y'hear me?"

He was overcome with the idea of wanting to go home to his mother's. He gripped the steering wheel hard, swerving a bit with the power of that longing. The cinnamon smell of her kitchen, the line of flowery teapots on the ledge between the living and dining rooms, the dried flowers that clustered in small, white bowls all through the house. He wanted to see her at the stove or the sewing machine and for her to look up, smiling, say "Hi, Sugar," and kiss his cheek.

It was all in the past, the whole of his family life, and that realization clouded his vision. He pulled over onto the shoulder of the highway. Cars, fast as ghosts, rumbled by. His car trembled with their presence. He fell forward against the steering wheel, against the keen edge of wanting.

He drove home in silence. The moment he entered his apartment, he smelled the rank boy-smell of sweat and stale cigarettes and grease. An electric feel in the air. Dixon faced the door, his back to the room, straightened his shoulders, did not move. Did not move.

He called out. No answer. He called again. His body vibrating. He turned into the room. Empty. Down the hall, into the kitchen. The pantry, the laundry room. Upstairs, he checked the rooms, the closets, under the bed.

Back in the living room, he found the note: "Listen up." It took a moment to understand. He crossed the room to his answering machine, hit play.

"You know, only reason your ass still here? It's more fun fucking witchu. You think, what, I'mma come meet you so you can set me up wit' the cops? Nah. Don't forget I'm the one got *your* ass. You put your hands on *me*. I got your whole life, right in my hands."

The smell of that boy in his house. The smell of Dixon's own fear overlaying it. He sprayed the air with freshener, holding his shirt over his nose. He called a locksmith to fit the door with a stronger deadbolt. He washed down counters, light switches, tabletops, threw out his toothbrush—better to be safe—cleaned floors on hands and knees, every light in the house burning fiercely, he cleaned against the tide of that kid. And none of it, none of it, was enough.

---

HE MIGHT HAVE BEEN DREAMING. IT MIGHT HAVE BEEN THE universe taking pity on him. Lena's voice rose like vapor from the phone late at night. "I am thinking of you."

"Where are you? Are you okay? It's one in the morning."

"Oh no! It's only ten in the night here. Seattle. Where are you?"

"On the other coast."

"Oh! Your country is too big. All these different times. Is like on the moon from here."

"I'm outside of D.C. Washington, D.C."

"Oh! I have been there. I love it with the blooming cherries."

"Cherry blossoms," he replied, laughing. He scooted upright, smoothing his T-shirt, making himself presentable.

"Ah, you know what it is," she tsked. "How are you, Dixon? Do you recover?"

Not "have you recovered," not a query in the past tense like all the others from well-meaning friends. *Do you?* Are you in the process? "Some days," he answered. "The truth? I can't find my way."

"It is that way, I remember. Did I tell you? My lover, he died on Aconcagua. The avalanche swept him away. I was right there. I see it now when I close my eyes," she said softly. "I feel so much what you go through now. It will get better, Dixon."

"Then you recover?" His voice quiet.

"I do."

"It's not like anything I ever thought."

"Yes, yes, it is not."

They sat in silence a long while.

She said, "I think about Nate a lot. 'Oh! He did touch me just there,' like slow, tender, then I go under just a minute. That is how he comes back to me."

His skin goose-bumped. "That's not all he was, you know. That's just the surface of him."

"Yes, but this is my one part. I thought you'd want to know I hold it fondly."

It dawned on him: "You fell for him."

Her answer was slow in coming. "I knew better. I saw through him, you know? But the way he held me. Ach! You are not sad to hear this, Dixon?"

He shook his head to dispel the image of Nate and her. "We did this to ourselves," he whispered. "We ruined ourselves. How do you do it, over and over?" He kicked out against the covers, freeing his feet. "I mean, why? You've seen what I've seen."

"They are not the same thing, the death, the mountain. The death, it happens, it is part of it. We don't go to die. We go because we are alive. The death, it's very, very sad. It is not the only thing the mountain has to give. I think. I think, Dixon, for you it wasn't love that sent you. It was something else. Something the mountain did not have to give to you."

His chest full. He closed his eyes. It might be her hand, the weight of it against his sternum. "He said the world would look different after being up there. That's what he promised." Before him, all cloud and endless sky. "It's all just so small, isn't it?"

"Only if you stay there." He heard rustling, a bed sheet maybe, the crisp slide of it across bare skin. He imagined her cradling the sheet around her body, digging her elbows beside herself to nestle in. "We sit with each other, okay?" She said "aw-ther": *we seat with each aw-ther.*

All night, dozing and sleeping, she was there beside him. All night, "Are you there?"

Near dawn, in a well of wakefulness, he confessed, "This reporter wants to do our story. He wants to tell . . . he wants to take our story, and, and . . ." His mouth so dry, it was hard to swallow.

"You do not have to share. Whatever happened is only yours."

His relief wide, he exhaled into the phone, which was warm

and slightly sour with morning breath, its skin moist against his cheek.

———

IT WAS MUCH LATER THAN NORMAL WHEN HE VISITED MARCUS the next evening, nearly at the end of visiting hours. He would have only ten or fifteen minutes with him. The day nurses who knew him were gone, and the evening nurse gave him the once-over. Dixon assured her, "I'd just like to say good night to him."

Dixon walked the sterile corridor to Marcus's room, glancing into the open doors along the hall. There were more visitors than in the afternoons. Tonight, the rooms were full of brothers who stood near hospital beds, hands thrust into their pockets, and daughters who leaned sideways across the beds as if they might crawl in beside their loved ones.

Marcus was lying unmoving and flat as usual, eyes open but unfocused. His breathing steady, his skin sallow in the artificial light.

Someone cleared his throat, and Dixon started. A man sat in a chair tucked into a corner between the armoire and the window. A large man, perched uncomfortably on a chair just too small, he sat forward. A familiar deep voice came upon Dixon slowly. "Hey, pardner."

Dixon was so startled he reached out to the doorframe to steady himself.

"It's just me, man," Herbert said quietly.

"You waiting for me?" In his confusion, Dixon shook his head rapidly.

"Naw. Boy deserves visitors up in a place like this." Herbert reached toward Marcus's bed and placed his hand on top of the boy's. The way Dixon usually did.

Dixon rubbed his forehead, an odd feeling of betrayal bubbling in him.

"Hate to see it, man, what happen to Marcus." Herbert's face dense, something Dixon could not read. "I understand the consequence." He looked at Dixon. "Not just for him."

The same nurse who had greeted him entered the room. "Gentlemen, we need to draw some blood." They both backed up, Herbert to his corner, Dixon to the doorframe, and watched the claret-red blood slush into four different vials. "All right, it's about time we get this one settled in for the night. You should say your goodbyes."

Dixon approached Marcus's bed. He kissed his forehead. "I'll come see you tomorrow." He imagined he held the boy's gaze.

"A'ight, pardner," Herbert said to Marcus. "Take it easy."

The two men left the room silently and headed toward the elevator. A slow anger churning in Dixon, he blurted out, "What's this about?"

Herbert retrieved a pack of cigarettes from his jacket pocket and twirled it in his hand. "Thought about Marcus's story. It's in the papers, you read it? Thought about the boy Shiloh, too. He prob'ly thinking he ain't do nothing so wrong. He figure, life woulda kicked that boy's ass. Maybe he done him a favor getting it over with. That's the kinda heart he got. I see somebody gone hafta take him in hand." His voice trailed off. His footsteps heavy beside Dixon.

"But why are you *here*? What's it got to do with you?"

"Yours ain't the only Marcus that ever been."

ixon wasn't sure how to approach Herbert the next day. He watched for an opening as Herbert sliced a tomato using a serrated knife, slicing fast and even, fingers tucked in. "Where'd you learn technique? Chef school?" Dixon asked.

"Hmph. Cordon Bleu *State Pen*." He glanced up at Dixon, obviously checking his reaction. "Dude in the joint was a master chef. Good with a knife." A slow smile crossing his face, he met Dixon's eyes again. "You didn't piss him off in the kitchen, let me just say that. So, look, you got a pro'lem with me visiting your boy, say so."

"Just surprised." He wanted to leave an opening for Herbert to explain.

"They catch that boy yet?"

"Not yet."

"Well, it's coming. Longer it go on, the harder it get for him. Bad things happen behind that."

"You should've seen Marcus before. He was a really cute kid.

Unrecognizable now. Shiloh, he still has his whole life ahead of him. Even if they give him ten, fifteen years, how's that fair?"

Herbert's look drew a wide arc around him. "Sure, he got things to answer for. But I ain't for a man doing time that ain't his."

"He deserves all the time he gets. Never thought I'd say this, but this isn't an ordinary kid."

"But that don't mean he oughta get thrown away."

"Not thrown away. But you gotta look at what he did! You gotta think about what he's likely to do again. He just, he just, broke all the rules." Dixon's body shook. "You can't get away with everything! You ought not do everything you think you're big enough to do!" Dixon panted. The mountain on his periphery, he squeezed his eyes shut. Once he calmed down, he focused on Herbert. "You're smacking the shit outta that steak," Dixon said.

Herbert eased up. "You either gotta have a conscious or a heart for justice. You can't have both at the same time. Your conscious gonna fuck you up, thinking 'Oh, it gotta be this way, gotta be all fair and square.' That's conscious. But it ain't always right. The world ain't a simple place."

"Okay," Dixon said, cautious. He wasn't sure they were in the same argument.

"Being a good man ain't always a straight-ahead choice." Herbert knocked the steak around, then began a low grumble. "You get under a man's skin, Dix. I 'on't wanna be wrestling all the time."

Herbert did not say good night to Dixon. He grabbed his things and headed for the door in a determined rush. Dixon had an anxious thought that he may not see him again. He walked outside, watching Herbert bound in long, hard strides for the bus stop.

CHARLAINA APPEARED AT HIS DOOR THE NEXT SATURDAY afternoon, her face riddled with confusion. "Dixon?" she asked. He reached for her elbow and guided her inside. She pulled away and stood across from him.

"I don't know where to start, really." She glanced around his living room as if she were looking for her lines, then frowned. "Do you know a Cal Fierston?" she blurted out.

He exhaled. "Shit." He made his way to the sofa.

"He found me. Came over and told me about the, the, mountain." She waved the mention of it away with one hand. "He showed me a photo of a man at the top. He says you told him it's Nate." She opened her hands in front of her, palms up. "I know it's you. I know you. I recognize you down to the way you hold your crooked little finger. Why wouldn't you tell me you reached the top, Dixon?"

He did not answer. He should never have taken off his damned glove. Pemba had urged him to do it and wave.

"This Cal wants to know how I feel about the whole thing, about you all going, about Nate . . . everything." She drew big circles in the air. "And then he shows me that photo that he thinks is Nate."

She stopped talking and let her words settle on him. He shrank under her gaze. "He says Nate, well *you*, you're the first Black man to reach the summit."

"The first Black man was South African, Sibusiso Vilane. First Black American was a woman, Sophia Danenberg."

"You're the first Black American man, right? That's, that's amazing. You did it, Dixon."

"It's Nate," he said weakly. He could not see the world in focus.

"No. It isn't." She sat beside him and took his hand. "I didn't tell that to that man. I think you should."

"I can't, Char."

"Oh, sweetie, why not?" She cupped his hand between both of hers.

"It's his summit. Let it be his."

She stroked his cheek, shaking her head at his words, at his ragged skin. All those weeks he had spent convalescing at her house, sleeping mostly, his cousin changed his bandages, fed him, did the caretaking he and his brother had come to expect from her. She had held herself like an anchor for him. Latching onto the sight of her, he might lose himself in the bone structure so like his mother's, the squared shoulders that belonged to his brother, all of what he had called "home" rising from this one woman. And yet he could not bring himself to tell her the truth. She repeated, "Why didn't you tell me you reached the summit?"

"Couldn't."

"You don't have anything to be ashamed of. I know you all worked hard to prepare."

He wagged his head back and forth, weighing his thoughts. "Knew just enough to be dangerous. Every mountain's a surprise, especially that one. Man, she just lets you think you can have her."

"She?"

"Yes, she. You think she's inanimate, that she's not paying you any mind. But the sherpas, they tell you quick when you get there, 'Respect Mother.' They ask her permission to climb. And everybody, all the Westerners indulge them. But those sherpas understand. You get too cocky, she just flicks you off her shoulder like a flea." He rocked toward her. "She's watching, seeing what she brings out in you. Then she pounces." He gave a quick snort of a laugh. "You know what you find on that mountain? God and the devil. You're all that stands between them." The world in front of him whited out.

She tugged at his fingers. "Don't close up."

"You don't know what you'll face up there. And I'm not even talking about, about, cold, or weather. See, it's that you don't know what the mountain will demand of you."

"I see."

"When you're climbing that mountain, you are peerless. Then, like the flick of a switch you descend, and you see the truth. You are blatantly mortal. I think that's why most people who die do it on the descent."

"You're not most people. You never were."

"But I am. I should be," he said and had to tamp down hard as that idea bubbled at the back of his throat. "Why didn't anyone make me be?"

"You just had better radar, somehow, this innate sense of the right thing. You're a good guy. We've depended on that."

Nate used to scold, "You've been a good little colored boy long enough." He closed his eyes. He is a boy again, a boy on his way from the darkened garage to the bright warmth of the kitchen, a boy who overhears his father's voice: "Nate seems to think it's not hip to study before an exam, and you know him, has to be 'hip' before anything else."

"They can't both be Dixon," his mother says, and they laugh. "But don't weigh Dixon down so, Eldridge. Give him flight, too."

"Lonette, he's a good boy."

"That's what I mean, let him be sometimes, Eldridge. Let him find his own level."

Dixon filled with resolve. "Don't say that, Char. 'Good.' Please don't ever say that about me again."

"It fits. I've never known anyone it fit more."

His father's voice echoed in Dixon's head, the memory of its bass and boom. "The Great and Powerful Oz," Nate would whisper to Dixon after one of their father's pronouncements. Nate always pushing the boundaries. Nate jumping from the car on a freezing morning at the bus stop to run to Marvelyn Dane's car and open the door for her, carry her books, lean in for a kiss. "Look at him," their father scoffed. "Thinks the best of him is between his legs. That's who he is." He had exhaled gruffly. Why had Dixon asked so eagerly, "Who am I, Dad?" His father had smiled, peered into the rearview mirror directly at Dixon in the back seat. "You're our quarterback, Dixon, you carry the ball." And hadn't he understood? That just as his father would repeat to Dixon "you carry the ball," he would chastise Nate, "Boy, who are you gonna be in this world?" Because everything, everything, was a momentous choice in their father's world. Be happy skinning tomatoes in the canning factory like the other colored boys (he would describe the way tomato acid and scalding water made your hands shrivel and peel, turning them into old-man hands in no time) or work three jobs to afford a college education. Decide the world was as small as that little town on the Eastern Shore of Maryland, every future spoken for, every man in his given lane, or veer wider to college, a path unknown enough to feel dangerous but necessary, a memory their father had recounted to Dixon and his brother with tears in his eyes. A man must make choices, affirmative steps toward his God-given life. A true man must choose as near to truth as he could manage.

Truth.

"You don't know what I did, Char," Dixon whispered. "I wanted to be an alpinist, then I violated their code."

"What happened up there?"

"You won't forgive me."

The two cops who stood at his door scanned Dixon—thin with a ravaged face, leaning unsteadily on a cane, not yet wearing his prosthetic—and they seemed momentarily unsure what to do. Dixon took in the starched blue of their uniforms, the light flashing off their badges. He had lived in quiet dread of this moment his whole life. All the ways he and his brother had been taught to avoid it. Say *Yessir, my license is in my inside pocket, may I reach for it or would you rather?* You roll the bass out of your voice while you answer the cops' questions. You stand stock-still and hold your bag up for inspection, lifting both arms, when the alarm goes off at the electronics store exit. You step back four paces from the doorbell once the woman appears and grabs at her robe, clutching it around her throat, step back and speak slowly, until you see the wave of shame cross her beautiful brown face: *Of course, you're the counselor from the school, please come on in.* There was a yellow-brick road of rules, and he had followed it.

"Dixon Bryant?" Officer Percy, his badge read. He had baby

blue eyes and big hands with wide thumbs like a basketball player. "Do you know Shiloh Evans?"

Here, then, a reckoning. Shiloh turning him in for that last day, that bullshit assault. "He was a student at my school." Dixon motioned toward his cane. "I'm on medical leave."

The cops seemed to relax, a few questions answered. "Accident?" Officer Percy asked.

"Mountain," Dixon replied and scanned their skeptical faces. "Climbing. Frostbite," he said. The cops stood with eyebrows raised.

The taller one was square-jawed. He smelled like pine aftershave. "He's been arrested. Your address was found in his GPS."

"Oh, oh," Dixon stammered. A cool spray of sweat on his upper lip. "I think he was here. It, yes, when I came home last week, a week ago, it seemed, it smelled like him. Smoky. He left a message on my answering machine, he said, you know, well first, I had gone to find him." He was blathering. *Take a breath!* "I knew he was wanted by the police, so I went to look for him. I wanted to persuade him to turn himself in," he lied. He felt his face flush. "Couldn't find him but I told some kids in his neighborhood to have him contact me. I think he thought I might be setting him up. He left a message on my machine, told me to go to hell."

"You have the message?" The tall officer headed toward Dixon's phone. He scanned up the stairway.

"No. I don't."

"And you didn't file charges? You decide to handle it on your own, Mr. Bryant?" The tall cop motioned to Dixon's cane. "Did it not go as easily as you thought?"

"What? No, I told you, I had frostbite. Lost a few toes."

"'Cause Shiloh Evans made somebody mad before he was turned in."

He'd been "persuaded," the officer told Dixon, dropped off at the precinct with a set of freshly bruised ribs, a bloodied face. Dixon's stomach lurched. "Can I—" He made his way across the room to the sofa. He sat, his hands balled into fists on top of his knees. How could he be upset about that fucking kid's bloody face? Maybe he was just pissed he hadn't been the one to bloody it. Maybe he was afraid that for all intents and purposes he had been.

"What can you tell us about Shiloh?" the baby-faced Officer Percy asked. He seemed the kinder of the two, one who might loosen the handcuffs on your wrists if they bit into the skin, maybe help Dixon with his prosthetic foot before arresting him. Did they know how he'd lunged at Shiloh? Dixon told them all he knew, everything about Marcus and how Shiloh stalked him. Everything that didn't indict him.

Herbert's voice echoed through him: *I see somebody gone hafta take him in hand.* Dixon tossed and turned all night. In dreams, he slammed Shiloh against the lockers, against a wall, against the blunt edge of a rock cliff, over and again. Even though he talked to himself this way: *You don't know what happened, just ask calmly,* the minute Dixon got to work the next morning and saw Herbert standing at the back door waiting to be let in, something surged in Dixon, and he bounded toward Herbert, breathless, "What did you do? What did I make you do?"

---

"I FEEL LIKE SOMETHING GOT OUTTA HAND," DIXON HEDGED. HE stood catty-corner to Herbert. "So . . ." He could not bring himself to ask. "Did I, I mean, I provoked you . . ."

"So this about you, huh?" Herbert snorted a disgusted laugh. "You figure you to blame for Marcus *and* Shiloh? You the kind of guy who ain't gone be happy till he hang from his cross, ain't you?" Herbert rearranged utensils on his cutting board, lining them up by height, then he stood back examining them. "It's some guys I know who, who . . ." Herbert's hand batted against the air, searching. "See, they get to these boys before the cops do, then we know they stay alive. Ya feel me?"

"Oh," Dixon said with a deep exhale, then another stab of alarm. Vigilantes?

"I tole you, I'm for a man paying for his deeds. Ain't for the reasons you thinking."

"Frankly, I don't know what I'm thinking."

"I don't know how that boy got hurt. Ain't how things are done. He musta, he musta . . . hate to hear it, for real." Herbert grabbed a handful of freshly washed knives, and water ran in rivulets down his forearm.

Dixon gazed at Herbert, taking him in with a wash of relief. "Why would these guys do this, I mean, take on somebody like Shiloh?"

"'Cause if they don't, who gonna?" Herbert wiped off the knives and placed them on a tray. Each thud against the tray echoed in Dixon. Herbert continued, "Look, man, you 'on't really know me. You know who I want to be, who I try to be. But what I come through? See, you know that, it change how you see me, most likely. I 'on't want that, man. I really don't."

Dixon felt a swell of compassion for his friend. "You're a good man, I see that."

Herbert grumbled. "Yeah, see, that's what'm talking 'bout."

Maybe he didn't really know his friend. Truth was, he seemed to live at the edge of life these days. The world inscrutable, shrouded by cloud. With winter at his heels, he sank into the cold, gave over to its inevitability—there was so little you could do to protect yourself. Down suits, balaclavas, plastic hand warmers? Useless, all that shit. Even now, he couldn't escape a bone chill. "Dixon, it's too cold in here," Charlaina would complain when she visited, then turn up the heat unnaturally high. The minute she left, he turned it down again. It was not, after all, any comfort to be warm. Nate was not warm. Dixon had left him with skin ashen from the cold, his eyes bulging and glazed. He must be solid ice now. The idea sank swiftly in Dixon's stomach, shockwaves shimmering through him.

He sat on the side of his bed, stared at his feet. "There's brown skin," Charlaina had told him months ago. "I've done some research. You don't have to settle for that." She had pointed toward the false foot. "They can match your own skin tone. Wouldn't that feel better?" Startled by the memory of her words, he stiffened. He had grown so used to seeing himself against the insult of that pale false foot. Who else could he be?

---

HIS LAPTOP OPEN ON THE SOFA ONE EVENING, A NOTIFICATION bell sounded, and an email popped across the screen. He expected somehow that it would be from Shiloh.

Dixon,

I was wrong what I said to you. I found this on the Internet.

*Other notable summits this year: First African American male summited on May 9, one of two brothers on Everest,*

*Nate and Bryant Dixon. Danzig Strifenbach, first*
*upper-limb amputee, summited on May 10 with the*
*world-renowned Bryton Baylor.*

They got it wrong. You must fix. You should tell to
the reporter. He can get it right.

Call you later.
Lena

His head might explode. He stared at the laptop screen a long
time. It had never occurred to him before to search for articles. He
knew something had been written, a short obit for Nate in the local
paper: "Local Man Dies Summiting Everest." Charlaina had shown
it to him after he returned home. Barely two paragraphs, mostly
about the number of people who had died climbing Everest, the
recounting of the 1996 disaster, a mention of George Mallory's
body being found in 1999. Nate, then, had been little more than a
vehicle for citing the dead.

He googled his name and "Mount Everest." An avalanche followed.

### Should I Feel Bad for the Dead on Everest?

https://www.wonkoutside.com>blogspot>news>4289>dead-on
-everest>24865

 . . . like **Dixon Bryant** and his brother Nate, who died on
the mountain . . . a mix of folly and arrogance leads
otherwise average men to test themselves on **Mount**
**Everest** . . .

**The True Cost of Climbing Mount Everest**

https://onguardnews.com/sports/winter/mt-everest/243

This year, with its usual efficiency, **Mount Everest** killed five people in as many days . . . along with climbing novices **Bryant** and Nate **Dixon**, accounts that leave us both pitying and shaking our heads . . .

**Of Privilege and Folly: The Fate of Mount Everest's Amateur Climbers**

https://www.usadailynews.com/opinion/column/danverson /climbers/amateurs/death

Proving **Everest** is an equal opportunity killer, this year's dead included African American Nate **Bryant**, who climbed along with his brother **Dixon**. Neither man summited . . .

**Editorial: Keep Amateurs Off Mount Everest**

https://www.outofdoorsliving.com/news/circuit/76534-OBD7q97

But no one wants to relent . . . needless tragedy. Brothers **Dixon** and Nate **Bryant**, two more "weekend warriors" who likely should have been turned back from attempting **Everest**'s summit . . .

He clicked on the first article and scrolled down to the comments.

*Who does this? What's wrong with these people?*

*All those dead people on Everest? I say it's natural selection at work!*

*What makes people crazy like this?*

*They'd be alive if they could just have kept their egos locked up.*

*Don't worry—Mother Nature sorted that shit out!*

He slammed shut the laptop.

---

*WHAT KIND OF PERSON DOES THIS?*

Even three days after he'd read that, he couldn't get over it. Someone had actually written that about them. What kind of person? As if it were psychopathic behavior. As if it were *ego, all ego*—isn't that what the guys at work had snickered behind his back: At his going-away party the previous December, Benny Lewis and Fred Pyle and Wiley Fitch, guys in their late forties like Dixon, had gathered around. "You're crazy, of course," Benny had said, lifting a glass of sparkling cider to Dixon, "but in a way I admire."

"I think you mean, marvel at. What the fuck, Dixon?" Wiley had joked.

Dolores Parsons had stuck her head into the little group, her broad cheeks blushing. "You know, Matthew Henson was a Maryland boy, too. You're keeping us on the map."

The men had cut their eyes at Dixon, a raise of the eyebrow, her crush on Dixon an open secret by then. Dixon had bowed his head slightly toward her—*don't embarrass her, don't encourage her.* How many times would someone mention Henson to him, as if they did not know conquering the North Pole and climbing Everest were not the same thing? Was Henson the only other crazy Black man anyone had heard of?

"I say, more power to ya," Benny had pronounced, and Wiley Fitch agreed.

Phil Pious had raised his glass: "To Dixon Bryant, that rare son of a bitch who does what we wish we had the guts to do, but a nice enough guy that we actually wish him well." And Dixon had overheard two colleagues whispering. "Who the hell wants to climb a goddamned mountain? That's nuts!" one said, and the other responded, "Ego, all ego."

HE HAD BARELY GOTTEN TO SLEEP ONE TUESDAY EVENING IN mid-December, not quite two months since Marcus's assault, when his phone rang. Groggy, he slapped around on the nightstand beside his bed until he found the phone. "My boy, my boy," he heard. Marcus had thrown a blood clot and had a stroke. The doctors had told his family to gather now to say goodbye. "I know my boy would want to see you," Mrs. Hollinger said. "His Mr. Dixon."

He rose from bed, dazed, and flailed around for his clothes. He sat at the edge of the bed and held his pants by the belt loops, unable to recall how to put them on.

Marcus had been moved from his old room to a ward without restrictions on visitors. The dying ward. Visitors rested, quiet, resigned, in the hallways, then went back to face death again. In Marcus's room, the lights were dimmed, the curtains drawn as if dying must be lured, as if it could not seize someone in the bright, hot blare of sun. Dixon lingered in the doorway. His fingers cold and stiff, he flexed and scrunched them over and over. Mrs.

Hollinger called to him, and throughout the packed room there was a brief flutter of introductions: aunts, cousins, grandmother, godmother. Marcus's younger twin brother and sister. His father, who did not move from where he sat, head in his hands. His father who had thought Marcus just needed to get used to dealing with trouble. Dixon did not go to him.

There were no noisy machines like in Marcus's old hospital room, no clear tubes or IV poles. There was nothing but the awful waiting. The nurses moved with little urgency. They did not say "Open your eyes for me" or "He's coming around." They said, "Only a reflex, ma'am, I'm sorry." They said, "No, he doesn't feel pain. No, he's not conscious."

Dixon moved closer to the bed. That sweet-faced boy. His skin so clean, a golden brown, as if he'd been scrubbed and polished for this last visit. But so very still. When he had touched the boy's collarbone in those early days in the hospital, Dixon could feel Marcus stirring. Now, nothing. Dixon trembled. He squatted down, his face beside Marcus's. "Don't go, don't leave us."

Dixon fell into the swell of visitors in the room, standing in a small circle, swaying side to side as if cradling their boy. Dixon numbing, his breath coming in small pants. The boy floated on the bed, half in, half out of life. A doctor arrived and said, "Are you ready to have that talk, Mrs. Hollinger? We have decisions we must make," and Marcus's mother asked, "How do they say that to you, like it's 'what color d'you want to paint the house, we gotta go buy the paint this afternoon?'"

Later, a doctor ushered them out of the room. "Let's let him rest."

From the hallway, Dixon heard the boy's mother wail, "He's gone! Oh, my boy!"

Dixon bolted from the building. He barely made it to his car before he wailed, "He killed him, the sonofabitch killed my boy." His words stirring a cool funnel cloud that congealed into hatred for Shiloh. Dixon punched the steering wheel, slapped at the dashboard, his knuckles ringing with pain, he punched himself into exhaustion.

All through that evening, the idea of Shiloh grew and hardened. In the middle of that night, he woke himself from sleep, growling.

Mrs. Hollinger's call startled him the next morning. He held his breath at the sound of her voice, paper-thin and eerily efficient, and for a moment he willed himself to believe the previous day had not happened. She wanted him to speak at Marcus's memorial service. "He would want that. He would love that." That evening, Dixon sat before his laptop and attempted to draft a eulogy once again. It had been both easier and harder to do this for Nate. Easier in that his head had been flooded with Nate things: his walk, his turns of phrase, his laugh. Harder because, of course, how was it to be done, that leave-taking? He focused on the screen.

Across the room, the television news blathered on. Had they said Marcus's name? "Prosecutors will now seek murder charges against Shiloh Evans, seen here at an earlier court date. He could receive a maximum twenty-five years to life without possibility of parole."

Dixon glared at the screen. Two bulky men with arms thick as tree trunks led a boy from the mouth of a building, its doors pulled back wide, spitting him out. They led the boy toward a police van. A boy. His face blurred out because of his age, but unmistakably a boy, slight and sunken in, his round head and skinny body clad in black clothing. A boy being led off in handcuffs. The image struck like a snake just at Dixon's throat. A sight you never got used to, a boy, his skin brown as yours, his shoulders hunched or thrown back defiant as Shiloh's were; it didn't matter. You became indicted by it, the creak and pop of your own wrist a rebellion against the idea of handcuffs.

Dixon got to his feet. Stared at the TV screen. He was just a kid—a *kid!* The boy glanced over his shoulder, quick, furtive, scared. What was he looking for? *Me,* Dixon thought, with a cool shudder, *it should be someone like me standing in that doorway watching after him.* The boy glancing back. That look enough to slough off skin so that Dixon stood naked before it.

His hands balled into fists, his fingertips digging into his palms, Dixon watched Shiloh stop near the van and glance behind at that empty doorway. As if Dixon turned with him: he sees himself, his face frozen with snow and ice, his down suit askew, Clive and Pemba lifting him under the arms, carrying him away.

Dixon blinked hard and there was Shiloh again, in chains. The only thing worse than watching Marcus die had to be seeing a boy plastered like that across the television screen. And this, this was no anonymous boy. This was his boy, his crime.

---

HIS STATE-ISSUED ID WOULD GIVE HIM EASY ACCESS, DIXON RE-alized. So the next day, he called out sick. It was 4:30 a.m., his usual wake-up time, the sky dark, and Dixon set out into that night, bundled against the dagger of early winter cold. This seemed a necessary trip. His pulse beating too fast, Dixon drove through largely empty suburban streets, listening to the soft whir of his tires on the blacktop.

Ironically, he took himself to a different diner in a town

forty-five miles away, a breakfast joint so like The Beaten Egg that he had to remind himself not to enter the kitchen. He lingered over his breakfast of eggs, hash browns, ham, and grits until 9 a.m.

The detention facility sat in a low clearing, wide open with high towers on all four sides offering unobstructed views for nearly a mile in any direction. Little chance of breaking out unobserved. The facility had two wings, one for adults, one for juveniles. He waited in the guard house with nearly a dozen people. A flash of fear-sweat broke above his upper lip. What if they flagged his school ID as suspended? The guard he handed his ID to sized him up, from his handwriting to his photo but only glanced at his guilty, sweaty face.

In the section for juveniles charged as adults, Dixon entered a cinderblock room, its windows high and small. About twenty small tables were bolted to the floor in perfect rows. He picked a table and folded his hands in front of him, his eyes steadily on the door. Guards patrolled the room, up and down the aisles, as wary of the visitors as they would later be of the prisoners. In the bright morning sun, which fell slantwise across the room, everyone washed out, black and brown and white, a blur of pale light cast across their faces.

One by one, the boys were led in. The door opened and closed behind them in quick succession. When Shiloh appeared, even though Dixon was staring right at him, he nearly did not see him. The boy, small and tentative, deflated. Just a boy, after all, in a place of bigger boys surrounded by guards, all men. Shiloh stepped quickly into the room, checking each side of him. The guard at the door pointed toward the table where Dixon sat, and when Shiloh saw Dixon, his eyes widened into an unreadable expression. The boy sauntered to the table and sat with a thud. Dixon skipped a breath. How hard that boy's face could hit you. He was sporting a fresh black eye.

"You?" Shiloh snorted. "Why I wanna see you?"

Dixon raised his eyebrows. He had no answer.

"Look at you, all happy and shit cause I'm up in here," he scoffed.

"Nothing to be happy about." Dixon's body buzzed, the sight of this boy churning him up. He focused on that impenetrable face. One scar nearly a dagger, then a cluster of puss-filled scars draped his nose like strung pearls. And then the black eye. It looked only hours old. "What happened, son?" Dixon pointed toward his own eye.

"Fell." Shiloh rolled his eyes.

"Into a fist, looks like."

Shiloh sucked his teeth. "Told you 'bout calling me 'son.'"

Dixon leaned forward. "It's not easy being the guppy, is it? You're surrounded by big fish here. Must have been how Marcus felt being chased by you."

Shiloh's gaze was fixed somewhere across the room. "Somebody always getting got. Next time, it's they turn."

"You got vengeance in your heart?" Dixon asked.

"Why, you worried? You send them mothafuckas that fucked me up?"

He froze.

"You not that smart." Shiloh hopped up in his seat, impatient, his face furrowing. "Look, whatchu doing here? You here 'bout Fat Ass?"

Dixon's throat constricted.

Shiloh shifted in his chair. "Whatchu just the visiting kind, huh?" He tilted his head to the side, his mouth tight. "You like them sick and shut-in visiting women from church, huh? Whatchu want, a cookie?"

"I want to know why you picked Marcus."

"Oh, 'cause I'm, like, 'troubled,' right," he made air quotes. "My lawyer talked 'bout that shit, getting sympathy from court or some shit." Shiloh sat forward and propped his elbows on the table. "How come you never come before? If I need sympathy, where you been? You take up for that fat-ass punk. He got people. Didn't nobody care 'bout me. Didn't nobody come for me." The boy blinked fast. He might cry.

Dixon's hand on the table, twitching.

Shiloh pulled back, a loud guffaw. "Bitch, you so easy. Ha! Now you all hurt. I ain't crying to you 'bout my life. Ain't that what Fat Ass did? He a whining little somabitch anyway. You want me to say I'm sorry 'bout that punk-ass? He died 'cause he weak. I ain't did that."

Dixon's legs bouncing restless under the table, he snapped. "You know, you may not see daylight again for the rest of your natural life." He was exaggerating, but he wanted to hit a chord.

Shiloh's expression registered fear before closing, hunkering down into a scowl. "I could take you wit' me. Y'know that?"

Dixon leaned forward, gave a relieved laugh: there it was. "I tried to stop you from beating the kid you are now accused of murdering. Who's going to listen to you?"

"Oh, I got my boys ready to say what they seen. You beat on me and I ain't do shit to you. I could take you down, man. I could have your job. Don't matter I'm in here. You know what I can do to you?" The boy's smile was wide, sadistic.

Dixon's blood rose. He spit out, "I killed my brother. I live with that every motherfucking day. Now, what do you think *you* can do to me?"

Shiloh glared. "Don't take me for no bitch." He studied Dixon just a minute, then pronounced, "I dismiss you." He flicked his hand, got up, and signaled to the guard.

Outside the detention center, Dixon sat a long time in his car, hands clasped tight in front of him. Of all the stupid things he had done lately, his visit to Shiloh was a high point. Had Dixon expected a scared boy begging for salvation? Truth was, he hadn't known what to expect. Truth: Shiloh was outside of Dixon's lane, a kid already distinguishing himself through his crimes. That's what he could never admit to Pamela, who had badgered him not to pass off the harder cases but to keep them and earn more money. He didn't want unsolvable trouble.

Frankly, he didn't have the imagination for it. He knew he could never comprehend, for instance, what it had taken for Marcus to stand at the bus stop each morning and afternoon, hunted, peering over his shoulder for no-end-in-sight trouble. Real trouble, which neither he nor Nate could fathom: Before the climb, when they and their teammates sat warm, snug, and eager in a conference room, Clive had shown them a photo of the South Col with a jagged red line imprinted above 26,000 feet: *Death Zone.* Every moment at that altitude, Clive admonished them, there was a little death, the body consuming itself from lack of oxygen. Hadn't Dixon whispered to Nate, "We got this!"

"And that's what makes you dangerous," that climber Jett had said to him in the Kathmandu bar. Dixon and Nate had manufactured their strife, that was so clear to him now. As if they had thought themselves immune to everyday trouble. They had forgotten the world and their vulnerable place in it: only guppies. Wouldn't Shiloh have been able to tell them: somebody always gettin' got.

That night, Dixon wandered his house. A bit out of his head, foggy and giddy and heartbroken. Nate's face before him, covered in ice crystals shimmering in the light. He was made of diamonds, he was hard rock, and Dixon's own voice replayed: *I killed my brother.* God, how had he let it happen?

# III.

# CHAPTER

## 16

*April 2011, Mount Everest*

Mornings on Everest, his waking disorientation replaced with a flutter in his stomach, Dixon nudged Nate awake, and the two put on jackets and shoes and squatted in the opening of their tent. The blush of sun slid across the face of the mountain, turning the snow rosy. The brothers watched in awe as if morning had never come to them before.

On climbing days, they pulled on layers of clothing, down climbing suits, inner and outer boots. They stepped into harnesses and fastened waist belts, careful to double the belt through its buckle to lock it. Dixon kept a quiet eye out for Nate so he didn't forget that last step, which could mean a slip of the harness followed by a sudden fall from the mountain. They strapped on crampons and head gear and goggles. Pemba and Angkaji checked them over like attentive parents, and the four men set out across a landscape as foreign and thrilling and foreboding as the moon.

Dixon and Nate had always understood they would climb this mountain more than once, spending weeks going up and down, ever higher, to get acclimatized to the altitude. All this before one final, breathtaking aim at the summit. They were ready for the routine. Dixon believed he understood patience, the sensual buzz of his thighs as he held himself suspended. *Ready. Set.* All this familiar ground. But in the long stretches between the smaller climbs, the dullness of suspended time required that he relax. In that waiting, doubt crept in.

Just above Base Camp in the Khumbu Icefall, where they ascended walls of ice on ropes affixed to the glacier, doubt bloomed in him; that is, his doubts about Nate. It was on their second acclimatizing journey up through the icefall to Camp 2 at 21,000 feet. In thinning air, under the sharpening pressure of a headache, Dixon paused to catch his breath after every step. Nate, who had much less trouble with the altitude, fell in beside him and mimicked his stops and starts. "We're our own drill team," he teased about their precision.

As he crossed over a makeshift bridge of aluminum ladders, Dixon remembered what his sherpa Pemba had told him: *One step, one step, one step, all the way across.*

Once he reached the other side, he turned back toward his brother, who bounded onto the ladder then became fretful, testing a rung and pulling back before committing to a step. Why the fuck did Nate have to confess he'd chickened out years ago on his first climb? Dixon held the edges of the ladder on his side of the crevasse as if that would secure his brother.

Nate's foot missed a rung on a ladder and he wobbled, leg hanging out to the side as he bobbled in the air an interminable time, then his legs seemed to give out and he dropped onto his knees, the ladder bouncing beneath him. "Shit!" he called. His hands gripped hard to the safety lines on either side of him alongside the ladder's rungs. Dixon sprang toward his brother. Clive grabbed Dixon around the waist and nearly slung him backward. "No! He's harnessed, he won't fall. Hear me, Nate? You won't fall."

Nate panted on all fours. His sherpa Angkaji called instructions to him. Pemba, who stood beside Dixon on the far side of the ladder, gave his approval at his brother's directions. "That is right, brudda, good, good."

Nate crawled forward, one hand, one knee, one hand, one knee across the ladder. Dixon's breath came in shallow pants until his brother tumbled onto the icy snow at his feet, breathing hard with terror. Dixon pulled him to his feet and embraced him, their down suits a hard distance between them. "Shit," Nate mumbled, "shit."

Dixon swallowed as hard as he could, but he couldn't keep it down. "You have to concentrate! You can't blank out for one goddamn minute."

"All right, all right," Nate said weakly.

―――――

THE BEST PART OF THE CLIMB WAS DIGGING HIS FEET INTO THE snowy ribs of the mountain. Each step was suffering then proving you could triumph. The wind a guttural bluster in his ears, Dixon's heart pounded in the crunch of his icy steps, pain bloomed behind his eyes. His body propelled him—he believed it would—his breathing labored and loud. Even amid his group, a thicket of climbers trudging in a loose pack, his was a singular experience.

He thought again of those guys back at his job, the ones whispering "ego" about him. He had turned that response around on its axis and decided it was not his truth. He understood the awful

mystery of this mountain. His stomach lurched. He had had diarrhea off and on since the trek to Base Camp. His lungs burned so
that he had to stop every few steps to take hard-fought breaths.
His leg muscles cramped at night. This was not ego. It burned off
in the fire of misery, a refiner's fire purifying him for his journey.
Whatever bragging rights he garnered were hard-earned.

The ice boulders teetering above him loomed sometimes as
large as houses. The sheer glassy beauty of ice surrounded him,
standing firm as brick. He trekked across the icy face of the
Khumbu, lost in the stretch and grip of his thigh muscles, attend-
ing to each tendon, each muscle alive as he climbed, one step, one
step, one step.

Nate trudged beside him, keeping pace.

"How's your head?" Dixon asked.

"Hurts," Nate answered, "not as bad as I thought, though."

Dixon's head felt like an axe had settled somewhere in his
skull, bearing in slow and sharp. Nate studied his snowy footsteps.
Dixon fell slightly behind. He glanced at the random ice blocks
nearby, the tufts of dingy snow along the path created by their
boots. He noticed something. A stick maybe.

Clive, their guide, caught up to Dixon. "Ice moves every day,
opens up like a crypt. Sometimes there are shoes, equipment. This
looks like old bone."

"Bone? Human?"

"Don't think about it. You'll see worse." Clive passed him,
waving his hand for Dixon to come along, but Dixon stood transfixed. The bone was short and ivory colored. It looked so small. A
finger, maybe?

"You okay?" Nate returned for him.

"Look."

"What?"

"Bone."

"Jesus. Why would you show me that?" Nate pulled away. Dixon thought his brother looked haunted.

***

ONE MORNING BETWEEN CLIMBS, DIXON LOUNGED IN FRONT OF his tent, listening to the ever-present shifting of the glacier. Around him men in flannel shirts and jeans like Marlboro Man ads stalked quietly between villages. Jocks in rugby shirts and well-worn hiking boots tossed a frisbee. A group of sherpas had a snowball fight. A guy juggled oranges, a small group puffed on some weed. Litter punctuated the pathways around camp or stood in tall pyramids held together by netting. Dixon was lost in the sights when Lena appeared. A tight expression on her face, she was clearly displeased. She bent down quietly gathering trash around her. She mumbled something that might have been Russian, then she said something so sharply it had to have been a swear.

"What language is that?" Dixon asked.

"Mostly Bulgarian. A little Russian," she grumbled, grabbing a discarded tin can. She sucked her teeth before looking at Dixon, a scowl, then a flash of smile. "Then Catalan, the best swear words," she confided. She glanced around at the tents, the swarms of people, the small, teeming city of Base Camp. "It's too much here, yes? This is not the mountain. Come, come. Get your brother." They found Nate lounging in the sun behind the tent. Lena instructed him and Dixon to gather their rucksacks and get ready for a hike. Dixon grabbed his lightest pack then paused, thought about it, and added an emergency kit before he put on his hiking boots.

Lena would lead the two men toward Pumori, she said, the

mountain where she was camped. "Is less crowded," she explained. Pumori was about a two-hour hike away, she told them. Dixon hesitated. "Let me run this by Clive," he said, and Nate's expression was so knowing that Dixon could hear his thoughts: *Ah, Dixon, doing the right thing.*

"Cool. That's a good conditioning hike," Clive responded. "Lots of climbers do that while they acclimatize. Good idea. Take plenty of water. Don't stay out too late, guys."

The three set out on their hike. They walked in silence for half an hour, the din of Base Camp receding. Lena led the way, Nate following close behind with Dixon pulling up the rear. He felt decidedly adolescent, a little sullen, watching the backs of their heads, the brief intentional veering into each other, the furtive touch of their bodies, the small jokes between them, Lena's laugh piercing the air. Maybe he should have stayed at Base Camp.

They fell into their individual rhythms as they trekked to Pumori, ascending about 1,000 feet above Everest's Base Camp. At least there was no real climbing, which made this trek a lot like ascending Kilimanjaro. *A big hike up a cold hill*, Jett had chided Dixon about climbing Kili. God, he didn't want to run into Jett again. He considered asking Lena if they would, then he thought: Of course! Because wasn't that where they were headed, to her base camp site with that team? "Shit," he said aloud.

"What, you are tired, Dixon? But this is nothing," Lena responded. She slipped back to him and tucked her arm under his, watched him for a few steps. "Ah, but you are fine. What do you complain about?"

"Nothing," he said.

Her eyes soft, amused. A dewy ring of sweat outlined her temples and widow's peak.

"Ah, just your thoughts, then," she said, squeezed his arm lightly, then bounded back to the front of their trio.

Pumori was a dome-shaped mountain of shale and dark boulders with glacial ice gleaming from its ridges. Its peak resembled a small nondescript rise, not quite a majestic mountain summit. Base Camp did not seem so different from Everest: the same rocky, dusty landscape, full of tents and people and their attendant noise. Dixon wondered what in the world Lena was thinking. Did she just want to lure them away? Was this Nate's idea after all? Well, there were fewer people here, he would concede that, a village rather than the city that was Everest Base Camp. Lena beckoned them to a rise that led to a wide cliff about five hundred feet up. "Can you do this?" she asked first, then answered her own question: "You can do. Follow me, up, yes?" The brothers looked at each other, incredulous. They did not have gear or crampons. Nate protested. Lena shrugged. "Is bare rock climbing to there. You know how?"

"Not really. Well, no," he said, and Dixon echoed that.

Lena smiled, a bright flash that nearly staggered Dixon. "I forget about you two. Okay, we do this." She produced rope and harnesses and carabiners from her large rucksack, sorting through and talking to herself about each one. The brothers exchanged bewildered then wary looks. Dixon felt young before her, inexperienced: a toddler awaiting his snowsuit and boots. Lena brought the gear to them. "We tie together, we belay. No sherpa, no fixed lines. We climb for real. Is just a short way up," she said. "Dixon, Nate, then me at the first. We all trust each other, okay?" Lena started up the mountain. "See where I go? You go, too." Her hands and feet wide, a firm touch, a testing of each rock's stability, and then she gripped with certainty. What appeared before them was a clear stairway up this slight bit of mountain, and it was hard not to imagine that Lena had created this magic. They climbed easily as they got a feel for the surfaces. The gray-streaked pieces were slickest, the ones that shimmered of silica were grittiest and easier to hold. They came to know the mountain.

At the top of the climb, they sat about eye level to the bottom of Everest's Khumbu Icefall, just visible if they leaned all the way out.

"Hey, mates! You come here for refuge from the big girl?" Jett, his English accent booming, waved to them from the end of the ledge. Beau and RedCurl sat beside him in front of their tent. Dixon was struck by the men's bigness—there was no other word for their visceral appetite for the world. The kind of men who jumped into the stream, then worried about whether they could swim. The world, they were sure, would accommodate them. Dixon heard his parents' voices echo through him, *Be careful, watch yourself, no foolishness now, you hear? Keep your eyes out for trouble. We can't let our guard down for a minute.* It really was miraculous that he and Nate were here on this mountain. Dixon sat up straighter.

The mountain men and the brothers exchanged pleasantries. Beau said, "Lena has a thing for newbies. She's like those old men who sniff babies' heads to steal their youth. She wants to watch you break your cherry on the mountain." He laughed.

"Okay, enough," Lena pronounced. "I bring them here for the peace of it." Lena shooed the others away. She and Dixon and Nate sat facing the slope of valley and jagged outcroppings before them.

"What do you guys do up here while you wait?" Nate asked.

Lena leaned into him. "We are with the mountain." She sat back, one leg folded under her, the other knee raised. A frown crossed Nate's face quickly, but the two men sat quietly. It was just after noon, the sun high and clear. "Do you hear her?" Lena asked. "Listen."

Dixon strained to hear. The wind exhaled a steady breath past his ears. The chatter of humans buzzed nearby. Restless, he shifted his legs, stretched his back. Lena placed a hand on his knee and pressed down to settle him. He summoned patience. Nate sat with legs stretched out in front of him, hands folded, clearly daydreaming. Lena nodded her encouragement to Dixon, and he redoubled his efforts toward stillness. The sun moved slowly across the sky, the valley below them fell away in concentric circles of rock and earth. Birds swooped and dove below them. He heard it. Something like a trickle of water, then a flowing gurgle, deep and clear and liquid, the mountain's voice. He took in a quick breath and when his eyes met Lena's, she gave a wide grin. She squeezed his knee, two short bursts. The sound a soft movement, he spread his hands wide on the rock below him, and he could feel it, he could swear, the current inside.

"Water?" he whispered.

"Yes, deep inside some of the caves. Mostly, though, it is the spirit."

Nate got up, dusted off his pants. "Need to stretch." He wandered over to Jett and Beau and RedCurl, who reclined in lounge chairs in front of their small tent. Nate squatted down near them.

"This is why we come, Dixon. Not just to get to the top. It is to be with her."

"Yes."

Communing, the mountain calling to him, what opened in Dixon was a swirling pool of heat. He stared at Lena, her beautiful olive skin, her capable hands. "Tell me," he asked softly. "Why Nate? Why not me?"

She folded both legs up, her arms wrapping around her knees. "He knows this with me is a small moment. But you, you would want to marry me." She laughed. "When I say goodbye to you, your heart will break. Your brother, he will kiss my hand, say I am beautiful, and wave goodbye. He will remember. But you, you will suffer."

His face burning, he stared down at the rock.

She leaned her face close to his, her hair falling across his cheek. "Don't break your heart, Dixon," she said.

Nate returned and sat on the other side of Lena. "So, you guys are heading up in a couple days?"

"That's right. Time to get a move on," she said.

"We're waiting for our window."

"Umm hmm," she said, as if she knew something they didn't. "I will come see you when I come down. Look." She pointed toward the sun, bright and orange. "You should get back, and I should get some rest. Tomorrow!" She raised her hands in a mock cheer. She turned to Nate, placed both hands on his cheeks, and kissed him hard and wide on the mouth. She met his eyes then rested her forehead against his. Dixon couldn't look away. He should. He should. She turned to Dixon, cupped his cheeks, her hands gritty and surprisingly warm, and kissed him, mouth closed, lips pressed against his. She set his lips to tingling. She lay her cheek against his, then pulled away.

"Here is how to go," she said, pointing to the left of where they had climbed. A ladder rested against the rock, lashed in with rope and screws. "Someone cheated." She pursed her lips. "But you can use now. I didn't want to make it too easy at first," she said, laughing. She waved and headed for her teammates.

Dixon and Nate did not speak on the trek back, each lost in his own universe.

---

THEY SPENT SEVERAL NIGHTS AT CAMP 2 AT THE BASE OF THE Lhotse Face, 21,000 feet above sea level but more than 8,000 feet shy of the summit. On this plateau at the waist of a glacier, more than one hundred tents full of men engaged in full-on suffering. And each of them was alone. Dixon lay exhausted, aching, in his team's tent. Wind slapped and scraped at the sides of the tent. All of them coughed, but none so violently as Cavit, the freckle-faced banker. Late into the second night, Cavit's coughing rose to a crescendo and then he cried out. Clive unzipped his sleeping bag and crawled to Cavit. The sound of rustling clothing was followed by Cavit's cry again, louder this time. "Broke a rib, I think," he said quietly, and Clive responded, "It happens. We'll send you down in the morning." Throughout the sleepless night, Cavit's moans punctuated their solitude. Dixon turned toward his brother and found him sitting up, arms tight around his knees, rocking. "Feel so naked. Like I'm missing a skin. Every mistake I ever made, playing through my head. That's what it does, doesn't it? This place?" Nate's eyes glowing wet.

Dixon recalled Nate swaying precariously over the crevasse in Khumbu. The image pounded along behind his eyes. "We don't have to do this. We can go," he said and without thinking, he turned his face in the direction of the mountain, as if its moonlit body beckoned through the wall of the tent.

"Just quit? That how you do things?" Nate said quietly. After a long while he said, "I'm a man who spent most of his life figuring out how to hit it and quit. Didn't Pamela complain to you all those years about your no-count brother? 'What is he this time? First, he's a banker. Then, he opens a health-food store. Then a data company. Now, what?'"

"Since when did I let somebody talk bad about you?"

"Never," Nate said, and sadness ebbed in his voice.

The next morning, Nate was restless, pacing, his hands dug deep into his pockets. Dixon called to him. "Hey, come with me." They hiked away from the center of camp, up along a slight rise of rocks overlooking it all. "Listen," Dixon commanded.

"What?"

"Lena taught me how to hear the mountain. It helps, man, it gives you a bond with her." Dixon described the sound, how it lived just beneath the rumble they were used to. They listened, three minutes, five.

Nate said, "You sure you didn't just hear what Lena wanted you to?" He laughed. "It's not real, you know, me and her. We're just . . ." He shrugged. "This is a hard place, you know? Listen, I know you're impatient but basically, you can handle the suffering. For me, it's just lonely, you know, in some deep, deep—" he trailed off. "It wasn't the ladder that tripped me up, it was the crevasse, all that emptiness down there, you know?"

Dixon shrugged. The crevasse had not seemed empty to him, but fully, unknowably populated.

"It startled me." His look earnest. "I wasn't prepared for that."

Dixon struggled for something to say. "I think, I think that's what the mountain's supposed to fill, see? Remember, that was your idea from the beginning. And I think that's what those alpinists were trying to tell us, so if we think like them—"

"Ah, Dixon, man, we aren't alpinists. We're clients. Don't kid yourself. We'll never be like them."

"Why not? They've got skills? So what, we trained. We know what we're doing! We're doing it right!" He hadn't realized he'd stood up.

Nate gazed up. "That's not what makes them alpinists." Dixon's face registered alarm. "That you don't know that is why you're not one."

AS THEY CLIMBED TOWARD CAMP 3 FOR THE FIRST TIME, THEY fought fatigue from using crampons on ice and rock. The hedge fund manager turned his feet too far inward as he walked so that his crampons ripped his down suit, which exhaled tufts of down like steam. On the Lhotse Face, that sheer, slick wall they ascended on a single rope, pulling themselves up by mechanical ascender, the hedge fund manager made painstakingly slow progress, unsure how to use his crampons during ascent. Dixon and Nate pressed against each other, rocking back and forth to keep blood flowing at 23,000 feet. Dixon recalled all their practice to avoid just this foolishness. Nate read his mind and said, "I'm grateful," his hand grasping Dixon's arm and lingering, the whole of their lives rushing between them.

Moving again, finally, they ascended the Face, and Dixon concentrated to keep a steady, if slow, rhythm. Plant the ice axe, kick into the ice with the toes of the crampons, pull up the body, ascend, rest. He panted in labored breaths and blew out steam like an ox. The rhythm sustained him. The air shot cold and dry up the nostrils, slicing into the skull and spreading wide and tight. His throat so dry he lost his voice. There had been so little air for so long. He had imagined that without oxygen he would feel light, but his body felt weighted even though he was thin, thin. Already a lean man, he had lost ten pounds in just a month on the mountain.

Camp 3 was a fresh hell with a staggering eye-level view of Himalayan peaks. The camp rested on a narrow ledge of onyx and snow that slanted downward, the pitch so steep that their tents had to be tied down and they had to remain attached to safety lines even when sleeping. Terrible gusts stole breath. Dixon was astounded by the amount of effort everything required: peeing, eating. Even walking around camp, he became nauseated but was too dehydrated to do more than dry-heave.

Dixon, Nate, and half of their teammates crowded into one big tent. At night, terrorized by the ballsy winds, they hunkered inside their sleeping bags and cradled the supplies that needed to stay unfrozen—gloves, inner boots, water bottles, cameras—an odd comfort in the physicality of inanimate things. Dixon and Nate lay side by side staring at each other, much as they had done as boys during particularly violent thunderstorms, alert and tethered.

In the airless hell inside the tent, the hair-curling smells of sweat and pee and shit and vomit merged into a low, stinging cloud. They could live in a low-lying equilibrium unless someone turned over or spilled a near-full pee bottle or simply opened a garment releasing a fresh blast of body odor that sharpened the axis of a headache. They would all release low groans and turn away helpless.

Worse, there was a relentlessness about being dirty here that exceeded anything he had ever experienced. His most meticulous habit had been to keep his nails clean. Pamela had been adamant: A man who tends to his hands can be trusted to tend to his touch. He got it. This was about sex. An intimate memory: Pamela filing his nails, rubbing lotion on his hands. It jarred him now that his nails were so caked with dirt, his cuticles ragged, puffy, and cracked. One morning, Dixon sat outside his tent, taking in the sun. "Filthy," he mumbled as he examined his hands. Another climber walking past said, "A delicate little thing, aren't you?"

"What was that?" Dixon's anger quickened. He stood up and towered over the other man. The stranger did a double take before his eyebrows raised, his chin squaring off. Neither man moved. Dixon would be damned if he'd blink first.

Nate approached cautiously along the narrow, flat perch of their camp. "Making friends?" he said and slid in easily beside his brother.

The mountain man said finally, "Naw, my friends can take a joke," and strolled away.

Nate sat down, and Dixon sank beside him. "Don't even know what that was about." Dixon scratched his cheek.

"Thin air. Makes you crazy," Nate rasped.

That night, as Dixon lay sleepless in his tent, Nate bent over in a torrent of dry hacking, his arms across his stomach as a brace. Dixon bent down alongside him as if that somehow would help. Long minutes until Nate calmed.

"What's that about, the cough?" Dixon pointed to Nate's throat as if the cough could be plucked off.

Nate gasped. "Must be the Khumbu Cough. Almost inevitable, they say." He swept a hand around, and like an illuminating wand it made all the coughing and groaning around them audible to Dixon. Half of their tentmates coughed. At least it wasn't a wet cough, that sure sign of congested lungs. The kind of thing that might signal edema and send you home. Or kill you. Dixon prepared tea for Nate from melted snow, then nudged him to drink it. Hot tea, a steaming bowl of water with a dollop of Vicks plopped into the center, a towel tented over his head. Like when they were kids. It calmed Nate's cough and soothed Dixon, too: he had fixed things.

———

THE BLAST LIKE DYNAMITE SHATTERED AN ORDINARY DAY OF cold and suffering at Camp 3. The ground rumbled beneath them. Dixon rose inside his tent and planted both feet on the ground as if that would secure him. Nate jumped up beside him.

Dixon peered out of his tent to see a deluge of snow and ice plummet just west of camp. Boulders of ice flew around them, flattening tents, puncturing oxygen bottles. After several long seconds, the ground settled. It was not their first avalanche—they happened daily—but this one had come closest to landing on top of them. The roaring petered out, replaced by a set of loud cries. People running, equipment rolling loose. A few feet ahead, several sherpas and guides gathered around a body, arms splayed out across the snow. His heart seized before Nate's hand landed on his shoulder and he relaxed: his brother was beside him, safe. Luke bounded toward them, his eyes wide. "He didn't see it coming." Reg came into view, lying in the snow: an arm, a shoulder, his mouth wide open, and finally his knee bent, his shin bone poking stark and jagged through his skin.

"Christ!" Nate said.

"Ice boulder. Took him down like a bowling ball," Luke explained.

"Jesus Christ," Nate repeated, an entreaty, and the three men stood helpless at the tent door under the blare of sun, in the relentless wind, the glacier on which they stood moaning and cracking.

Dixon glanced around camp. Reg was not the only victim. Their camp had become a triage unit. Clusters of injured people lay scattered around them in small, tight bands like the one surrounding Reg. Medics darted back and forth between groups, assessing injuries. Dixon stood outside his tent on the edge of all this, unsure what to do, balling his hands into fists and releasing them over and over. A dazed man cradling his arm staggered past, his clothing white with snow. Another was rushed to a tent on a cot-turned-stretcher. At least no one was inside the two flattened tents, but they proved a chilling carnage, their silver tent poles bent and broken, splayed out on the snow in a tangle of blue polyurethane sheeting. Cans of food spilled from the split mouth of a broken tent, a different kind of litter than he was used to seeing. Not trash but useful things, necessary things: a spilled bag of ground coffee, a flattened urinal cup, a lover's photograph dog-eared and cherished. Things that reminded Dixon of home, of solid earth, the certainty of his life pulling away from him.

Medics shouted into cell phones to doctors down below at Base Camp, getting instructions to treat the wounded. Dixon watched as two medics sedated Reg, whose eyes rolled back into his head, his moaning a low exhale, and then the medics doused his broken leg with Betadine before binding it tightly in bandages. Reg's body shuddered. He called, "No, no, I can't miss her again." The medics made fast work of splinting Reg's leg before carrying him to the team tent. Reg, semi-conscious, twisted his head back and forth against the pain. Dixon dropped to his knees beside him. He deliberately did not think of bad omens.

Luke and Nate joined Dixon, and the three men guarded Reg. Snowdrift blew through the tent flap and danced around them, a light dusting from the churned-up mountain. Soon, the wind began to claw at the tent, and spiderwebs of ice multiplied along its skin. The men shivered in the cold. Their bodies ached. They sat on their haunches, hovering over Reg in his morphine-induced sleep.

"This is horrible," Luke whispered. "This is unbelievable." His voice echoing Dixon's own thoughts, Luke rocked down and up, deeper, sharper each time, his voice keening. "What are we doing here? God in heaven, what have we done?"

During the sleepless night's descent into suffering, Dixon, Nate, and Luke took turns beside Reg. It had been more dangerous to move Reg, the path back down the mountain needing to be checked by the sherpas first, than to keep him at Camp 3 overnight. The team medic, a grave-looking young man with a Fu Manchu mustache, kept Reg sedated. Regardless, Reg would rouse and wag his head back and forth in the night, his words clear even through the haze of the oxygen mask, "So close, so close," yearning for his mountain, his voice like a dagger to Dixon. He or Luke or Nate might offer their hand to Reg, placing it inside his and letting Reg squeeze out his frustration before he fell unconscious again. A cold, desolate night, the wind a growl stalking the tent, punctuated by a shake of its sides. Dixon lay awake, feeling for the first time like prey.

First thing in the morning, Clive finalized arrangements to have Reg sent down the mountain. Clive and the young medic gathered sherpas to secure Reg on a stretcher. "Can't we help?" Dixon and Luke asked. "Just keep him calm, distracted. Save your strength," Clive replied. Reg's eyes shut tight, he was clearly awake and steeling himself.

Pemba, who held seniority throughout the camp, gave the

sherpas instructions for ensuring Reg was secured. "Not to worry, Dixon," he said very softly, using Dixon's name for the first time. "We will take care with your friend. Is very sad, very sad, and everything, but he will recover. You will move on, yes?" His voice consoling and encouraging in a fatherly way. He gave Dixon two "buck up there" pats, the kind Dixon might have given his boys at school. He wondered if it felt more consoling to his kids than it did to him just then. For the first time, he doubted it.

Dixon, Nate, and Luke made sure Reg was bundled in his warmest clothing. As Dixon tucked a fleece blanket around Reg's shoulders, Reg opened his eyes, looking Dixon dead on, his look plaintive, made all the more desperate by the cumbersome oxygen mask scrunching up his face. What was he trying to say? A warning against the mountain? A message for her: *I will come for you again?* Before Dixon could decipher, four sherpas hoisted Reg's stretcher and carried him away. Reg moaned. Not from pain, Dixon was certain. From the loss of her, his mountain—again. The fear of that fate rumbled through Dixon's gut: he would not be Reg. He would not be left behind.

The descent to Camp 2 the next day came as a partial reprieve. The wind was quiet enough to allow sleep. In the blur of his teammates' earphones spilling their sound and DVD players that cast a bluish glow, each man on his own moon, Dixon said to Nate, "Just want this over with. I just want to get there and get it done."

Nate snorted a laugh and propped his arms behind his head. "You never learned to enjoy the conquest."

Dixon cut an eye toward him.

"Only looks easy from the outside, but there's an art to it. Haven't you been watching me all these years?" He started to cough. He curled onto his side until he recovered.

Dixon brought Nate the water they had made from melted snow, watched as his brother drank, as he cleared his throat. "Listen, we're going down to Base Camp in the morning, you know. That cough should clear up. If it doesn't . . ."

"You have to just watch a woman first," Nate continued. "See what her style is." He swallowed, tried to breathe normally. "Gotta make her see you. Like, dancing with her, right? You put your arms around her shoulders, not her waist. See? That way she has to raise her head. Look at you. Into your eyes. Make that contact, don't turn away. Let her see you. Dance ends, you smile, thank her, back away, but keep your eyes on her. Because a woman wants to be seen." He coughed, then cleared his throat.

"If that cough doesn't clear up, Nate . . ."

"Now, she won't forget you. Even if she wants to. She knows you saw her, see, you didn't shy away. We're not gonna shy away." He sat up, eye to eye with Dixon. "We're gonna wait for good weather, and we're coming strong for her, this mountain, 'Hey Goddess, we're here.' Just remember what I told you, bro, a woman likes to be swept away some time."

**CHAPTER**

17

*May 2011, Mount Everest*

At last, after six weeks, they were officially ready to summit. All the acclimatizing runs completed, the teams held a rowdy party at Base Camp with dancing, music, alcohol, a wild release of exuberance, a push against fear. Dixon and Nate danced late into the night, ignoring their aching toes and savoring their intermediate triumph. Now all they could do was rest and await clear weather for the summit push. Wait and dream, a collective, solitary endeavor. Dixon had stopped calling home, resorting instead to generic "the weather is fine, all is well" missives. He had come to guard his mountain life jealously despite its brutality. Dixon and his fellow climbers continued to struggle to eat and sleep. Doug, a teammate and first-time climber, sat in the sleeping tent their second night back at Base Camp, head in his hands. Pemba said to him, "Bad sign. Means to hold up unhappiness." In the morning, when Dixon awakened, he found Doug quietly packing his duffel bags. He turned to Dixon, shook his head, and started down the trail toward Lukla and the flight to Kathmandu.

Clive discussed their reduced numbers at dinner. Not only Doug and Cavit the banker, who had been evacuated earlier with high-altitude pulmonary edema on the second acclimatization run, but also another old-time climber, Phil, had gone. And of course there was Reg. Clive said, "No judgment about anyone who leaves. Everyone has to do what's right for them." Dixon turned that thought over and around.

Late in the afternoon, Kira called. "Daddy, are you done yet?" she asked. She sounded so much like the little girl she once was that he could nearly feel her sitting on his lap, throwing her arms around his neck, her sweat and breath seeping into his bones. She had heard of the avalanche.

"Please don't worry, sweetheart. I'll be home to you soon," he said.

"Dixon?" Pamela's voice called. "Please don't take any unnecessary risks."

Her voice left him flummoxed, a spin of surprise and gratitude.

"We're thinking of you and Nate constantly. Please be careful."

Nate laughed when Dixon told him about the call. "Well, damn, we must really be in the shit if 'Pamela, not Pam' is worried about us. Hell, maybe you shoulda climbed a few more mountains while you were married to that woman. She mighta appreciated what she had."

Two days and two commonplace Everest avalanches later, Clive parked himself in the communications tent, deciphering weather patterns and jet streams as if studying tea leaves. Dixon stared into the tent. His face furrowed, Clive examined the long sheets of dashes and darts like an EKG of the world. "Where's my damn climbing window?" he muttered. Dixon listened, his body goose-bumped. If the weather never broke, it would be over, no question. They could go home. He imagined the joy on Kira's face. But he knew: he would have to return to this mountain.

He was not in charge of himself. Nate saw it, he knew, and in a strange way it seemed to please Nate.

Dixon dug his toe into the gravel outside the communications tent, then he headed to Nate, who sat straddling a lounge chair near their sleeping tent. Across the camp, the prostitutes began to filter in. Young girls. Someone's daughters.

"So, you ready to head up tomorrow?" Nate asked. His eyes held firm to the small prostitute. Her long jet-black hair was swept to one side. She wore Uggs, a short denim skirt, and a flesh-colored T-shirt so tight you could see the outlines of ribs and nipples.

"Yep. We need *rest* tonight."

Nate said nothing but kept his eyes on the young girl. She walked toward Nate like a beacon.

"What're you looking at?" Dixon snapped.

"Same as you." Nate stretched out his legs. "Little girl lost."

"Who would pay a whore in the dirtiest goddamn place you've ever been?" His eyes dead on Nate. Anger, sudden and sharp, a knife slicing through him. Lena's kiss, teasing him, sweet and tender and without any passion for him whatsoever.

"I have no idea." The girl and her pimp approached, and Nate waved them away.

"Lena's up the mountain. You're on your own," he spit out.

"What're you talking about?"

Dixon's agitation rose. His throat clenched. "You lied to me. You said you climbed."

Nate pinched his nose, his face drawing in. "You're right. I should have come clean. I apologize. I was wrong. Cowardly." His face was eager. "But I'm ready this time, Dixon. You made me ready."

"Yeah, so you could come up here, and, and . . ." The white light of anger sparked across his vision.

Nate closed a magazine, folded his hands on top of it. His left brow arched.

"You've always done whatever you wanted. And you get away with it!"

Nate stared at him a long time. "How else you gonna be so holy, Dixon, if you don't have me? Only sins you've got to confess are mine."

"You made me want this!" Dixon shouted. He uncoiled like a spring, rising and kicking a chair before he headed off.

They kept a determined distance at dinner. The other climbers glanced at the space between them, but no one said a thing, and the meal tent descended into the monotonous clinks of forks on metal trays, occasional talk that petered out. Dixon thought they were really in silent avoidance of him and Nate because the brothers had disturbed some natural order. He walked a tightrope of danger, and the image appeared so clearly before him it took a minute to realize that image was Nate's conjuring: "You think you live so far above us," he had spat at Dixon so many times during their youth. Dixon remembered this: his mother in her seemingly benign introductions, lining up her boys as they squirmed in Sunday suits before the appraising eyes of church ladies or just the fucking corner store grocer. "This is my number one son," she would say, her hands caressing Nate's shoulders. "And this is my number two son," she would say, patting Dixon's shoulders, and he would bristle toward the irreversible positioning of birth. But on this mountain sculpted by desire, Dixon's hunger the stronger, he became number one son, and the idea beat in him.

———

AFTER CLIVE ANNOUNCED THAT THEY WOULD FINALLY HEAD for the summit at dawn, Dixon and Nate packed their gear, Dixon making sure Nate packed according to the list he had given him. He strained his neck to see whether Nate packed the correct climbing shoes—the lightweight ones for high on the mountain. Nate, aware of him, turned himself away. But it was too old a bargain between them, and eventually Nate gave in, shifting so Dixon could see he was doing the right thing.

In the yellow glow of their tent, Nate sat beside Dixon, sat down hard, giving in. "That guy I was, that you *thought* I was, I haven't been that guy for a long while. I was a kid then, Dixon." He shrugged. "Quiet as it's kept, I haven't dated anybody for about a year. Just how it goes."

"You've always got tales."

"Old tales." He stared at Dixon a long while. "'Cause you need 'em."

That answer left Dixon flustered, resisting it.

"I wasn't the only one who needed this trip. You're gonna climb fucking Mount Everest, man. It's like, it's like, earning that Superman badge you wear all the goddamn time."

Dixon let out an embarrassed laugh.

"What's so wrong with enjoying that? Huh? I mean, you do understand pleasure? You always seemed to fear it so much. Like,

like you thought if you gave in you could never stop. Like it might destroy you. You know how that always killed me, man? This mountain. I want this for you, Dixon. You deserve it."

———

LENA CALLED THEM AT BASE CAMP THAT NIGHT BEFORE THEY headed to the summit. Actually, she called Nate and they talked a long time, Dixon outside the communications tent watching Nate cradle the satellite phone. Then Nate motioned for Dixon. "She wants you," he said.

"Newbie, you are on your way now. Enjoy her. Listen, I want to tell you. You are strong. You have the, how you say in English . . ." She sucked her teeth and mumbled in another language. "The chops! That's it, the climbing chops! I see that in you."

"You think so?" It felt like an anointing, this recognition from a true alpinist.

"Yes, yes, but this is the danger. You must not get carried away with yourself. You have to let her have her way, Dixon. She will tell you if she wants you. If she doesn't want, you must turn back. Understand? It is important."

"Yes, I think I get it." He paused. "Did you tell him that, too?"

A soft laugh. "Yes, but I told you, he knows how to let go."

———

THE MISERY OF NAVIGATING THE KHUMBU ICEFALL PASSED UN-remarkably as they ascended for the last time. The ice yawned beneath them as they clattered once more across the ladders spanning the crevasses. By the time they reached the Western Cwm, the icy valley burgeoning with sun, Dixon realized the climb was indeed easier this time. He greeted his mountain, joyful in his suffering and endurance.

There was also comfort in the camaraderie between the two sets of brothers, Dixon and Nate, Pemba and Angkaji. They moved in concert, tucking into the mountain as they climbed, shoulders forward, one jagged line. Nate and Angkaji in front and Pemba and Dixon behind, then Pemba and Dixon might overtake the other two, that switch prompting teasing hand gestures, their breathing too labored for much discussion. Still, it was a lovely small universe, a nearly umbilical safety rope.

From Camp 1, they headed to Camp 2 to rest the first night, and then soldiered on to Camp 3, which was a bit like re-entering the landscape of a bad dream. Nate's cough resumed, leaving him winded. Clive sat beside Nate in their tent the evening after they reached Camp 3. "How's it going, partner? How bad is it?"

"Not as bad as last time. Nothing coming up when I cough," Nate said.

"I'm putting you on oxygen tonight. If the Os don't help, we'll have to have a conversation."

As they left Camp 3 the next day, they entered uncharted territory, moving toward their final camp before the summit. They climbed across Yellow Band, a dark patch of mustard-colored rock, slick and smooth as marble. Luke climbed beside Dixon. "Think I could dig out some rock to take home, eh?"

Dixon glanced at him. "You mean, carry something else, something that heavy? That's altitude talking."

Luke frowned and said, "Right, right," but he stared a long while at the veiny marble of the rock. "Won't fit in my rucksack."

The air below Camp 4 smelled of whiteness, of snow and ice, a brisk scent. The face of the moon must be this pure white, Dixon thought, its air must burn off like the snow that swept sideways from the rock. Icy white crystals rough as sand etched Dixon's goggles. As he passed through the snowfield of the Geneva Spur, the sun beat hot on him, making him sweat inside his down suit, while the wind chilled and jolted him, threatening to lift him like a kite. He gripped tight to the fixed ropes. One step, breathe. One step, breathe. His whole body the breath, the lungs, the beating in his ears.

At 26,300 feet, Camp 4 occupied a slim perch of desiccated rock, a bowl once underwater millions of years ago, now holding the fossils of mountain climbs. Oxygen bottles were strewn orange and red and yellow and blue across the slate-colored rock. Dixon could peer down across the sleek Lhotse Face. Beside him, the 7,000-foot drop to Tibet on one side, a 4,000-foot drop to the Western Cwm on the other. He perched on the tip of the mountain's finger.

Their tent was lashed to the mountain. Dixon and his teammates collapsed inside. At least now they could all begin supplemental oxygen. They dug through the pile of oxygen masks and tanks like starving children clawing at a meal. The mask felt awkward and clumsy, but even the faintest whiff of oxygen relaxed Dixon's shoulders, easing the sheer weight of his body. Nate gave him a thumbs-up.

They lay sleepless awaiting midnight when they would begin their final attack on the summit. Sleepless like men awaiting execution or reprieve. Nate and Dixon studied each other, fixing on each other's breath and movements, the small smooth scar above Dixon's right eyebrow, the chicken pox mark on Nate's left cheek, the familiar territory of their known worlds.

The team rose at midnight in the glow of their tent, amid the frightful chatter of the wind's teeth, and packed their gear, slipped on their crampons, and moved sluggishly toward the top of the world. Before they set out, Pemba and Angkaji hovered over Dixon and Nate, checking that their crampons were on properly, that their backpacks were balanced, that their harnesses were double-looped, that their oxygen tanks were set correctly. The sherpa brothers talked to each other in their usual shorthand, a language that required much bowing on Angkaji's part, although Pemba's voice was full of tenderness. Nate said to Dixon, "They look out for us like their own."

They began the twelve-hour ascent in darkness, each climber encased in down and fleece, goggles and oxygen mask, the small, tight arc of light cast by a headlamp. They shivered in the ungodly cold—it was unfathomable that they could be this cold and still alive.

Within a few hundred feet, they were slowed by a long queue of climbers waiting to ascend fixed ropes. Stalled, they watched other climbers struggle to the top of the ropes with the added encumbrance of an oxygen tank. Even the trained climbers moved slowly, but the untrained, those novice clients they had been warned about in the bar in Kathmandu, took nearly two hours to do what should have taken forty-five minutes.

The path widened briefly, and the few alpinists among them unclipped from the fixed ropes, anchored themselves to one another, and climbed, bypassing the stalled clients, then swung back onto the ropes above the traffic jams. What gorgeous madness! Dixon used to peel away from the pack as he ran, accelerating the body so easily, an exquisite engine. Now, instead, he waited in line, stamping his feet, pounding on his arms against the cold, waiting dutifully like the novice he was. Envy poured through him.

Finally, he ascended. As the moon hung bald and bright, Dixon traveled slow, hallucinatory along a rocky plateau of sharpened black rock. His head encircled by the sound of his own halting breaths, the steady hiss of the oxygen tank. Amid the long slope of stones, the brittle crest of the mountain, he kicked into ice and rock. In this new world, bodies began to appear. Curled on their sides in the snow, their frozen faces gray as old ice, icicles weeping from their cheeks. Another, and another, clothed, mid-climb, dead. Because they were above rescue here in the Death Zone. Dixon trudged past a chorten, a small pile of stones marking a grave. At least, he thought, something private in that death, some small dignity. He had known about the bodies—who had not heard? He had seen them from a distance farther down the mountain. But these were so close and indistinguishable from the living: the dead fully clothed in down suits, reclining. And he passed them by. He passed them, awaiting his own shame at that, but he felt only numbness as if the cold had burned away his soul. That these bodies around him were dead seemed not a far stretch. The dead, the living, on Everest there was less than a veil between them.

A patch of fresh snowfall seemed a stroke of luck since it was easier to climb into snow but more exhausting, plowing through virgin snow that hit him just below the knee. He punched in his ice axe, hoisted his leg and kicked into the snow, paused, held himself upright with one hand on the snowbank, dragged his body along, stepping, pausing, planting the ice axe, kicking in, rising, over and again, for hours. He was an astronaut tripping and tumbling across the face of a foreign planet.

Nate was falling behind. He stumbled, rested on his knees, his body shuddering as he coughed. Dixon slogged back to him. He bent over his brother, his gloved hand on Nate's back. He waited as

Nate rested. The cold radiated from Dixon's bones, rode up and out of him as if it fed the mountain air. "Do you need to go down?" Dixon's voice managed to rise above the wind. Nate rose, shook his head, gave a thumbs-up, and resumed the climb. Dixon stayed beside him.

"He will do better now," Pemba said, smiling at Dixon. The two sets of brothers stood together a moment, the sherpas fussing over Dixon and Nate's rucksacks, shifting and adjusting them. "Older brudda, we do not like to be behind." Pemba gave his customary giggle. Angkaji agreed and Pemba's voice rose with the encouragement. "See? My younger brudda knows. But it is the problem, and everything. One of us must be behind, you from your brudda, or me from my brudda."

"Older brudda has it good," Angkaji said, leaning in. "Is first in mudda's heart, but second son is for fadda, yes?" The sherpa brothers laughed conspiratorially.

"You've got a point," Nate said, but Dixon wasn't convinced. He shrugged.

"Is all right," Angkaji said to Dixon. "We get away with more. Fadda is on to first son. See through them like mudda cannot." Dixon could hear his father's constant mantra about Nate, *Boy, I've got work to do with you.*

Ascending again, the long spans of repetitive motion and short rests became meditative, and time moved quickly. Clive and the other climbers spread around them, each climber shadowed by a sherpa. Dixon's team had passed the most congested clump of climbers, those who had stalled from exhaustion or lack of preparedness. Clive kept a close eye on them, hanging back occasionally to spur them on. "Okay?" he mouthed and the brothers affirmed. "A little behind pace," he said, pointing to the celestial glow of headlamps from other climbers along the ridge behind them. "Don't want to get caught up in that mess."

Pushing along in the haze of rote motion, Nate sometimes veered too far right or left so that Angkaji had to pull tight on the safety rope and nudge him back to the center of the route. Nate's cough rattled through him regularly. About 5 a.m., they rested. "Almost halfway up," Dixon said to Nate, who tapped his watch. They had been climbing for five hours. About six more hours at this pace and they would reach the summit.

The sun began to rise. Nate tapped Dixon on the arm, motioned first toward the break along the horizon and then toward the ground. The brothers sat on their packs, waiting. Nate hooked his arm around Dixon's and leaned into him. The light spread as fingers across the mountain, reaching for them. Nate lowered his oxygen mask and croaked out, "This, this!" The sunlight lifted onto his face, Nate's face golden as the ripened sun fanned toward Dixon. When the sun reached him, he bowed, grateful. Pemba slapped at their arms. "Too much waiting," he said and motioned toward the climbers who trudged past.

In daylight now, they climbed for two more hours until they reached the open expanse of the Balcony, a wide bridge between mountain ridges. Dixon and Nate paused to take in the view above so much of the world, the slope of mountains, the curve of the atmosphere becoming visible. Pemba and Angkaji noted the brothers' nearly spent oxygen tanks. Pemba frowned and said, "Should be lasting till South Summit. You must slow down the breath." He and Angkaji helped the brothers switch to fresh tanks. That momentary absence of oxygen felt like a descent down a bottomless well. Dixon gulped and coughed. Nate waved his arms, panicked, his legs stiffening. "Breathe, Matthew Henson One, breathe,"

Angkaji said as he attached the tank to its hose. Nate inhaled and his body relaxed.

Beyond the Balcony, they fell into deep, thick snow, sinking sometimes up to their thighs. Poor Luke, so much shorter than Dixon, was often encased to his waist and squirming helplessly like a man in quicksand. Slow, hard going for a long time. At last, the snow receded and they were once again on hardpack and ice, the limbs of rock protruding around them. Dixon noticed how very mean the high reaches of the mountain had become, hard and craggy and steep. She had toughened herself, bolstering her resistance to him. Snow blew from her cliffs in waves. Snow slapped Dixon's cheeks, the gust of the wind so loud he felt dizzy.

Not far ahead along the sharp knife of rock that formed the upper edges of the mountain, the team was stopped once again by a crowd of climbers before the South Summit. Just beyond them lay the Hillary Step, the last real obstacle before the summit. In this way station before the South Summit, climbers negotiated slowly, kicking their crampons into the jagged rock and pulling themselves up along ropes. Exhausting work, especially after trudging uphill for more than seven hours, lugging oxygen tanks and gear. Dixon and Nate waited in the long line. The aching in Dixon's feet grew sharp, and he tried to flex his toes against it. The toe-warmer batteries must have died. He danced slowly in place to fight the cold. After forty-five minutes without any progress, two climbers from a British expedition turned around and headed back down the mountain. "This is certain death!" one of them said. They had actually left—Dixon couldn't get over it, and he kept waiting for them to scramble back to their place in line. A jolt of envy that they could so easily walk away. So close, so fucking close!

Nearly half an hour more into their wait in that infernal line,

Nate could no longer control his coughs. They came in long, gasping bursts every few minutes. "We're gonna get in trouble," Nate gasped. "Home late again."

Dixon didn't understand. "You mean Clive?"

Nate nodded.

Of course, Dixon thought, but they weren't yet at the turnaround time, where any climber could be turned back if it was too late to summit and get back down before dark, or if he was too ill, or if the guide thought he just couldn't make it. Dixon looked at his watch. There was time.

Nate shivered and fiddled with his oxygen mask, his suit, his goggles. Like he itched all over.

"What is it?" Dixon reached out to help Nate adjust his mask. "Better?"

Nate quaked. He doubled over with each cough. Clive made his way toward him. "You, I don't like your cough," he said and motioned to Pemba and Angkaji, who were urging the sherpas from another team to get their climbers moving faster. The two sherpas came over to convene with Clive.

"Dad's really mad," Nate gasped out. He propped his hands on his legs. He was bent over and breathing far too hard, even with the oxygen mask.

Dixon's thoughts felt mushy.

"But I did not know," Angkaji protested weakly.

"Is your job to know!" Pemba barked so that Angkaji bowed his head and folded his hands in front of him.

"You're done for, partner," Clive said to Nate. "Where's your meds?"

Dixon pointed to Nate's left pocket, to the hypodermic needles of nifedipine and dexamethasone he had placed there. See, they were prepared for this, Dixon reminded himself, *We are ready.* Clive gave Nate an injection.

"I am sorry, Matthew Henson Two," Pemba said, "but brudda must go down."

"It's that bad? So fast?" Dixon's chest tightened. "Oh God."

"He shiver, he cough. Must get him down from mountain."

Dixon broke a sweat down the center of his spine. He had never imagined doing this without his brother. "Nate?" He waded toward him. "Nate? You gotta go down, man. You hear me?"

"Home? Okay," Nate croaked. "C'mon."

*C'mon.* Dixon paused, alarm sparking in his chest.

"Before curfew. Let's. Go." He caught hold of Dixon's sleeve and began to tug.

Dixon struggled to catch his breath. They were so fucking close, two hours, maybe. He could hear her, he could taste the snow at the summit, sweet and icy. "I can't." He tapped at Nate's hand.

Nate stared at Dixon a long time, then tightened his grip and yanked. Dixon's feet slid easily across the ice toward Nate.

"No!" Panic surged in Dixon as he slid down the mountain. "Stop!" He tried to pry Nate's hand from his sleeve.

Nate latched on with the other hand. "We have to go home," he said.

An enervated slow-motion push and pull, each man winded but Nate alarmingly strong. He yanked at Dixon, Dixon yanked back, and they two-stepped across the snow, Nate with the upper hand, pulling Dixon down the incline, five, ten, fifteen feet. Leaving his mountain. His face turned from the summit, he saw the hordes heading up the slope with unimaginable speed, poised to replace him. Dread washed through him. The wind might be his own protest, knocking and howling as it did. Dixon snatched free with one arm and shoved against Nate, Dixon's feet sliding. It seemed one good leap and he would be down the mountain, his chance gone. Reg's anguished face flashed before him, Reg muttering as they took him away, "I can't lose her, I can't lose her." Dixon lifted his arm, bent his elbow, and jabbed it into Nate's shoulder, knocking him backward, Nate flailing with one hand still holding tight to Dixon so that Dixon staggered with him, a backward waltz until they both collapsed.

The two straining to breathe, lying in the snow, the weight of oxygen tanks making it impossible to get up. Angkaji and Pemba took so long to come. Dixon peered into Nate's face, his eyes wide, frightened. Dixon saw stars. The sherpas sat them up and checked their oxygen tanks, turning them up for a few moments, allowing Dixon and Nate to catch their breath, then adjusting them back down again.

Nate's face so frightened. "Will you leave me?"

Dixon pleaded, "It's for us!"

Nate's shoulders sank. He folded himself in.

The sherpas scooped the brothers under their arms and helped them stand. Pemba said emphatically, "Matthew Henson One, you must go down. You must go down." He turned to Dixon. "You must decide."

Dixon glanced toward Clive, who was engrossed in conversation on the walkie-talkie. "I'm sending them down now," Clive said loudly.

"You are strong, then you will go. You not sure? You go down with brudda."

Dixon did not move. He wasn't really leaving him, he wasn't. He was putting him in good care—see? Angkaji would care for him. It was just the same as if it were him, he thought, he was not abandoning his brother. He winced, the lie wild and bucking inside him.

"I will take care, Matthew Henson Two." Angkaji tapped Dixon's arm. "You must conquer your mountain." Angkaji turned Nate by the shoulder and pointed him down the path. Nate walked forward a few steps, turned back to Dixon. "What will Dad say?" Nate asked, and Angkaji reassured him, "Is all right." Nate reached out his hand to Dixon. "You're not coming?"

Dixon trembled. He wasn't abandoning him, he wasn't. He wasn't that kind of man.

"Come, come, I go with you," Angkaji urged, standing between Dixon and Nate. "I come." He began to walk Nate down again. This time when Nate stopped and turned back to Dixon, he waved, holding up his hand a long time.

Dixon sank onto his knees in the snow, panting.

"Too much breathe," Pemba chided and fiddled with Dixon's oxygen gauge.

"Deep breaths, partner, slow it down." Clive clasped Dixon's shoulder. "I know this isn't what you bargained on. You wanna go on? You wanna go with your brother? Your call."

On his knees, swaying in each gust of wind, Dixon watched Angkaji lead his brother back down the path, Nate listing to one side. Dixon felt the cool wire of fear. His body jerked toward Nate. How could he let go? That was exactly how it seemed: letting go of a rope that pulled fast and hard through his hands. Dixon grew lightheaded, dizzy. His brother stumbled down the path. Dixon's body lashed open, the wind beating hard against him, he examined his down suit. Was there a gash in the lining? The snow around him like down, clusters of it fleeing him and soon he would freeze in place, turn to stone. Do not look back like Lot's wife, or you will freeze, a block of ice. No, it was salt. A pillar of salt. A mound of snow. Nate growing smaller on his way down the mountain. He reached out his hand toward Nate's back, then pushed down on the snow to help himself stand. He told himself, I'll just get this done and get back to him. Won't be long now, won't be long.

CHAPTER

18

*May 9, 2011, Mount Everest: Summit Day*

Dixon and Pemba ascended the rope toward the South Summit. From there, the path to the top of the world became visible. Dixon's heart leapt. *I will make it.* It welled in his throat. He coughed a long, hard time until Clive glared at him. "You, too?"

"No," Dixon said with all the strength he could muster.

Up along a steep bulge of slate, across the cushioning bank of new snow, up and up, his ascent along the rope so steep that he rose almost perpendicular. Heady, spinning, there was only sky holding him up. The wind punched against him. It swiped at his feet. He might be plucked off the mountain in a sudden breath and become a speck dancing out into the sky. Above the South Summit, the world consisted only of mountaintops and cloud and steep drop-offs, a 10,000-foot drop into Tibet on one side or Nepal on the other. He swallowed against dizziness, dug his crampons into the rock, slid the jumar, and lifted himself. In this steepest part of the climb, he was tired, anxious, but he made steady, slow progress along the Hillary Step, the forty feet of vertical rock that lay between him and the top of the world.

He fixed on what was in front of him: a green pack, a red snow-suit, the body of yet another dead climber still fixed to old rope, dangling beside him. "'Yea, though I walk through the valley of the shadow of death, I will fear no evil,'" he chanted.

In the numbing cold, there was no body. No brother. No world. Only the yawning hunger that rose into breath. He had carried his brother all his life, and in these last vertical feet, on the knife edge of the world, he balanced solo.

Atop the Hillary Step, no competing peak remained, and Dixon already stood above all things. He traversed a series of hills, climbed beside wind-swept cornices of snow that lined the path to the summit, enchanted, glittering swoops and swirls gleaming in the sun. Pemba, just slightly in front of him, said, "One step, one step, almost there." They trudged up, down, Dixon's crampons squeaking on snow as if on Styrofoam. The path smoothed out and the snowy mound of the summit appeared about the size of a ta-bletop, its edges sloping slightly and its surface strewn with color-ful prayer flags and stuffed animals and photos.

There was nowhere left to climb. The summit felt sudden after so many hours of forward motion. Climbers milled about, jubilant, awed, a crowded, disorganized group. Individuals slipped impa-tiently past one another to get to the very tip of the mountain. Waves of photos and flags washed across Dixon's feet.

"For. Me." Dixon eked out and pulled off his oxygen mask, his breath a long pull from a dry lake, the feeling of rising suddenly from underwater into the staggering hand of gravity. He grabbed a slab of snow and icy rock from below his feet and shoved it into a pocket of his down suit.

The short, angled tip of the mountain rested beneath his feet. This was the feel of the top of the world. Number one son. He waited. For something. For his mother, his father. For God himself. Waited for exuberance. But the mountain dismissed him like an unwanted suitor, and that slight washed over him as a deepening chill. Shouldn't the world open itself to him here, shouldn't he be able to know the whole of earth? He saw its curvature, but its towns and rivers and oceans, its valleys and plains, its people were obscured, all its fine, dazzling detail too far removed. There were only the truncated tops of mountains, floating disembodied in a soup of cloud. There was nothing here that cared for him.

He was king of small perches, of rocky places.

A wide, expansive nothingness. He removed his glove and reached out his hand—*Nate, Nate*—and began to cry.

Pemba grabbed Dixon's hand. "Yes, it's happy, happy time," he said. "I take your picture." He removed the camera from Dixon's pack. "Want to give thumbs-up?" Dixon misunderstood. Instead, he held up his hand, a stop sign. Pemba asked, "Want to send email?" and fiddled with the phone screen. He called down to their team manager at Base Camp, "It is Pemba. Made it to top with Matthew Henson, and everything." A swell of cheering and congratulations, then a familiar voice on the line, "You did it!" Lena's voice rose through the throng at Base Camp.

It was 1:45 p.m. when Dixon began to descend. Clive and two other clients were just behind him. They were part of the last wave of summiters from their team that day, although a steady throng headed up to the top, behind schedule. Dixon became more aware of the cold, of the breathtaking height, of the waning supply of oxygen in his tank. He staggered toward a long, grumbling line of climbers trying to descend the Hillary Step. They waited, silent, single file, some of them sitting on their haunches and rocking slightly. Dixon had not felt his toes for so long. He noted it with dulled alarm. He thought he moved them, wriggling blood back into them, but could not be sure. Nearly an hour passed before Clive stormed to the top of the line and began to argue with another guide. "My guys are freezing here! What the fuck is the problem on this rope?" He returned shortly and motioned to Pemba. "Somebody below blocking the rope. We've gotta move him so we can climb down." After another half hour, Clive announced it was time to move. Down the haggard rope, into the sun's last blazing hours, Dixon's feet dug into rock that felt like bone, and the high-pitched call of wind at his back was nearly human. He slid toward a figure in a yellow snowsuit clipped into a length of old rope that dangled beside Dixon. Was he descending, ascending?

"Must keep going," Pemba told him. Dixon maneuvered past the man. Only when he was beside him did Dixon see his face, one eye swollen shut, his left cheek caked with blood, his body shuddering into unconsciousness. Dixon nearly lost his foothold. In the dulling afternoon light, as if the cold had restored him to malleable flesh, he saw the line between himself and this man was thin, faulty.

"Don't we do something?" he said to Pemba after they had descended the rope. "Can't we call someone?" Alpinists would do something.

"Nothing to be done. Too high up. We unclip him, move him later. But now, must move," Pemba said. "Get down to brudda. Yes, we go. Okay?"

"Nate."

JUST BELOW THE BALCONY, PEMBA, DIXON, AND CLIVE ENCOUN-
tered Nate and Angkaji creeping along, walking one step then
stopping a long time. Dixon felt a brief surge of energy and moved
quickly to Nate, latching onto his arm. He might burst with relief.

"Jesus Christ, this is only how far you've got?" Clive got in
Nate's face to examine him.

"For long time we walk, slow, slow, resting lots. Then he say he
is waiting for brudda. I cannot get him to move. Coughing, too,
and pull off goggles too much. Cannot see good now, he say," Angkaji told them.

Pemba barked at him in Nepalese. Angkaji's face looked
stricken, whether with shame or fear, Dixon could not tell. Angkaji pointed to his own ankle. He lifted his boot, which was only
partly laced, and let them all peer inside at his swollen ankle bulging against the boot. "I am so sorry," he said, and explained he had
badly injured his ankle. Pemba knelt to touch the ankle, and Angkaji cried out. "Oh, brudda," Pemba said. "Why you not call me?"
They spoke in their native tongue, intimate tones. Pemba's hands
cupped around his brother's ankle as he squatted down and peered
up at him, his face lined with distress.

Nate's body became racked with his cough, the force of it
bending him nearly face-first into the snow.

"Shit, we've gotta get you down," Clive mumbled. "Nate, you
coughing anything up? Let's see." Clive and Dixon lifted Nate from
the snow, Clive removing Nate's mask, which was sprayed with
foamy pink sputum. "God," Clive said. He pulled out his satellite
phone and called the doctor at Base Camp for advice. Pemba and
Angkaji remained in tense conversation.

Vibrating with alarm, Dixon wrapped his arm tight around Nate's, who struggled away from him. Nate peeled off his headgear, tugging at his hat, and when he could not remove it, he snatched off his goggles and tossed them aside. He lifted his axe, planted it, attempted to pull himself forward, but fell onto his back in the snow. He replaced his oxygen mask, breathed in repeatedly, staring at the sky. All the while Dixon flailed, trying to stop him but unable to move fast enough, far enough, Nate continually out of reach. Nate's head back, the echo of a cry. Dixon dropped down beside him.

"Son of a bitch," Clive said. "Where are his goggles?" Pemba searched for them as climbers snaked around and between them. Finally, Pemba said, "Lost, boss."

"All right, just close your eyes." Clive placed his hands over Nate's eyes.

"You know what this means," he said to Pemba, who understood.

"What?" Dixon asked.

"Ah, he's blinded himself. Took off his goggles too much. Going to have to short-rope him. This is serious, Dixon. Nate," Clive said, "listen, I'm giving you another shot for the HAPE. Then we're short-roping you. Listen to Pemba, all right? Do what he says."

Pemba and Clive latched Nate between them using rope and carabiners. In his head Dixon replayed: HAPE, high-altitude pulmonary edema. Nate had waited for him and now he had HAPE. Jesus, what had he done?

Pemba, who was latched behind Nate, called out the steps for Nate. "Lift leg, Matthew Henson One, left leg, right leg, rest, left leg, right leg, rest." Angkaji lifted his head to Dixon—had Dixon realized the man was so small? "I have failed," he said, quietly, and fell in behind Dixon, limping and leaning heavily on a walking stick. The two followed the short-rope team. In that way, for the next four hours, they crept down the South Col, traversing the long slope as night began to descend.

The path was narrow, steep, rocky. Midway down, they were met by two other sherpas and clients from their team. The climbers heaved with each exhausted breath. They acknowledged Dixon and Nate quickly, wanting none of their misfortune. Clive talked with the sherpas.

Dixon leaned into Nate. "Remember that time after practice, riding the dirt bikes down the highway?"

Nate eked out, "Tell Dad I'm sorry. For everything."

"They'll keep heading down," Clive told Dixon once the others had passed them. "They'll be ready for us at high camp."

"Can't they help? Can't someone help?" Dixon begged. Clive looked away.

They continued their descent. None of it got easier, not breathing, not walking. How could he have left him? The weight of that idea staggering, Dixon stopped in his tracks. Angkaji pushed against his arm. "Please move, Matthew Henson Two. It is cold." A whorish memory: the summit beneath his feet. Dixon swiped at it, his hands flying in front of his goggles. "Do not take off!" Pemba called back over his shoulder. "You go blind like brudda."

Near dark, too far from Camp 4 with no help coming, Nate dropped to his knees, coughing, and curled into the fetal position. Dixon's feet useless frozen slabs, his exhaustion profound, he crawled to Nate. "You with me?" Dixon asked over and over.

Nate snatched off his mask. "Where's my brother?"

"It's me," Dixon said, but he realized his voice was high and hoarse and did not sound familiar.

"Time for his track meet, gotta see him fly. He flies, he flies."

"Nate, it's me."

"He's Zeus."

"I'm gonna get you off this mountain, a'ight?"

Clive and Pemba conferred, Angkaji sunken onto the snow at their feet. Clive phoned the team doctor. "Gamow bag's at camp," he said. "Too far."

Gamow bag. Dixon searched his memory: the red pressurized cylinder they carried with them in high camp. That would do it, that would save him. They would place Nate inside to simulate lower altitude and give him oxygen until he could be carried safely down to Base Camp.

Nate sat up and scooted back along the ice toward a ledge of rock. He propped himself there. He coughed violently, scattering bursts of pink sputum across the snow. "Where's my brother?" he rasped. "Get. Dixon."

"It's me," Dixon repeated, "I'm with you."

"Tell my brother," Nate whispered, "I didn't quit." Nate's body convulsed, his breath a long, gurgling rumble.

"No! No!" Dixon grabbed Nate and turned toward Clive. "Help him! Save him!"

Angkaji began to rise, forgetting his ankle, pushing off with it. An awful snap, clean and crisp, and he screamed in agony and crumpled to the ground. Clive and Pemba at Nate's side, Clive on his knees, Pemba halfway between standing and kneeling, his hands on Nate, his attention on Angkaji, an anguished look on his face. "Go," Clive said, and Pemba headed for his brother.

Nate's seizure eased, he moaned slightly, his lips moving. Dixon bent toward his brother: "Tell me, tell me, Nate, what can I do?" His brother's clouded eyes, bulging now, the long rasp of his breathing. Let's get up, man, let's get outta here, Dixon thought and tried to sit Nate up but he was limp. Dixon jostled his brother's arms, the hands cupped and stiff. "Up, up, c'mon." Clive was on the phone again, bent over, whispering. He glanced at Nate. Nate's mouth twittering, talking, his eyes bulging.

Clive returned to Dixon. "Listen, partner, this is bad. He's got multiple edema. See his eyes? That's his brain. Probably a bleed."

Dixon frowned. "No, no, he's just cold." He began to unzip his own jacket. He would drape it over Nate. That's all he needed.

Clive clutched Dixon's hand, stopped him from unzipping the jacket. "This is the hardest. I'm so sorry. There's nothing we can do. We have to let him go."

"Go? Where?" Dixon's head in fog, his hand still wrapped around his jacket zipper, that hand arrested by Clive's.

Angkaji shivered in Pemba's arms.

Clive squeezed Dixon's hand. "C'mon. We must."

"He's alive," Dixon said.

"Not for long. He doesn't know you're here. He won't know you're gone. He's not with us."

"He'll know. I'll know." Dixon snatched his hand from Clive and latched onto Nate. His lips moving, Nate talked in Dixon's direction but made no sound.

"Dixon, he's dying. And we can't wait. We'll all be too far gone. Look, in this cold, sick as he is, it's like sleeping. He's just fallen into sleep."

Dixon hugged Nate, laying his body against his, trying to warm him. "He's talking, see, he's okay."

"His teeth are chattering. Look. Another seizure. C'mon, Dixon, you don't want to watch this."

"You're making the wrong choice," Dixon said. "Take Nate, not me." If they got Nate down, then Dixon could wait here. He'd be fine until they got back for him. He was sure of it. His face pressed against Nate's, whose seizure rattled them both. Nate's shallow breaths against his face. Dixon could hear him talking: *Get my brother. Get my brother.* "I'm here," he answered, "I'll save us. I can do it. I'll redeem myself."

Clive tugged at Dixon. "We're running out of time. Look, Angkaji's gonna lose that leg if we don't get him down. The bone's exposed. And you've got frostbite on your face. We gotta go, partner. Say goodbye." Clive tugged at Dixon's collar.

His arms around Nate's neck, the small, dull glimmer of life: Nate's lips moving, his clouded eyes, the irises burned white from the sun. "I'll carry him," he said.

Clive sat back helpless as Dixon tried to wedge himself under Nate and lift him. The effort knocked him down. He nearly passed out, lying just this side of consciousness, the feeling of light and dark sliding across his eyes. A long time before he found a breath, his exposed cheek lying in the snow, freezing, numbing. He lay flat out, panting. He crawled on top of Nate, who saw him, he was sure he did. Dixon grasped Nate's collar, his face against Nate's, which was a rubbery cold mallet. Dixon banged his forehead softly against it. "Forgive me," he whispered.

Clive pulled at him. "Get up now, c'mon. Now. Now."

He did not remember letting go, but he was on his knees, above Nate. "It's not in me, it's not in me to leave him. Not again. Not now."

"You're not gonna be able to walk, if you stay down there. I can't carry you. We gotta go. We gotta, Dixon. Right now."

The slight movement of Nate's eyes, back and forth, his lips twittering. He dangled between life and death, and the idea that he would die alone, or worse that he might linger, abandoned, racked Dixon. *Give him peace!* He shuddered, took off his gloves, and placed one hand over Nate's mouth; with the other he pinched his nose shut. Nate's body bucked. His sputum bubbled onto Dixon's hands, oozed through his fingers. Nate's breath rasped and rattled and Dixon, feeling himself awaken from a nightmare, snatched his hand away. He gasped. Nate coughed, seized, his body rising and falling in the snow.

The view from the summit flashed into Dixon's head, the endless billowing clouds, the unexpected loneliness at the top of the world. "She betrayed us!" he whispered to Nate, whose breathing grew wispy. Dixon called Nate's name over and over. Nate, whose eyes had softened, whose face remained frozen in grimace, Nate who fell from the precipice like all those bodies along the South Col, the brothers and dreamers who formed the bones of this mountain. Exhausted, Dixon lay down beside Nate and took him into his arms.

Clive and Pemba stood on either side of Dixon and lifted him. Nate drifted from Dixon's grasp, arms out stiff, torso erect. Dixon's body so thoroughly cold he could not resist Clive and Pemba. Pemba short-roped Dixon behind Clive. Dixon stared at Nate lying flat out in the snow, his face to the sky, eyes open.

Pemba finished tying Dixon's rope and went toward Angkaji, who spoke in urgent entreaty. Pemba bowed to his brother, then backed up toward Nate. When he was just above him, Pemba dragged Nate slowly, a zigzag of effort, toward a ledge and propped him against it. Pemba returned to Dixon. He did not look him in the eye. "Brudda is nearly there. He rest." Dixon thought: Yes, he will rest, and then he will meet us. He will come. He must come. Clive tugged at the rope, dragging Dixon forward, Dixon who strained his head toward Nate and moaned "Rise! Rise!" and Angkaji in his brother's arms, they set off toward Camp 4. Before long, Dixon could no longer see Nate. The battered foursome descended an incline, Dixon dragging heavily, Clive grunting and pulling him along. Dixon's hands on Clive's shoulders, he trailed behind the big man, latching on, a follower one last time.

On the icy floor of Camp 4, the teammates who greeted them set to work reviving Dixon's body with hot tea, cool towels on his frost-burned cheeks, cold baths for his frostbitten toes. He did not move. He did not speak. Even when he needed to pee, he quietly wet his pants and was not ashamed.

Pemba cradled Dixon's head, feeding him tea. Sometime next morning, Dixon awakened to Pemba shaking him. He showed him a photo, a mound of packed snow marked by a chorten of blackened rocks. Pemba and two other sherpas had returned to the place where Nate lay and covered him with snow, a furtive burial. "He rest now," Pemba said. Angkaji lay beside Dixon, his face cast down.

Dixon awoke hours later. He could hardly sit up. He could not walk. He could barely breathe, even with the oxygen tank. "Leave me here," he mumbled. "I'll wait for him. He'll come."

Dixon woke again as he was lifted onto a stretcher to be carried down the mountain, then evacuated to Lukla by helicopter.

On his stretcher, awaiting helicopter retrieval from the mountain, Dixon opened his eyes, took one last look at her, and the wire in him began to vibrate, a high-pitched tune, discordant, wailing through the icy walls of the glaciers, winding and spiraling to the mountaintop.

"Sedative," the camp doctor called. "Now, please!" She bent over Dixon. "All right, all right. Shush, shush. There, there."

Light, dark, bodies close and far away, voices, then the rush of wind. Dixon felt himself being lifted, weightless. He dangled in thin air at the whim of God.

# IV.

n January, Cal Fierston appeared at the diner as if he knew it was Herbert's day off and Dixon was unprotected. Cal sat at the counter. The set of his shoulders told Dixon this man had all day to wait. "I don't understand," Dixon began as he walked behind the counter facing Cal. "Is somebody paying you for this story? I mean, you're like a dog with a bone."

"As a matter of fact, I get paid to write other stories that I'm neglecting because I want to tell your story."

Dixon looked around him at the placid faces of people enjoying their breakfasts, sipping coffee, living in their own little lanes. "What does it matter?"

"I tell you what, in a couple months, it won't." Cal's nostrils flared, the hairs wriggling inside. "There's a big expedition from National Geographic heading up, taking what they think will be the first Black American man to the summit."

Dixon's stomach clenched.

"Because somehow they don't know about you and Nate.

You're a rumor, but that's it, Dixon. If Phil Henderson makes it, you'll have a hell of a time staking your claim. He's well-known. Well financed. You don't have any other allies but me. You need to get your story out before he climbs. In two months, March, you know, Everest season begins."

Dixon swayed back and forth from the idea. His lips parted but he could not speak. He hated that mountain now as intimately as he had loved it, but he hadn't imagined it could be taken from him.

"Look, I know you're learning to navigate loss. Believe me, I get that. More than you know. But this story matters. You owe it to Nate," he said. "You have to push your brother's claim to this mountain, Dixon."

Heat tunneled up from Dixon's feet and bloomed through his body. Who the fuck did this man think he was to hurl his dead brother at him?

Once Cal had left, Dixon walked from the grill to the back room and stared out the long vertical windows. The day was gray and cold, the asphalt ashen with rock-salt residue. He leaned his forehead against the window. His skin absorbed the cold. *Speak now or forever hold your peace.* Nate had mocked seriousness before Dixon's wedding. *Say the word, man, and I'll save you. They get to "Speak now or forever hold your peace," I'll jump up, "Run, Dixon, run!"* He had burst into laughter, and the two brothers had jostled their way into a tight hug. Speak now. Or else. It was amazing to think there might be anything left to lose from that beshitted mountain. He turned his frostbitten cheek against the glass, his cheek flush with new skin slowly regaining its melanin. New skin that had not known mountain cold. "What do I do? Tell me, tell me. What do you want from me?" he whispered and awaited Nate's answer.

That night, he tossed in bed. Nate would have told him he needed a woman. He wouldn't necessarily be wrong. All those years when Pamela starved him, she had pushed him away in the night, too, a quick sweep of her hand denying his erection, her back to him, her body closed. After the divorce, there had been mostly divorcees as hungry and wary as he. They'd kept him at an emotional distance but close at night. A body cupped inside the well of his own body. The curve of a thigh, the indent of a waist, a slope of breasts. Lena. Those days she did not wear a bra, her small, round breasts spread into a full arc, her nipples imprinted against her T-shirt. That night, as so often then, he imagined it was her hand gripping him, her thigh, her pleasure.

AT WORK THE NEXT DAY, HERBERT HOVERED AT THE EDGE OF Dixon. "So, Dix man, that boy in jail, that killed Marcus, what you know 'bout him?"

"Always looking for trouble. Well, he's got the black eye now to prove it."

"You seen him?"

It caught Dixon out. He answered slowly. "Yeah. I went to visit."

"Isthatright?" Herbert kept his eyes on Dixon.

Dixon shrugged. "I'll tell you one thing, he wasn't happy to see me. Dumb move on my part."

"Maybe. Maybe." Herbert grew pensive. He laid his hand flat on the counter then patted it slowly.

The next day, Herbert brought up Shiloh again. "You think he got a decent lawyer? You think his people got it like that, you know, got the money to get him one?"

Dixon was annoyed at being made to think of Shiloh again. "Don't know anything about it."

"He need a decent lawyer. I ain't saying he don't have to pay for what he done to Marcus, now. He do. But he need a lawyer that don't see him as garbage." Herbert lectured to the ham and steaks spread out before him.

"What's this about? Why're you worrying about him?" Dixon asked.

"He did ter'ble things, but he still a kid."

Dixon shifted his shoulders, stretched his neck against the idea of saving Shiloh. "Marcus was a really good kid. Why pick on him?"

"Akst him, next time you see him."

Dixon looked up sharply. "Oh, I'm not going back there."

Herbert stepped away from his grill. "Why not?"

The visit to Shiloh had unsettled Dixon for days afterward. That unrepentant bastard. Dixon had had a flash of something like fire, the feeling that he could snatch that boy up and choke him. A fire in his hands. The burn of memory. His hands across Nate's mouth and nose, squeezing. At night, he often lay awake, his hands pressed flat under his head. One by one, he would hold up each hand in a wash of moonlight, looking for evidence of its unthinkable deeds.

On his day off that week, he searched online court records and reminded himself of every detail of the case. Shiloh had been harassing Marcus daily, sitting wide-legged on the steps of the bodega near Marcus's bus stop waiting for him. He would call him names—*hey Fat Ass, hey faggot, hey little fuck*—or pelt him with small rocks, orange peels, sunflower seeds. The day of the attack, Shiloh was actually pacing at the bus stop, witnesses said, looking "menacing." Kids could see him from inside the school bus. They crowded the aisles to watch. Marcus's friends surrounded him and tried to sneak him away in the center of the group, but when Shiloh pounced, the group scattered. Shiloh chased Marcus. He punched him first before grabbing Marcus's coat and yanking it backward like a lasso. One of Marcus's friends ran home to get his father, who came outside and found Marcus. Mrs. Robbie, an elderly woman watching from her bedroom window, said when Marcus got up to run, Shiloh tripped him. Marcus struck his head when he fell. Shiloh stood over him a minute, laughed, then looked panicked and called out Marcus's name repeatedly before running away.

"Did he ever say why Marcus?" Dixon called Benny Lewis after reading the full case report.

"I heard—this could be just a rumor, I shouldn't say—but, I heard when the cops told him how badly Marcus was hurt, he said he'd just given him 'an old-fashioned ass-whipping like everybody else gets.' I remember because I thought, 'What's happened in this kid's life?'"

"Who does he think he is, Ike Turner? 'I didn't beat my wife any more than the average man beats his wife.'"

"Exactly."

What Dixon knew about Shiloh's life: His mother murdered, he was raised by an aunt and uncle. Got into small skirmishes that escalated so that he ended up doing a tour of state youth facilities until, exhausted, the state authorities released him.

At night, when Dixon attempted to focus on memories of Nate alive and healthy, Shiloh managed to interrupt. Shiloh the interloper. Dixon was tied to Shiloh by something chafing and dogged. Because, somehow, Dixon had taken the boy on.

LENA ASKED AGAIN, "DO YOU RECOVER?" HER TENSES LIKE SLOW time travel, her call coming deep in the night, as Dixon lay alone in the dark with his hand coiled around the receiver. "It was different for me," she said. "I lost my lover in that avalanche, I lost my sex."

"What?" He blinked, startled. He was glad she could not see him.

"My sex, all things about my body that he knew. Like which breast is too sensitive, where I hide the scar from a surgery, how I feel about the wide of my hips. You are different. You lost, I think, your history. Do you have another brother, a sister?"

He explained about Charlaina.

"Then it's not all gone."

"Have you ever, I mean, have you gotten your sex back?"

Her voice a half laugh. "Of course. There was your brother, remember? But it's not like I had, never the same. Maybe I didn't get my body back completely. I don't know."

He lay curled on his side, his chin propped on his arm. He hesitated. Remembered the way she had of running her tongue absently over her lips in a slow circle. "Can we talk about your body?"

"Oh! You are like your brother, more than I thought. *Tsk-tsk.*"

Caught off guard, oddly soothed, he laughed aloud, his head thrown back.

"On the mountain, I think you are client but want to be a little bit alpinist. I think I can show you. It is kind of thrilling. Your brother, he didn't have that same, I don't know, what do you call it?"

"Did I disappoint you, then? Did you expect—"

"Wait, wait, you tell me things, then I let you talk whatever you want. Did you call to that reporter guy?"

"He came to me. I didn't really talk to him, but he told me some other group is climbing next month. Someone else might . . ." He cleared his throat. Why was it so hard to say? The words bitter. "Take our claim. First Black American man to summit."

"Oh! You cannot let that happen, Dixon, all your work, all your brother's. You must tell!"

"I don't know how," he said softly.

"Practice. You can tell it to me."

He shook his head fast. There was the spinning he sometimes felt when he stood up too quickly. An inner ear disorder diagnosed after the climb as a post-traumatic vertigo. He grabbed the bridge of his nose then exhaled hard into the phone. "I abandoned my brother. I left him behind. What else can I possibly tell?"

"That you survived."

"I haven't yet."

"Oh, but you have. Why else do you think you should be so miserable? The truth can be like that. It won't go away just because you don't say."

"I can't."

"Say the truth."

"I'm not ready."

"The truth doesn't wait on you. Oh! Don't be arrogant! What is it you fear?"

He thought a long time, then blurted out, "Ego."

———

THE STRIKING THING AT NATE'S MEMORIAL SERVICE HAD BEEN when everyone had stopped crying. At first, before the service began, lifelong friends and a slate of people from Nate's adult life had filled the chapel, and everyone had wept. The portrait of Nate mid-laugh had seized them all as they arrived. Women reached out to stroke the portrait's cheek. Mourners wept onto Dixon's shoulders. His body shook in that subterranean way of grief. Skeet had stayed closest to Dixon that day. There wasn't a cup of water or a tissue or a chair that Skeet didn't provide for him. Tending, hovering.

Once the service began, the tears dried up, and Dixon felt surrounded by a steely silence. And then the whispers started: *What were they thinking? What kind of foolishness was this? Did they have a death wish? Who did they think they were? Some arrogant shit. Of all the ways a Black man can die.* The whispers stinging him into numbness. "Don't listen, don't listen," Skeet said, but then he had to bite his lip.

That night, Skeet had shown up at Charlaina's. Loud, obviously drunk, he screamed, "Why'd you let him, Dixon? Why'd you let him go? You knew better than to let him climb, you always knew better, that was your *job*, man! Why? Why?" Skeet's voice echoing up the stairs toward Dixon's bedroom. Charlaina begged him to shut up and go home. Dixon lay in bed, his heart thumping. His limbs heavy and immobile, paralyzed by that accusation. "Why'd you let him do it, Dixon?"

Now, after Dixon had ignored Skeet's earlier calls, it was Skeet who wouldn't talk to Dixon. Tania, Skeet's wife, made excuses when Dixon called: "He doesn't sleep, he doesn't eat, Dixon. He's a mess," as if his suffering should be reassuring.

"Everyone, everything is slipping away," Dixon told Lena one night.

"Sometimes you must let go. But listen. I am here," she whispered.

HERBERT STUDIED HIM THE NEXT DAY. "WHO YOU THINKING 'bout? You got a secret girl? You got that look, that 'sweetest pain' kind of suffering going on. Something new for you." Herbert shook with a deep laugh. They stood in the back doorway to the kitchen on an incongruously warm winter day.

Dixon wagged his head side to side. A sudden, unbearable memory of Lena's skin ran up his spine like a stick dragged across fence posts. "Yeah, you got me. This woman from the mountain. Guess she's churning me up."

"Hmph. You ain't had it like this in a while, huh? You ain't have this, like, back in the day, for your wife?"

"I mean, I loved my wife, of course."

"But you ain't loooooved her." Herbert leaned in, laughing.

Just for a minute, he might be laughing with Nate. He caught his breath. The idea of Lena like a hitch in his side. "It's not, no, it's not . . . I'm just, you know . . ." He paused. "She was my brother's girl, sort of. She was with him on the mountain, not me. Never me."

Herbert raised both eyebrows, then nodded slow. "But she a comfort. Ain't nothing wrong with that, man. Really."

But he was certain there was.

"What? He gone. Y'all just comforting each other, right?" Herbert's face full of concern. "Man, ain't you ever just been happy? Just, let yourself be happy?"

Dixon turned that idea over like a stone and found no way to measure it, and it occurred to him: It was not his province. He had been content. He had built the "good" life—good job, good home, good reputation—he'd been raised to have. He felt at his best when there was order, when he could discern the right course. This for Dixon had been the equivalent of "happy." How could he have imagined that definition could contain a mountain? He had stretched toward Everest with a physical ache and left his life listing to one side. Now, that inner vibration of right and wrong he had counted on all his life lay somewhere he could not quite reach. "I'm just waiting for my life to make sense," he confided.

Herbert cupped Dixon's shoulder then gave it a shake. "Work your shit out, boy."

IN EARLY FEBRUARY, IT WAS HERBERT'S TURN TO CONFESS. "Need to tell you something." Herbert rubbed his jaw. "Your boy up in lock up? I had him checked out."

It took a moment for Dixon to realize Herbert was talking about Shiloh.

"That Scared Straight thing they do on young'uns in the joint? One my boys was running the program, see, so I had your boy included." Herbert made a face. "He ain't ready. He ain't 'bout to be broke. He gone learn the hard way." Herbert stood across a great distance now. "Hate to see a young boy heart so set."

"Why'd you do it?"

"Good question." Herbert fumbled with the serving spoons on the chrome countertop beside the grill. He did not answer.

DIXON AND HERBERT WERE HOSING DOWN THE GRILL PARTS OUT back, despite the return of brisk winds, the deep misery of grayed skies and genuine cold. One hand dug deep into a pocket, the other holding the hoses, they swore intermittently when the sprays ricocheted onto them. "Handle your shit!" Herbert scolded and sprayed toward Dixon's feet as punishment, and Dixon returned the spray. It wasn't long before both men were soaked, cold, battling like boys, chasing each other with the hoses. Inside the locker room, peeling out of their wet clothes, laughing, each of them declared victory over the other. "I gotcha, motherfucker," Herbert said, laughing. "Don't mess with the big dog!" and he barked.

"You are two of the dumbest motherfuckers I ever saw." Their boss Hoss tossed them spare T-shirts and sweatpants. "Now you idiots gonna catch the pneumonia, and I got no backups for the both of you, dammit!"

"No worries, we come in, sneeze all over the grill, mix it in with the eggs, won't nobody know 'bout that extra spice." Herbert laughed.

"You think you're funny. Keep it up, get my ass closed down by the health department." Hoss walked away mumbling, "Dumb motherfuckers."

"Better toss my stuff in the dryer," Dixon said.

"Why, you got some big date?" Herbert laughed, and when Dixon sat sheepish, Herbert sighed. "It's out your hands, Dix man. It's nothing you can do with that boy."

Dixon blinked. How the hell did Herbert read him like that?

"Look, I believe you do all you can do, but a man show you he don't want your help, then he don't want it."

"I hear that. I've believed that. But this kid," Dixon said, frowning, "can't seem to shake him."

As Dixon sat again in the youth jail's waiting room, he felt singular. Seeking something he could not put his finger on.

Shiloh sauntered to Dixon's table but didn't sit. Only a month since the boy had been here; it seemed like forever. The boy towered there, hands in his pockets. He appeared to have grown an inch in the few weeks since Dixon last saw him. His bruises were healed, his eye no longer black. "What?!" Shiloh barked at Dixon. A guard came over and pushed down on Shiloh's shoulder to make him sit. "Whatchu want? How you keep getting in?"

"You look better." Dixon pointed to Shiloh's eye.

"You disappointed?"

"No, glad to see it."

"You come up in here like you got somethin' to say."

"I wanna know why Marcus? What was it about him?"

"I ain't like him."

"Yes, but why?"

"'Cause."

"That's not a reason. I really want to know."

"You all into my business and shit, fronting like you give a damn. You couldn't wait to get me the fuck out your office. You was just looking for a way to bust me up out that mug, wasn't you? Yeah, yeah. I know 'bout you."

Dixon's voice quavering. "I guess you think you have me all figured out. You feel like you have the upper hand. Maybe you do. You haven't answered my question. I really want to know what you were thinking."

"What was you thinking when you was 'bout to choke the shit outta me, huh? Was you worried 'bout me then?"

He stared at Shiloh, who saw through him: He recognized Dixon as the kind of man who could leave him behind. A gut check.

Shiloh rolled his eyes. "Bitch, you 'on't know nothing 'bout my life."

His breathing audible, Dixon looked around the room at the

overwhelming calm of other visitors. What did they accept that he could not? Nate's voice: *Give in.* A dull illumination grew clearer. "You're right. I don't know about your life. Speak on it."

The boy looked agitated. "You tryina trap me? Whatchu doin'?"

"I'm saying, you are right." Dixon sat back in his chair. He felt weightless. "Enlighten me."

Shiloh sat up in his chair, a little hop as he got situated. Dixon was clearly getting under his skin. "I 'on't know you."

"That's the point. I don't know you either. So tell me, son, who are you?"

Shiloh glared at him awhile. "What you want from me?"

Feeling animated now, Dixon leaned toward the boy. "Go 'head. Tell me your life. Tell me, whatever you want. Tell me, tell me all of it, tell me about your family, your aunt and uncle, tell me about your mother—"

"Fuck you!" Shiloh hollered and jumped from his chair. "Guard!" he shouted before he headed toward the door.

The next day, Herbert took Dixon's measure. "So, Dix man, what you suffering over today?"

"You got my routine down, huh?" Dixon laughed at himself. "The mountain's got me. Didn't get any sleep last night."

"Man, you left your mark, sound like to me, from what that reporter said. Ain't that a good thing?"

"That Cal Fierston, he's hounding me."

"It's hard for you, huh? I mean, your brother and all, I know. But what, it's hard for you to fail at this mountain? You don't picture me as the kinda dude have failed a lot in his life. AmIright?"

"Everybody fails at something."

"That don't make it easy, though, do it?" Herbert shook his head slightly.

"You know, you may be the only one outside my family who has any sympathy for me."

"That's 'cause you a new kinda failure, one that come outta privilege. We ain't learned what to do with you yet. Guys like me, we marked for failing from the time we young. Talking 'bout Shiloh, too. That's what he living up to. Hell, that make him a success in his book, right? That 'see I told you I wa'n't shit' book." He let out a short, hard laugh. "See, that's what I'm talking about failure, man, that deep shit that keep you down. You the kinda guy we looking to to pull us out, right? Ain't that the role you got? Ain't that what you feeling guilty about? So tell me this, why you can't do both? Why you can't go with your brother so he make it to the top of the world *and* take care your business back here, far as you can? Seem to me you did that. I mean, can't a Black man have a goddamn mountain, if he want? Give a man his mountain, man, give it to him."

Herbert's words buzzed through Dixon's chest. "It isn't his. It's mine."

Herbert propped both hands on the butcher block counter. "Oh? Oh! Now, that make sense to me, Dix man. You all into denying yourself something, ain't you?" Herbert looked away. When he turned back to Dixon, his face had softened. "I ain't saying I understand all that mountain-climbing shit, I ain't even gonna front like that make sense to me. But I know when a man is running. You, Dix man, are like natural-born to run. That's what you ain't know 'bout yourself, ain't it? You 'on't hafta answer."

They passed the rest of their shift in silence, Dixon keeping as busy as he possibly could. At the end of the day, as they began their clean-up duties, Herbert said, "You like, a pioneer, man. Back in the day, you'da got the cover of *Ebony*."

Dixon pushed it off. "I thought you had to be Beyoncé to get a cover these days."

"Why you don't want nobody to know?"

"What does it matter?"

"Well, it's got to matter to you first. But I'm sure it do. I know it do."

―――――

HE HAD PLANNED TO GO HOME AFTER WORK. BUT IN JUST A MO-ment's hesitation as he pulled out of the diner parking lot, he turned left instead of right, and he knew then where he was headed.

"Tell me about your life, since you say I don't know it. Tell me something. Who's your best friend? Tell me about your mother." Dixon sat before Shiloh in the same chair as always, getting the same glare he had come to expect.

"Man, I ain't cuss you out enough 'bout that? Fuck you." Shiloh sucked his teeth, his arms folded tight across his chest. He scanned the visitor's room. "Why 'on't you give up some information, huh? You got all these damn questions. How 'bout you, huh? What high school you went to?"

"Kenridge."

Shiloh's eyebrow rose, as if he knew the place. "Where you stay at?"

"Fieldstone Crossing."

"Them big houses?" He frowned, rocked a bit in his chair, his arms wrapped tight across his chest.

Dixon hedged. "Not so big, I mean, compared to how they build them nowadays." He stopped. What a privileged man's view of the world. He looked away from the boy.

"Hmph. You have your own room?"

Dixon nodded.

"You ain't have no brothas and sistas, then, huh? You a spoiled little rich boy."

He said finally, "A brother."

"Y'all ain't share a room?" Shiloh sat forward now, concentrating, trying to get the full picture. Dixon shook his head. "Damn. Y'all had it like that?" Shiloh sounded childish, then caught himself. "That's why your ass soft, you ain't have to do shit. You had a maid when you was little? One o' them nannies?"

"Nah. We had chores, cleaning the house, walking the dogs, cutting grass. We weren't spoiled."

"Y'all had a dog?"

"Two. Frazier and Ali." He remembered his dad lobbying for the names Malcolm and Martin.

"What kind? Not some little punk-ass little pussy dog."

"Chocolate labs." Dixon lifted his hand to measure the height of the dogs.

"Hmph." Shiloh nodded approval. "I wanted me a German shepherd. All black. Name him Satan." He cracked himself up. Dixon imagined the sight of this short kid with a dog three-quarters his height. "That shit be fierce, yo."

"Big dog. Needs lots of space to run."

"Backyard. You have that? You leave 'em outside?"

"Doghouse in the backyard."

"A dog need shelter." Shiloh rocked in his chair: a self-soothing gesture, Dixon noted. "Let me akst you, you leave him way far back in the yard or up close to the house? Do he get scared outside?"

Dixon sat forward toward the boy. "Well, a little ways back but not so far that he can't see the house and know you're there, not so far you can't see if he's okay."

"Uh-huh, uh-huh," Shiloh agreed, his brow screwed up. "Shit, my neighborhood? You can't leave that dog outside. They be fucking with 'im and shit. Tryina steal him, set his ass on fire, fuck

255

with his food. My dog, he hafta be a house dog. Let him sleep in with me. Matter fac' don't let him out my sight. Yo. Tell them mothafuckas at school he a, a, whatchu callit? Blind people kinda dog?"

"Seeing-eye dog. You'd have to actually have a problem with your vision."

"Shit, I can fake that." He reached around as if he couldn't see. "I can do that Stevie Wonder shit." He rolled his head from side to side.

Dixon laughed. "You got it figured out, huh?"

Shiloh stopped abruptly. "Yeah. I thought about it. They nice dogs, though, loyal, man, real loyal. And like, they train real easy 'cause they smart, real smart. And they be friendly, right, if you come correct, but don't fuck wit' em, don't fuck wit' they master. Especially not they master. I said they loyal right?"

"You did."

Shiloh gazed off, pouting. Just like any kid. And then he jumped up. "Don't nobody need no damn dog." He kicked his chair and got ready to leave. "Hey. Don't go thinking we best friends. Get the fuck out."

He didn't exactly like Shiloh, but he no longer hated him. Maybe that was the best he could do.

As he walked away, the hardness of the floor seemed to bore its way through Dixon's shoes so that he limped, favoring his partial foot. The musky smell seeped from the concrete walls and mingled with the undercurrent of body odor, the dull light in late afternoon. Dixon thought of tombs, a thought underscored by the distant echo of slamming cell doors whenever someone entered or left the room. There was no mistaking where he was.

"I hate that place," he told Herbert.

"You went back, huh?"

Dixon ignored him. "I'm not sure any kid oughta be there. I mean, just the way it smells, you know?"

A long pause. "Yep. A shithole," Herbert mumbled. "And don't think they ain't know that, don't think they ain't make it like that on purpose. Want you to feel like a animal. And most the time, you do. You do."

Herbert began to fade away then. He talked very little that day and the next and the one after that, taciturn and closed, erupting every now and then in a tirade about the pace of orders or the stickiness of the floor—"What, can't nobody but me mop this bitch once in a while?"—snapping at Dixon if he pointed out a steak was too rare—"then *you* do this, shit." Dixon stood back from it, waiting for Herbert to return. Because he had morphed, his attitude, his body even, hulking over the grill, a kind of menace rising as shadow across his shoulders. "You a'ight, big man?" Dixon might ask, and Herbert would grimace. Or, he might nudge Herbert, "Long Legs says hi," and the old Herbert would rise up a minute, flash a smile, and then he was gone, fallen back down and away. It went on like this for more than a week, long enough for Dixon to begin to grieve his loss.

Herbert called in sick two days in a row. Hoss was vocal about it, about "how you stupid motherfuckers got yourselves sick and now I've got to suffer, like I got the cold." He filled in for Herbert at the grill with none of the grace, style, or rhythm. More than a few plates were sent back. "What am I suppose to do about this? You tell your friend," Hoss barked at Dixon, "to get his ass well and get back here. I mean it. He's got to the end of the week." Dixon didn't want to tell him that he didn't have Herbert's phone number, that he didn't exactly know where he lived, or—worse—that he feared he might not find him there even if he had known.

IN SHILOH'S CASE FILE, THERE WAS ONE RECURRING NAME. Chris Temple had been Shiloh's caseworker years earlier. She seemed to have had ongoing contact with that kid. Through the state directory, Dixon tracked down her phone number and called her one day in mid-February.

"You know, I was hoping someone would call me about him. I'd have preferred it to be his defense attorney," Chris Temple said.

On a damp Wednesday afternoon, he awaited her at a café. The seats were chenille-covered couches and what looked like daybeds covered in faux leather. The tables were pulled up close to the couches, the kind of low, wide tables made for banging your shins. Soft jazz whirled overhead. Chris Temple was a prim woman, petite, with a small purple handbag she clutched with both hands in front of her as she stood in the doorway scanning the room for Dixon. She wore a cape and small-brimmed hat adorned with a flower and Dixon nearly laughed: she looked like Mary Poppins. He caught her eye and stood to wave her over. She unbuttoned her cape, removed it with a flag-twirl, and sat at the opposite end of the sofa from him. She revealed a tote bag that had been hidden under the cape.

He jumped right in, eager. "What's his real story? Is it true he attacked his aunt or a foster mother or somebody?"

Her eyes widened a bit as she took him in. "No, no, that was a recanted story by another child in the foster home who told that same tale about several other children."

"His mom died right in front of him?"

"No, another myth. He grew up with his aunt and uncle, the Giddings. According to the aunt, Shiloh's mother dropped out of junior college to be with Shiloh's father, then he died in the service soon after she got pregnant, and Shiloh and his mother moved in with her. When he was around three, his mother left him with the aunt while she went to work out of state. His mother was murdered the next year while she was away. Shiloh was about four. Basically, he was raised by his aunt, the mother's sister, but they just, I don't know, didn't bond, perhaps. She told me he used to say to her, 'You're not as pretty as my mother.'" Chris Temple retrieved a thick brown file from a tote bag, placed it on the table, then slid it toward Dixon. Her eyes dead on him. "I told you, I couldn't let go. He sucks you in, doesn't he?"

Shiloh's life contained in one thick file. Things Dixon already knew. The school counselors' notes on his acting out, on his art therapy, on Intervention Circle. Also new information like results of psychological testing: situational depression and oppositional defiant disorder. Allergy testing: none. Enzymes, blood work: normal. Things Chris Temple should not have had in her possession. Dixon pored over the pages. Nothing in this damn file made him much different from tons of other kids who fucked up.

There were pictures of the aunt's tidy bungalow. Dixon peered at a photo of the dining room. A massive oak table anchored the room, its walls full of plaques with Bible verses and crosses with a white Jesus hanging from them. Talismans against trouble. The ubiquitous footsteps in the sand plaque signifying Jesus's steps, the footsteps tinged red like a child's Crayola had swiped across them. Beside them on the wall, a photo of what must have been Shiloh's mother, a glossy glamour shot of a beautiful young woman. On the photo's frame was written, "Beloved Sister and Mother, Gone by God's Will."

Chris Temple touched the edge of the file. "When I was his

counselor, I visited the home so often I nearly saw it in dreams. Later, once I was a state caseworker, he ended up in my caseload. I went there again when he had to be removed from the home. Kicking holes in the wall, threatening his cousins, disrespecting his teachers at school. Just full of rage. Then he got caught shoplifting and that kicked off everything. He's done four stints in juvy, plus one of those awful boot camps. Twice he's been in foster homes, but they always return him to the aunt and uncle as if he's 'fixed.' He comes home angrier, kicks bigger holes in the wall. It's just so frustrating. See his IQ?" Chris Temple flipped through the papers. "I thought perhaps he was above or below. But no. Dead normal, the high side of normal, in fact." She stared at Dixon. "I initiated these tests. I paid for them. Chasing the devil."

Dixon perused the file. A photo of Shiloh at six or seven wearing a pirate's hat, arms folded tight across his chest, an eyebrow cocked as if to say, *Look at this shit.* Perhaps what Shiloh loathed about Marcus was his hopefulness. Dixon held up the photo, his look quizzical.

"Don't ask." She swallowed. "I was trying to take him on a fun outing like any other little boy. He was never quite like any other little boy."

Dixon stared at the photo. Not a cute kid, one sharp around the edges, a cut-glass boy. "Damn. This kid. What is it with him? Nothing's so singular about his story," he said.

"I think—can I tell you something? I think this child makes us dislike him so much that we become ashamed. Some part of us wants nothing to do with him and that makes us afraid."

"Of what?" He frowned, hoping she had some concrete answer.

She shrugged. "Because it costs us. When I first met him, I was brand new to the job and full of idealistic claptrap about what I was going to do. I nearly . . . I lost things, parts of myself for this child, *this* child. Do you understand what I mean? Finally, I had to pull away. When I returned to him, he cursed me out. He didn't need me, he said. I thought, 'This is good, he's working out his mommy issues and that transference could set him free.' I couldn't fathom his anger was actually meant for me. I'm telling you this to help you."

"I'm not new to this. I know you can't help everybody. You save the ones who can be saved, who want to be saved," he said and blanched.

"No, I don't know that. I'm in the camp that says never give up on a kid."

"He doesn't want our help." He was talking to himself now.

"But he's a child, how can you stop?" They held each other's gaze a long time, a challenge.

Dixon stretched his neck. "I probably shouldn't even be doing this. I definitely shouldn't be visiting him. Somebody's going to object eventually. Then what?"

"Who's watching? He's a thorn in the side, Dixon. Nobody really cares."

---

AT HOME THAT EVENING, HE WALKED AROUND HIS YARD. SOLAR lights cast deep shadows on the flagstone path. A few intrepid pansies shivered in the February chill. There had been a time when he could know unerringly what was right. A bitter swell in his throat. What was he to do about Shiloh? It was a test Dixon had not studied for.

Wasn't his life full of tests? His next one appeared a few minutes later: his daughter. She entered swiftly and sat at attention in his living room, something needing to be said but he couldn't imagine what. Not yet herself, she wore glasses (not contacts) with plain black frames. Unremarkable jeans, a dark sweater. One gold bangle, which he fixated on, as if it might one day multiply into her old flamboyance. Kira kneaded her hands, rambling about school, about how hard it was to concentrate this term, how her friends said she was in a kind of fog, and then she blurted out, "Are we literally never gonna talk about it?"

All the unspoken things of their lives rushing by. He honestly had thought so little about her grief. He'd imagined her relief that he had come back alive might overrule the sadness. Selfishly, he had thought this overwhelming grief about Nate was mostly, if not all, his. But there it was on her: her eyes sunken. God, had she lost weight? It stunned him.

"I mean, will we ever be able to talk about the climb? Because it means we never talk about Uncle Nate. Doesn't he deserve it?"

He wouldn't lie to her. He never had. That had been his rule, especially once the marriage started to tank, especially once she began asking why he and her mother didn't get along anymore: "Daddy, don't you love each other?" He had told the truth, some version of it: "I'll always love her for giving me you." Evasive reassurance he'd picked up from some sitcom. As she grew older, he'd admit, "We're having trouble living together, but that's different from not loving each other." And finally, "It's a past love, not one with a future." He could not deliberately lie to her. Her face soft with sorrow. Had he noticed how much she looked like Nate, the shape of her face, the brows, right down to the dimples? "I'm not ready to talk about it," he said.

"Mom thinks you're embarrassed because he made it and you didn't. You're not, right?"

"No."

"But you can't talk about what happened?" She paused. "Even to me?"

He shook his head. How would she be able to forgive him? "But you can, Monkey. You should. You really should."

"About him making it to the top?"

His voice came through a tunnel. He felt so far away. "About your uncle Nate climbing. Yes. Celebrate him."

———

HE DID NOT RECOGNIZE HERBERT. AS DIXON LEFT WORK AND headed into the indifferent light of a rainy near-spring afternoon three days later, he was met by a hulking man near the back door of the diner, a tall, broad-shouldered man in a hoodie, faceless, shadowed. Dixon jumped back, his body preparing to run in the split second before Herbert lifted the hood up and away, revealing his face, the pure suffering of it so piercing that Dixon lunged for his friend and embraced him.

They went back into the empty diner, not bothering to turn on the lights. The room felt skeletal, as if the light might add flesh to the hard bones of countertop and booth, but the bareness suited them. They sat at a table far back, hidden from the wide front window. Herbert, his arms tucked close to the sides, receded. After a few quiet moments, Dixon got up to make coffee, and they both drank in silence through one cup and then another.

"My life snuck up on me, man," Herbert said finally. "Thought I worked all that shit out, man, but, you know, sometime . . ." Herbert rubbed his fingers around the top of his coffee cup.

Quiet again, a gully of time flowed by, wide and deep. Dixon turned his face toward the window, the slant of light stark across the sky. A chill shook him.

"Back in the joint, I had to write a letter to my young self. This class I took, trying to get it together for parole. Just a assignment. But then I see, this class went to the heart. I mean, you write to that knucklehead self that got you where you at. You tell 'em what you wished you had knew, right? It's deep, man. Had to go read it again behind all this, all your boy's shit."

"What did you write?"

"'Don't do it.' What else to say after you do some pointless shit? Don't do it."

Dixon couldn't bring himself to ask what "pointless shit" Herbert had done. It was enough to know that Herbert had spent seventeen years in prison. He only wanted to take his friend cleanly in this moment. And yet, that is not how we come, Dixon knew. We are fraught, we are weighted. Before Dixon had confessed all to him, Herbert had never once asked him about his foot. There had been opportunities to ask, times when Dixon's foot swelled as if it had thawed but retained the water, awaiting another good, hard freeze. At those times, Herbert might nod to Dixon's foot with silent reverence, but he never asked. Dixon would not ask Herbert about his time. Even if Dixon understood he was really driven by fear of what he might not be able to forgive.

"It's a helpless feelin', man, being now and seeing back then. Make you want to do some time travel. It tear you up and, then, but, then you gotta let that shit go. Suffering don't change nothin'." He looked at Dixon. "You think suffering is salvation itself." He drank a long swig of coffee. "Listen. What you aksed a while back? You aksed, how you live, you know, once you know what you capable of, r'member? You can't block out what you been, man, but you gotta . . ." Herbert paused. "You s'pose to be able to see your crime, accept responsibility, right, before you move on and be a man. But it's a curse. 'Cause you see it in front of you sometimes, so real what you had did, and it bring a man to his knees. If he got a heart. That boy, Shiloh. He ain't ready. I know cause I wa'n't. He think the worst of him is the best he got. He wear that like it make him, it lift him up in his world, it keep him safe. Maybe it do for right now. But it's like some acid, eat into your soul, man. He ain't gone fine his way till he become a man. You like the Bible, don'tcha? You know what it say, 'When I was a child, I thought as a child. When I became a man, I put away childish things.' And something 'bout seeing through a mirror darkly now, but then it will be face to face? All 'bout vision, man, 'bout learning to see. He have to look up and see his life have slipped away. Then he gotta forgive hisself. Till that, ain't a fucking thing you can do 'bout it. Y'hear me? Ain't a fucking thing."

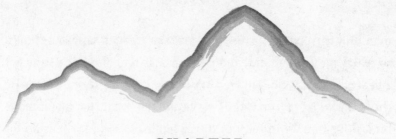

CHAPTER

21

When he arrived at the detention center, Dixon noticed that Shiloh seemed changed. That anxious, jittery boy with the bruised face had molted into a new self. Shiloh strolled long and lean toward the table where Dixon waited, the boy looking to the side, then over a shoulder, a glance behind, gauging the room and cutting an eye toward this one and that one, receiving the slow chin-lift of respect. He had earned his spot in this place.

Shiloh sat, his body sinking into its particular language of *So, what you want?* He sported two fresh cuts along his cheek, a bandage beside his ear.

"How ya been?" Dixon began.

Shiloh shrugged. "Shit, what you care?" He rolled his eyes, glanced around the room, and let his gaze linger on the guards near the door.

"Did you tell somebody about those cuts on your face?"

"Fuck you."

"Talk to your caseworker. Maybe they can move you to another facility."

"Been to all them others. Ain't no place no better." He stared at Dixon a long while. "Tell me something. How come you always come up in here like that, like you scared, and shit?"

Dixon hesitated. "Do I?"

"You got that smell on you. What you got to be scared 'bout?" He leaned forward into Dixon's space. "You scared-a me?"

Dixon didn't flinch. "For you, maybe."

Shiloh's face registered surprise, a snap of his neck. "What the fuck that mean?"

"Fear. Goes hand in hand with trouble." He felt giddy, light-headed. He shook his head. "Only person I ever knew who could juggle trouble, man, was my brother Nate, my big brother. Acted like life was a three-ring circus, each one had somebody eating fire or, or, juggling knives and he was just walking between them, skirting in and out, watching the show. Was like that all his life."

"Where he at now?"

He struggled to find his voice. "Gone."

"That the one you say you kilt?"

He lifted his shoulders, a weary shrug.

Shiloh studied Dixon, then his face showed some openness.

"Hey. Tell me something. You know what. Tell me about your mom."

"Why you keep aksing?" Shiloh sounded more weary than angry. "Don't nobody talk 'bout her, it's like, it's like, if it wasn't for me, she wasn't even here. Ain't no clothes, no jewelry, ain't but, like fo' pi'tures of her, and shit. I aksed my Granny once before Granny die, 'What was my momma like?' right, and Granny tell me five things. Five things. Like that's all she was." He rocked forward.

"What were the five things?"

"Why should I tell you?"

"So you're not the only one who knows. So I'm your witness."

Shiloh shifted in his seat, frowning, his hands clasped in front of him. Dixon waited. Shiloh cast a long stare, weighing it. His voice grew low. "She love eating all them bright red kinda cherries out the jar and then she leave the juice, like she think nobody could tell. She won a spelling bee in fifth grade for the whole county. She like to sing 'Go Tell It on the Mountain' 'cause she said she like to think they was shouting on the mountain like the choir did in church." He exhaled a short laugh. "She want to be a nurse. She want to get married and have five babies and a big house wit' a white picket fence. And that's all I know."

"There's a lot there. What she dreamed about, her sense of humor . . ."

"It ain't her."

Dixon knew what he meant. It wasn't Shiloh and her. "I hear you."

"All I ever seen o' her was her dead."

"You weren't there, I thought."

"Then how come I r'member her bloody and shit? They say I ain't seen her die, but I r'member her lying there. I seen it. They say, 'You wasn't even there.' They try and say it was the car accident where my face got cut. But she dead in my mind, and I seen it and that's all I r'member seeing of her."

So that was what accounted for his face. Why wasn't that in any of the files? Dixon remembered his older cousin Jed after a car accident in those days before safety glass. Jed, whose face had gone through the windshield, had small shards of glass embedded in his face, and the nurses and doctors extracted them with tweezers while he moaned and whimpered. Why the hell was Dixon in the room? He would've been five or six years old. Did it even happen that way? He remembered hiding his face against Nate's arm. But this much he knew was true: when Jed was released from the hospital, his face looked like ground meat and the bloody smell made Dixon gag.

"I seen that shit. Don't nobody believe me."

"I believe you," Dixon said.

Shiloh stared off a long time, his arms tight around himself, rocking again in that self-soothing way. This was hardest, to *see* him. Yet this was what Dixon had been seeking, what he had insisted on. "That's an awful thing, son. You can't unsee it, you can't not know. I'm sorry."

"I remember how she smell," he nearly whispered. "How she hold my hand at night till I fall asleep. How she sing, 'This little light a mine,' how she shine, she shine." Shiloh closed his eyes, swallowed. Within reach, Dixon might grab him now, stop the slow, inevitable fall. He might. Too late, too late, the boy grew agitated, rearing back in his seat, stretching beyond Dixon's reach, bouncing up and then sitting on his hands. "Don't tell nobody my shit. And I 'on't need your fucking pity." He spit out the last part.

"It's not pity. I won't tell, don't worry."

"What I got to worry 'bout? You the one need to worry. My boy up in here, he say, you pro'ly ain't suppose to be talking to me. I tell my lawyer, I can get you busted. Oh yeah," the boy said with satisfaction.

Dixon didn't move.

Shiloh's low grunt of pleasure. He rose. "You can go now. And keep your fucking mouth shut."

HE WASN'T SURE HE SHOULD TRY THIS, BUT HE'D GROWN BORED of old-lady push-ups and partial squats. It was time to run again. Thing was, he knew the rules: Warm up. Stretch in the middle. Don't ask your body to train on lousy fuel. Hydrate. So why, he kept asking himself, wasn't he following the rules? He pounded his feet hard along the pavement and over to the park opposite his house. Almost immediately, pain carved a path from the stubs of his toes to his heel, trenched its way toward his ankle, and knifed into his calf. But he did not stop, as if the pain was his very aim all along. His eyes welled up. Half a mile—only half a fucking mile— and he faltered, stumbling and hitting the ground hard and skidding along his leg. He could feel blood spilling down his shin. He hopped to the grass beside the sidewalk and fell over onto his side, yanked up his pantleg. His foot, a bar of hot metal. The blessing of frostbite, he recalled, was the utter absence of pain, which was of course the death knell.

The park was empty. He could hear traffic on the other side of a row of trees, salvation so close, so distant. Five minutes, ten. Knees bent, elbows wrapped around them, he rocked back and forth. Invisible. The ground was cold and hard, a familiar comfort and punishment.

A black German shepherd bounded into the park. Shiloh's imagined dog. Dixon laughed, and it snapped him out of his reverie. He gathered himself to stand. The dog came beside him, licking at the dried blood on his leg. "Vampire dog," he said. The dog whimpered in condolence and let Dixon rest one hand on his back briefly as he hopped, stopped, hopped, this dog become his guardian. At the edge of the park, the dog bowed his head and trotted away.

Dixon lay awake that night. February was ending, and March slid fast toward him, a shelf of rock dislodging, teetering. He drifted to sleep and the memory of an avalanche moved through him, the wave of snow and cold, the deep, guttural call of the mountain. He felt lashed to the bed, and when he kicked out, freeing himself, he felt the sensation of falling, the disorientation lodging itself so firmly that even the next day he could not get his bearings. He stood in the middle of the diner's walk-in freezer, a blast of cold at his back. A pale layer of ice on the boxes of frozen potatoes, a drift of snow easily wiped away, and yet he stared transfixed. Beyond it something yellow as the tents at Base Camp, as blue as sky, the whole treacherous terrible beautiful world just there.

"Yo, Dix man, can't you find them potatoes?" Herbert's voice bellowed into the freezer. Dixon snapped out of his trance. He grabbed two boxes of frozen French fries and headed out, closing the door hard behind him.

"Whatchu do, forget why you was in there?" Herbert asked.

Dixon nodded, returning from the mountain.

"Say, you seen your boy Hardhead?"

"Yeah. That's the right word for him." He considered how Shiloh had become both more vulnerable and more unreachable at the same time. "He's in another world."

"Always was. Another world from you. You was in the big house, he was in the field. Me? I was in a rougher place than even your Shiloh. Wa'n't no suburbs, now. Them old projects down southeast? Bailey Farms? Maaaan, I seen photos of Soweto looked better."

"That's rough." He thought of the letter Herbert said he had written to his younger self. Would Dixon recognize that boy as Herbert?

"It's your circumstance, ain't got to be your mindset. But it was mines. It's your boy Hardhead's, too." Herbert's face deflated. They sank into silence, Dixon fighting his way back from his mountain, Herbert fighting his way out of Bailey Farms.

Dixon knew then he needed Herbert's help. It was their turn to finish cleaning and lock up at the end of the workday. When they had finished and were at their lockers packing to go, Dixon sat on a low, wide bench. He told Herbert about Cal Fierston's last update.

"All you gave for that mountain, you gone let somebody else take it?" Herbert sat close beside Dixon and folded his hands in front of him. "What happened up there, man?"

"You, you can't breathe, you can't think, your body is swollen, aching, your limbs are turning black and dying. And you just want it so bad. So bad. But it's nothing, man, nothing compared to—he didn't die in my arms. He was dying, but he wasn't gone. And I left him, I left him. I was reckless with my brother's life. How do I get to be a hero behind that?" Dixon bent over, Herbert's hand firm on his back.

"Ah, you got to come through this, man, you got to reach the other shore. Don't give out," he whispered, "keep pulling for it."

———

HERBERT ARRIVED LATE THE NEXT DAY, WRAPPED IN HIS HOODIE with a leather vest over it, both garments pulled tight as a shield. He was in the back room changing into his apron, pulling it on slowly like maybe his skin was glass. Dixon stood beside his friend, immovable, like shelter. Herbert, his chin tucked toward his chest, eyes fixed on the apron, brought its ties slowly around his waist and said simply, "Hey," which resonated like gratitude.

Throughout the workday, Dixon kept an eye on Herbert, and it felt so ironic, doing for him what he had done so long for Dixon, something as simple as a slight push of the stool toward Dixon when he was favoring that foot. A way Herbert had of taking Dixon's pulse. And now he must return the favor.

They were in the locker room after their shift preparing to leave for the day. Dixon wasn't ready to let Herbert out of his sight. "Wanna beer, Big Man?"

Herbert cut his eye to Dixon. "It's three o'clock. You startin' early, huh?"

"All right. Coffee. Soda. Something."

They headed to a sports bar a short drive from the diner. Too early for liquor, according to Herbert, unless they decided to shoot pool—that, Herbert informed Dixon, required at least a beer. Herbert proceeded to beat Dixon mercilessly for two games, Dixon barely getting to move the pool stick from where it rested on the floor, his hands folded on top of it. He watched Herbert play and told him about his last visit to Shiloh, except for the five things. He wouldn't break the boy's confidence.

"You see something in that boy," Herbert said, then pronounced, "Eight ball, corner pocket."

Dixon swigged his beer. "What d'you mean?"

Herbert made his shot, finishing the game, and he and Dixon gathered the balls to set up for the next round. "I mean, I know what I see. Bunch of dudes I had knew. Whatchu see? Brother, uncle, cousin, best friend?"

"Nobody really, he's not quite like anybody I've known before, come to think of it."

"I doubt that. He a old story."

"Can I break the set for a change? Only way I'll get to play." Dixon chalked up his stick. "I know, by the way, that he's not new. I've had plenty kids who fucked up their lives. But this one, Shiloh, he's not the same. Most boys, there's some part of them you can grab hold of, pull 'em back. But him? I mean, he doesn't doubt." Dixon sank three balls and the cue ball. He sighed and went to sit down on a stool to the right of the table.

Herbert did not move toward the table. He stood dreamy, his eyes vacant. After a while, he sucked in a breath. "He a boy made up his mind 'bout hisself. And now, his whole world built on proving he ain't wrong."

It reverberated in Dixon, that cool, thin wire in him alive again. "That's me. That's been me." He gathered himself, and it felt like this: pulling up an arm here, a leg there, that feeling after being so cold on the mountain of reclaiming your body bit by bit, seeing what worked, what did not.

They finished the game in silence; rather, Herbert finished. Dixon sat on that high stool, his body bound tight. How long had he sat that way? Once on a flight from Denver to D.C., he had been assigned a middle seat between a very pregnant woman and a large man, and he had prided himself on fitting into that spot, his elbows dug into his chest, arms against his ribcage instead of on the armrests beside him. When they landed and he unfurled himself and stood, finally, in the aisle, stooping to avoid hitting his head on the ceiling, the woman had said, "Dear god, I felt so sorry for you. You looked absolutely miserable." He had laughed, incredulous, because she had not gotten the point. He had done it! It was required of him, and he had done it!

After Herbert had finished beating Dixon at pool, they stood at the bar waiting to pay their tab. Herbert reached inside his hoodie, hesitated a minute, a quiver passing over his face, some internal argument that he seemed to be losing. Then he pulled an envelope from his jacket and set it before Dixon on the bar. He patted it, and then backed away. A thing plucked fresh and beating. Herbert's letter. It carried Dixon to Nate unexpectedly, to the last moment of holding him, of burying his face against his brother's, which was so cold and hard, Clive hollering at Dixon to let go, and Nate's lips still moving Dixon was certain: *Tell my brother I didn't give up.*

Dixon clutched the letter, then slipped it into his inside jacket pocket against his chest.

IT WAS OVER, CHRIS TEMPLE TOLD HIM. SHILOH HAD ACCEPTED a plea deal that took life without parole off the table. "It's as good as we can hope for," Chris said over the phone, and Dixon couldn't help blurting out, "We?"

"Yes," she said emphatically, "those of us who actually care about him."

How did he get in that camp? "How do I get out," he said aloud after he'd hung up. Fifteen to twenty-five years, up for parole in twelve. Was that fair? Could anything be fair in exchange for Marcus's life?

He sat on the edge of a chair, pumping his hands into fists. On the edge of a happen, as his grandmother would say. His living room quiet as evening settled in. It did not feel welcoming. He wished he was in his family's den sitting with his brother and their dad, their mother in the kitchen baking her fabulous cakes, calling in, "I know no one has his feet on my coffee table." All of them watching TV, which was no small thing. All their lives, their father had battled with TV, his jaw set on edge, saying, "Look at that mess. Now, who do you know, what grown Black man is named Huggy Bear?" "Why is everybody a pimp on this station?" But when Dixon was about twenty-one, there was a TV show about a Black man who inherits his father's restaurant, and his father saw in that man, remarkably, his best self: bookish, even-tempered, standing tall in the world. The character, unlike the others they recalled, was neither poor and happy about it nor undereducated and filthy rich. He seemed just a man, one who knew who he was, living among others who did, too; no buffoonery, no shucking and jiving. He lived clean and clear, his father liked to say, and Dixon gathered he meant there was a cloak that had fallen from him. Dixon could see that image, the TV character alone on a bare stage, untying a ribbon at his neck and a cloak dropping away so that he stood perfectly himself, a remarkably simple act of bravery. Every week, then, the boys watched not the TV so much as their father, who would remark, "He's just a man, and why shouldn't he get to be?" The whole of the world came to rest in that room, Dixon and his brother and father, his mother just at the edge, pausing, to watch a free man.

Dixon could not remember feeling truly free.

NEARLY MARCH FIRST. THREE WEEKS TILL EVEREST SEASON, and he might lose his claim to that goddamned mountain. It might be a relief, having it all taken away. Fitting, too. But just as swiftly that idea felt unbearable. He thought about it all through afternoon supper one Sunday at Charlaina's, the words rising to his lips—"I'm about to miss my claim to Everest"—then falling away. After supper, he and Charlaina lounged in her solarium, the sun dancing warm against their skin. They sprawled across the plush sofa, their legs stretched out on the massive ottoman before them. That is, his legs stretched out, Charlaina's feet just propped at the edge, barely reaching. He laughed, her feet arched as if she stood on tiptoe. "Char, tell the truth. He was your favorite."

She glanced at him and then away. "Actually, I hardly thought of you separately. I mean, you were one entity to me, you know. Nixon."

He smiled.

"Then you were NateandDixon. Truth be told, I'm having to learn to see you now, I'm ashamed to say, to see you not as half but whole. I would've had to for him, too." She sipped her wine, then ran her finger around the rim of her glass. The glass hummed a high-pitched tune. "I'm going to tell you something. Listen, Dixon, listen to me. I haven't been sure whether to say but I think it'll help. Are you listening?"

"Yes," he whispered, eyes closed, a palpitation beating in his throat.

"About a month before you left for that mountain. He told me, Nate told me when I asked him how on earth he could be doing this, how he could think this was a good idea, I mean, I really gave it to him, I told him, I said awful things to try and shock him, I said, 'You're nobody's athlete,' I said, oh, Dixon, I said to him, 'You'll never make it to the top, you know, Dixon will be the one and you'll lose to your little brother again, do you want that?' and you know what he said? He said, 'I know that.' He said, 'Of course I know that, Char. This is for him. I want him to have this.' Dixon, that's why he wouldn't let you say no. You made it. You have to claim it as yours. He put you there."

She reached into her pocket, then handed him a white hand-kerchief with neat bric-a-brac edging, her finger motioning to his cheeks, his runny nose. Apparently, he was crying.

"I used to know how to live, Char."

They sat quiet a long while. The sun began to set, streaking purple and fiery red across the horizon. He felt himself sliding down with it, a steady retreat. Falling, still, as if instead of climbing to the top of the world, he had set in motion a perpetual tumble away from it.

"Mom made me promise something," he began. His mother, that way she had looked at them, a slight squint as if trying to put them in just the right light. She had pulled Dixon aside when he was about ten. That year, Nate had had a series of run-ins with teachers for saying smart-aleck stuff that made the whole class laugh. Nearly every week, Dixon might find his brother on the bench outside the principal's office, one of their parents having been summoned. An anticipatory knot formed in Dixon's belly, a loose fist waiting to clench whenever he rounded the corner near the office. Would he come across his brother sitting on that iron bench with his head down, his legs swinging useless, and his expression so easily read: *Why did I do it* again?

One day in late October that year, nearly six weeks into Nate's reign of terror, Dixon sat beside Nate on the iron bench as their mother talked with the principal inside the office. She emerged tight-lipped, her hand gripping her shoulder bag to steady herself. She seemed beyond the point of anger—hadn't they punished and beseeched Nate enough by now? She pointed Nate toward the exit. Nate gave Dixon a sorrowful look. Once Nate was out of sight, their mother leaned down to Dixon, her voice quavering. "You must watch out for him. I know you're the younger one, but you've got the compass, Dixon. Lead the way. Promise me," she had whispered, the desperation in her voice, her hot, sweet breath. *Promise me.*

All this he told to Charlaina. She placed her palm on his knee. "I know. I heard my mother complaining about it to my dad. She thought it was cruel. She used to say, 'Don't keep calling that boy the "good one." It damns him and his brother.'" She grasped her empty glass with both hands, stared down into it. "I lied. I saw you separately, I did. You were so dutiful to him, Dixon." She gazed at him. "So I took it, I made it my job to look after you." Her voice full of emotion. "Oh, Dixon, did I fail you?"

His hands in his lap, limp, palms up. "Char, I think the world doesn't work that way. No matter what we do."

"Nobody told us." Her voice cracked.

"I left him. Not quite dead. Calling after me, maybe. I think I heard him."

A soft gasp. "What?"

"I couldn't lift him, I could barely walk. He was half-dead. Coughing up blood." He looked at her as he spoke, her face stricken. "They made me. I would've died, too."

She turned her head from him, turned far to the other side, her chin pressed against her shoulder. He heard her ragged breathing.

"He couldn't really have been talking, he was unconscious, nearly dead, but I heard it, I hear it. I hear it."

"Stop. Stop." Her hands on his cheeks.

"I hear him, I still hear him."

"Quiet, now." Her forehead against his, they wept.

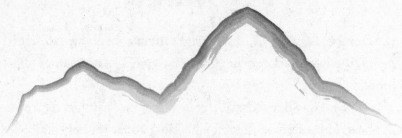

Young Man,

I am about to show you your life. You can imagine me your
fortuneteller if you want. But beleve I am on your side.

Because I know you Young Man. I am you. I am writing
to you from the afterlife of a 17 year bit. That is 17 years behind steel bars and concrete and razor wire to think on every
minute every second every blink of a eye every wipe of a brow
every twitch of a muscle that lead to where you at. Im 46 years
old. No steady woman, no homies left. Working two shit jobs
and lucky to have em. Just got me a piece a car. Before that I
was a grown man with a bicycle. Live in one room with a hot
plate. And this a good life. My one room used to be a cell, my
job used to be keeping a eye on where every big motherfucka
who want to be king in the joint was every minute of the day
watching over my shoulder for when they come at me. Being

*told when to pee when to eat when to sleep when to be a man. And that aint the hardest part is it? Cause you steady praying God give you relief cause you starting to feel the consequnse of all you have did.*

*You had made yourself a problem, a menace to society, like they say. How that feel in your real heart when you all alone late night, do that give you comfort? I know it don't I know it twist like that razor wire you live behind and you thinking ain't nothing you know how to do about it.*

*That's why I have to school you see cause I want to be clear. That thing you feeling Young Man like something have blown apart inside and now you free-bleeding let me tell you what that is. Ashame. A word that if you don't know you gonna learn soon enough. Penance too will be another one of your new words. You getting a bad vocabulerey.*

*Let me tell you something you dont know: You got good in you. It just need to be trained, like you do anything you love train em up. You got to raise your good. You got to give it room dont fear it will make you weak. You be mad raging now but all you gone be left with is this Ashame. You got to let go the shame let go the rage. Stop. Sit still just sit still.*

*You got to let them people who trying to help you help you. Otherwise its a long ugly life. Im telling you Im <u>begging</u> you dont just suffer years and years alone.*

*Signed, Mr. Dixon friend Herbert*

The afternoon settled in clear and mild, the sun pale in the early March sky. Shiloh's allocution to accept the plea bargain would be the following week.

"Your punk-ass again." Shiloh leaned to the side in his chair, arms folded over his chest.

"You don't ease up, do you?" Dixon sighed.

"On you? Why should I? Whatchu want now?"

"You know, we go over this every time I come. Nothing's changed." Dixon had looked at Marcus's photo this morning and had arrived shored up by his anger. "Next week, the jig is up," Dixon said.

Shiloh frowned. "What that mean? Some kinda code?"

"It's an old expression."

"'Cause you old." He rolled his eyes.

"One week until you get sentenced. How're you feeling about that?"

"Kiss my ass," Shiloh said. Dixon laughed to himself. What, no "fuck you" followed by bolting from the table? He must be softening. Shiloh sucked his teeth. "What you know 'bout it? You come 'round to celebrate?"

"You've got an attitude today. I don't see anything to celebrate. Marcus is still dead."

Shiloh glared at him and then away. He said nothing for a long time. "You sent me that weak-ass letter. 'Signed Mr. Dixon friend Herbert.' Why you think I care some old dude got locked up?"

He frowned at the boy. "You're just all in your own way, aren't you? My friend was trying to offer you some insight. But you don't want help, do you?"

"When I aksed you for shit?"

"Everything you do shows how much help you need."

"So you get some old-head con send me a letter. What, he my best friend now? Shiloh ain't stupid, now. I ain't gonna be crying like some little bitch 'bout myself."

"You would if you had sense. Son, you are about to take a plea, and you're going away for a long time."

"What, you here to make sure, ain't you? You want me begging you, you want me, what, like that fat-ass bitch of yours? He was all like, 'please please.' Don't nobody care!"

Dixon's body tightened. "He begged you to stop?"

Shiloh began to rock slowly. "Fat-ass mothafucka. Whining-ass bastard." His eyes widened. Dixon was certain the scene played before the boy's eyes.

One hand gripping the seat of his chair, reining himself in, Dixon's voice quavering. "He. Begged. You."

Shiloh pursed his lips, a flash of terror passing over his face. He took in a hard breath and pulled back in his chair. "Everything my fault, huh?" The gears in the boy visible, cranking and churning, he hollered out, "He ain't have to go dying on me! How he do me like that? Now I gotta suffer for that!" His face ragged, raging, an awful mirror.

A bolt of anger and Dixon was on his feet. "You didn't see how badly hurt he was? You had the chance to do something! You could've *done* something! But you left him!"

"He the one fell! He killed hisself!" Shiloh kicked out the chair as he rose. "You 'on't want a nigga be angry?" He slapped his chest so hard Dixon felt the thump. "You want me just sit back and take it? I'm tired of it! I'm tired of it!"

One move, a smooth easy snatch across the table, and Dixon had him. The boy gasped, a flash of fear. Dixon loomed over him. Dixon had Shiloh by the collar, both hands full of the fabric of his jumpsuit. The boy's bones sharp and fragile as a chicken's.

A guard rushed toward Dixon, another yanked at Shiloh. A

hand around Dixon's neck, a sharp jab to his solar plexus, a series of gasps for air.

Shiloh collapsed backward. All the jabbering going on, the guards, the visitors, the boys yelling and jeering. Two guards held Dixon, bracing him. "Press charges," he heard someone yelling at Shiloh. A cold fear racked Dixon. Shiloh, his breath calming, stared at Dixon, wide-eyed.

They carted Dixon off to the warden's office. There might be charges pressed, did he understand? The warden was a man of about sixty, his mustache wide and pure gray. He leaned over his desk toward Dixon, hurling questions at a staccato clip. Had Dixon been ill? Was he all right? Did he need a doctor? Dixon sank into the chair and closed his eyes. He heard the clank of cell doors, the beat of loud voices, a boy's wail climbing the walls, primal, raging.

---

"BOY, YOU REALLY LIKE YOUR SUFFERING," HERBERT SCOLDED after Dixon told him about his latest visit to Shiloh. "You going to jail now?"

"Got to pay a fine and I'm banned from visiting that place. Had to produce a letter saying I have PTSD." He reminded himself to call and thank Benny Lewis.

"Dix man, what I'mma do with you?"

"He flipped out about the letter."

"I ain't surprised. He ain't ready yet, but so long as he keep it. He'll come to it. He'll come to it." Herbert fiddled around with a knife, a ladle, a grill scraper, touching and turning each one as if they spoke to him. "I was a raging man a long time. A long time. You wanna know why I be looking out for you? I see you, man, all up in the wilderness. Tell you something else. You aksed, why would some guys go hunting for that boy, try to get him to turn himself in, you know, get right with his consequences. I ain't think you'd understand then, but I know you do now. I tell you why. 'Cause he our burden."

That evening when Dixon pulled into the parking spot in front of his townhouse, he found Skeet waiting in the car beside him. Skeet stared straight ahead, motionless as if he were set in stone. A long time before he emerged. Drawn, thin, his mustache full of white, his wide chest deflated, Skeet must've lost thirty pounds.

Inside Dixon's house, Skeet downed a shot glass of whiskey. He sat at an angle in a dining chair next to Dixon, Skeet's body half on, half off the chair so Dixon wondered if he might bolt at any moment. "I wanted to believe, you know?" Skeet poured another whiskey. "I didn't want to be the one who says 'No, don't do it,' who tells you not to try. That's not who he ever was to me. So I swallowed it." His look plaintive. "He tried, Dixon, he tried so hard. I never saw him try harder."

"I know." The silence vibrating with Nate's presence.

"I thought, maybe, you know, why not? He could do so much in life. He had talents." Skeet gave a wry laugh. "The greatest one was making us believe in him." They poured more whiskey. Skeet drank his quickly. Dixon sloshed his around and stared into it. "Dixon, you know I didn't mean it, before, at Char's. I was just out of my head."

"I know."

"How you doing? How are you, man?" He touched Dixon's hand.

The wide familiarity in that touch opened him. "I wanna run.

But." He took off his shoe, then the prosthetic. Skeet's hand over his mouth. "Fell last time." He snorted a laugh. "The man he once was—"

"Uh uh," Skeet cut him off. "That's not the world we're gonna live in."

———

"I DIDN'T WANT TO CLIMB MOUNTAINS," LENA EXPLAINED. "They are nice to look at, but who needs to climb a fucking mountain?" She said *foc-king* with a hard g, which amused him.

"Me either," Dixon said. "This guy I used to work with, Julian, was from Seattle. Talked about mountains all the time, 'You don't know what it does to your life to live at the foot of Rainier.'"

"Oh, they are always from Seattle," she said knowingly.

"I didn't really pay attention, but then the year my marriage was crashing and burning, he looked at me one day, said, 'I know what you need.' He started talking up this trip to Kilimanjaro." Julian, sitting plain and easy in front of Dixon in the teachers' lounge, within the din of coffee brewing and laughter swirling, papers being shuffled, the quotidian life surrounding them, yet Julian's face seemed bathed in wonder as he recalled mountains. "It seemed exotic," Dixon explained. The solitude, the life of the body, Julian told Dixon, would bring him clarity. "I needed a time-out. And it was Africa, which seemed like a spiritual journey, you know." He remembered dreaming of the stark beauty, of anticipating a homecoming. "I don't know, I just knew I could do it."

"I am like you, I think. I did it because I could. I tried it, being a big shot, you know, with my friends and also I didn't want Christoph going without me, with that Iliana on the trip, that one! My

Christoph, he was just like your brother, you know what I mean?"
She faded off a minute. "So I go, and look at me, I am good! Strong
lungs but I don't know what the hell I'm doing. I get stuck trying
to get over a ledge, Christo get so mad at me! I come home, I learn
my stuff. I'm never going to get laughed at again. But it took a long
time to learn the mountain, not the climb, but her. Like I showed
you, remember?"

"Christoph, is he the one who died?"

"Yes. It had been told to us, 'Is unstable ice today, wait,' but we
were so in a hurry, too young, ack! We think, 'We can do it.' You
know, Dixon, what it is to be beat by the mountain. It is not because I am a woman, or small, or speak the wrong language. It is
because I am. Some days she does not want you. That is all. Is the
only true equality in the world, yes?" She paused a long while.
"Dixon, you must stop suffering. You break my heart."

"You didn't want to break my heart." He lay flat on his back in
the dark, the phone cradled in the crook of his neck. "I remember
you kissed me hard after you said that."

"No, I didn't want *you* to break your heart. I didn't really have
nothing to do with it. I still don't."

"What do you mean?"

Her sigh sounded impatient.

Sinking down in bed, his hand on his stomach, hot, flat, smooth.
"Come to me. Come see me."

"Oh," a soft exhale.

He pictured her standing before him, a thin veil of fabric, a
thing he could just reach.

"You want too much," she whispered. The muffled sound, a
hand washing over the receiver. "I am all the way to Seattle."

"It's not as far as Nepal. I'll come to you, then."

"By then, I will be gone. Home to Sofia. Then to another mountain."

"Wait for me."

"We don't climb the same mountain. I will pass you by. Dixon, you must tell the reporter. Tell him the truth. Then you won't need me."

He hung up deflated, exhaustion creeping over him. His eyes closed, there was Nate, indistinguishable in a mound of snow, his hair and clothing white, even his skin glossy with the sheen of frost.

He sat upright. What if he wasn't meant to carry the mountain alone? Then it was right to come clean. To give it away—he thought of it that way, of giving his summit away, a purge—what if that might make him whole again?

CHAPTER

23

The diner seemed the only safe place to do this. Dixon certainly wasn't going to ask Cal Fierston to come to his house. Better to invite Cal to meet him late afternoon. The place would be nearly empty. Since Dixon and Herbert were on closing, they could stay as long as they wanted.

Dixon sat across from Cal in a sunny booth near the back, knowing that just behind the swinging doors Herbert leaned against the countertop, listening, head down, arms folded. Cal spread out on the table between them a spiral notebook, his iPhone, a ballpoint with a chewed end, and the photo of Dixon at the summit. Dixon told the story of Nate dying on the mountain. Nearly the whole truth of the climb. The lie of it—the photo—lay faceup on the table.

When Dixon was done, with a long exhale Cal said, "That's an awful story. I'm sorry, Dixon." He took off his glasses, wiped the lenses clean on his shirttail, and put them back on. "You know, you're not the only man to lose a brother on a mountain. There's a famous climber, you must know the story—"

"I know. It doesn't matter. This is the one that happened to me." Dixon pressed his hands into the sticky Naugahyde seat. He avoided looking at the summit photo. He could feel how numb his chin had been in the cold, the weight of the ice on his mustache.

Cal Fierston sat back in his seat. He rolled a pen under his fingers. "What drove you to do the climb? You never really said."

"He did. He wanted it. I didn't so much." He frowned at himself. This wasn't quite true.

"Do you still have the desire, I mean, since you didn't summit? You didn't, correct?" Cal put a finger on the photo and slid it closer to Dixon.

Outside the window, the swaying of tree branches, their fresh green leaves rustling in the breeze, formed a busy language muted by the thick glass. The photo called to him. Why wouldn't Cal put it away? The photo like a beacon, he squinted against its light. His body emitted a low hum of electricity. "We thought it was freedom. It looks like freedom, anyway." He stopped, words swirling inside him.

"You feel duped?"

"Yes." Dixon sat on his hands. It was such an ancient feeling, spiraling up through his body. He felt prickly, flushed, like he might throw up.

"Because of what? Explain it to me."

Dixon took a breath to steady himself. "This was between us, I think, me and Nate. It got away from us somehow." At the top of the world, he had lived on borrowed air and transcended his known world. He began his descent then, falling away from himself. This fucking lie. There was no one to protect, there was nothing but unpardonable truth. Electricity sparked through the core of him. He remained the boy who could not rest with a lie. A heaving breath, then he folded toward the table, exhausted. He tapped the photo with one finger. "This," he exhaled, "is me."

———

THE NEXT DAY, AN ORDINARY MID-MARCH MORNING, DIXON headed for Court Room A on the fourth floor of the County Court-house, a place he found disappointingly modern, full of matte aluminum and blond hardwood. He had imagined it with high-domed ceilings and murals of gods and judges in flowing robes, their fingers raised to scold.

The hallway was long and plain, linoleum not marble. He climbed the wide industrial stairs to the third floor, headed to Court Room A, entered the crowded room, and sat two rows from the back. Mrs. Hollinger stood among a throng at the front of the room, and when she saw Dixon, she walked slow and straight-backed toward him. She made everyone in the courtroom see her suffering, dazzling and awful, in her quiet sighs, in her misshapen, wrung-out sweater.

Dixon rose and headed toward her. She was followed by nearly a dozen people. He recognized some of their faces from Marcus's room the night he died. Across each of their T-shirts a photo of Marcus was emblazoned, Marcus's face bright and full in the crin-kled fabric. How could they stand to carry their dead like that? Dixon cringed, then thought of all the ways to carry one's dead. Mrs. Hollinger reached him finally and grasped both his hands in hers. "Marcus's Mr. Dixon," she announced, and the group mur-mured approval, greetings. His throat felt raw and dry. He eked out hellos.

"Well, there's justice coming today, Mr. Dixon," Marcus's mother said. "That boy gets put away. Hallelujah." Her chorus echoed her hallelujahs. Dixon bowed his head. He didn't feel triumphant, he didn't feel justified. Mrs. Hollinger began, "I wished, I hoped I got to say something, you know, speaking up for my son. But they don't do that since the boy already admit he's guilty. Can I, Mr. Dixon, can I tell you what I have to say?" She stepped closer. Her breath minty and warm. "Well, I'da tole them he was all the hope we had, you know." Her eyes were filmed with memory.

A stutter in his belly, Dixon swayed slightly forward, which Mrs. Hollinger took as invitation, and she plunged her body into his in a tight, hard hug. Just like Marcus.

Back in his pew, Dixon half listened as the proceedings began. He took the measure of the room. There were only two people he knew for certain were there for Shiloh. First was Chris Temple and the other was Shiloh's aunt. She looked both self-righteous and resigned. An impenetrable-looking woman. He was so distracted trying to get a read on her that he missed Shiloh's uneventful entrance. When Dixon looked eventually at the defendant's table, at the skinny boy in an ill-fitting suit in which he seemed to be drowning, it startled him. There were shackles around the boy's ankles.

Shiloh sat down gingerly, grabbing the sides of the chair. His eye blackened again. It seemed to be the other eye, a fresh bruise. He was small and battered, but the hardened expression he wore loomed large enough for both his own aunt and Mrs. Hollinger to fold their arms, to shift their bodies away from him. How could a boy, just one boy, carry all that weight? The weight of fear and distrust and his own hardened anger about it? Even his lawyer seemed to keep a cool distance from Shiloh, warned off by his sullenness. By something else, too, something tired and lost and failing.

The boy's face immoveable. He sat bolt upright, but his legs trembled so hard that his shackles rattled. The sharp sound circled the room and landed on Dixon.

Much of what happened next blurred by: the entrance of the judge and his initial questions, the opening statements. Dixon floated, underwater. Again, he wondered why there was no gilding in the courtroom, no stained glass. No evidence of the fear of law or God. Sure, the judge tried his best with his sweeping black robe, the high lectern of the bench. But he was less godlike than, say, Dixon's boyhood preacher, who seemed to descend from heaven each time he left the pulpit, his black robe adorned with a velvet collar, that embroidered gold cross along the yoke a gleaming burden, the drape of his full sleeves arcing like wings.

The D.A. Tito Aguilar gestured and spoke in a deep, purposeful bass, a tone filled with the gravity of the day. He was dark-haired with a wide streak of silver at both temples. He seemed to glance often toward Dixon.

From behind him, a firm, flat palm landed against Dixon's shoulder. Instinctively, he expected to see Nate. Herbert clapped his shoulder again and took a seat in the row behind.

Dixon kept his eyes on the back of Shiloh's head. A lollipop of a head swelling over his ridiculously slight body. The judge's opening remarks droned in the background to the rattle of Shiloh's shackles, that sound betraying the boy. It was all that Dixon could hear but then the judge mentioned Marcus's name, and his mother cried out, "My boy! My boy!" And the mention of Marcus, the idea of him, electrified Dixon's pulse.

He picked a spot on the far side of the room, near a bank of high windows, and let his mind rest there. *You have to have a safe perch, a deep ledge that is stable and tucked back against the slate arms of the mountain. That's where you pitch your tent, out of the wind alleys, clear of obvious loose rocks and snow. You shelter but in the open. It is after all just a ledge, pitched high and jutting straight out into the sky. All thin blue sky and shallow air below, the limitations of gravity made clear: it will not buoy you, it will not cushion you from a hard tumble, it will not save you.*

―――――

CAL FIERSTON'S BACK STRAIGHTENED, THEN HE BENT FORWARD across the table toward Dixon. "So you *have* been lying to me." Each man's finger on an edge of the summit photo, they pinned it to the table between them. "Why own up to it now?"

A sorrowful laugh burst from Dixon. "I can't help myself."

"Clearly, this had to be you, from everything I was told. But you insisted it was Nate. Frankly, that was more intriguing than the truth." He paused. "Heartbreaking, really. Why did you want it to be him?"

"Don't blame him. I don't want him blamed."

"You think you're protecting him, then, is that it? Some people might think you're protecting yourself."

Dixon felt small, helplessly caught.

"It might seem you didn't want the blame for your brother's death. Is that it? Well, from what I've learned, it wasn't your fault. It was a series of terrible mishaps, the kind the mountain just offers no margin of forgiveness for. Are you listening? You shouldn't fear the truth."

"Why does this matter to you?"

"Why not? You're a school psychologist, and you go to climb Mount Everest. You're an average guy who did an extraordinary thing, especially for a Black man."

Dixon sucked in a hard breath. A feeling of exhaustion started mid-chest and seeped into every part of his body. *For a Black man.* Because he was expected to represent them all. "What did you say before about aftermath, something about wanting to tell that?"

"I think it's important. I mean, how you live after things happen. We all need to understand that."

"That's your thing, then, that's what's making you want to do this? Did you lose someone on a mountain?"

Cal stared out of the window awhile, then said, "No."

"So is this what you write about usually? Do you, what, do you have a following?"

Cal cleared his throat. "I'm, I'm establishing one."

"I see. You're trying to make a name for yourself." He squeezed hard on the bridge of his nose. "So you want me to be known for my worst mistake. And how do I live after that?"

---

SHILOH'S LAWYER STOOD FIRST, THEN BECKONED SHILOH TO get to his feet. The judge peered at the boy. Did he understand the deal he had agreed to? Yes? Then it was time to tell the court what happened.

"We was tussling it up, me and my boy." Shiloh tossed his head to an imaginary person.

"He wasn't 'your boy'!" Marcus's mother shouted, and a chorus of groans rose around her.

The judge smacked his gavel. "You will please refrain from outbursts. If they continue, I'll have to clear the courtroom."

His lawyer in his ear, talking fast, inaudible, Shiloh nodded and started again. "We was tusslin'. Kinda rough. It was—" His shoulders rose and fell slightly. "He fell and hit his head. I ain't mean, you know, I ain't know he was gone die and all. I ain't meant for him to die."

The Hollingers were wiping their eyes. Shiloh's back to Dixon, who read the knotted ropes of the boy's shoulders, the way he shrank down and then rose back up into himself.

"Young man," the judge interrupted, "let's start again. You need to tell us precisely what happened and what role you played in it."

Shiloh glanced around once, his gaze landing on Dixon, the boy's eyes hooded, a light sweat on his brow, and then his face broke into a momentary wave of panic. Dixon locked onto the boy, who looked at Dixon with such pleading. What did he want? Dixon grew agitated, uncomfortable, and looked away. There, in the doorway, stood Nate, his Nate, not dead, not suffering, Nate dimpled and smiling, wearing his favorite double-breasted suit, dark-navy gabardine, and camel-leather shoes, Nate with a hand in his pocket like always. He leaned against the doorframe long and lean, one leg crossed in front of the other. Dixon's hand up to his mouth, his breathing too hard and fast. He rose quickly, banging his knee against the seat in front of him, shuffling and scrambling to get to Nate. Shiloh's eyes on him. Nate in the doorway. Dixon must get to him. Now.

---

CAL SAT QUIET, PATIENT, WAITING FOR DIXON TO EXPLAIN. THE sunlight diffuse, it was much later than Dixon had thought. "You can't imagine where you're getting the energy from. You're, you're outside of yourself and just trudging up that mountain because you don't know how to stop. Maybe you can't imagine what else to do, not in some, some heroic way, but a kind of robotic, senseless, I don't know what to call it. Hypnotism, maybe. There's no other world, no other consequence, no other responsibility but getting to that fucking summit. You're in bondage. You cannot stop. You go and go. You're in a tunnel, you're heading for that light and the train might be coming, but it just might not be, and you're getting closer and that's how it is. Then there it is, the summit."

"Exalting, yes?"

He gripped his hands together. He whispered, "No. The loneliest place I've ever been."

"Dixon, isn't there any part you can celebrate?"

"I want to be proud. I might be one day. For my brother's sake. I don't know. Now, I hate that I did it."

Cal sat, hands folded. "You mean, you hate that you did it alone."

Dixon swallowed and his voice left him, a thin ribbon spiraling out of his body and hovering above them. He followed its movement. Then he began to sob.

⸻

DIXON SPRINTED FROM THE COURTROOM AND INTO THE HALL-way, panting, sweating. He scanned the corridor, listening for Nate. Before now, there had been no real visitations from Nate, only haunting visions of him half-frozen, not yet dead, still waiting to be found on the shoulder of their mountain. "Nate, where are you?" he whispered.

He inhaled deeply, letting the air swell his lungs. Hallucinations. Jesus, what was next? *Get a grip*, he told himself. *He is not here. He's gone. He's gone.* He sank down onto a bench at the back of the corridor.

Herbert sat down beside Dixon, sat just like him, hands folded between spread-apart knees. They might be in prayer. Groups of people hustled back and forth down the corridor. Whispers, raised voices, muffled tears.

Herbert said, "He a little dude. I ain't expect that. He gone hafta keep swinging a while, keep the big boys off him. That ain't on you, by the way, so don't go feeling some kinda way 'bout it."

The hallway bright and antiseptic-smelling, Dixon thought they might be in a hospital corridor, they might be awaiting some awful news. "You should've known Marcus. Really gifted at math. Compassionate. Took up a collection for a kid whose house had burned down. But you know what? He was goofy, too, man, a little pitiful. He could split his pants in front of the whole class but laugh about it, like really let it roll off him. When he got excited, he spit, laughing and spraying, then he'd cover his mouth and yell, 'I'm spitting,' and laugh louder."

Herbert banged his leg softly into Dixon's. "You had love for that boy."

"I did."

"Tell me something. Have doing the right thing always came easy to you?"

"I guess, maybe," he croaked out. "Yes."

"Well, I'm tryina get used to it. I mean, if I'm in Marcus people's place? I'd want that boy under the jail, rest of his life. But I don't have that luxury of not knowing how it feel to be sitting there seeing what you have did and how you have lost your life, man. That moment, it'll come back to young'un, middle of the night, early in the morning. It's hard man, it's hard."

Dixon sat up straight. "You said, a long time ago, you either have to have a heart for justice or a conscience, but you can't have both. But you have to have both, I think."

"And that don't fuck you up?" Herbert's voice was quiet.

"Yes. It's supposed to."

Dixon walked back into the courtroom just in time to see Shiloh stand and accept his fate. Twenty-five years, the maximum, served first in juvenile jail until he reached eighteen and the remainder in adult prison. Did the boy rage or weep? Along the rugged landscape of Shiloh's face, what was on display? Dixon, like most everyone in the courtroom except the judge, saw only the back of Shiloh's head, the boy standing bolt upright, his narrow shoulders straining to fill out his suit. He had glanced backward once straight at Dixon, blinked, then turned away. That boy Dixon had seen as evil personified. *This* boy, his chains bellowing through the room. This boy in whom Dixon recognized the thing he could never quite identify before. The thing that had compelled Dixon. He locked eyes with Shiloh and saw it: a wild, voracious grief.

———

SKEET APPEARED AT HIS DOOR A FEW DAYS LATER—"YOU ready?"—and drove them to the trails in Great Falls Park. "I know you love it here," he said once they had arrived. They stretched a long while before jogging along a low trail. Skeet quietly monitored Dixon as they gained speed and elevation. Dixon had bandaged his foot to give him better cushion so the foot didn't pain him, but the work of running bit into his thigh and calf muscles. It felt good.

Ahead of him a group of riders on sleek racing bikes wound their way up the trail. Dixon ran toward the heart of the group and then the riders accelerated and sped like birds, beating against gravity and disappearing over the crest of the hill.

Dixon pushed himself forward, Skeet right beside him. He didn't remember Skeet being a runner, but clearly he had a good stride. Dixon could tell Skeet was holding himself back, letting Dixon set the pace. So Dixon accelerated both to see if he could and if Skeet could keep up. Dixon felt winded but only a twinge of pain. Skeet was right on his heels. Dixon slowed, and Skeet did, too. "You got some chops, huh? When did you start running?" he asked Skeet.

Skeet's smile was sheepish. "Always did. Just had sense enough not to race you back then. Came into my own in grad school. Long distance, mostly, just to work out stress."

"Did Nate know?"

"Umm hmm." He raised his eyebrows in affirmation.

"Figures. He was your boy."

Skeet slowed, hands on hips. "You were, too. I always liked you more than you did me."

Dixon was happy to walk a minute, catch his breath. "What do you mean? I liked you fine."

"I mean, you had him. There wasn't any other room."

"I don't think that's true. You were *his* friend, right? In all his classes. You all had that girl-chasing thing and, and the business club and all that."

"I studied with you. I was a bookworm. You don't remember?"

Dixon shrugged. Sure, he remembered Skeet studying with him, but once Nate came along, then it was all Nate.

Skeet cracked his knuckles. "I used to feel like, like, you thought you were babysitting me. You were being polite, letting me study with you but then the minute Nate came in the room, you were like, 'I'm outta here.'"

"I was always heading to practice. You two always had something to get up to, I mean, it was good he had you, right?"

Skeet kicked at the ground. "I was as much your friend as anybody."

"Where's this coming from?"

"I was part of this, too, you know. It wasn't just you and him, it was, it was everybody you know, you took us up that mountain, man, don't you know that? No, I wasn't with you but I was *with* you. I've always been with you."

It felt surreal, all this anger from Skeet. Dixon waved a hand in front of his face. "You're mad at me."

"I'm mad at you. I'm mad at you." Skeet was in his face. "I don't need you sending, sending generic 'thank you for your support' cards that I know Char mailed for you, like I'm some stranger." His breathing jagged.

Dixon thought about Cal Fierston's article. Now was the time to tell Skeet. Now was absolutely not the time.

Skeet sank back against the edge of the hill, his hands behind him. He looked small. "I lost my friend." His face glowing wet.

They stood at the top of the trail, wind striking against them. Dixon gazed across the canyon. In the deep gorge of the river below, several small bullet-shaped islands dotted the water, their forests only bare sticks. The hills on either side of the river rose brown and rocky. All earth. Springtime earth, softening from the hardpack of winter. Muddy, cold. It was only going to get harder from here, more truth to shoulder.

"Jesus Christ," Dixon said, "can't we just run?"

## CHAPTER

24

*May 2011, Mount Everest*

At the start of that year when they had prepared so meticulously for Everest, Dixon and Nate had completed their paperwork together, sitting at Dixon's dining table, forms spread around them, the solemn look of two boys completing an exam. When it came time for the Body Disposal Preference Form, each man had grown quiet, and then Nate broke the silence with a loud guffaw. "They really want you serious about this shit, huh?" They had joked about Nate's life insurance policy, about how Dixon was the beneficiary. "That hundred grand isn't going to get good to you on top of that mountain, is it?" Nate asked, and Dixon shot back, "Hell, why wait? I could take you now." The form had seemed a fail-safe, an amulet against bad things. If you carried it with you and laid it at the mountain's feet, weren't you conceding her power? Wouldn't that alone spare you?

Unspared at the end of his climb, lying inside the helicopter from Base Camp to Lukla, leaving Everest behind, Dixon watched the mountain as the plane lifted off and teetered toward the Icefall. Facing the back of the aircraft, he saw Everest recede. He stared at it the way a child leaves a turbulent but beloved home forever. He strained to find Nate's spot along an upper ridge. He might be standing now, signaling for Dixon's help. Dixon lifted his head. "Back! Back!" he called.

A nurse beside him said soothing things he couldn't fully hear over the engine. She pushed down on his shoulder, urged him to lay flat. But he had to keep his eyes on it, he had to face it down, the slate ridges that rose from the snow, that skated and wound around the face of the mountain. An escape route, a roller coaster track. "Ride, Nate, ride," he called. "Come home, come home."

In Lukla, he lay on a stretcher awaiting the transport plane to Kathmandu. The sky, the palest blue, the sheerest cloud. The pounding in his head fell silent. His ears popped in the relative quiet, seeking the persistence of wind. He was falling now from the mountain. His breathing slowed, the air dense in his nostrils, he smelled dung and spices and earth.

"Dixon! Dixon!" He turned his head toward the familiar voice. There was Angkaji on a stretcher, an attendant pushing him forward, Angkaji's hand outstretched to Dixon, his face wet with tears, he cried, "Oh, am so sorry. I wish to take back time, I would not fail you all. Now, I must carry it." Angkaji latched onto Dixon, his hand like fury, like sorrow, and the feeling spiraled through Dixon sharp as an auger, the two men side by side now, falling into the grieving, Angkaji moaning, "brudda, brudda."

## CHAPTER

## 25

*This is Dixon Bryant, the first African American man to summit Mount Everest. It's taken him a year to tell his story.*

So Cal Fierston's magazine article began. It appeared in print on April first. Dixon couldn't help noting the date, April Fool's Day; it seemed somehow fitting. It was a year after his journey and deep into a new Everest climbing season. He was, then, new-old news. A grainy black-and-white photo that Cal had taken in the diner made Dixon look haunted and grim. He didn't read the article. He sent it first to Herbert, who read it and said, "Yeah, pardner, it sounds like what you tole me, anyway. Seem like he got it right." With that endorsement, Dixon forwarded it to Charlaina, Pamela, Kira, and Skeet. Then he waited.

Before the interview with Cal, Dixon felt he might be a man carrying a cement block across his middle. The weight had not been dispelled entirely by telling the truth, merely shifted, say, to a thing hoisted on a hip like a small child. He might imagine it eventually could be held in the crook of an arm, the palm of the hand, but not gone. Never gone.

He waited, seated on his sofa, expecting an avalanche of response. Charlaina was first, calling to say, "Open the door," and there she was. She wrapped her arms around him, cradling his head, saying, "Good for you, Dixon, good for you." Pamela called. "It seemed ironic that it would be him to reach the top. But I see, now, how implausible that was."

Kira was the only one angry: "I feel like I don't know you. How could you just lie? To me!" Her big gold earrings swayed, her bangle-clad arms waved animated and sad in a way so like her mother. He thought of all that would need to be repaired between them. It might not be a bad thing. A quickening idea. Fine, let her tear down his image. He imagined her finally seeing him ravaged and thin and broken and understanding this was who he had become. And then as quickly, he glanced into the mirror near the front door and saw it was his own vision that needed adjusting. He was not so thin anymore, his cheeks healed. But the loss of Nate had etched itself on his face in perceptible fissures and lines. He sat patiently and let his daughter rage. When she was done, he said, "I'm sorry, sweetheart. I'm not perfect. I did the best I could at the time."

Local reporters began to call, mostly the ones who had run one-paragraph stories on Nate's death the previous year. A small flurry of interest each day from local newspapers like the *County Gazette* or regional once-a-week tabloids like *Maryland Now!* Certainly not *Newsweek* or *Time* or the Nightly News. Not even *Ebony* or *Jet,* those chroniclers of all things Black. He began to joke about it with Herbert. "Wonder who it'll be today. Yesterday, it was my college newspaper, you believe that?"

"You wa'n't a Boy Scout, was you? Maybe you be down for a merit badge," Herbert joked.

"Don't laugh. Could be."

"You gone let it go to your head?"

"Couldn't possibly. There's the other side, the comments online about the story, about me, matter fact."

"Why you keep reading those, man? You that used to being liked by e'er'body?"

"I've worked at it hard, all my life."

"Do it serve you, man?"

The funny thing was that he did not mind the media calls. For a solid week, he came home from work, changed his clothes, sat on the straight-backed chair beside the telephone table, and ascended to Everest.

The second week, Dixon came home and turned on his answering machine: *You have no messages.* A sinking in the pit of his stomach. Just like that, his story had run its course. "Is that it?" he asked aloud on the third day. "Nate? Is that it?"

On his computer, he scrolled the many Everest blogs and climbing sites. He found a small entry on "Everest Stats" that was about the size and scope of an obit:

**2011, May 9: Dixon Bryant, first African American male to reach the summit. With DX8 Expeditions.**

The world was in the midst of a new Everest climbing season, with a new set of stories to be written, but he couldn't help feeling like a man who had stood frozen on the high diving board being coaxed to jump, and now that he soared midair toward the pool, the water had drained, the crowd had dispersed, and he was left to career wildly down.

His father's image filled his vision, his father as he always saw him first, his shoulders squared and filling the frame of the world. When Dixon was a child, those shoulders seemed impervious, the way his father towered above him, his shoulders an umbrella over his sons. In that shelter, the boys had grown from sturdy shoots into men, formed in his shadow, held to his light.

Not long before his death, Dixon's father had beckoned him to his bedside. "I'm proud of you boys that you dreamed bigger, all those steps beyond what I knew back in my day. Your mother, she was always asking, 'What'll feed their souls?' and I was asking, 'What'll they be? How will they live? Who will respect them?' I didn't want you getting too big for your britches. Me, you know, I'm practical. I was born with my feet planted in the Eastern Shore of Maryland, swampy land, sulfur-smelling, you know, but it was sweet to me, all that tall corn and crape myrtle and jasmine, yes, that jasmine bush on a summer night, full of fireflies like the stars had come down to me. You see, that's how much of earth I've been. It was all I could do to dream a life away from the farm, from the 'yessir, no sir.' Now see, your mother and I gave you something sturdy to take off from."

His father had drifted off, eyes closed. When he opened them again, he reached out for Dixon's hand. "I do worry about you, son. I don't know if I gave you choices enough. I stretched as far as I could, and here you and your brother are. Businessman, owns his own company. Psychologist. *Dr.* Bryant. Listen, I wanted something else for you, too, son. I don't know that I understood how to give it. I hope I had vision enough to give it. Your mother, worrying over your souls, I wanted you to be men, follow the straight and narrow, see? Shoulder your responsibilities. But your mother used to tell me, 'Let 'em fly, Eldridge, let 'em fly.'"

One evening on the mountain at Camp 3, that precarious ledge above the sheer drop to the Western Cwm, Dixon and Nate had sat lightheaded and giddy and stunned by their own audacity. The air crisp and thin and the setting sun blazing purple and orange streamers across the sky. They sat as they most always did, so close side by side that they banged into each other with the slightest movement. Dixon whispered, "Daddy would've had a fit about this trip."

Nate laughed. "But Mommy would've understood." The two brothers gazed up at the sky, and Nate whispered, "Let 'em fly, Eldridge, let 'em fly."

---

ANGELA PRESTON, THE SCIENCE TEACHER AT HIS OLD SCHOOL, Angela with her full, heart-shaped mouth, wrote to him: "Congratulations!" She wrote in bold letters she had re-traced several times. "I hope you'll tell the boys about it next year!" By next fall, the kids who knew him would have left for high school. The story would be his again to share as he saw fit.

He drove to his old school. The closer he got, the quieter he felt, as if he were a child told to sit up straight, get in order. With the front of the school locked up tight for the weekend, he drove around back to a patch of cars near the gymnasium. An afternoon basketball game, must be. Students and parents slammed car doors and headed toward the gym, laughing, walking fast in the early spring chill. He listened as the cheers from inside the gym swelled, the sound lifting inside him. Couldn't he feel the rhythm of that place, his own self-assigned, exalted place within it?

He turned the key in the ignition and drove away. At a stop-light, he noticed ahead of him an elementary school, kids playing in the schoolyard. He rolled down his window. The sound of them, the wild abandon, the glee, the absolute dangerous glee. He rolled down the other windows, letting the sound echo through his car. Once the light changed, he pulled over to the curb in front of the school. The kids seemed wild, hungry, skirting childhood's line between terror and joy. A boy balanced across the top of the monkey bars, his fearlessness and certainty their own grace, the boy lifting one foot and lingering, weightless, midair. Oh, what daring could do! The freedom of the boy rising, elevated, the sweep of surprise and joy across his narrow face. On the ground, a circle of boys paused to admire the boy midair, the free boy, finding his own height and gravity, holding that mesmerizing moment. Audacious, thrilling, terrifying. The world must be that way sometimes. The boys ran across the playground leaping toward the next moment. Dixon leaned over his steering wheel, smiling, laughing. What if he could start over?

IN THE SMALL STUDY OFF HIS LIVING ROOM, DIXON FINALLY sorted through boxes of Nate's belongings. He locked himself away in that room for nearly two days, standing in a sea of papers and treasures like Nate's first business card, his passport, the program from his college graduation, and a poster of Everest's South Col with the camps up to the summit clearly marked. Dixon had kept a duplicate of this on his own wall the year before, tracing the route in the final months of their preparation, worshipping it, dreaming of it, conquering it night after night before he drifted off to sleep.

"What was the best of it?" Lena had prodded. "You have to find that, too. You have to tell to yourself that."

He would never forget the way the sun came over the mountain's peak, the sudden indescribable grace of it, illumined and golden above the world. On those mornings sitting beside Nate, bound together in awakening, there had been sheer joy. That was what Nate had envisioned for them, *for him*. This was the way Dixon wanted Everest to come to him: a gift, a memory of his brother beside him on the far side of the world, the two of them suspended on the earth's fingertip. Dixon propped the poster of Everest against a box and sat on his knees. He lowered his head, and then raised his fist, slowly at first and then holding it high in deference to her power.

SKEET HAD SAID NOTHING ABOUT THE ARTICLE EVEN THOUGH they continued to run together. Perhaps they could just leave it lay, but anxiety built in Dixon while they ran so that when they had finished one day, Dixon was overflowing. "Did you read it?"

Skeet did not look at Dixon. "Worse than I imagined."

Dixon collapsed down onto the rocky footpath, trembling. "He waited for me. You understand? That's what killed him."

Skeet sat beside Dixon.

"I left him in the first place for that goddamned summit. That's what I'd take back. That's what I dream. I put my arm around him, I turn my back on her, not him, and we head down and come home together. *Together.* I made the wrong choice."

"Or. You did it for both of you."

Dixon's head on his knees a long time, staving off nausea. "That's the lie I told myself. I did it for me. I have to live with that."

Skeet crossed his legs in thought. "You used to do this thing,

used to drive him crazy. We were at the Y, remember Marco's surprise party? Coupla cute girls over by the pool, Nate says, 'C'mon,'
we head over and we start walking, right, all of us, but then you ease
up, let him walk in front. He slows down so you can catch up, you
slow down, too, and it goes on like that, like you can't see yourself
in front. He's staring at you, and I remember his face looks almost
hurt, then he brushes it off, goes on over to the girls. I remember
because I guess, I don't know, you know, I wanted to fit in, so I did
that to him one time and he blew up at me. 'You ever think I don't
want to be out in front all the goddamn time?' He was pissed."

Dixon twisted a foot in the dirt. He wasn't sure he believed
Skeet.

"You listening? As I said: Or, you did it for both of you. For
once."

———

THE POSTCARD ARRIVED ON A FRIDAY, DOG-EARED AT ONE COR-
ner, lightly crumpled. On the front, a photo of an idyllic mountain
scene that might have come from the children's tale *Heidi* in the
Alps, complete with sheep and a log cabin against the stark beauty
of snowcapped peaks.

*Dixon,*

*This photo is the best I can do for mountains. Corny, huh?*
*Good for you on the article. I am very happy you did it.*
*I am off now to train for Karakoram for June.*
*This life, it goes on.*

*Lena*

He set the postcard on the side table. The mountain snow like pale-blue glass. A memory. He opened the table's small drawer and slipped the postcard inside.

---

THE NEXT SATURDAY, A NEARLY TWO-HOUR DRIVE AWAITED him, so Dixon set out early. He drove toward Western Maryland, leaving the congestion of D.C.'s Beltway and winding north toward the blue haze of the Catoctin Mountains. Benign-looking mountains, he reminded himself, not particularly tall, nothing to fear. He could nearly surrender to their beauty, a wide, undulating blue band etched across the sky. He could nearly let himself relax into their distance, just nearly, a thing like stretching a muscle before the burn snaps you back. Not yet but perhaps soon.

He mulled over the call from Cal Fierston the night before. Apparently, Phil Henderson had to turn around before the summit because of altitude sickness. There would be no new Black man on Everest this year. Did Dixon want to comment about that? "I wish him well," Dixon had said and then, "No. I wish him peace."

He left the interstate and followed the two-lane state roads, their edges full of gravel and wildflowers in riotous bloom, spring announcing itself in the yellow leaves of forsythia. He was a long way from home. It must be hard to be a kid here alone, he thought. The juvenile center where Shiloh would serve the first part of his sentence was old and squat, not far from a maximum-security facility for men, a preview of where Shiloh would serve out the bulk of his term after coming of age.

Shiloh sat down in front of Dixon. "You," he said, which sounded nearly like welcome. In fact, there was the faintest whiff of relief. Could Shiloh be glad to see Dixon? The boy scanned the room, and Dixon followed his gaze. The walls were thick cinder-block painted a dull tan and chipping from floor to ceiling. The concrete floors beneath them were the same dull tan but, overhead, the high slanted ceilings were supported by thick old-wood beams. Dixon sat on one side of a plexiglass partition that rose about two feet from the middle of the table. Shiloh slumped in his chair on the other side, arms folded across his chest.

"You're looking better." Dixon pointed to Shiloh's face, which was healing, no sign of swelling and the bruising grown faint.

"Hmm." Shiloh, wide-legged in his chair, scratched his chin. He remained spindly but his face had narrowed, closing itself toward manhood.

"How've you been?"

"Locked the fuck up." He cocked his head. "How you been? Free?"

This smart-mouthed kid.

"Don't go forgetting, I gave you that. I coulda tole on you more. You still think won't nobody listen to me?"

As Dixon studied that boy's face, he realized how well he could read it now. That slight tilt of his chin. He meant *I didn't want you forgetting me.* "I'm sure somebody will listen." And then, "I'm listening."

"Your boy that wrote that letter, he out now? He done his bit? Guess he a man," Shiloh said.

"You think that makes him a man?"

"Oh, that's right, you here to set me straight."

Dixon smiled. He stretched out his fingers on the scarred wooden table before him. "Keep the letter. You'll want to read it again."

Looking away, arms folded, Shiloh scowled then puckered his lips, brooding.

"So, tell me about this place."

Shiloh came back to him slowly, a cold engine cranking until it caught, then he gave his opinions on the food, the guards, the bed linen, the strict rules about yard and exercise privileges and schoolwork. "It's prison basically," he finished with a verbal finality that matched the set of his chin.

"That it is." An odd feeling, not to hate this boy, not to fear him.

"Tell me something. You made that shit up about leaving school for some mountain, right? What, you had cancer or somethin'? That's why you come back looking like that, all spindly and shit?"

Dixon let slip a short laugh. "And here I was thinking I looked better. I'm recovering from the mountain climb." He swallowed, then inhaled. "I'm the first Black American man to summit Mount Everest."

Shiloh slanted his head to the side.

"I climbed Mount Everest. I stood at the top of the world. That's why I look like this. Frostbite. Lost some toes."

"You fucked up, ain't you?"

"Yeah." Dixon's laugh burst short and loud. "Yeah, I'm fucked up."

"Ain't this some shit. And you here to help me." Shiloh squeezed his folded arms, shook his legs back and forth. "How come you did that?"

"It was, it was, audacious," he said and let the word echo. "You know that word? Means bold, unexpected." Shiloh stared at him. "Off the chain," Dixon added.

"You famous?"

He shrugged. "Not so you'd notice."

He examined Dixon a long while with the slightest hint of awe. "Ain't it dangerous?"

"Yes." He paused. "My brother. Died."

A mild shock on Shiloh's face, a raise of his eyebrows, then a sweep of comprehension. He got it, he got it, Dixon was sure, the hubris and suffering and triumph and grief, the wanting to be counted.

They didn't speak a long time.

"What's the top of the world like?"

"Terrible," Dixon said automatically, then reconsidered. "Stunning. Like nothing you can imagine." The boy with him fully. "I'll tell you about it someday." The boy's eyes locked on Dixon, who added, "Don't go thinking we're best friends."

The curl of a smile formed at the edge of Shiloh's mouth. "True that."

Shiloh settled back. "I'm 'bout to do a bit, for real. Twenty-five years. Your boy that wrote me that letter, what, he a do-gooder like you, huh?"

"No, just a brother who's been there."

"He do his time, he come home all like, changed, and shit and his people give him a damn parade?" He gave a disgusted snort. "And, what, he go to church now, and, and his momma, his momma all 'that's my boy.' So he think that's gone be my life?" Shiloh turned his face away from Dixon, his tongue poking out the side of his mouth. His chest heaved once.

Dixon fell toward him. "I'm sorry for your loss." Shiloh's body stiffened, he looked about to strike, his shoulders high and sharp.

He was the wrong boy. He was the one left.

A guard announced that their time was up. The boy gave the guard a fast once-over before he stood. "Hey," Shiloh said to the

315

guard, "you see that crazy mountain-climbing somabitch there? Y'all need to watch him." He began to walk away. He stopped and turned to Dixon, a flash in his eyes: "I ain't gone be your bitch."

Dixon, his laugh small and slow, said, "I know you won't."

There would be a reckoning, there would be justice for Marcus. Shiloh would be kept here at the far edge of the state, tucked into the mountains behind barbed wire. He might easily be left behind. But Dixon would come. He would *want* to come see this boy who did not adore him, who tolerated his presence without particular joy. Dixon would bring Herbert. They would sit shoulder to shoulder in front of the boy, patient, seeking, until they found him.

# ACKNOWLEDGMENTS

Writing this book has been a long labor of love and revision, and I have many people to thank. First, I must start with my agent, Alexa Stark, and my editor, Pilar Garcia-Brown, both of whom embraced this book as I hoped someone would. For their faith, enthusiasm, wisdom, and humor, I am deeply grateful. I'd also like to thank Ella Kurki and LeeAnn Pemberton at Dutton for all their detailed work.

Over the course of writing and rewriting this book, I've had invaluable support from the Rona Jaffe Writers Award, along with time, space, and support from Hedgebrook, the Porches, the Sozopol Fiction Seminar, and the Maryland Arts Council.

Thank you to the writer friends who have read and reread the drafts of this book: Stephanie Allen, Jeremiah Chamberlin, Melanie Hatter, Donna Hemans, Travis Holland, Elizabeth Kostova, Nicole Maranhas, and Sharon Pomerantz. Thank you also to American University Law Dean Roger Fairfax for providing a thought-provoking dialogue on the juvenile justice system. For their insights about running, many thanks to my cousins Al Owens and Ronnie Carter. For their long-term support, thank you to Martha Cooley, Lewis Flanagan, Ann McClellan, Jil Persons, Martha Southgate, Sherry Weaver, and Mary Kay Zuravleff.

My curiosity about mountain climbing stems from the infamous mountain disaster in 1996, so I am indebted to Jon Krakauer's *Into Thin Air* as well as to David Breashears's film *Storm Over Everest*. I was helped immeasurably by conversations with alpinist Steve Swenson and critical review by climber Rob McClellan. What a surprise to find that climbers and trekkers lurked among my friends! Thank you, Travis, Jeremy, and John Bishop. I've read more books and watched more videos about training for and climbing Mount Everest than I can name, but the ones most useful to me include Conrad Anker's *The Call of Everest*, Broughton Coburn's *Everest: Mountain Without Mercy*, Maria Coffey's *Fragile Edge*, Christine Gee's (et al.) *Everest: Reflections from the Top*, Mark Horrell's *The Chomolungma Diaries*, Lacey Kohlmoos's *How to Climb Mount Everest with Your Boyfriend/Girlfriend Without Dying or Killing Each Other*, Jon E. Lewis's *The Mammoth Book of Eyewitness Everest*, Sherry B. Ortner's *Life and Death on Mt. Everest*, Mark Pfetzer's *Within Reach: My Everest Story*, Barbara J. Scot's *The Violet Shyness of Their Eyes: Notes from Nepal*, Ed Viesturs's *The Mountain: My Time on Everest*, the novels *Above All Things* by Tanis Rideout and *Solo Faces* by James Salter, and the DVDs *Train to Climb Mt. Rainier or Any High Peak*, *Everest: The Death Zone*, *Mountain of Dreams, Mountain of Doom*, and *When the Mountain Calls, Show Up*.

Finally, I must thank my family members, who taught me the importance of storytelling, especially my cousins who showed me how Black men care for, laugh with, champion, and love one another. A special thank-you to my beloved uncle Chuck Kiah for his grace at high hurdles, his humor, his insight about our responsibilities to one another, his annoying falsetto singing, and his unerring love. Finally, to my mother, father, and sister, my devotion and gratitude are boundless.

# ABOUT THE AUTHOR

Karen Outen's fiction has appeared in *Glimmer Train*, *North American Review*, *Essence*, and elsewhere. She is a 2018 recipient of the Rona Jaffe Foundation Writers Award and has been a fellow at both the Institute for the Humanities at the University of Michigan and the Pew Fellowships in the Arts. She received an MFA from the University of Michigan.